www.clocktowerbooks.com
ClocktowerBooks

Siberian Girl:

A Romantic Historical Espionage Thriller

(Memories of Love and War 1942-1992)

A Novel By

John T. Cullen

www.johntcullen.com

London Under Attack During World War Two
Collage with Inset of Adapted Version of
Dante Gabriel Rosetti's Mnemosyne (London, 1881)

Contents

Dedication
2016-2017 Editions

For

Gary and Rae Kerzner

With Thanks And Affection
For Many Years of
Friendship and Support

Special Celebration
At the Wedding in July 2016 of
Rebecca Theise and Chaz Firestone
May They Enjoy Many Years
Of Happiness and Success Together

JTC

Prolog: Ghosts of Siberia

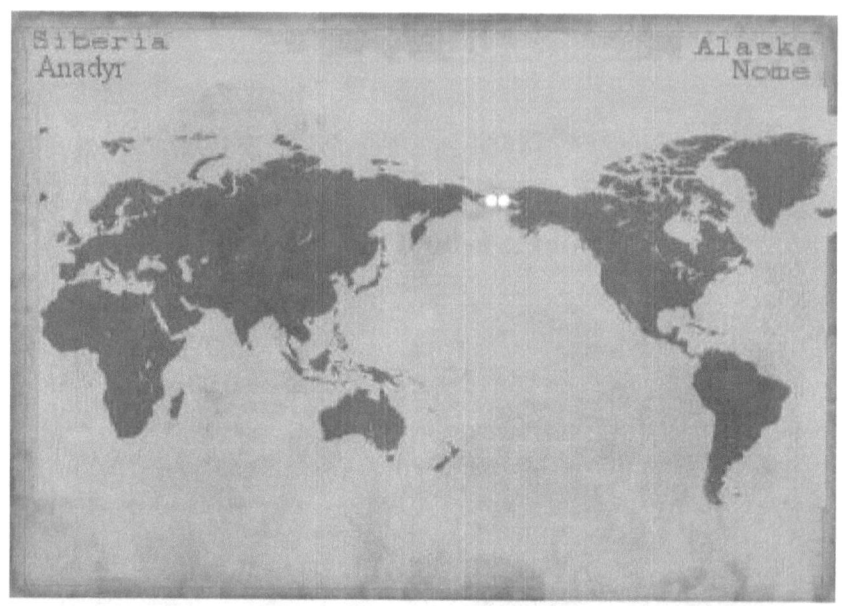

Siberia
Anadyr

Alaska
Nome

1992—*Umnitsa*—A Good and Clever Girl

On the last leg of the thundering Aeroflot flight from Moscow to Siberia, Marianne prepared herself for her life's moment of greatest and final honesty with herself... *Siberian girl.*

The urn of ashes sat overhead in a compartment, along with luggage, coats, and satchels of food and duty-free treasures. Her only possessions on this trip, leaving behind chateaux and family in France, were a coat, a small suitcase, and the ashes of a lost lifetime.

She was no longer a brassy tabloid princess with nine lives, no longer tracked by shouting paparazzi and beaming in the attention of tracking flash bulbs. She hugged herself, in her beige, high-necked pullover and jeans, and tried to be as small and modest as possible in her seat.

She kept herself all alone among vibrant passengers—a few blond, blue-eyed Slavs; most of them Yupik, Inuit, and other Siberian Asiatics. They wore a mix of Western dress and colorful native costume, as they crowded around in family groups with laughter, talk, and cigarette smoke. Like Marianne, they were coming home from distant places. Unlike Marianne, they were not living interrupted lives in search of lost truths and loves.

She had found the yin of her beginning and end; now she would close the circle by bringing the yin to the yang, and complete her life so she could start to life, for the first time, as her own person. She remembered very little of her mother, except her love and affection, and the endearment she would call Marianne while hugging her. It was a very Russian word of subtle meanings: *Umnitsa*…my good little girl, my clever little girl…

Marianne smiled amid welling tears, feeling her shoulders start to quake with a barely controlled mix of feelings from grief to elation.

The plane would soon land on remote Chukotka Peninsula, and she would set foot in the tiny Arctic capital of Anadyr—for the first time since her departure as an orphan, aged four, so many years earlier.

After a lifetime of parties, news feeds, hangovers, blackouts, and the whole blur—she was now an anonymous traveler, a middle aged woman, still stunningly beautiful, but mature and graying, with reading glasses and deceptively calm eyes.

She was approaching the edge of the world, and a return to her beginnings. This was the right thing to do--the right place to go.

Overwhelmed, and fearing a thorough, wracking cry, she hurried along the Ilyushin Il-62 passenger jet's crowded aisle to wash her face at the W.C. sink. After so many hours of travel, it would be refreshing—even if it overwhelmed, at last, any further resistance to a long built-up sense of profound helplessness and loss. She consoled herself by thinking: *I have three such good sons. What did I do to deserve them?* She'd been pretty much a lousy mother. Under the all-seeing eye of their grandmother, and fabulous family wealth, the boys had raised themselves and were now successful men. No suicides, no depression. They were strong men, who sometimes seemed almost like father figures to their wayward, yet beloved mother. *But was I a good daughter?* Marianne thought as the first sobs began to pound like sledge hammers inside her diaphragm, breaking out into air and light. If she could be done being a daughter, maybe she could fully function as a mother, what was left of her time and that mission. What had her sons' *grand-mère*, her adoptive mother, said with a knowing grin while chain smoking in the garden in Provençe? "Look at me. If nothing else, you can become a good grandmother one day." The old woman, born with the new century, and now in her 90s, had lived a profligate youth herself, and her outcome had been no children and a suicidal husband. But not before they had traveled to Siberia and adopted a little four year old Caucasian girl who would mother three sons and keep the family line going stronger than ever. *Am I a player, or just a passer-through?* Marianne asked herself on the way to the loo. It was a question she'd asked a thousand times since the fatal accident at the Red Bull air races in Barcelona, years ago, that had claimed her young playboy husband, Count Didier. She had been snatched from the Arctic grave of her mother, and she had redeemed herself by being a mothering bed of three male heirs, but she was still a half-formed soul in need of the finished shaping. Now she was close to the end of her journey. Just a few more days, and she could at last become a complete person. Fire in the forge, sparks and dross flying away while hammers banged the glowing steel—so the steel mill, so Marianne's heart.

The engines' thunder and whining almost made a symphony. A chorale seemed to sing amid the rushing wind, but it was an illusion of memory and expectation. There was no Bolshoi hidden in the air conditioning ducts or in the cargo caverns—only heartless Siberian air, full of Arctic ghosts, spattered by brutal Russian engines at 10,000 feet that courageously met power with power.

At age 46, Anechka looked like what she was—a well-heeled Westerner—in her yellowish hiking boots, slender-figured tight jeans, purple sweater over travel-sweaty camisole. She might look like one of the new Russians as well. The new Russia—the Soviet Union had just been dissolved—was filled with adventurers. Most were shady, some downright deadly. Marianne was not one of these. She was acutely aware of looking different—yet in her heart, she knew she belonged here more than anywhere else on earth. It was her birth place. She was coming home to her mother, the soil, and in the soil. And yet she could stay. Mama would understand. A tear rolled down one cheek.

Her light but bulky military-style parka with faux-fur collar was jammed into the luggage compartment over her seat, along with the white, ceramic jar of ashes that was half her reason for making this journey.

The other half of her reason lay enurned in her heart, which she touched with her fist as she sidled down the aisle—a woman on a mission.

📖

'Why do you make this trip alone, a woman who barely understands Russian?'

So asks the pretty young police woman—a Sergeant Lena Varov--in Anadyr police station, after Marianne arrives and presents her papers—she also needs a trustworthy local guide.

'Are you not afraid?'

'Not any longer,' *Marianne replies, standing before the duty desk while the young sergeant's brother and cousin, both constables, look on while smoking harsh cigarettes. They have silently violent eyes.*

📖

Marianne felt her own foreignness, over the soil of her birthplace, as she tiptoed down the rubber-matted aisle, past smiling and nodding Aeroflot stewardesses, toward the little lighted W.C. sign. She was French, but her natural father had been a U.S. Navy officer and spy during World War II, and her mother had been one of the three important women in his life at the time. She spoke perfect English. Some called her the American.

Long ago, on the soil below where she had come into the world amid Arctic darkness and Stalin's personal vendetta, her mother had called her by a Russian endearment—*Umnitsa*—good or clever girl. It had taken her half a century, but now she had proven it to be a true name for herself. She had only one thing left to prove it absolutely and totally forever. That meant taking the ashes to a grave that lay on the edge of the Siberian Sea.

📖

'I'm no longer afraid,' Marianne says of personal matters beyond the girl's understanding.

'I am not either,' Lenka says, meaning something very different from her own small world here in the vastness at the world's edge. 'My name is Elena—you can call me Lenka. Everyone does in this little town, where everyone knows everyone else. At least until foreigners and bizenis men showed up, now that Communism is finished. Now this is the murder capital of Chukotka Peninsula.'

Marianne clings to the jar of ashes and offers a reassuring smile. "I have nothing to worry about, since I am with the police.'

Lenka's look darkens, but she says nothing. Her cousin and brother exchange startled looks, as if they are culprits who have been found out. Marianne has no doubt they smoke an occasional marijuana cigarette on duty—she smelled it on her way into the station. Suspicious smoke wafted around the building's corner from in back.

'Are you the police chief as well?' Marianne asks flippantly. She admires this businesslike young woman who clearly runs the show here.

Lenka looks directly and frankly into Marianne's eyes. She gives her a surprised or surprising look. It is like sunshine flashing in baby-blue glass. 'The police commissioner was murdered in a drug deal last year—two streets away in broad daylight. Big shootout with bizenis men from Vladivostok. Nobody wants to be police chief here anymore.'

Marianne wonders if it had been a drug bust or a drug deal. She doesn't dare to ask.

📖

Marianne's straight hair, chopped to a page boy style, was losing its rinsed color amid her new Diogenes penitence and search for light. Her hair, though turning gray, was still thick, and parted in the center—all she needed was a tall, colorful Sami cap to look like an aging hippie queen of an earlier generation. Her face had lost its unflinching addiction to flashbulb lights, and now looked plain and pretty and almost serene. Her warm but concerned gray-blue eyes only betrayed that she had miles to go before she slept. Hidden in her carry-on, in the luggage rack above her seat, was the ceramic jar of ashes she was bringing home.

📖

'You bring ashes to put on beach, is that right?'

'Not on the beach, exactly. My mother's grave is on a small, old cemetery near the sand bar.'

'And you are American?'

'No—yes—French, but my father was American.'

'Then you are American,' Lenka says authoritatively while checking over Marianne's paperwork at the desk in the small police station. Things are simple in Lenka's small world.

Marianne says: 'I am Chukot, because I was born here.'

The pretty young blonde looks up with bright blue eyes under a ledge of rebellious blonde hair pinned with combs. Lenka's uniform cap lies on the desk near the police radio and a duty roster. She has a little pink plastic flower on one of her combs, high up on the line of her part—no coloring or rinse there, Marianne notes—it's the girl's natural hair color. She is still so young. Her skin is pale and soft as snow, except for a natural rose-blush on her cheeks. Her cheeks are not broad, nor are her eyes almond-shaped— she could pass for a college student from Amsterdam or London or Kansas City, but she has never been beyond the Chukotka Peninsula—the only part of the Russian Federation in the Western Hemisphere, a few hours' flight across the Aleutians to Alaska (though Marianne's tortuous path has taken her the long way, from the west, via Paris and Moscow). 'I am Slav,' Lenka says defiantly, 'from Latvia—okay, it's two generations ago.' She does not want to be thought of as Asian, though she is.

Marianne takes her turn to ask a question. 'Why were your grandparents sent here?'

Lenka quickly retraces the limits of her schooling—there too, she has never been much beyond the Anadyr Estuary: 'Something happened in World War II. Stalin and the Five Year Plans—the reforms and all—you know.'

'Yes, I know all too well.' Marianne looks at this small, thin girl, in her uniform, with gun and cuffs and spray, who is young enough to be her daughter, and half a foot shorter than herself. 'My mother also,' she tells the slender police sergeant.

📖

Lenka looks up from Marianne's paperwork, and slides it across the desk to its owner. 'So, you will take ashes to cemetery.' It is a question.

'Yes, and I need someone to guide me there. I will pay.'

'I can guide you,' Lenka says. 'You pay one hundred U.S. dollars.'

'Yes,' Marianne says quickly, surprised that the policewoman asks so little.

'No, Lenka,' object the two young constables who are her relatives.
'We don't have time this morning,' says her brother Anatoly.
'You forget our bizenis,' says her cousin Mikhail.
'We have time for both,' Lenka tells them sharply, and that ends the
discussion. No wonder she is the sergeant and they are constables.
Marianne wonders what their business deal might be. She gets a dark
feeling. Her dark feelings have never been wrong.

📖

The arc of her journey was near its end. Events of today had been set in motion lifetimes ago. An arrow shot into the air in Stalin's age was about to hit the ground in Yeltsin's age. Marianne touched her cheeks with probing fingertips. She herself was that arrow. The ground was the soil of her birth—Mother Russia. She was returning to her mother, and bringing her father back to the woman who had never stopped loving him—nor had he ever stopped loving her—though he was married to two women in fact if not on paper.

Love, like Mother Russia, was larger than any human life—vast, and unfathomable. Love and war were the mother and father of gods and goddesses. Human mythologies since the Ice Ages had endlessly repeated this epic marriage song, the most primitive and powerful of all cosmic ideations that propelled the warriors of Sumer and Troy, of Rome and the World Wars. It was true then, and it was true now. Marianne, world traveler and seeker, had heard their siren songs over the horizons of the earth and the seas. The truth spoke to her soul, and told her she was nearly finished with her journey. Soon, the arrow would rest. She would be free. The whales and sirens of the sea would sing on, long after she too lay with her mother and father, until the very end of time. To have lived was glorious, if it meant to have heard the song of the universe and its deities.

Just as there were reasons for how and why she had been born, and lived her life, and circled the globe in search of her long-lost father, now there was a reason why she had returned to the womb of Siberia, and in fact to this small, cold refuge high above the clouds, so near the stars. It began with a violent shaking of her shoulder blades, as if someone were beating her. It was totally out of control. She clung to the sink with both white-knuckled hands as deep, racking sobs rose from her guts like whales breaching the frizzy, icy Bering Sea surface. It was a crying that had waited, like a white wolf among pine trees, to race forth and devour her with its ripping teeth. Sheltered by a Soviet-era door with torn placards, she cried loudly and uncontrollably. She heard the sound of herself, which was like a wounded forest animal dying in agony. All those glittering media eyes, flashbulb smiles, topless Monagasque sun tans, paparazzo Vespa rides, white whirling gowns at Paris or London balls, and a tiny girl in a torn dress, holding her beautiful but dying young mother's hand as they gazed together across the frigid, wind-ripped sea toward America under the

Milky Way…now it all crashed down in a cacophany of truth. The chorale in the air conditioning ducts howled around her, while a concerned attendant banged on the door and yelled *Is something wrong in there?*

📖

'You have no fear?' Lenka asks as she signals to her brother Anatoly, and tosses the keys to the squad car to her cousin Mikhail.

Marianne shakes her head. 'Do you?' she asks in an ironic tone.

Lenka shrugs. 'We live life as everyone must—whatever is handed to a person.' She picks up her cap and a padded uniform coat with stuffing leaking from frayed edges. The four tromp across the wooden floor, out onto a plank porch, and down worn concrete stairs onto a gravel street.

Lenka, even under her gray-blue fatigue cap, is the smallest of the four, while Marianne next taller. Anatoly and Mikhail stand just under six feet. The two men carry the wide saucer caps common to Russian uniforms, ready to throw them unworn into the back of the police car. Mikhail has blond hair like his sister, and blue eyes, but a scarred and beard-stubbled face with uneven teeth, one of which is broken and brown. Anatoly has longish brown hair that curls over his dirty gray-blue uniform collar.

Both young men wear black clip-on neckties, but Mikhail displays a fine golden cross in the Orthodox manner, with one straight and one skewed lateral bar, which lies on the knot of his tie from a fine chain. 'Given by my mother,' he explains fervently in response to Marianne's praise for its beauty. Everything about these Siberians, Marianne thinks, is fervent and secretive. They seem intense and pent up. They are the police, and she has no reason not to trust them, but she has an uneasy feeling.

The air is cold, with a chill wind that keens in the barren hills.

Anadyr seems typical of small, barren settlements along both polar circles around the globe. Along its harbor lies a collection of rusting, capsized steel deep sea fishing trawlers. A few modern ships come or go with silent purpose on the flat, silvery waters of the Anadyr Estuary. Multi-colored Soviet era housing blocks stand shoulder to shoulder in the downtown area. Everything quickly recedes on all sides into frozen waste and drab hills before there is a chance for flowers or urbanity to crop up.

📖

After the longest, hardest cry of her life, Marianne washed her face slowly, looking into the W.C. mirror on the jet passenger plane. She felt numb, yet hopeful, even painfully reborn. It was a relief to have quaked with sobbing and tears, to have closed the curtains on her past life, to be ready for a new start, to feel drained and newly born.

Hearing *din-din-din* warning signals that the plane was about to start descending for its landing at Anadyr, Marianne took one last look in the bathroom mirror. She was beyond the question *why*.

Opening the door, she made her way forward to her seat. She heard a routine speech rattled off by the male co-pilot as the plane angled sharply forward to its landing. Opening the door, she sidled back to her seat amid a carpet of yawning faces, fingers wiping eyes, mothers comforting squalling babies, men finishing a last cigarette in the smoke-thick air. In less than an hour, she expected to be on the ground with her luggage. She would drop it at the plain, modern hotel near the airport, and then head into town to see a certain Sergeant Lena Varov who had been looked up for her by someone at the Russian embassy in Paris. What could go wrong with a woman cop? Marianne would need a safe, armed local guard to help her find her mother's grave on the 40 kilometer sand bar between the Anadyr Estuary and the Bering Sea. Who better than the police?

As the plane thundered down to a landing at Anadyr-Ugolny Airport, Marianne studied her maps and notes again. It was very difficult to obtain an accurate map of granular, precise detail for her destination. She would have to rely on this Sergeant Varov for local guidance. Marianne read that the flight distance between Anadyr and Nome, Alaska in the U.S. is 506 miles (815 km). By contrast, between Moscow and Anadyr lies 3,861 miles (6,214 km). The Bering Sea is a marginal body of water of the Northern Pacific Ocean. The Russian-U.S. border is a little over 300 miles east of Anadyr in the Bering Sea.

Stalin had chosen cleverly—Anadyr, administrative capital of Chukotka Autonomous Okrug (Region), the baited trap for Tim Nordhall, with Anna and Anechka Timofeyeva as the cheese. But not too cleverly, because the trap had never been sprung.

📖

Marianne waits in the police station of Anadyr, wearing slim-legged jeans and bulky parka. She has graying, page-boy cropped hair, a long handsome face, and gray-blue eyes. If there is anything at all Slavic about her face, it is the slightly almond-shaped eyes and broad cheekbones she inherited from her mother. It is a subtle Asian effect, seen in many Western Europeans, a result of millennia of invasions from the East.

By her choice, Marianne has finally put the paparazzi behind her and can blend anonymously among the people of the world in her travels. She holds the ceramic jar of ashes on one arm like a baby.

The three Anadyr police wait as Lenka must organize things before the ride to the sand bar and cemetery at the mouth of Anadyr Estuary.

Slight and blonde, girlish yet authoritative, Lenka is a young woman who has taken charge when the world around her is falling apart. Lenka tosses the patrol car keys to her brother Anatoly and cousin Mikhail. Lenka makes a phone call while the two constables trudge outside to get the patrol car.

Lenka speaks by radio with the regional police dispatcher. Marianne sits on a hard wooden bench by a worn wooden window. Lenka has a sweet voice, like honey, but hard around the edges like dried sugar. The window is streaky, and has greenish paint spatters along its edges to match the socialist era wall décor. An electric samovar bubbles nearby. The room is filled with smells of tea and cigarette smoke, as well rotting wood imported decades ago to build this precinct station.

As Marianne watches through the window, she sees Anatoly and Mikhail outside—loading boxes into the back of a second police cruiser, this one a small Land Rover-type, parked behind a smaller Lada. Both vehicles are blue and white, with colored emergency light bars on top.

'We go now,' Lenka declares as she rebuckles her pistol belt. Putting her cap on over her blonde hair, she comes around the desk and wags her fingers in a hold-hands motion. Her tone is nurturing. She holds out a hand, as if Marianne were a child. 'Come, Anna Maria Didier. We visit your mother.'

'Thank you,' Marianne says, rising, and grateful for Lenka's warmth and humanity. She squeezes the girl's hand briefly, but does not hold it. She is afraid.

📖

Marianne had read about her birth place. Though she had not been back here in forty years, it seemed familiar. There was the great Anadyr Bay in the Bering Sea, and east of it the large Anadyr Estuary. On the southern shore, a peninsula jutted north, almost cutting off the outer bay from the Anadyr River that flowed from west to east into an inner bay. At the tip of the peninsula, which separated the inner and outer bays, was the administrative capital of Russia's largest autonomous *okrug* or administrative region— Anadyr, population about 13,000—a relative metropolis in this vast Arctic emptiness dotted mostly by remote little aboriginal villages.

The Ugolny airport complex lay across the bay on Chukotka Peninsula itself. In the distance to the south, across the estuary, seen from the northern shore, Anadyr looked like a miniature metropolis complete with tiny buildings set against a stark and barren wilderness. The two shores were several miles apart, and reachable by ferry during the summer months. When the water was frozen over, most of the rest of the year, the two population centers were connected by an air hop—with both chopper or fixed wing taxi service available.

Marianne, traveling west from Paris to the remotest peninsula in Far Eastern Russia, had crossed twelve time zones to reach Anadyr. She could have traveled less than 500 miles from Nome, Alaska heading east. The international boundary between the United States and Russia was barely 150 miles east of Anadyr, in mid-ocean. Regular flights now connected Nome in the United States with Anadyr in the Russian Federation.

The old military and cargo airport of Anadyr-Ugolny had been converted into a compact but sparkling modern transit point. When Marianne deplaned, she carried her one suitcase in her left hand, and a carryall with her toiletries and the urn in her right hand.

The terminal building looked new and smelled clean. It had a map of the world on its rubberized floor. The equipment all around was modern as well, and local personnel were very friendly and efficient. The new Russia was gearing up to take in billions of hard currency dollars Westerners were willing to spend—including those returning home from lives of exile abroad, and those laundering money in all the major cities from drugs, human trafficking, gun smuggling, and every other imaginable crime.

Although the politics and paranoia were gone, one was still expected to have a handler. This was not some dour spook on the KGB payroll—the KGB itself no longer existed, but was now a tenuous ghost of its former self, split into smaller rival agencies.

Marianne's handler was a tall, thin man wearing a tan tweed suit, and carrying a raincoat slung over one arm.

He recognized her from a photograph, and introduced himself with a small bow as Nayden Marinov, an important official. "As arranged by your travel agency," he added with a friendly little bow.

"I'm delighted," Marianne said. She wondered how it happened that this man had been selected to be her guide. There was something too purposeful and knowing about him for her to feel entirely at ease.

Something about him…*what is it?*…she felt a deep pang of unease that grew, second by second, and then stuck in an unsettled twilight between wondering and not knowing.

A blue-suited Yupik red-cap, who might have passed for a native U.S. American, scooted skillfully in line. Samsonov gestured for the man to put Marianne's two bags on his shiny steel cart.

"You must be very tired," Marinov said to Marianne.

"I am," Marianne said, drawing in a huge gasp of oxygen. The air was cold and brisk as they stepped into the Arctic landscape. She'd seen this scenario elsewhere—in Greenland, in Patagonia, in Finland, in Quebec—a biting, frigid sea washing up on rocky beaches where ice crackled over crystal puddles; forbidding bluish-gray cliffs topped off by a rolling landscape of barren hills and valleys. These places always seemed to be rimmed with distant mountain ranges of frigid gunmetal color, swimming in a haze of near-freezing vapor.

"You should stay at the airport hotel," Marinov said. "It is modern and clean."

"Yes, I already booked a room there," Marianne said. "I have to spend some time across the bay in Anadyr, but my real business is here on the north side."

"It can all be arranged, Madame." His eyes had a way of not meeting her gaze, as much as possible.

"Call me Marianne."

"Very nice, thank you. I'm Nayden."

"Nayden," she repeated. "Your English is very good."

"Thank you. Nayden means 'Found' in English."

"Found," she said as they walked along the tarmac to the sheltering arms of the hotel. "As in lost and found?"

"It's ironic," he said. "You could well say that."

"It's certainly true about me," she said. "How did you happen to be assigned to me, Nayden?"

"It's a long story."

"Your English is American, though your name is Russian."

"I lived in Seattle, Washington for many years."

"Were you a spy?"

He laughed. "No, I ran away from this crappy place and started a real life."

"In the freedom of the United States." As a Frenchwoman, she respected the idea, but couldn't help placing an ironic twist on the cliché.

"Yes."

"And now, Nayden, you live—?"

"—In Los Angeles. I get around. I'm in the sales business."

"So you did what for how long in Seattle?" What was 'sales business'? An American would have said "I'm in business" or "I'm in sales," but never both. Maybe it was a strange Russian concept, lost in translation. She judged him to be about her age, not bad looking, with a slightly swarthy complexion and Mediterranean-like features. But he had blondish hair, and dark, slate-blue eyes the color of a cold sea. What was it about this guy? She felt a strange sort of bond with him, from somewhere deep in the soul. Must be the strange power of Russia in general, and Siberia in particular, like the musk of an animal or the bristling abundance of a bear's fur. Like even the overripe woodsiness of the paper towels in the Ilyushin's toilet. Russia not only made you aware of itself—it overwhelmed you. And she was tired. That must be what was going on deep inside her.

Nayden said: "I taught Russian, Geography, and History at a high school."

"For how long?"

"Thirty years in all."

"Married?"

"Divorced. I have four children, all now in their twenties and in college or working, all in California or Washington State. I go back to visit every few months. My ex and I are on speaking terms, and the kids are now grown up. I am free to do what I want."

"So you come to visit Anadyr. Of all the places on earth, I cannot imagine why."

"Because I was born here."

A chill ran through her. He was about her age. "Did I ever know you as a child?"

"It's possible."

"You lived here in town as a child?"

"Yes."

"You don't mind that I ask so many questions?"

He shrugged. "Everything in due time. Water finds its own level, as they say in the United States."

The conversation trailed off in a stalemate. They trudged along behind the porter, who pushed his cart with her luggage on it to the new hotel area beside the terminal. For a few moments, they endured biting wind and blowing, frozen grit. Moments later, they were in a modern hotel lobby— modest, functional, but clean—that smelled of floor polish and cooked, salty cabbage.

"You are a man who takes care of everything."

"You have children, Marianne?"

"Three sons, two married, one a career officer in the French navy, all professionals in great careers. The oldest is Tim, the next Louis, the youngest Bernard. I have three grandchildren as well."

"Lucky you. Wealthy family?"

"That too."

"And Mr.—?"

"Widowed. He died in a plane crash, racing in Spain. Something rich men do." That memory of Barcelona was a ruddy blur in her mind. A smouldering hole in the ground, full of twisted scrap and upturned soil, along with a spray of small body parts. Ambulance crew led speechless Marianne away, while fire fighters retrieved what was left for burial, later held in the family mausoleum in Provençe. Nicolas had been the only male heir, and with his death both family fortunes flowed to Marianne for her sons. Months of depression and despair. A turning point. From there, the play scene was never the same again. In a way, Marianne could thank Nicolas for pointing the way to a new life. She'd gotten wilder than ever for a while, until she'd had to stay with a middle-aged friend whose 18 year old daughter had just died of a heroin overdose in a Brussels flop house. That had been the other shoe to drop.

"I am sorry to hear about it."

"It was long ago."

"And you never remarried?"

"I was an international playgirl. My husband and I were both tabloid stars without ever meaning to be. We just played and played."

She began to suspect that he knew a lot more about her than he was telling her. Like a fox, she decided to keep still, be clever, and watch him. Words and questions were cheap. Curiosity killed the cat. She would catch him, maybe, if he lied or something. She'd play it by ear.

The porter led them across the hotel lobby on a durable, merlot-colored carpet. Nayden tipped the man, who left her luggage for a bellman to next pick up, on the next Western-style tipping leg to her room upstairs.

Nayden Marinov showed no sign of getting pushy about her privacy, her bed, sex, or anything of that sort. He remained formal, aloof, and yet somehow uncomfortably, mysteriously familiar. He said: "Wait here—I'll talk to the concierge and get you all set up."

Amused, Marianne waited by her luggage. She could have checked in herself, and carried her own bags up in the elevator. But protocol was protocol. She'd been in Moscow only recently, to visit with the retired, former KGB colonel, Uncle Viktor. She knew how bad things could be— although these Arctic wastelands had a unique talent for redefining 'awful' in new ways. Life was harsh in these places. She shivered to think how lucky she had been that, after Mama's death, the rich Parisian couple had adopted her.

Nayden returned, surreptitiously putting his wallet in a pocket under his coat. He must have tipped someone again.

"I will reimburse you for all expenses," she said.

"Don't worry—I'm running a tab. You'll need to sign for me at the end. Can I buy you coffee and a sandwich? The food isn't bad here in the cafeteria."

"Sure. Travel builds up an appetite."

They sat at coral-red, functional tables and chairs in a lounge overlooking the main runway. Between them on the table sat two coffee services and two plates of fish delicacies with good bread and butter. Coffee, tea, and beer beckoned from glass windows set in stainless steel serving trays.

"You didn't need this," Marianne said, meaning the job.

He squirmed pleasantly. "No, I didn't. It's just…something that came along. I was curious. I couldn't resist."

"Are you satisfied?"

"They call you the American," he said, "but you speak with a slight French accent. You are educated, and you studied American English."

"I am French. You're right. You are a detective. Are you sure you are not a spy?"

He grinned. "Sometimes we are all spies. Especially we former Soviets."

"But you must feel more American after thirty years in Seattle."

"I do." He spoke reassuringly. "I'm a stranger here, as much as you are." Seeing her look, he added: "Something made you come back here also. I don't have to explain myself too much."

"No you don't," she said. She stirred her coffee thoughtfully. "I came here with the ashes of my father. I am going to bury him next to my mother, who has lain out there on a god forsaken sand spit for nearly half a century. Actually, half his ashes stayed in San Francisco with the two women who were his wives." She paused a second to gauge his reaction. When there wasn't one, she knew he knew a lot about her, her father, and her background. She got chills up and down her spine. But what did any of it matter any more, with Stalin dead nearly fifty years and the hunt for her father concluded in the most final way possible. "I have the other half of the ashes. His women gave them to me, in an urn. I chose my way of burying them…to bring them to the woman he never stopped loving."

"Very dramatic," Nayden said softly and guardedly. "Very beautiful. I commend you on the poetry with which you live your life." For a moment, she could hear a Russian accent in his voice. *The truth never leaves you, no matter if you wash a thousand times, drive all night, or burn your clothes.* As the old joke went: *No matter where I go, there I am.*

"Will you go back to the U. S. any time soon?"

"In due time," he said. "Everything in due time."

Pleasantries petered out, and Nayden got that dark, furtive look again as he stabbed and slashed his bread to butter and spread it.

"In due time," she echoed. "You know something you aren't telling me."

He stopped in mid-slash and looked at her directly, face to face. "I had to see you."

She regarded him speculatively. "Refresh my memory. Did I know you back then?"

He resumed preparing his fish sandwich. "I am two years younger than you, Anechka. I barely remember you, except from stories told to me by Auntie Dora. You were four when the French couple came to take you away. You might not remember the little boy who hung around Auntie Dora's tavern…"

Marianne's heart skipped a beat as a thousand dark images flooded her memory. "Auntie Dora! Oh my god." Did she remember a little boy? No—just drunken fishermen and sailors, bar fights, cigarette smoke, the smells of fresh beer and stale beer puke, not to mention the river of urine foaming in the alley out back on its way into the Anadyr estuary if it didn't freeze along the way, crossing the gravelly harbor road by a little tin-lined sluice that cars and trucks drove over. How vivid some things were—but how dim most of it was.

"Yes, Auntie Dora," Nayden said as he reached for his mug of steaming black coffee. "Auntie Dora was my mother for real. Your mother married her good-for-nothing brother, because he had local Communist Party connections. Not membership, mind you, but criminal connections."

"He used to beat my poor mother and yell at her," Marianne said with a dull, dark sense of pain that would never go away. "Luckily he was at sea much of the time, fishing. And then he drowned in the Siberian Sea."

Nayden shrugged. "Nobody missed him, I'm sure. You don't remember me? I suppose I was just a toddler then."

Marianne shook her head. She tried to remember, but nothing came.

For a moment, Nayden sounded bitter. "I remember you not as a person, but as a girl who got away. I envied you when I played behind the same bar where you used to play." Marianne barely heard him talking, so overcome was she with memories.

She remembered standing on the seashore by moonlight with her mother, who pointed across the sea and said: *San Francisco. There is your father, my love forever.* It was the seashore on the Ugolny or north side, near the sand spit where her grave would be under the Milky Way forever.

Marianne—Anechka—looked up in memory, at her mother, and asked in a little girl voice: *Is he coming to get us, Mama?*

One day he will, sweetie. One day, Umnitsa, he will come for us.

Umnitsa in Russian was a term of affection, meaning 'good girl' or 'clever girl'. It was one of the few Russian words she would remember in the decades to come. Russia was like a distant dream, shimmering in smoke, very dark and stormy like the Arctic Ocean—it might as well never have happened. Now that the flood gates were open, it most assuredly happened, every tormented and lost minute.

Does he love us, Mama?

Yes, baby. Your Papa loves you.

Will he beat up Uncle Vadim when he comes?

Sweetie, Uncle Vadim went to sea and will never come back. I don't even think about him any more.

You think about Papa?

All the time, baby.

Will Auntie Dora be mad at us about Uncle Vadim?

No, baby, Auntie Dora was always angry with Uncle Vadim. She helps us out a lot. Auntie Dora loves you too, my little Umnitsa.

Marianne had few real memories—just jumbled images and short mental film clips. In some of them, she stood on the shore with her mother, looking east toward America. In others, she stood on the wood-plank floor behind the bar in Auntie Dora's rough and tumble tavern for sailors and fishermen on the docks of Anadyr. There was always rough tobacco smoke, night time, chiaroscuro light, men's booming laughter, the clinking of glasses and tang of raw vodka in the air. Occasionally the fight or the whiff of puke. There was always a washing machine-tumble of voices and gloom and laughter, but Auntie Dora was like a tugboat, an iceberg, an indomitable force moving through wild and dangerous seas of life. She would give Anechka a sweet, or sit her on a stool so the roughest of men could coo at her and think of their daughters far away—some actually cried—and then came the accordion and the shouting, the dancing so the wooden floor boards shook, and grown men crying and singing together. Some would not come home from the Arctic seas. Death looked in every window.

Then, one day, mama was very ill. A doctor with a black bag, wearing a militia colonel's uniform, came and sat by her bedside. An Orthodox priest brought last rites. Auntie Dora and her surviving relatives sheltered Anechka through all of it. Soon after, mama lay in a cemetery on a slight hill near the hook of the great sandbar that stretches south across the mouth of Anadyr Estuary. The wind was always so raw and cruel. The galaxy was always so magnificent—it was like looking toward America and lost Papa—Timofey, the American.

The man Stalin had sent to kill Timofey came to Anechka's rescue. Uncle Victor Mutsev had no desire to kill a man he had known in London, whom he admired for his decency and goodness. By then, the tools of Stalin were turning against the man of steel. Auntie Dora was already old, and having a hard time raising her niece. Her drowned, drunken sailor brother, Vadim, had been penalized posthumously by having his pension denied because he died drunk—falling into a fishing net and being dragged a hundred nautical miles behind the trawler before anyone realized he was missing. That meant Anna Timofeyevna would receive nothing from the state. Auntie Dora's family were decent, hard working people, and they struggled to raise the little Umnitsa as one of their own. She was like a little blue-gray-eyed monkey, the towheaded child, everyone's pet at the bar or at this uncle or that aunt's house. Finally, seeing their difficulty, Stalin's man had come forth. Wealthy Europeans were traveling around the U.S.S.R. adopting orphans. One such family from Paris had come, expecting to adopt a bright young boy of Anechka's age, but the boy turned out to be feeble because of his mother's drinking during her pregnancy—she'd died in childbirth at the local hospital after being rushed there in a police cruiser from the drunk tank. So, instead, with limited time, and enormous disappointment, the wealthy French husband and wife were about to board their plane bound for Moscow, when Auntie Dora and Uncle Viktor approached them at the airport and informed them of a beautiful, precocious little orphan of mixed European-American parentage who might just fit the bill for them. She would not be a son to whom they could pass their aristocratic titles, but she would be splendid and regal when she came of age. Uncle Viktor had a golden tongue, and spun great fairy tales for them. During his long stay in the Arctic winter of Anadyr, waiting to assassinate the little girl's father if he finally showed up as Stalin had planned, Viktor had become fond of Auntie Dora—and more so, carnally, knowing her sister Lyudmila, a local beauty—and he was more aware than anyone else of Anechka's precarious situation. She really was a good and clever girl, a true *umnitsa*, and he did not want to see her waste away in a state orphanage, maybe to die young, or to be married to another drunken, cruel idiot like Vadim, or spend her life in a vodka or fish processing factory with krill for brains.

"Was Auntie Dora your mother?" she asked Nayden.

"She was," he said simply. There was nothing more to be gotten out of him. They left the table and walked together to the elevator, each *en route* to their own hotel room and life.

"Have you met Viktor Mutsev?" Nayden asked as they headed to the heliport. The day was bright, though a cold and blustery dry wind kicked up little devils of dust and grit on the flaky concrete runway with its sheets of fine ice.

"Yes, finally. I may have met him as a child, but I don't remember. He looked after me, though. So did Auntie Dora."

"He looked after many people," Nayden said. "I'm told he lived her for a time, waiting for your father so he could assassinate him."

"What aren't you telling me?" she asked, confronting him by the elevator.

"All in due time." The door rumbled open, letting out a family of European tourists in fur caps and heavy parkas, who looked well-fed and relaxed. "This is as far as I go."

"What about tomorrow?" She did not feel like riding in the elevator with him.

"Before you leave, we may talk again. I have to think about some things." So saying, he left her standing alone and baffled in the lobby while the elevator door closed on his pale face and haunted eyes.

The next morning, Marianne sat breakfast alone—black coffee, rolls, butter and marmalade, orange juice in the American style. She also took a sausage, a poached egg, and a chunk of white fish marinated in vinegar and parsley. Everything was delicious. She'd slept deeply, exhausted from her emotional storm, and woke up famished. She had low expectations of finding any landmarks across the estuary, in Anadyr, that she would recognize. Ancient Siberia was a fog in her memory, interspersed with a few fleeting, blurry memories: the bar, the beach, the sea, the stars.

Her appointment at the police department to see a Sergeant Lena Marinov did appear briefly to see her off. She spotted him standing on the runway with a circle of dark-suited, hard-faced men. They had a sort of politburo look about them. She kept her distance. When he looked over at her, she did wave—an involuntary reflex. He excused himself from his bizenis associates and strolled over to greet her. The helicopter engine was rumbling softly, and the long, sagging lift blades spun languidly. Mechanics were still checking out the open engine cowling on one side. But the pilots climbed on board, and a driver on a yellow towmotor arrived to pull the boarding stairs away. The engines made a few banging sounds, and black gouts of smoke spat from the exhaust grills. The prop blades turned faster.

"Did you sleep well?"

"Like a log."

"Ah, what a beautiful touch of home, to hear your U.S. English."

"I have to go. See you later?"

"Enjoy your visit to Anadyr. Nothing is like it was. I already checked."

"I would have thought you'd offer to show me around over there."

"I'm staying away, for reasons of my own. There's nothing there for me. Just a bit of heart-ache."

"Maybe I'll find the same heart-ache too.'

"Everything around here makes the heart ache."

She waved as the engines started to roar, and the blades began to whirl. Wind blew around them both in the prop wash.

Nayden stood with his hands in his coat pockets, while Marianne already was several steps up the ladder into the helicopter. "Anadyr is bad business for me. I don't think Auntie Dora's tavern still stands. You won't find anything at all that you remember."

"I have to make the journey," she told him. "I've been around the world. Now I have to make this last little leg of the trip."

"I understand," he said. "You have my number."

"Thanks for everything."

He laughed. "We're not quite done yet. I have to see you safely off on the plane back to Alaska and then the Contiguous 48."

"There you go, sounding so American."

"But I am, more so than you, Frenchwoman."

"My father was a U.S. citizen. That makes me more American than you, buddy."

"Buddy," he echoed. "So American of you. Sibling rivalry at every turn."

"What?"

"You win." He waved.

Is it possible? She staggered up the stairs into the welcoming, diesel warmth with its smells of seat leather and military cleaning agents. Siberia had further horrible secrets to dish out. She felt the same kobolds clawing inside her gut as during the Aeolian howling on the Ilyushin airliner yesterday.

He called after her: "I'm staying at the airport hotel one floor up from you. Just call me or ask the concierge. I'll be here another few days."

"I want to see you before I leave," she commanded in a near-hysterical tone. She barked harshly at him. "You be there!"

"Yes, I will be there for you."

"And then?"

"I'm heading back to the United States. I have business there. We will not see each other again after this. I know you'd want it this way, and it's for the best. Believe me, for your sake."

Bizenis? She wondered. She regarded the knot of dark-eyed, stony faced men awaiting Nayden at the other end of the runway.

She said: "I'll be heading home as well in a few days. I'll see you tomorrow, when I'm done with my purpose for coming here."

"I will help you all that I can."

Without responding, Marianne fairly threw herself into the chopper to end the conversation. The interior smelled of upholstery, oil, and cabbage. Several women fussed over small children, and their men sat stolidly holding packages, while the copilot made sure they were strapped in and wouldn't fall out over the estuary.

Anadyr was quite as Nayden had predicted: a desperate, bleak outpost with a few brightly colored blocks of apartments to give it some artificial cheer. Marianne had few reference points in her distant, hazy memory—just images of inside the warm, smoky tavern and the frozen black water outside. In this grim daylight, overcast the color of bluish-gray fish scales, nothing matched the map in her soul, no landmark, not a single sign post of her past. Where she thought Auntie Dora's tavern had been—she could not even remember its name—she found rows of long abandoned concrete ruins that once had been fish processing plants.

Her appointment to walk into the police station was for early the next morning. Disappointed, though not surprised, and perhaps a little relieved to have this over with, she boarded the last, mid-afternoon helo for Ugolny. As the chopper clattered over choppy estuary waters, she looked ahead to a long, hot bath and an early bed time. She wanted to be rested and awake for tomorrow's heart-wrenching journey.

Later, back in Ugolny at the airport hotel, she took a long, hot, soapy bath. She rested in the safety of her locked bathroom, enclosed by warm tiles (almost like the comfort of being behind Auntie Dora's bar). Floating in blue water, in an oversized and luxurious tub, she closed her eyes.

What do I feel?
Nothing much, with this overload.
Am I afraid?
Of course.
But why should I be?
The truth shall set you free.
She thought of the grave.
But the truth is only the beginning. From there, you must travel back to the beginning, and start over. In time it will dawn on you: life is an endless circle, like in the T. S. Eliot *Four Quartets*.

It was like being stuck on a heavy wash cycle, waiting for *rinse* to endlessly trade places with *suds*. She grinned wanly, with little humor, but glad to have that small life preserver of sanity.

As long as I can laugh, I am alive. Laughter makes us free.
She imagined a barren plot of land on which a few weeds waved in the rough air. She dreamed of a silence that had lain over the sand bar for half a century, and would lie there as long as the galaxy wheeled overhead at night, and as long as San Francisco beckoned thousands of miles over the curvature of the ocean. Mama would hold her hand and reassure her—there was nothing to fear from the dead. Only from the living, who ran like wolves in the forest around her. The predators never rested. Their eyes and teeth glittered in the polar moonlight.

After an uneventful helicopter ride across choppy waters hypnotically twinkling with Arctic sunlight, she landed at the heliport in Anadyr. Carrying the urn of ashes in her gray Adidas carryon, she trudged through half-frozen slush to the police station.

As she approached the low, concrete-block structure on a hill street, she smelled a whiff of marijuana smoke. With one foot on the concrete step, and a hand reaching out to the door knob, she paused and sniffed. Yes, it was unmistakeable. At a police station?

She entered, and saw the small blonde woman at the desk, who looked up from some paperwork with a sharp *Da?*

"I am Marianne Didier, from Paris," she said in English, the universal language.

"I am Sergeant Varov," said the girl. "I was expecting you."

Marianne hefted her grip with the urn in it. "I have an appointment."

"Yes." The woman closed her books and folded her hands on the front counter. A back door opened, and two young men came in. They wore constabular uniforms, and looked a bit sheepish. Marianne guessed they were at least slightly stoned, probably from a very bad grade of *trávka* or weed. Then again, Siberia was vast. Theoretically, you could grow entire Kansases and Minnesotas full of eight foot high *cannabis sativa*, and nobody would ever notice. The trouble would be getting past the *bizenis* men to market. Hence, the police were smoking bad dope here. The two young constables eyed Marianne with suspicious, veiled eyes. They looked violent and scary. She was glad Lenka Varov stood between her and them.

"Meet my brother Anatoly," Lenka said, "and my cousin Mikhail."

"Hello," said Marianne. She put her satchel on the counter, and managed a weak grin and a wave. "Nice to meet you."

"And you," said the stoned policemen, like cats standing shoulder to shoulder.

"So," Lenka said. "You need guides to help you find mother's grave and leave ashes. Native people here would respect your intentions greatly."

"Guides," Marianne said with lawyerlike precision. "A guide."

Lenka was brusque and self-assured. "We have bizenis elsewhere. We will go together."

The two men argued with her briefly, saying there was not time, but she overruled them. A dollar was a dollar. A hundred dollars was a hundred more than they had in their pockets right now. She gestured, and they hurried back outside to load suitcases of something into the back of the patrol cruiser, which looked like a Land Rover knockoff.

Marianne sat on a bench by a window, and looked idly outside while cradling her satchel and the urn in it.

Mikhail hollered something from the driveway.

"We go now to see the grave," Lenka said, grabbing her hat. "Come." She extended a hand, as if Marianne were a child. "Must be very sad for you. Will be over soon."

Her day was proving strangely convoluted, but Marianne was prepared to go along with anything. This was not her day—it belonged to god, the universe, to reality, whatever. She was a passenger, not the driver. So it was with the police car. Sergeant Varov had made the arrangements, including having Marianne meet them in Anadyr rather than Ugolny, which would have been much easier for Marianne.

They changed vehicles on a shadowy side street, which looked as though sunlight never penetrated here. Big piles of plowed snow rose on either side of the frigid street, covered with black dust. The air smelled of coal smoke. Smoke-colored clouds were ripe with more snow.

Now in a new Land Rover knockoff, they rode to the harbor. Mikhail drove, while Lenka rode shotgun in front. Anatoly sat in the rear bucket seats with Marianne, looking none too happy. Or maybe he was stressed about something. He kept chewing his lip and acting nervous. His eyes flickered from one thing to another. The holstered automatic dangling from his belt looked none too reassuring. Marianne noticed machine pistols under the seats, along with boxes and belts of ammo, polishing rags, cleaning rods, and related weapons paraphernalia. They were sitting on a veritable armory, and yet she did not feel entirely safe.

At the harbor, they barely slowed down for stop signs and red lights. Mikhail drove rapidly and nervously. The rover bounced on its tight chassis as it headed to the open, gaping mouth of the estuary ferry, a large white motor vessel with black hull and red Plimsoll line at the water level. Rust streaks bled down her hull. Bilge water spurted from pump holes in her sides. But she was a big, brawny ship with a powerful engine and robust beam or width, prepared for any sort of sea storm.

The passage was calm. Marianne was lulled by the mix of basso profundo engine noise and the shrieks of large, wheeling gulls. The steel deck throbbed under her boots. She and Lenka stood silently on the deck, letting the cold wind blow through their hair. The two policemen smoked cigarettes some distance down the railing.

In Ugolny, they drove up the ramp onto dry land. Not far away, Marianne could see the rolling fin of a large jet readying for takeoff.

"We have no real roads here," said Lenka. "I have seen films of streets in Moscow and Europe. It's amazing! Here, we have no main road along the south shore. On the north side, where we are going, is frozen gravel road as far as sand bar on coast, where your mother's dear grave lies. We will take you there."

The men understood enough English to argue some more.

Lenka barked back at them, but seemed to be wavering.

"Okay," Lenka said, turning to Marianne as if Marianne had been part of the conversation. "How long you want to stay?"

Marianne sighed. "I don't know. I have not seen my mother's grave before, and I probably never will see it again. A while, I think."

"An hour?" Lenka prodded. "Two hours?"

"I'd like to get some coffee and a sandwich, and stay about two hours."

"Okay," Lenka said. She explained to her boys, who grew more tense. Mikhail slammed the car into low gear with a curse as they turned into a parking lot. Lenka climbed out and went into a restaurant. Fifteen minutes later, she emerged, laden with plastic bags of food and drink. For another fifteen minutes, the car filled with the smells of black coffee, chilled marinated fish, cabbage, potatoes, and onions. Outside, huge gulls paraded around looking for scraps. A Yupik family eating at a picnic area shooed off a stray dog that had cautiously slunk close for a look at their scraps.

Soon enough, the car was en route again.

They drove at a rapid clip through a barren landscape of rolling hills and short, bitten-off grass and brush. Snow capped the distant hills. Off on their right, the sea lay like a leaden blanket. Wan sunlight shimmered over the rippling water from sullen clouds.

As Lenka had promised, a frozen gravel road made a winding ribbon above the sand line, following the shore inside the estuary. Ahead, a long spit grew on the horizon and then resolved into a shapeless sand bar.

At a crossroads, one path ran north and the other south on the sand bar. There, on a low hill, among boulders, were a number of mingled rocks and broken grave stones. In the center, just thirty feet or so above sea level, stood a weathered shrine of concrete blocks with a faded blue dome the size of a diving helmet, and an Orthodox cross atop that. The cross, with its characteristic two beams—one straight, the smaller one oblique under it— had been painted white, perhaps annually in some ceremony, but was reduced almost entirely to its natural gray stone color. The elements out here, Marianne thought, must be unimaginable, between winds and floods and storms.

"We go now," Lenka said. She spoke to the two men, who alternated between fits and sullen silence. They were clearly all wired up about something.

There was a long walk across a low tidal flat. Lenka walked beside Marianne. Both women had their hands in their pockets. It could have been a leisurely stroll, except for the anxious, impatient noises made by the two men.

Marianne glanced back, to see Mikhail and Anatoly leaning against the police cruiser. They were smoking cigarettes as they waited, hopping from foot to foot. They looked repeatedly at their wristwatches, and glared after their female relative. "What is with them?" Marianne asked with a touch of annoyance.

Lenka made a dismissive gesture with one hand. "Think nothing of them, *Gospoja*." The Russian word for Mistress rolled on her tongue, sounding like *gaspajah* to Marianne's ears. "They are boys who never grew up."

"Tell me about your parents," Lenka said.

Marianne was too overcome with emotion, lugging her satchel, to speak coherently. She saw ahead the rise of gravel, the boulders, the cross, the graves. The embassy man had told her over the phone in Paris that her mother's grave was marked with a freshly hewn marker, to make it easy for

Tim Nordhall to find it should he ever come after the fact. At least, so the embassy man had been told by his sources in Novossibirsk, who had never been to Anadyr but checked with Lenka Varov's office in the Western Hemisphere, thousands of miles for Novossibirsk. And Lenka Varov had only been to the cemetery a few times in her own life.

The men started shouting.

Lenka stopped, causing Marianne to reluctantly cease plowing her boots through a mix of sand, snow, and gravel.

Nearby, wind rustled over the sea and rattled in Marianne's ears. She could barely hear the men shouting.

Lenka waved to them, saying in Russian that she would be right there.

Mikhail was on a portable phone, walking up and down nodding and gesticulating, as if someone were yelling at him.

Anatoly kept waving, jumping, shouting urgently to his sister.

"Listen, *Gospoja* Didier," Lenka said. "I got to go now."

"It's okay," Marianne said. "I think I can find the grave. Will you come back in two hours?"

"*Da, da.* Two hours. I come back. We come back." Lenka backed away, making gestures of relax, relax with both hands. She kept making reassurances and then turned to run back along the beach.

Marianne, now alone, trudged on. She came to the rise and stopped.

Behind her, she heard the distant slam of car doors. She saw the police cruiser do a fast U-turn and wheel away in a cloud of dust on a high, dry portion of the gravel road. They were headed back in the direction of Ugolny.

Consumed with her mission, Marianne put it out of her thoughts. Stumbling on the uneven ground, she fell twice. Her palms were rough and painful from gravel burns. The skin in her palms looked red from both the scrapes and the cold.

The stone was not hard to find. It was larger, cleaner, and more recent than most of the others. Some were old and cracked, with cyrillic lettering dating to the early explorers of the 1800s. She found the gravestone of her mother lying on its side near the top of the rise, not far from the shrine and the Orthodox cross.

If the embassy man had heard the stone was fresh and new, he did not realize that half a century of hard weather lay between the age of Stalin and that of Yeltsin. The stone was unbroken—the only one intact, that she saw—but it was a sour shade of smoky gray, streaked with salt and pitted with efflorescence. It was covered with a patina of mosses and lichens in green, white, and rust-reddish. But her dear, sweet name was clearly visible, etched in moss, in the Latin alphabet.

Some fresh flowers, wrapped in cellophane from the airport gift shop, lay beside the stone. Someone had come here, very recently—maybe this morning or yesterday—and brought the flowers. They'd left the flowers in a crack between the stone and the gravel under it, pinning the flowers down with a few small stones to prevent wind from savaging them prematurely. Everything here would quickly weather and blow away, that much was clear. The flowers were expensive carnations, flown in from some warmer place on earth along the Siberian air routes, maybe even from Alaska—or, she speculated, from Seattle. Right now, it didn't matter.

It was herself, her lost childhood, that she had come to redeem.

Marianne threw herself on the cold stone, sobbing, and lost herself in time. She cried hard, more so than even the massive cry she'd had in the airplane's toilet. If her shoulder blades ached after that, they would be in pain after this. It was like a violent, out of control beating.

She was blind with grief and longing for the lost, long ago past. She should have had a mother and a father, and yet both were torn from her. Now her decades of numbness, the crazy drinking and partying, were torn from her soul in turn, leaving the fresh wounds of the late 1940s. Just past toddlerdom, she'd had no choice or understanding, no guilt or control, in matters so long ago. She could not say far away, because it was right here. She had come back to the focus and the epicenter of her life's childhood crash and burn.

Still sobbing, she rose after a long time.

Why had she not thought to bring a little shovel or a pick? She cried anew at the stubborn Siberian resistance to any slightest comfort or reason. How could she force his ashes into the frozen ground? She clawed at it until her nails broke and the skin around her fingertips hung in shreds. The scrapes in her palms hurt worse than ever. Now they actually bled. She took a sharp rock the size of a melon and beat the ground, trying to break it. She sobbed, she groaned, she cursed, she implored. She spoke soothingly, beseeching her mother. Oh please, dear mama. Just this little favor for me. I came so far to see you and bring him here for you, for both of you to be together. Okay, to make me happy too. Is that so much to ask.

"Go to hell!" she screamed hoarsely at the harsh sky overhead.

Only a few screeching gulls mocked her as they circled looking for a fish kill, or maybe a poor crab scuttling among the lichen-blotted rocks and pocked ice sheets like window shards. The tide was low, and a smell of cold rotting kelp made the very air unattractive.

She stood and contemplated the satchel. Taking the urn from it, she threw the satchel away. It landed out of sight somewhere on the far side of the cemetery rise.

She had come to redeem her soul and her lost childhood. Sniffling, but dry of tears, she unscrewed the lid of the urn. It was surprisingly light. The ashes inside were thick and flaky, the color of the sky above.

For a moment, she thought of dumping them. The wind would blow them away, but then did it not blow everything away? But not the spirit of the dead woman who lay here, a young life snuffed out so cruelly. Regarding the logic of the flowers, she just dribbled a few ashes into cracks in the ground. She screwed the lid back on, and laid the urn carefully alongside the grave stone. On second thought, she laid it down on the other side, away from the flowers. This was her moment, not his. He had no doubt already cried over her, if he had tears for such things. She used her wounded hands to painfully scrape enough gravel close to almost cover the urn. The local people, if any came here, were spirit worshipers, animists, who would not disturb a place like this out of fear for their own souls. The urn might lie here a year, a century, a thousand years—however long it took for the sun, and the air, and the water, and the earth to grind everything down to dust and return it to the drifting galactic fog of eternity among the stars.

When there was nothing more to do, when there were no more tears, when she was exhausted from loss and grief, Marianne knew her journey was finished. Now life could begin again.

She blew her two loved ones a final kiss, and strode back across the beach toward the gravel road.

No sign of Lenka and her brother and her cousin or the police cruiser.

As she strode along, numb and without feeling, Marianne looked at her wristwatch—not with the impatience shown earlier by Mikhail and Anatoly as they looked at theirs.

Two hours had passed, and Lenka should be back to pick her up any time now. That had been the agreement.

No sign of anyone.

Marianne was growing thirsty. She had cried all the salt out of her system, and all her water. She was dehydrated. So much water all around—in the salt-pocked ice, in the sea, in the taunting clouds—and nothing to drink.

Hands in her pockets, she walked in steady, long strides. She hunched her shoulders to make her parka bigger around herself, and shelter herself from the elements.

Time now to return to France, and to look after the *grande maison* in Paris, the Maison Troisroses near Avignon, and her three boys. She had grandchildren now—where had she been all this time? Grand-mère would be chain-smoking out of concern.

Then, too, from her travels around the world in search of Tim Nordhall, and her conversations with so many people, she had a whole box of notes. She'd been in the habit of scribbling furious, cryptic notes in pencil, ballpoint, or even mascara on whatever was handy—note paper, card stock torn from old cigarette cartons, napkins, anything that came to hand. Now it was time to collage them, to piece it all together in a logical time frame, at least, if not for herself, then for her sons and their children. They should all be proud of the legacy of Tim Nordhall, and the sacrifices of the woman he had never stopped loving, nor had mama ever stopped thinking of her lover in the far West. Or east, from Siberia.

As she approached the gravel road, a sleek European luxury car pulled up. Its elegant, dark-green metal gleamed in sunlight.

If not the police, then who?

She had a strong feeling.

The car pulled up, and its lone passenger stepped out of the driver's side.

Her hunch was right—it was Nayden Marinov.

The last awful shoe was yet to drop.

Let it—she was ready, even eager, to put all this behind her.

He stood with his hands in the pockets of his long coat, which hung loosely and easily around his tall frame. He looked ruggedly, criminally handsome with his dark hair blowing in the wind, and sunglasses parked on top of his forehead. He looked youthful for a man in his mid forties. His face betrayed little emotion. He was a man who had long buried his emotions and their moral sinews. His eyes had a flat, leaden, calculating confidence to them. If he smiled, it was almost a grimace.

"Where are the police?" she called out as she drew near.

"They won't be coming for you," he called back to her.

He extended a helping hand, but she ignored it, preferring to clamber up the berm to the main gravel road surface on her own power.

"I came to rescue you," he said.

"Thank you. I appreciate that. And the flowers."

He said nothing. He waited until she had walked around the car. He made no move to open the door or offer any more polite gestures. When she was seated inside, and buckled up, he got in and slammed the door shut. The car started up with a rustle of expensive machinery. The car inside smelled of leather, and fine oils.

The smell of drug money, she thought. *The irresistible song of bizenis.*

"I am going to drive you to the airport and see you take off from here. I don't want you to look back, or ever return here."

They rode in silence through the unchanging, empty landscape.

"Thanks," she said simply.

"I owe you something."

"That's on your dime."

"I understand." He leaned forward to wipe condensation off the windshield with a rag from under the seat. The car was a rental from the airport—the best they had, of course.

"It was nice to meet you, Mr. Samsonov."

"You figured it out." He hardly seemed surprised. He kept his hands on the steering wheel. His eyes only briefly flickered in her direction. He was a chess playing type. He'd calculated all this ahead of time. He was the type of man who planned his emotions ahead of time. You had to, to survive in his business.

"You left your credit card on the table when you paid for dinner yesterday evening."

"Maybe it was a Freudian desire to help you learn the truth. About me. About Anadyr."

"My mother suffered here," Marianne said. "That is all that really matters." She looked at him. "Your mother."

He nodded. "This is a little armpit of hell, yes."

"Don't make light of it."

"I'm not," he said sharply. "There we go already. Sibling rivalry, like I said. It must be in the air."

She did not say it, but she wondered if Samsonov—Uncle Vadim—had raped her to make her pregnant, or if she had consented to have sex with him for his name, his ration card, and his meager seaman's pay. Mama must have been desperate. If Marianne had any tears left she would have cried again.

"Look," he said, "I know you think I am a terrible guy. I am a very terrible guy. It's true. But you are my sister, and I will get you out of here alive and in one piece."

He pulled out a huge Makarov hand gun, which he laid on the seat between them. From another pocket, he pulled out two clips of spare ammunition, which he laid beside the gun. He pulled the rag over them, which he had used to wipe the windows.

Marianne gripped the seat around her with white knuckles. What was this now? She remembered the arsenal in the police cruiser.

"We will come to a militia checkpoint up the road in a minute," Nayden said. "I got through without a hitch coming this way."

"Because your thugs let you through. I can already guess the whole story."

"You have a big imagination," he said warily, eyeballing the road ahead and behind, looking for signs of an ambush. "Whatever you're thinking, think the worst and you are probably right."

"Lenka..." she said, filled with concern. She'd begun to like the brisk little cop. She'd already had fantasies of Lenka returning to Latvia one day, now that the Iron Curtain was gone, and of marrying a blond, blue-eyed man from Riga perhaps. Starting a new life where her grandparents had left off before Stalin's purges and mass relocations of entire peoples.

It was not to be.

"Oh my god," Marianne said, holding her hands before her mouth. Her eyes bulged at the sight before them.

A number of heavily armed Spetsnaz special forces in white Arctic camouflage stood by the sides of the road. On the road itself were blue and green uniformed local militia police in fatigue caps and olive-drab battle dress.

In the center of the road were two cars.

One was the police cruiser, lying on its side riddled with bullet holes.

About 100 meters away sat a second car, a small white sedan, burning hard, and flat on the road surface as its tires had been shot away and were now on fire. Blacker than black, smoke poured out from its seats, its tires, its oils and benzine, and the three or four bizenis thugs inside. Before dying, Lenka and Mikhail and Anatoly had made an accounting of themselves.

Anatoly and Mikhail lay by the police cruiser, shredded by bullets, piles of raw meat, broken bones, and torn clothing. Their faces were caved in and unrecognizable. They lay on their sides, fetally, roughly facing each other.

Lenka's face looked as though she were asleep, pale and calm-eyed. Her small body likewise had been torn into a mangle of ripped clothing, shattered bones, and opened up ribs. She lay face up, with her arms sprawled over her head, and her legs crossed at the knees. Her pearly little teeth were visible between blue lips, and she still had little pink, plastic flower ties in her blonde hair.

A few pasty militia men, unshaven and cynical-faced, bent to look in the car—more to ogle the pretty Western woman and the fancy interior driven by an impressive looking *bizenis* man, than look for anything suspicious.

Seconds later, the wreckage lay behind them.

Slowly, Marianne took her hands from her face, breathing less raggedly.

"Sorry you had to see that," Nayden said. "You got done what you came here to do, that's the main thing."

"That girl...Lenka..."

"Don't grieve over her. Russia is full of them. Back in the 1940s, the whole world was one big mass of Lenkas."

"You were involved in this," Marianne said through gritted teeth.

"I was looking out for my own interests. Those three were crooked cops who tried to knuckle in on big business way beyond their scope."

"Who ambushed them?" She hit her brother repeated on the arms with her fist, in a futile gesture of rage and revulsion. Yes, she was grieving for Lenka, and her grandparents, and all the millions of people harmed by the Hitlers and Stalins of the world, unto the nth generation, long after their own disgusting animal deaths.

Nayden brushed his sister's impotent fists away. "Stop it. I'm just an investor."

"You came here to look after your business, not after me."

"Not quite. I was contacted by an old uncle of ours, who lived here when we were small. Your father's assassin, though he threw his guns away and returned to Moscow."

"Uncle Viktor," she intoned.

"Yes. I have never met him, but he spoke very passionately and persuasively to me that he is too old to come here himself, but he knew I was coming here on business—apparently not too difficult to track if you have connections around the world—and all but demanded that I look after you. That's when he told me that you are my half-sister."

"I wish it were not true."

"It won't be for very long. I'm going to do you a big favor and disappear from your life. I have done my job here. I have taken care of you..." He put the gun and the ammo away as he spoke. "...and of my own business as well. You are outraged right now, and emotionally drained, but figure I did you a big favor today. If you had tagged along with those three cops, you might be dead right now. Instead, you get to fly back to Paris and pick up your life where you left off. You have your sons, your houses, your money, and your grandchildren. And, in case you are wondering, I am not jealous. I've made my own money, my own way. Nobody came and adopted me. I shot and stabbed my way out of this hell hole. You can hold it against me all you want. But you know how fucking miserable life was. Do you remember that? Do you? Answer me!"

He reached across and squeezed her forearm in his fist so tightly that it hurt. She did not resist, but melted back into crying mode. It was a dry, lippy, hazy-eyed cry at the memory of the drunken sailors, the dancing, the rape of her mother by Vadim Samsonov, the birth of this monster in some back chamber of Auntie Dora's tavern. Maybe what hurt most was that the woman whose memory she had cherished almost like her mother, the woman who Nayden had fibbed and claimed as his own mother because his real mother had been taken from him, that Aunt Dora had probably been quite a crook in her own right. God knew how many bodies had ended up in the Anadyr on their way to the fishes or the great bay in the Bering Sea. But she'd had to be tough to survive, Auntie Dora. And she'd always been so kind and loving to the little ones.

Beyond all that, Marianne's heart broke at the thought of her own failure in life…

The airport hove into view, and Nayden pulled up at the edge of the tarmac. An U.S. Alaska Airlines 737 was just then boarding. Nayden handed her a paper book of tickets. "Take these and get on board."

"My stuff…"

"Everything is packed and on its way to Nome. Don't go near the hotel. I have enemies around here. You see what happened to your friend Lenka. I don't want to see you lying in the road too."

She climbed out on rubbery legs. "Oh my god. What do I say to you?"

He regarded her from the car with those leaden eyes. "Bye, sister."

She stared at him, trying to say the words, but they would not come.

"We're done," he said. "There's nothing more to do or say. We're finished. I left flowers, you left ashes. Neither of us is perfect, by a long shot, but we're both survivors. Go on. Good bye."

She slammed the door and stood there, while he wasted no time driving away. The last she ever saw of him was the receding brake lights of the Mercedes as he paused to let a baggage cart rumble by ahead of him— probably carrying her suitcase, and the copious notes she planned to assemble into a journey, a legacy for her children and grandchildren, once she got safely back to France…which would be tomorrow, perhaps, or the day after. She would miss nothing here. Nothing at all.

She'd proven that she was indeed mama's good and clever little girl child. Like a faint echo of rose petals pressed amid important pages in a long-closed book, she could faintly recall the voice and tone when her mother called her *Umnitsa*.

As she boarded the flight on an exposed, open air ladder, with her hair blowing in the wind, she felt a cold, empty sense of freedom. It was the hollowness of starting life over again. But at least she was privileged to do that. She would go back to the beginning, unearth her notes, and start compiling the story of herself, and before that her father and mother, so that the wheel came full circle and never stopped turning.

2006—Marianne's Journal

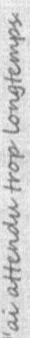

-- i --

  I have delayed too long before committing
these memories to paper—for my sons and
their children, if nobody else.

  Now that I know the complete truth about
l'affaire Nordhall, as much as it can ever be
known, I have retired--not to the *Maison
Grande* in Paris, but to Maison Troisroses in
the seclusion of Provençe--to compile my notes
and quotes, and create what permanent record
I might. I owe at least that much to my sons
and their posterity.

  More selfishly, I owe at least as much to
myself, since the circle of my life is inscribed
within the story of my father, his women, and
his war with Josef Stalin over the atomic bomb.

-- ii --

Anadyr was a baited trap—but the prey never came, not to bury the love of his life, nor even to rescue me. Had my father known where to find us, things would have been different, but not necessarily any better.

As it was, he did not know I existed, and by a most cruel twist of fate, he thought she had once again abandoned him—which was never true. She did what she had to do in her tangled net of warring puppet strings.

Stalin had banished her to Anadyr, so far from Moscow, so near to U.S. territory, as bait—in hope of luring my elusive father to a terrible revenge death to be inflicted by the dictator's goons. The man of steel was already then dying. His bow was slack. History swept past him as it does with all of us.

-- iii --

Speak, Memory—take me back in time, past the moment of my birth on a remote shore of the Bering Sea, to a warm but dangerous place called San Francisco during the greatest of all wars, of which my beautiful mother told me before she died so young.

In San Francisco, where I was conceived in 1945, I was—as the American expression goes—but a glint in my handsome daddy's eye and, in that same moment, a shiver in my beautiful mommy's step when the arrow pierced her heart once again.

Their first moment together actually came earlier during that great Iliad—in London right after the Blitz, when it seemed the good world they'd all known was coming to an end, and nothing was what it seemed. But then, that is what this song is all about— love and war—the sirens of love and war, that sing upon the seas of the world.

Their moment in London was as quickly lost as it occurred, in the unstoppably churning breakers of time—when atoms seamlessly rearrange themselves in a luminous soup—time at its irreducible minimum being a condensate without shape or form, shade without color, paralysed force, gesture without motion—never stopping for definition, nor even broadcasting transient coordinates, like those lonely war ships full of men far out at sea.

Parle, Mémoire— me prendre dans le temps, passé le moment ma naissance sur un rivage à distance de la mer de Béring, à

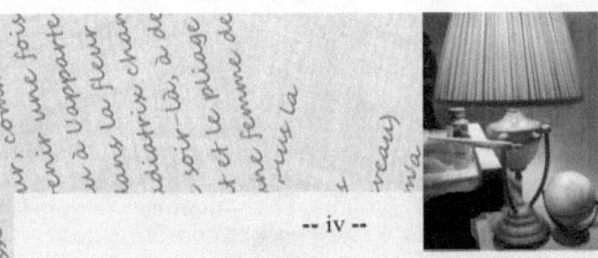

-- iv --

That shadow of all shadows, jaguar in the night, Uncle Viktor, he told me—when he let me find him many years later in Moscow after the Cold War, where I brought him coffee and cigarettes and raspberry jam from the West—he told me that the universe is an infinite and eternal circle.

"Everything ends as it begins, and in the end is its beginning," Viktor told me over Russian vodka, American cigarettes, and Finnish marmalade in his miserable cold-water flat, while the lights were out over Chertanovo's brooding high rise tenements.

In my later years I have become a woman of introspection rather than action. Uncle Viktor had many well-worn books in his flat, among them the love story of Yuri Zhivago and Larissa Guishar—the beautiful, immortal, yet tragic Lara. Many of these were controversial and forbidden books in Stalin's morbid universe. But Uncle Viktor was widely read, having traveled and lived in the supposedly corrupt and decaying West so many years.

2

Strange how the most corrupt and venal of people will tell their people that up is down, down is up, evil is wonderful, and good is to be avoided, all in the name of phony patriotism and phony moralities. Uncle Viktor figured it out for himself, in London and New York and San Francisco, decades before any of his baffled and brainwashed contemporaries cracked the code of lies. What a pack of nonsense the *nomenklatura* wrote in the papers and spouted in the media to keep people stupid and enslaved. They must have laughed, driving around in fine cars, with their hard currency, and Western goods hidden in the trunk, while hard-working common people suffered and lived lives of abject illogic—willingly, if that is possible, since they knew nothing better.

Stalin murdered and betrayed many persons--and just as many would take their revenge on him if they could. If anyone betrayed Stalin, it was his favorite spy, Viktor Mutsev. Then again, Stalin nearly had Uncle Viktor rubbed out in his rage that Viktor did not bring him my father's head on a silver table service. In the end, for my mother's sake, Uncle Viktor and the

American CIA conspired to hide my father and his two surviving women somewhere, deep in the heart of America. All of this is part of my story. I finally understood why he never came for us. It was a relief to know that he never knew. He was a quiet, easy going man of profound courage—he would have split the sea to come for us if only he had known the truth a lot earlier.

3

As the long Muscovite evening wore on, in early spring 1992, Uncle Viktor (Colonel Mutsev) and I sat at his plain wooden table. We heard icy cold wind and hard rain drops rattling the windows, listened to traffic noise and distant train horns, and hoped his granddaughter Marinka would come home alive yet once more from some punkish drug rage near Arbat.

In the tedious way of old men, Viktor found his eyeglasses and hovered in the dark (the electricity was out again) searching on the wall amid his books. Pedantically, he forced me to be patient, though I trembled with impatience, while he took down a well-worn volume of T. S. Eliot. He opened it as we sat with an oil lantern on the table at our elbows. He pointed a Destroyer's clay-colored life-and-death finger (reminding me of the Creator in the Sistine Chapel ceiling) to the opening page of *Four Quartets*, beginning at the beginning of *Burnt Norton*:

Time present and time past

Are both perhaps present in time future

And time future contained in time past.

I was already becoming an amateur *philosophe*, as my beloved Grandmère said a woman must become once the last blush is off the bloomed rose, and she passes the pivotal age of 45. I came to Viktor's shabby apartment during that 1992 evening in the last shimmering bloom of my life as a tabloid gladiatrix sung by paparazzi. I left there later that evening, bound for Sheremetyevo, in the wilting and folding gauze of my developing new aura as a woman of reflection...and of tranquility, thank heaven, which deepened as the last crashing chords of a great symphony rumbled through a rapt theater, and Stalin's poisoned arrow at last fell into indifferent soil.

-- V --

We each walk down our own long corridors of many closed doors. We open a door on some impulse, having no idea what lies beyond. We step into the unknown which in time becomes the familiar past, but the door remains a passage to our unknowable future. Only the moment around us is illumined, more with questions than with answers, while larger time remains dark. It is best that we do not look beyond the breath-taking beauty of the moment.

In the farthest-looking telescope, just as in the closest-looking microscope, we become only atoms once again. Everything is revealed, but nothing is known, because nothing matters anymore when everything has been settled and done; when the equations of life—of time and action, of love and war— have been reduced and canceled to their lowest common orbits.

Like my father on that West African beach, with the smoke and stench of war still in the blue air, I embrace the granularity of the moment. Wounded though he was, and staggering with a gun in his hand, he relished the feel of wet sand between his bare toes. He swathed himself in balmy air and fresh wind as the golden atoms of the day reconstituted themselves—as they inevitably do, time being an endless machine of uncountable and immeasurable infinitesimal parts.

-- vi --

When Viktor and I spoke in that Moscow flat, now
many years ago in itself, Stalin's nightmare state had
finally been nullified by its victims and their
befuddled leaders. My journey around the world, in
search of my long-lost true father, was nearly at its
goal. Viktor and I spoke honestly and fearlessly for
hours over Russian vodka, American cigarettes,
Russian bread, German butter, Canadian cookies, and
Finnish marmalade. Everything was on the table.
There were no more secrets. Viktor should know
about life and death, just as my father should know
about time, and love, and clocks. As one of Stalin's top
assets, Viktor had killed many men and women, being
a triple agent through night and fog, and licensed to
kill without reflection, humanity, or guilt, like a god.
Uncle Viktor said: "Everything ends as it begins, and
in the end is its beginning."

I found peace in that, at last. Our lives are finite,
but they turn in circles forever, like the hands on a
clock. Hours, minutes, and seconds are each bound up
in the great cosmic clockwork mechanism in which no
part is alone, and all are part of the infinite totality of
a chain that has no beginning or end. Like an orbiting
Sputnik, the wanderer always finds herself again in
the place where she was not long ago, or even far back
on an Arctic shore, alone with the poor, beautiful
woman who died too soon and forever lies there in the
granular sand, with only a few weeds and gulls to
dance around her final bed.

-- vii --

I will take you even further back, *mon journal*, to
the moment when my father was a young U.S. navy
officer who quasi-died in the sea after a German
torpedo attack. He was a young clockmaker from New
Haven, and confused as young people always are by
hope and hormones. He'd left behind in New Haven a
beautiful red-haired girl he would never see again,
and did not have a woman in his life. Time stopped for
him on the sunny green sea where dead men's corpses
floated still burning. His clock was stopped but his
heart kept ticking. He was the only man on his ship to
return from the dead. Time gradually fixed his clock
and his life resumed its orbit among the spheres.

How did he know he was actually alive? I would
say because he felt a great irrational urge to survive,
which is our natural instinct as humans. Maybe he felt
some great purpose, because in the end he helped
save the world from Stalin and atomic war. Stalin
never forgave him, and had men like Viktor hunting
my father for years. Only everything became
smooshed in the cool condensate of time and atoms,
and nothing was as it seemed, except the terrible loss I
had known first-hand as a child in remote Anadyr.

-- viii --

My father may not have known right then what his purpose in life was meant to be, but he was drawn to life, buffeted like Odysseus. What really matters is that he spoke prayers while he scrubbed his sword in salt water--actually, a rusty pistol he found in a smashed lifeboat that beached, still-born, without having reborn a soul. Maybe the salt water was tears, shed for all the shipmates who died horribly before his eyes, in fire and oil, whom the useless boat might have saved. I even know that the legend on its broken little bow read *H.M.S. Sturmer.* But that was the steel warship, which never made it near shore after the torpedo atack, of which my father was the only survivor.

-- ix --

I was able to put his story together from my own notes, and from the words of people I met along my journey to the truth of my life:

—the aged U-boat commander and his beautiful granddaughter in West Berlin;

--the old spy master and his still beautiful wife in Canterbury; we spoke in a tourist diner near the cathedral, while the pealing of the angel bells--of the Oxfords and Dunstans in Arundel Tower--made me sob uncontrollably for their unstinting beauty and my broken heart, while Haywarden's wife handed me paper napkins from a dispenser;

--my cold and distant aunt in New Haven, who was yet, by time-trained reflex, sworn to Federal secrecy because Stalin's agents had hunted my father for so many years—she loved him, and trusted nobody; I could have been a spy, sent to assassinate him--that was the magnitude of Stalin's personal hatred for my father;

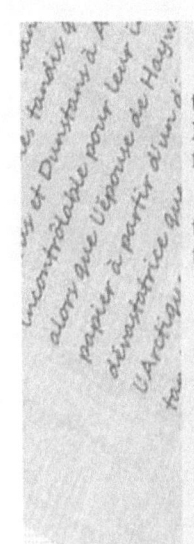

2

--Uncle Viktor himself, caring only for his darkly tattooed and nickel-studded granddaughter in a Moscow slum and glad to get a pound of fresh coffee from the West;

--the one-eyed man near San Francisco who knew the whole story, and drove my soul the last few miles to its light;

--and finally the rest, which will be clear as I finish this journal and its enormous appendix, the story of Tim Nordhall himself, and his women, and his adventures in the global wars of 1939-1991.

Each interview led me to the next, according to a road map I thought had been planned by Jaguar, but in fact was a collaboration with his former deadly enemy, a one-eyed American station chief of whom I have more to tell—who, along with Haywarden, worked for Wild Bill Donovan and OSS, and later for the CIA.

-- X --

The need for secrecy in *l'affaire du main en bois* (the wooden hand of Ivor Crane) ground to a halt with Stalin's death in 1953, but these things have a way of leading a life of their own, in the darkness, for decades afterward. Stalin was already a sick old man by 1945, and the world was a far better place with his demise (from smoking, stroke, and sheer malignancy) barely eight years later. Uncle Viktor said that Stalin kept a picture of my father and his three women in his office toilet, to remind him, as he shat, that this was the man who took the atomic bomb from him in 1945 when he thought he first had it in his grasp. A man and two women got away, but my mother (sometimes called the third woman in the relevant espionage circles) was the unlucky one. Who knows how things might have turned out if she had not been traded by certain U.S. agents to the NKVD on that foggy night in San Francisco.

Detective Howard Lemon delivered her to the NKVD on this dock near Hunter's Point with her one little suitcase, when she was pregnant with me. Mr. Lemon did this with true American outrage over injustice--sadly, even angrily.

Howard Lemon would later tell people you could hear sirens whispering on the distant oceanic horizon, ships calling each other far out at sea, which reminded him of those wartime radio broadcasts from London, by Walter Winchell, that always began with "Good evening Mr. and Mrs. America, from border to border, and coast to coast, and all the ships at sea. Let's go to press..."

And to press we shall go, my little journal.

-- xi --

I was a middle-aged woman by the time I came to that same dock, north of Hunter's Point, inside San Francisco Bay, with four companions. We stopped at the point where Howard Lemon, on orders from above, nearly half a century earlier, had delivered my mother to be taken away by the NKVD.

I helped my father out of the car. Viktor's American counterpart drove us there. With us were the two women my father married, in spirit if not on paper. He was a duogamist molded, golem-like, though very handsome, amid war's strange beauty and wonder. That was in the exceptional plasma forge of those momentous months in 1945, when anything was possible. San Francisco, in the summer of that year, was the intersection point of two vast wars—the final moments of World War II, and the true beginning of the Cold War. If that was Iliad, the rest was Odyssey, though all metaphors are imperfect by definition. Those months also saw the founding, in that place, of the United Nations—the martialing point for history's first atomic war—and the full orchestra of Stalin's nightmare symphony. San Francisco might be a city of love during those final wartime months, but it was also a glistening and dangerous place of car chases in the night, of flying bullets, and of terrified eyes hovering in the shelter of rainy doorways.

-- xii --

With my companions, that evening in 1992 when peace and
levity floated across the water, I was still attractive, but the
paparazzi had long gone from my life. I drove them out like a plague
of rats. Not even a shade of pale beside Mama's long ago beauty, I
stood at that same spot and looked across the sea. I looked west
toward Siberia, where I knew a little girl of four once stood on that
other beach, near Anadyr, holding her mother's hand. That little girl
looked eastward into eternity, above the sea and under the stars, to
where her mother pointed. Her mother said in a low voice while the
waves of the North Pacific Ocean thundered under a sliver moon:
"That way is America, and San Francisco, and your father. That way
are all good things, and I don't know how to get them back if ever

2

again. I meant well, but I made such a mess of everything." She may have been sad, but I remember not much guilt about her—everything she did was as it had to be done. Optimists and boosters will say that is the greatest excuse of all time, while those given to fate and tragedy will say choice is only an illusion; that the wheel of events turns, and our lives cascade like water on a mill stream. And don't the stars and even the galaxies of the universe do just that as well? And the atoms in their tiny forge? It was the one clock my daddy could not fix—the cosmos itself, but what a magnificent ambition if he even thought of such a thing. If I am his daughter, his meat and blood, and I think this, then is it not likely that Daddy did? I never got to ask him that, though when I finally found him, we did talk about the weather, and about love, and about life—and always about his beloved, lost Anna.

That little girl was filled with wonder—feeling none of her mother's sense of loss, or her tragedy. My mother was just 30 years old then, and dying of tuberculosis, so young, and some would say she was one of the most beautiful women who ever lived. But then, any man in love will say that. Of that I am convinced. Despite the betrayals, and the engines of state grinding inexorably, she was the great love of his life. That I know in my heart. That is why I close now, having buried them together at last. But now, at the end, I return to the beginning. I must tell my story from the start, as best I can, filling in what details I continue to learn.

I had best let the story tell itself.

My father as a young man was washed ashore on a forsaken coast along the western bow of Africa, where lions roamed under blue sky dotted with pinfeather clouds, where eternal sea weeps upon infinite sand, where the warriors and empires of mankind lie down to die...

Part One: Africa 1942

Type: UK 1943 River Class Frigate/Imp War Museum

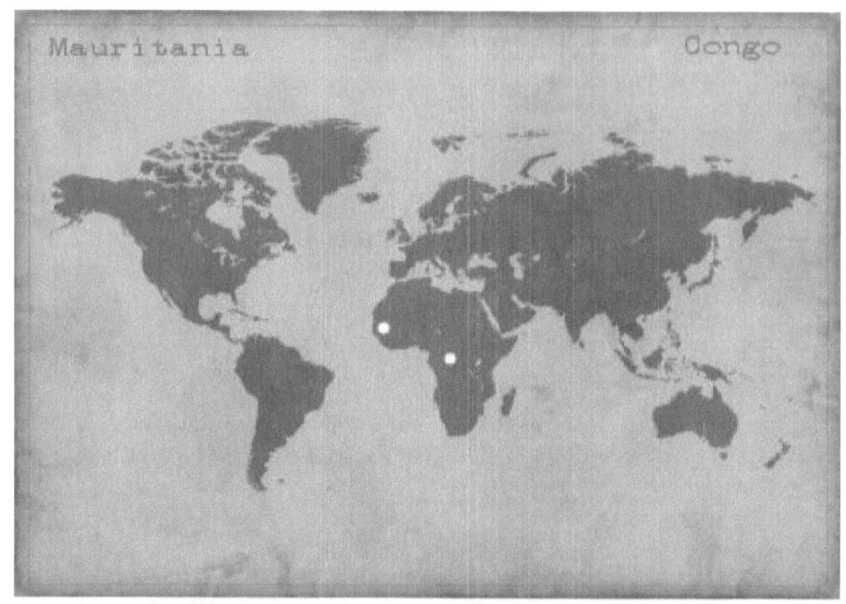

Beach with Lions

A pride of Barbary lions—six magnificent, tawny cats, the last of their kind on Earth—appeared on a West African beach one late afternoon in 1942. They were the last few survivors of their kind, whom the chaos and opportunities of war had flushed out of the hinterlands of the Atlas and Chouf Mountains. They were the biggest, most beautiful subspecies of lions, hunted to the verge of extinction even in ancient Roman times. They had killed and been killed for centuries in Roman arenas around the Mediterranean. In the Colosseum they had been the fabled eaters of Christians. Of all lions, they had the fullest, darkest, thickest manes, which covered not only their necks but also the forward part of the torso, and reached deep down along their bellies. They had distinctive angular faces and large amber eyes that lent them heightened nobility even among lions. It was thought the last of these Barbary lions had been shot in the 1920s. Were anyone on this deserted West African beach today, he would not know it to see these six.

The lions strode at their own confident, unhurried pace, looking about for lunch, trouble, or whatever aroused their interest. Being cats, they communicated with one another by subtle body language—like closing the eyes to signal assurance, pleasure in one another's company, contentment that things were as they should be. The late afternoon air was alive with buzzing insects, and the lions flicked their tails in testy zigzags as they blinked at each other.

The sandy coast stretched 2,000 miles south from Gibraltar, around the marshy bend of Abidjan in Ghana, to the tropical jungles of equatorial Africa. In the east, over the rips and tears of the rocky Sahel, black night rose out of *Trab el-Hajra*, the 'Country of Stone.' In the west, the sky was still as blue as the ocean rolling underneath it. High in the powder-blue sky, a full moon presented its own ghostly cameo of deserts and mists. On the beach, where the lions paraded on their evening hunt, a fine haze rolled in, and the sand smelled of dying mussels and drying kelp—the tide was ebbing. Huge breakers crashed and groaned on forlorn hooks and sweeps while gulls wheeled, cawing. The tawny squiggle of sand was the same color as the slowly padding lions—beach and lions were made for each other eons ago. This world was theirs, though they were the last few of their kind.

New predators had arrived, and these new predators were at war with each other. Off on the South Atlantic, explosions were audible. Flashes of light tore through the red and orange sunset on the ocean horizon, but the lions barely took notice—only sniffing briefly with a widening of the nostrils, a challenging growl, a glance from cold golden eyes, to question whether those low boxing thunders meant rain was coming. But there was no rain smell, just a tinge of burning oil smoke carrying more odors of the new predators who now ruled the earth. Sometimes, faint screams of their dying warriors echoed across the sea. The cats did not blink for them.

Berlin, 1991: U-Boot Captain and Countess

The old U-boot warrior was always punctual, and the Countess had a reputation for always being late. Knowing this, he was not surprised when he found himself waiting in the 20th floor sky-dining room of the Hotel Magdeburg late one evening. In any case, the view was lovely, and he had his 24-year old granddaughter Bernadette with him. The girl was a tall, lovely brunette with wide blue eyes and creamy skin. She was studying medicine at the Free University of Berlin, *Benjamin Franklin Klinikum*, and he was proud of her; for that, and because she took good care of him. She was a good girl. She had driven him here, parked the car, patiently walked to the elevator with him, and now sat close by him *plaudernd*—chatting. He kept one hand on his cane, and the other linked with hers, as they admired how the high 19th Century rooftops all around were stippled with a fine lacing of early snow.

Seidlitz and Berna had already eaten one marzipan torte each, and had drunk one cup of hot coffee, when Madame Didier finally strode in from the elevator.

The restaurant was nearly empty, waiting out the last hour before closing for the night. It occupied an entire floor in the office tower, with a well-lit glass and aluminum snack bar in the middle and elegant little tables with white linen cloths overlooking the charms of Charlottenburg on all sides. The only sounds were the occasional sweeping sound of the kitchen door opening and falling shut as the sole waiter on duty passed through; or the cleaning lady complaining about her ankles in the kitchen; or the steady whoosh of the central air system blowing in a clean dry warmth.

"*Bitte*," said Madame Didier as she hurried across the carpeted floor extending her hand. "*Entschuldigen Sie doch*. I'm so sorry."

"It's nothing at all," said Seidlitz, as he and Berna rose and they three shook hands before sitting down at the small table again with its rose in a glass, its old mustard stain on the linen, its half-full coffee cups and smeared cake plates.

"Thank you for agreeing to meet with me," she said.

Seidlitz nodded sharply, with a snappy bow of the head, to show that he was entirely at her service. She was every bit as lovely as the tabloids tattled she was. He'd seen pictures of her in a bikini at Cannes, or in a turtleneck at Davos, or with an actor in sunglasses on the *Étoile* in Paris, the city where she now lived. How could anyone be impatient with a woman like this? She was 45, still fresh and crisp if only more ripe and worldly, and wore her golden-brunette hair stiffly teased up into a white band that crossed from ear to ear. Her clothing and jewelry were understated and pricey. Her perfume painted a light violet mood with just the right after-note.

She bit her lip and got right to it. "I wrote to you at some length about my problem."

Berna spoke up, stirring a spoonful of sugar in to her grandfather's tea. "If you don't mind, I will be bold and interrupt. My grandfather and I have been very anxious to meet with you, and we want to help as best we can. But so many years have passed now."

Madame Didier acknowledged this. "Bit by bit, I am trying to narrow down my search for my real father. Luckily I am in a position and can afford the travel and expense. If I am in the least causing you any expense—" She produced a wallet full of credit cards.

Seidlitz laughed gently. "No, no, Madame."

"Very well." She put the wallet away, but left one card to pay for everyone. She spoke more delicately and sensitively than he felt she needed to: "I understand that after the war you did meet with the families of the *Sturmer* men." He could picture them, sturdy British sailors in their old World War II warship named after a coastal city with such a Germanic sounding name—the sort of irony a hunched and bleary Hitler had been fond of wistfully remarking about to his field marshals, while poring over maps of his crumbling empire—that his enemies had good Germanic names like Eisenhower (Eisenhauer, a smith, a beater of iron), Nimitz (nice Prussian *Junker* name), even the Dutch or Flemish Roosevelt, 'Field of Roses'.

"Oh yes," Seidlitz said, leaning both hands on the cane between his knees. Berna leaned against him, putting one arm protectively over his shoulder and the other on his forearm. Her long blonde hair hung down over her light blue sweater.

"I can imagine how sensitive it is."

He touched the corner of his eye, where a tear always sprang up at the long-ago memory. "It is unimaginable," he said in a strangled voice. "At first it was unbearable to see them. Then I was surprised that they understood that that was war and now is peace. We were on warships and both did what we had to do at the time. I did not want to take their sons and husbands and brothers from them. I learned that they understood this and respected me for coming to them after the war."

"It must be very difficult for everyone," she said.

"You have your own problems," he said. Berna squeezed his hand, warning him not to say too much. His knowledge came mainly from those grocery store scandal sheets and the gossip hour on television.

She nodded. "I did not know my father was not my father until I was your age, Berna. My mother married a poor man who drowned off a fishing boat. We lived in Siberia when I was a baby, outside Anadyr on the Chukhot Peninsula on the Arctic Sea. My mother, who loved me very much and used to sing lullabies to me and call me *Umnitsa*, Good Girl—she died of it soon after in 1949. I have only vague memories of life in Anadyr as a small child. Mostly it seems it was always dark and cold and we had not enough to eat. My mother married a man named Vadim Samsonov, a simple and rather brutal sailor who drank all the time and beat her. He drowned when he fell off a fishing boat off Siberia. When my mother died, his sister raised me—my Auntie Dora. She was part Russian and part Yupik. She made sure I was adopted by Westerners, because she could not raise me by herself and run a tavern and all. My luck was to be taken in by a wealthy French family. The tabloids tell the rest."

Berna stirred her coffee with a kind, practical hand. She would make a fair-minded doctor, her grandfather thought as he listened attentively. Berna said: "I have never known deprivation, so it is all foreign to me, but I imagine your mother suffered considerably."

"Everyone did," Madame Didier said in her German, which had a strong French accent.

"You must have a beautiful home in Neuilly," Berna said with innocent admiration. She could have added others, all well-known to paparazzi, on Lake Constance, in Provence, on the Ligurian Riviera, and more.

Madame Didier nodded with a certain mixture of sad pride. "I have three boys, who are all doing very well. One is in the French Navy, one is a wealthy corporate CEO, and one is an atomic scientist. They make me proud and happy. I have two grandchildren by now. But I always wanted a lovely girl like you, and now it is too late for me."

Berna impulsively reached out and took the woman's hand. *That is the doctor in her*, Seidlitz thought. "Maybe I can visit with you on my next trip to Paris. I sometimes make a holiday there."

"By all means, come see us and we'll take you for a drive to Versailles or maybe we'll stroll in the Luxembourg Gardens and see the *Orsay*."

"I'd love that!"

"Are the alligators still so big in the Berlin Zoo?" the Countess asked.

Seidlitz and Berna both laughed. "They feed them so much!"

Berna said: "Your mother now, she had a lovely daughter."

Madame Didier beamed. "You say the right things, Berna."

Seidlitz tapped his cane lightly on the carpet, thinking about *H.M.S. Sturmer*. "I was filled with the utmost anxiety when I received your letter saying that possibly your real father might have survived the sinking. The official report was that she went down with all hands, and that is what the plaque in Canterbury says, as well as the records at the Royal Navy Museum in London, which I have visited from time to time." He kept tapping that cane. "When you are an old man, and you killed many beautiful young men in your youth, you go with old blind eyes to run your fingers over their names as if you and they could have a conversation. But my tongue wanders. So you think your real father survived the sinking?"

Madame Didier sighed deeply, folding her hands on her lap. "That is one of the many mysteries about this, Herr Seidlitz. I am hoping that we will see some light as we put the many tiny pieces of this puzzle together."

Berna added: "And the atomic espionage?"

Seidlitz said: "We'll get to that in good time, *Kindl*. That's another matter and another time, in the last days of the war—Fehler's boat, *U-234*, which he surrendered to the Allies in May of 45. He was carrying a load of atomic bomb materials, and a *Luftwaffe* general, and a couple of Messerschmitt jets to Japan for bombing Los Angeles and San Francisco. The war could have turned out quite differently. I have spoken with him a number of times. He is an old man of 80 now, living here with his wife and children. What an adventure he had! What a bold and humorous man!" He tapped his cane again, and leaned on it with the weight of terrible memories that never went away.

HMS Sturmer 1942

H.M.S. Sturmer, a British destroyer escort, rose and fell in mild summer seas while pouring out a long, thick banner of black smoke from her single stack. A thirty-year-old U.S. naval officer and, by turns, his top secret Huff Duff equipment, sailed unceremoniously through the air in a bosun's chair from a U.S. destroyer. A young clockmaker and trainee teacher from New England, he'd never been farther from home than a two-hour train ride to New York City or Boston. He'd been commissioned in the U.S. Navy only a year ago, and found global warfare a breathtaking adventure. Bloody and scary though it be, the war took him far from his land of quiet village greens and white-steepled churches. It also took him from a future he found stifling, with a beautiful but root-bound high school sweetheart and a choice of equally grim careers—either continuing to make clocks in a brick, Victorian-era factory on a Dickensian-turgid river, or teaching science and engineering in a similar building once he finished his four year degree at Teacher's College. The future yawned before him, dark and mysterious, and he somehow felt there must be something more than what New Haven had to offer.

Wearing a yellow oilcloth jacket and boots over his dark blue uniform, Tim gripped harsh canvas straps as sailors on both sides guided him on his perilous path. More than 100 feet below were the foam-laced waters of the Atlantic. Lieutenant (j.g.) Tim Nordhall was a good swimmer, having grown up lobstering and oystering in the groins and coves of his native New Haven. He didn't fear the water but regarded with alarm the steep gray-rusty iron sides and rails of the two ships rocking in close proximity to each other on a sea that seemed to snort and buck like a nervous mustang. One hit against those steel plates, and he was as good as gone. But the ordeal was over in less than five minutes as he stepped on board and saluted the ship's colors, requesting permission to come on board in time-honored etiquette.

H.M.S. Sturmer was a 306-foot long River Class frigate—one of hundreds hastily riveted together at John Brown shipyard as *U-boot* kills reached frightful proportions. She was a destroyer escort, a smaller and slower version of the destroyer, intended to escort convoys through treacherous waters. Capable of making 20 knots, she carried two paired three-inch deck guns, one fore, one aft, and twin torpedo launching tubes.

The British officers welcomed Tim with grins and handshakes. Their grizzled beards and sun-reddened cheeks revealed rough humor and camaraderie. They wore tan loden overcoats and navy-gray shallow helmets, as well as binoculars and web gear. Tim's sea bag followed across. A sailor carried it below to Tim's cabin. The Brits were seasoned warriors, always looking for the slightest edge against their merciless *U-boot* adversaries. They pumped Tim for information about the new class of Huff Duff coming across in wooden crates. Royal Navy sailors swarmed around the equipment, and several bearded warrant officers already had technical manuals in hand as they directed the crates to be moved amidships for mounting on the small deck platform.

Tim found his hosts most congenial. A bosun's mate saw him to his small cabin near the captain's. It was something of an honor to have one's own niche in a ship this small, with 140 men jammed on her in every oily nook and cranny. The ship was a coal-burner, and when cruising at full steam she laid down a long black plume of smoke that left soot and tar on every surface.

Within a day, the warrants had Tim's new Huff Duff in its final operational shakedown phase. Tim found them to be highly competent technicians, while he himself was a two-year college man with a rudimentary engineering background that he found barely matched theirs. They were a grinning, feisty lot, these Brits. There was always someone with a joke, or a harmonica, or a story about home. The working hours were endless, and sleep came in small bursts here and there, but the men were young and would just as soon stop for a game of cards. The daily grog ration lightened things a bit, though Tim wasn't much of a drinker or smoker. He ended up telling about girls back home, particularly Sally Levesque who taught English at Hillhouse High School and lived in Hamden. Tim related his dissatisfaction with life as it appeared to be laid out for him—pretty redhead and all. Sometimes, he dreamed of joining a theater company and performing or writing or at least managing stage props—but that, and writing original plays or novels, was entirely outside his social class and framework. Growing up, he would have been ridiculed and hounded had he strayed from the norms—so his theater ambition would probably forever remain a deflected dream. He substituted for this with a love of movies—and taking pretty girls to them turned out to be quite pleasurable. Still, in his blood was that raw, industrial scenery that was today the latest craze—the stage play of the imagination, played with few or no props, left only to words, gestures, and imagination while the audience sat around in a circle, as if at a Stone Age campfire. Several men were from London, a city of history and theaters. They knew of New York City, and Broadway—and New Haven's famous off-Broadway Schubert Theater, where many a famous stage production went through its pre-New York sea trials. New Haven, furthermore, home of Yale University, was a city of high culture if a person could step across the divide between town and gown. Tim's compromise, dished out by life and circumstance, had been to attend teacher's college. Maybe after the war he'd teach. But the Navy had given him a whole new set of options. The clock maker of New Haven was now a technical intelligence expert in the U.S. Navy, with breath-taking new possibilities for growth and advancement. He was trapped in a never-land between land and sea, between Sally and a cold bunk, between life and theater, between fact and fiction, between war and peace, betwixt and between. In a way, it was exciting to live from moment to moment. War did that to a man's life. It also took life, and rarely gave it back. The Brits, Welsh, Scots, Irish, Manx, even an Indian and a South African, and two Canadians of no discernible 'accent,' all had their stories to tell as well. If nothing else, he was learning that it was a small world, and that people everywhere had about the same hopes and dreams. Even, probably, the Germans and the Japs, one supposed, though one never got to talk to one, and vice-versa. There was a lot to wonder about. Many a man lay awake late at night, even dog tired after working a long watch with little relief or even decent grub. The twilight bunks were lit with a reddish glow here, there, as a man lay with one arm behind his head and looked into the blackness above, pondering his place in the universe. Whatever one might say about being at sea during a shooting war, it made you think. It made you reconsider everything, and wonder a lot.

Tim learned about Jerry Harris's blonde Edna in Manchester, who had a cage full of finches that enjoyed sitting in the window twittering to the Sunday morning church bells on a sunny day. And Ben Meyer's Shula who was already assistant bookkeeper in the family carpet business in Southwark. Or Harvey Kinnan's red-haired Nuala who was a nurse at Guy's Hospital and had lost a hand in the Blitz but was still a lovely bird in her whites. "Do you plan to go back and wed your Sally then?" Harvey would ask, his young freckled face wide with innocence and his mouth agape to reveal a missing middle tooth. Dark-bearded Jerry Harris seemed a more dour man who tended to stare, but Tim imagined Edna with her finches must keep him in line, like a sunbeam across his glowering stare. About Sally Tim did not have an honest answer, either for himself or Harv. When you got away from home, Tim was discovering, you started to change, and the ones you left behind often did not change with you. His letter exchanges with Sally had begun to wane after the first year away.

Work and war and responsibility kept Tim too busy to spend much time thinking. Many ships had the new RADARs on them, but they were limited in range and often inaccurate. Huff Duff, or High Frequency/Direction Finding (HD/HF), was an entirely different tool with over 600 miles (1000 km) range. Using an unusual cage-shaped sender/receiver mounted on a mast, Huff Duff could intercept German radio traffic and triangulate the approximate location of *U-boot* packs. A round picture tube similar to a RADAR screen revealed the location of the signal being sent. Already, as these units were being refined in crash R&D projects on both sides of the Atlantic, the effect on the northern convoy routes was measurable—*U-boot*s were beginning to run for their lives. A ship with Huff Duff could use shore-based as well as ship-based Huff Duff units, some located as far away as in the Bahamas, others in newly liberated North Africa, to zero in on wolf packs and then send aerial bombers or antisubmarine ships to kill the killers. Now the latest American version was being tested in the South Atlantic as the Allies gained their balance and started hunting the enemy who had been sinking hundreds of Lend-Lease ships.

Tim felt like one of the pack as he joined his hosts on the bridge, wearing his own sandy loden coat and flat helmet. The warrants were in complete technical control of their operation. Tim's job was to compile technical statistics on the unit's performance, and to write a detailed journal over 100 pages long, with appendices. To this end, he had the relative privacy of a small cabin, and a typewriter with a supply of paper and ribbons. After a four-week cruise, they were due in the Bahamas for a well-earned and anticipated R&R, during which Tim would debrief U.S. and Commonwealth officers on the strong and weak points of the new technology.

Already, they had a possible kill a hundred miles away, off Cape Verde, and they steamed south at top speed. The warrants triangulated, using a sender at Tobruk and another at the Gambia, and a flight of Lancaster bombers had been sent to investigate a possible *U-boot* nest.

Then disaster struck.

On the first day of the second week of Tim's cruise aboard *Sturmer*, just as the ship's bell rang and the smell of tea and cakes wafted up to the bridge, a tremendous explosion rocked the tail section of the ship. Another followed immediately after, tearing off the bow.

Tim had been standing at the rail amidships, enjoying a chat with two young sailors who were telling stories of the pubs and of their families and girlfriends in Leeds, and a brisk sea breeze blew. It was a sunny day, and Tim felt as if he were on a luxury cruise, if only one could order a good cup of American coffee and maybe a handful of chocolates from home.

The next moment, Tim smashed against a bulkhead. Everything went black. He heard the truncated scream of one of the young sailors as both men disappeared in a gout of flying glass and blood and bits of flesh. By a miracle, Tim found himself intact—he'd been blown into a cavity that had once housed small collapsible life rafts but now contained only rolled-up deck canvas. Jammed awkwardly between two rolls of this sun shield, he had survived when the other two boys clearly hadn't made it. At first Tim thought he was blind, but he realized his vision was being obscured by a mix of oil and blood smeared like porridge on his face. Stunned, he at first thought he must be missing his arms, but he found them firmly attached and was able to raise his hands to wipe the gore off his face. Already, *Sturmer* was listing badly, and it looked as if the sea would swallow Tim when she rolled over.

The *U-boot* they were hunting had found them first. Two or three torpedoes, and the dirty work was done.

Now he heard men screaming as he untangled himself and got on his feet. The steel deck was listing badly, and he pulled himself up a ladder to the upper decks, straddling an upended and shattered lifeboat that would be of no use.

Events unfolded with blinding speed now, all wrapped in a white froth of thrown waves as the ship started sinking and the sea surface bubbled up closer by the minute. He caught glimpses of faces in the water, drowning men, arms reaching for ropes and hawsers and anything else to grab, mouths spitting water but taking in more water instead of the air they hoped to breathe. Wounded men, helpless, were drowning in six inches of water on the inundated decks, pinned under floating debris, and they looked up with huge imploring eyes as if it were just a shop window between themselves and the air they needed to breathe. He thought he recognized Jerry Harris's dour bearded face staring in black accusation up at Tim, at the world he was about to lose, before the sea closed over the man.

Tim slipped on the blood-smeared deck as the ship shifted, and banged his ribs on a steel mooring-winch. Doubled over, he slipped down into the boiling cold water. His breath was knocked out of him. Not a sound could escape his mouth, though he tried to scream. Then his mouth filled with harsh, salty water. He felt hands grasping at him with rubbery dying terror, cold fingers like little fish gnawing at him, trying to get under his shirt or grasp his belt.

For a minute or so, he was underwater. This was it. He was done for. He'd hold on as long as he could, in this moment between life and death, but when the pressure got too much he'd open his mouth to gasp for air and instead take in a lungful of water and black out. He heard the clanking of the ship's engines, still firing away on at least one boiler. He heard the grinding of her worm gear as it crunched away in a shaft full of abrasive seawater cutting through her packing grease. He heard the screams of trapped men who faced certain death from drowning just minutes away. He heard the tortured groan of tons of steel realigning itself now that the ship's structural integrity had been destroyed. How deep was the sea here? What would it be like to sink down as the darkness quickly took him?

Then she rolled the other way, settling by what was left of the bow, so that the stern rose momentarily.

He felt the weight of water crashing away, and got several great lungs full of cold air, all in a blur.

As the stern rose up, he spread-eagled against the aft gun turret. In that instant, he caught sight of the *U-boot*. She surfaced about a quarter mile away, a fish rising from the sea, streaming foam and water, with rich twirls of magnificent bottle-green sea flying around her sail. The commander might put out some rubber rafts if he had them. The Germans sometimes stayed to rescue, but nowadays the Krauts were on the run, and it was dubious the Kraut would risk his boat and complement to save enemy sailors, particularly in sight of land.

Sky and sea whirled blender-like. Tim lost consciousness again as he fell.

The way he figured it afterward, the stern had risen up, then briefly hung in the sky with him straddling a gun mount. Then she'd rocked once in a swell, throwing him clear, before sliding without another sideways motion straight down, bow-first, on the long descent a mile down to whatever slimy plain would become her eternal cemetery.

Tim had on his life vest, and that saved him. He came to, minutes after falling into the water, and found himself bobbing up and down in an oil slick among debris—a large tin of tea, some wooden crates of linen and bread, waterlogged mattresses, and motionless bodies.

Then he heard shouts. A few men had gathered around a rubber life raft from the *Sturmer*. Tim scissor-kicked toward them. His ribs ached, and the sea was cold, but he was alive. He was intact.

Several of the men were wounded. One died as Tim arrived—just closed his eyes, sort of let go, and disappeared under the waves. Desperately, others grasped at the rope around the dinghy. Tim smelled wet wool, old tobacco, and fresh metallic blood. There was a smell these open wounds had, like gutted fish with the salt water in them. The wounded were too weak to scream as the chemicals and oils from the ship filled their gashes; they just emitted a low moan at best and hung on. One shivered violently, so that his blackened lips flapped and threw off a spray of oil; imminent death was written in his eyes, and when Tim looked away at the blinding sun, and back, the man had disappeared as if he'd never been. How much of this was all a dazed illusion, Tim wondered, wishing he could clear his head.

The ship was gone. So was the *U-boot*.

There was a brief conversation amid gasps for air and wet sputters. Tim calculated that *Sturmer* had not had a chance to get a signal off. With luck, someone would come looking for them. It was midday, and that meant probably a good twenty-four hours bobbing through the night, maybe a day or two, if searchers came at all. It was a huge stretch of ocean, full of hostile *U-boot*s and not enough Allied traffic to do a proper search.

Soon it was just three of them, Tim and red-haired Harvey and another sailor. All the other men were gone. Drowned. That, even though the sun was warm and the sea sparkled like gold.

They clung to the rubber dinghy until it began to deflate, becoming just another bit of debris.

Tim drifted in and out of consciousness. He expected he was at death's door like the others. Some had perished quickly from terrible wounds and burns. He and the other two would gradually weaken from thirst, hunger, despair, and exhaustion, and drift off to eternity and nothingness. Or would there be angels with trumpets? For some odd reason, the golden-red glow of the sea reminded Tim of quiet Sunday afternoons in New Haven, during Indian Summer when the rich trees were still green, and the air retained a lingering ripeness of summer, but weakly so; underneath it all something was changing, some powerful body chemistry signaled that autumn was roiling up, and the leaves were dying inwardly. One felt the very elements of one's body and blood transforming themselves in a rhythm as grand as the movement of the world around its sun and the Newtonian tick-tock of machinery in a Copernican universe.

"There's land over there," Harvey said, bringing Tim out of his reverie, and they began swimming.

"If there are sharks, we're done for," said the other.

"We'd be long done if it wasn't for the oil in the sea," said Harvey.

"Let's stick together," Tim ordered. Instinctively, he towed the dinghy along, and it offered just a tiny bit of buoyancy. In it, he knew, were first aid and other emergency supplies. He was most hoping for matches.

The sound of crashing water grew louder.

"A beach!" the other man said.

"Surf," Harvey said, looking pale through his freckles.

Tim stopped and looked, feeling the water surging around him. He was tired now. They'd been shocked and in the water for a good two hours already. "Breakwater!" he shouted.

"Tired," Harvey said with a groan, closing his eyes. Tim noticed now that his friend had a wound in his side. He took Harvey by the chin and began swimming slowly and methodically toward the sound of crashing water, which could not be too far from land.

Then raging water took hold of them, spinning them in foamy, bumpy gyres.

Tim watched mutely as the other sailor was ripped away, flying down and around a barnacle-crusted rock that rose like a mushroom out of the continental shelf. The tide must be in full movement, Tim thought. Best to stay back until it crested or troughed, rather than get battered to pieces here. He heard Harvey scream and felt him torn from his grasp. Helplessly, he watched as his friend was sucked away into the maelstrom. Tim let himself go limp, lying sideways and kicking weakly. He let go and just prayed to live from one moment to the next.

Again he felt that golden glow, that presence of death, and he saw again the gleaming little New England church roofs and neo-Gothic Yale towers around his hometown. He saw himself again with his girlfriend, Sally Levesque. Maybe they were driving home from a football game, with autumn leaves rustling in the streets a foot deep in places, and they had between them the afterglow of heavy petting, maybe even of the occasional guilty sex. And yet he felt so desperate to escape, to scream, to struggle to the surface like just now. Sally Levesque almost seemed to be sitting in a convertible in the ocean, sinking while he rose, and he could sense the quiet accusation radiating from her eyes. It wasn't her fault, he realized. She was too shallow, God forgive him, too lacking in courage to escape the monotony of a life lived from crib to cemetery amid that same somber brick Colonial architecture. She was born and raised to be a good woman in that atmosphere, and he was the bad one, he was the one who should feel guilty, for throwing it all away. It was over between them now, anyway. She had been unable to handle his departure for Navy duty, and had taken up with a boy from West Haven who shared her tightly knitted French-Canadian Catholic universe, who had been rejected from active duty because of flat feet and was now a police lieutenant guarding the Green from vagrants and South Street beach from enemy submarines.

Tim cried out and raised a hand into the sky, but an undertow took him down, twirled him around so that the fine sand at the bottom polished him like a jeweler's rag on a lens. Tim gave in to his wrongs, confessed his shortcomings, and prepared to die; but it wasn't his time yet.

He did not have long to struggle. The undertow took him out another hundred feet. Then the undertow vanished, leaving him in steadily rising and falling swells. He stood treading water and gasping for breath. He had lost his shoes and clothes by now, but shreds of his shirt still clung to his shoulders along with the life jacket, shielding him from the blazing sun. He lay back and concentrated on just keeping his face out of the water, which the design of the life jacket helped him do.

He became detached, feeling as though he were floating in air rather than water. It was a curious sort of air, soapy green, but piss-yellow when the sun shone through it, and full of kelp shadows. He floated motionlessly. He was free of Sally Levesque, free of New Haven, free of the clock factory, free of whatever it might have been. The mighty summer ocean off the southern coast of Africa had cleansed him, and then put him within sight of land almost like Jonah being belched out by his whale.

Dreamlike, without being part of the scene, he watched three razor-sharp sharks tearing Harvey's body apart, the legs one way, the arms another, the russet-gold head and the torso floating downward out of sight until another shark did a magnificent hooking dive and disappeared with it.

Tim floated motionlessly amid the kelp, knowing he would not die here. Slowly, the incoming tide brought him around so that the back of his head rested on the firm sand.

Berlin, 1991: Countess over Torten

"You have a Russian name also," Berna said looking through the photographs that Madame Didier had taken from her purse. Outside, on the high black slate rooftops, snow created stipples and filigrees in intricate patterns under a lovely ink-blue night sky. The quarter moon looked like a gold sword out of the Arabian Nights.

"Yes, several. My mother and Auntie Dora always called me *Umnitsa*, which means Good Girl," Madame Didier said self-consciously. "Auntie Dora took care of me after my mother died. But Auntie Dora ran a tavern, and didn't have time for me. Then the French came. They were wealthy old-school aristos who had lost their only child in a car crash. They came to adopt a little boy, but he proved to be feeble—so instead, in this cruel world, Auntie Dora gave me to them, and I became their only child. They loved me as well as any man and woman could. They spoiled me, I'd say."

"And they are gone?" Seidlitz asked gently.

Marianne nodded. A tear ran down each cheek and she sniffled a bit. Her parents had died more than ten years earlier, and were buried in the 17th Century family mausoleum near Avignon. She idly fingered a little cellophane book of color photos. The ever-tactful Berna took the photos and showed them to her grandfather. "Look, Opa, these are Madame Didier's three boys." He put on his reading glasses, and admired three fine young men looking out in the world with happiness and self-confidence. "Handsome young men," he said, nodding, and Berna appreciatively handed the photos back. "You should be proud, Madame."

"Thank you." She put the photos back in her purse. She changed topics as she did so. "Did you have any idea that there was a survivor?"

He shook his head. The thought upset him very much. "I had no idea until many years after the war. I feel I have lost a great opportunity in not meeting him. And you think he is your father?"

She looked pained. "Yes, I am sure of it now, at last, after many years of searching. His name was kept secret for many years, but I believe is a man named Tim Nordhall. I need to find him now, if he is still alive somewhere."

"You are traveling all over the world in search of one clue or another," Seidlitz said sympathetically and thoughtfully. "I wish I knew more. I only heard about Nordhall from Fehler, who went with me to a meeting of *Sturmer* next of kin in Canterbury. That would have been, oh, probably 1955 or 57, I forget—and Fehler had been talking with a man named Heyday or Highway, one of those English names, whom he met over a beer at that reunion, and who also may have been a double agent. Yes, it is all quite confusing, and still swallowed up in official secrecy even now, half a century after the war. Even now that East Germany has ceased to exist, and now even the Soviet Union is history, you would think that they would all give up their ghosts and secrets." The old captain looked around, lost in his memories, and suddenly finding himself in this place now. "Very *gemütlich* here," he said, looking around at the dark restaurant, its silent tables, its windows bright with a sea of city lights and neon dusted with faint traces of white that outlined the edges of black slate roof tiles. As always, a sea of traffic flowed underneath with an apparent total lack of concern—for every life was in crisis, and no stranger had time to wonder about someone else's puzzle from another time.

Berna had a silver and turquoise barrette between her lips, and used both hands to fold her long blonde hair back into a ponytail.

Madame Didier pushed a crumb around on the linen. "I have been to San Francisco, London, Berlin, Brussels, anywhere I can think of. Every time I think I am closing in on my real father, he slips away again, like a ghost."

"I am sorry to hear that," Seidlitz said.

Berna said: "You are so wealthy and beautiful, and yet unhappy. How sad."

"I have a lot to be thankful for; you are right."

Berna had finished tying her hair back and sat drumming rock rhythms on her jeans. "We can be happy sitting here, warm and dry, having coffee."

"At least we are alive, those of us who made it," Seidlitz said. He rubbed his granddaughter's back affectionately.

"Recently," Madame Didier said, "I came into possession of some papers including some diaries kept by my father. The papers were recovered from my Auntie's family in Siberia, and originally belonged to my mother. It seems she was in love with Tim Nordhall to her dying day, and wrote a stack of love letters to him that she never sent." She felt flustered. "It seems Nordhall fell in love with not one but two women, or is that just more myth like so much about him?"

"Nothing was unusual in wartime," the captain said, shrugging lightly. "Not even a man with two women."

Berna giggled. "Or two women with one husband."

Madame Didier shrugged, feeling as always the fatalistic weight of the unchangeable past. "There are still so many puzzling details, but I know for certain that the NKGB or GRU kidnapped my mother right out of her residence on Nob Hill in San Francisco when she was pregnant with me, and that's how I ended up in the Soviet Union."

"A dreadful fate," the old man said, pursing his lips as he no doubt reviewed a thousand painful memories of his own.

"Yes. My poor mother. She ended up marrying a man in Siberia who drank heavily and was mean to her, but he brought home a small paycheck and that kept us from starving to death. Those were hard years. I'm told he fell off a fishing boat in the North Pacific in 1947 and drowned. My mother never married again. Not that she had much time, because she died the next year."

There was a silence as they all digested this information from the chaotic aftermath of the world war.

"Where do you go next?" Berna said.

Outside, the wind blew a long veil of snow across the slate rooftops.

Castaway

I am alive, Tim thought as he felt the weight of the land assert itself. *Somehow I have survived and all the others are dead.* Slowly, he rolled over onto his side, feeling sickness and grief. He lay doubled over, feeling the sun drying the shreds of his clothing. He smelled dying kelp, rotting mussels. He heard the loud buzzing of countless flies. On his sun baked, salt-crusted lips and nose, on his cracking skin, flies and ants crawled but he was too weak to swat them. He lolled dizzily as the water drained away, leaving him to dry in the sun. He was alive, at least, to smell and feel these things.

He raised himself up and looked out to sea. A smudge of black smoke stained a violet evening sky. Night was coming, and he began to feel cold. He was too weak to jump up, but he lay back and inhaled great gulps of living air as if it were some wonderful champagne. He lay gasping the marvelous near-liquid called air while the planet wheeled in the heavens and then sun began to turn large and orange on the western horizon, over the fatal sea.

He again saw Jerry Harris's dark beard and eyes fading under the waves. Again he saw red-haired Harvey Kinnan torn to pieces by sharks. He cried out "No!" and beat his forehead against the sand, sobbing. He pounded his fist down again and again, thinking of the finches and the one-handed nurse and all the aching holes this war was leaving in a billion lives around the world. These others had given their all, and he had been given a new life. He must make something of it, for his sake and theirs.

He rose, staggering, and wandered through stranded kelp until he came to the rubber dinghy. It looked inflated, but flattened when he crawled on his hands and knees into its shelter. No shelter there. He found the laces holding shut the emergency kit, and fumbled with the hard, dry strings until slowly they pried loose. He used his teeth to try and bite through them. Finally, he braced his feet against the inside of the raft and pulled with all his might, until the cabinet spilled its contents into the boat. There was a first aid kit, a flare gun, a bottle of water—he fumbled with the water, uncorking the tin lid and tilting it back to drink and spat—it was contaminated with seawater and oil. A hideous taste filled his mouth, making his thirst worse. The sea biscuits were stale, moldy, wet, ruined. The medical kit, same. Iodine and mercury and other chemicals all run together, soaking the bandages, and the small bottles of salve broken, shattered. He groaned with frustration, pawing through the wreckage. Nothing at all useful there.

Wait, one thing. A web holster, an old Webley Mark IV .38 revolver, rust on the handle, six rounds. He took off the life jacket, laid it aside. He put on the web gear, first one arm then the other, so that the gun dangled loosely under his left shoulder. The straps crossed over his back and met in a clasp on his belly. At least he had that, unless it blew up in his face if he ever needed to fire it.

He rose and looked about. *Where am I?*

Africa.

That was all he knew.

He was someplace on the western coast of Africa. He tried to remember his geography—anything. Africa was shaped kind of like a prehistoric skull, facing east. The back of the brain case was Western Africa, and on it was what? Inland would be Mali. He was 1,000 miles of desert away from Timbuktu. The Atlas Mountain range stretched north into Morocco, amid endless desert. Hitler's adventures on the Dark Continent were almost finished. Montgomery and Eisenhower were just mopping up the last German and Italian legions in Africa, driving Rommel back to Europe. *Now my adventures are just beginning,* Tim thought as he slogged along. He must find shelter for the night, water, food. Next, he needed to find a U.S. consul somewhere to repatriate him.

A golden evening set in. Haze blew in off the sea, and the wet sand shone like gold. About two miles down the coast, Tim saw a building of some kind. It looked like a ruined tower. Naked except for shreds of his shirt, remnants of his pants, and the web belt with the old gun, he walked on bare feet in the sand the way he'd done in Milford or West Haven as a boy. In those days you'd get hot dogs and root beer at a stand, and the merry-go-round at Savin Rock blared with music and laughter. Here, all was silent, like the time before time when the world still stood empty, or like an empty time after the end of the world.

Marianne in New Haven, 1991: Catherine Nordhall

The Boeing 747 with Marianne Didier, Countess Troisroses on board approached North America on the North Atlantic route from London across Greenland. The plane made a customs stop in Bangor, Maine and then made a hop to Bradley Field in Hartford, Connecticut en route to points irrelevant. Marianne had not slept well the night before. She'd dozed on the plane and felt tired, but was anxious to meet her possible relatives in New Haven. The weather was rainy and chill, with a damp, icy wind blowing down from Canada, across the Great Lakes and upstate New York, into New England. Under a leaden sky, she rode in a limousine about a half hour from Hartford to New Haven. At the coast, she hardly noticed the annoying traffic, concentrating instead on the picturesque little villages visible through bare trees, and beyond them Long Island Sound, with a fuzzy, dark, misty Long Island lying in the distance.

Gino Franzese and his wife of many years, Catherine Nordhall-Franzese, came to meet her in a light blue Cadillac driven by their oldest son, Frankie. Catherine was Tim Nordhall's sister, now a woman of 72 with medical problems but a still-chipper attitude. "That would make you my aunt," Marianne told Catherine.

"I haven't seen my brother and his wife in years," Catherine said. "I don't know if I can help you at all, dear." She seemed oddly cold, guarded, and distant. These New Haven relatives all did—at ground zero of Tim's birth and formative years, his clock-making apprenticeship, his broken engagement with a lovely redhead named Sally Levesque—all the paths not taken, and Marianne longed to find out the reasons.

"I'm trying to find my father and his..." Marianne said softly. *Wife or wives?* She wondered, but dared not ask for fear of offending her hosts. And her hosts seemed distant for some reason. Were they afraid of strangers, or was there something to hide?

Gino was 77, heavy-set, balding, a big silent man with a dutiful expression, heavy hands that staid powerfully knitted together under an overhanging paunch, and small lips that stayed quietly pursed though his quick eyes missed nothing. Francis, Frankie, already a graying man in his mid-40s (Marianne's age) looked sleeker and more businesslike. He was edging his father out of a lucrative construction business as Gino grew tired. "I travel a bit," Gino said humbly, "like maybe Canada or one day London.

Nothing like all of your travels, I'm sure." It was practically the longest sentence he spoke during their few hours together.

"You're welcome to stay at our house if you'd like," Catherine said airily. Her eyes betrayed deeper, suspicious thoughts: *You didn't bring a playboy friend? Have you remarried, you hoore?* (a New Havenism, of antique Colonial English or Dutch roots).

"That is so generous of you," Marianne said feeling a bit embarrassed. "Do you know, I have to be on a flight to San Francisco tonight for a meeting tomorrow. Why don't we make it next time when I can really enjoy your company?"

"We'd love that," Frankie said, waving his hands as he maneuvered the large car along New Haven's maze of narrow one-way streets where every parking space was taken. It was a weekday around noon, and the sidewalks were jammed with Yale University students and faculty on their lunch break—going either to some downtown restaurant for a quick bite, or to one of the college dining halls or the university Commons. The New Haven Green looked soggy, with its three old Revolutionary War churches fuzzed over by a growing haze of drizzle. New Haven was a city of umbrellas today, of early darkness inscribed with neon blurs and squiggles.

"Why do you think my brother might be your dad, sweetie?" Catherine said with a speculative, calculating glance. Marianne sensed obligation here, and an urgency to get her on that plane and away from here. The walls of obtuseness closing in from all sides suggested that the less she learned here, the better.

She related her story again from the kidnapping of her pregnant mother in the last days of World War 2, forced by Soviet agents to board a Soviet freighter *Kalinin* in San Francisco, and abducted by the NKGB on Stalin's orders to Siberia, to the death of her mother, and her adoption by a wealthy French family. Catherine blanched as she listened, and her chin actually trembled.

"My mother died before I could really speak with her," Marianne said as if reciting an old drama, simply because it needed to be conveyed. "I had an auntie in Anadyr, an old woman of Russian and Inuit stock..."

"What stock?" Gino asked politely but blankly.

"Siberian," Marianne said. "Auntie Dora. She ran a tavern in a sailors' part of town, and she took us in. My mother washed dishes and served beer and swept floors, until winter took her away. I was barely three when she died in 1949, so I never really knew her. I lived with Auntie until I was about five, and she told me my father was a wonderful adventurer in San Francisco during the war. She said he had two wives, and was handsome enough to have all the women on earth.

"Two wives!" Catherine said with a mix of displeasure and incredulity. "That doesn't sound like my brother." If she knew anything, she was not going to tell.

Marianne backpedaled. "Well, these were the stories Auntie Dora used to tell on winter nights. And what would Auntie Dora know? She lived her whole life within a few miles of where she was born."

"Was she a Communist?" Frankie asked.

Marianne realized she must be careful not to exceed the intellectual capacity of these simple, brainwashed people. She shook her head. "Politics meant nothing to her. She was just a very kind elderly woman full of stories. Anyway, this French count and his wife came looking for furs and other rich things, and Auntie gave me to them because they lacked a daughter. They came to adopt a little boy, but he proved to be feeble-minded. They didn't want to leave empty handed, so they settled for me." What more to tell them? Marianne fell silent, thinking of her life—a story of dire poverty one day, great wealth the next—adopted, living in a chateau in Alsace or a mansion in Paris or a palace in Provence. Her new family also owned a chalet in Davos; bungalow in Cannes, factories in Marseille, other industrial interests in Madrid, Turin, Vienna, and even Canada. But she always wanted to know who her real father was, and that hunger tormented her all these years. Knowing the jealousy it might raise, she glossed over her wealth.

"I'll bet they settled for a girl, but you made them happy," Gino said.

"You have three strapping sons," Catherine said. "You accomplished something there." *You hoore*, was the uncoupled and unspoken caboose of her sentence. Marianne could taste her aunt's New England Puritan (even though Catholic) disapproval, but she was used to being smeared in the press day by day. She had endured it for many years. It was a passing cloud, like weather. "Well," Catherine said, reflecting on the unspoken tale of infamous Cinderella wealth without any particular feeling for history or for the visitor's sufferings, the loss of her mother, any of it. Marianne did not hold it against her. She had known many persons of narrower experience in her time, and sometimes they even managed to quarry more richness out of a small life than some worldlier persons managed to extract over many time zones and exotically named seas or far locales. "We weren't exactly well off. My brother—your father, if it's true what you claim—managed to scrimp and save and put himself through two years at Connecticut Teachers' College. It was the Depression, you know. He loved engineering. There were no jobs before the war, but he managed to get something in a clock factory down along the Quinnipiac River. The factory burned down years ago now, I forget, when, Gino?"

Gino's hands twitched dutifully. "Oh, I'd say 1975 at the latest."

"Gino says 1975," Catherine told Marianne as though people did not hear Gino when he spoke—although Gino had built an impressive business with those big hands and preoccupied eyes.

Marianne nodded from her seat beside Frankie in the front. "With so many years gone by, so much evidence is washed away."

"Washed away by time," Frankie said.

"We all get washed away," Catherine said, and Gino nodded, giving a twitch of the hands, tapping bent fingers together, as if playing a chord on some invisible tiny accordion.

"I would like to know what kind of man he was. Or is. And where he is."

Catherine looked at her oddly. "I don't know where he is. I haven't seen him since right after the war. He came out to visit with a woman he said he had married. Nice looking young gal, I can't remember her name or even what she looked like. Something fishy about the whole thing, but I could never put my finger on it." If Catherine was a liar, she was good at it, Marianne thought.

"Did you and your brother have a disagreement?"

Catherine shrugged. "We always fought, but all siblings do. No, it was something else. I never figured it out. He had something to hide. Didn't he, Gino?"

Gino nodded, gave that steepled-fingertips twitch.

"Gino agrees. There was so much going on during the war." Catherine shook her head. "I don't think we ever knew the half of it."

"I'd appreciate anything you can tell me."

Catherine said: "We were all sworn to secrecy. We knew he was in Africa for a while, then in London, and finally in San Francisco. My mom and I, rest her soul, we were the only ones who knew, and we were told he could be killed if anyone found out he was doing important work for the Government, so we kept our mouths shut. That's all I know."

Nothing but secrets, Marianne thought, *and you are still keeping your mouth shut.* How well they must have hidden it all these years. So many dark secrets had been born in that vast modern *Iliad* called World War II.

Catherine made a wry mouth, thinking dreamily of her memories. "He was always a strong, handsome boy. The girls really liked him."

"Good looking," Gino said—nod, twitch, and all.

"A handsome man," Catherine said.

They drove slowly downhill through narrow streets. "This is where the factory was where Uncle Tim worked as a boy, the clock place," Frankie said, pulling up on a licorice-colored pad of wet asphalt edged with trash and weeds. "A bunch of family members were lucky enough to get jobs there during the Depression and then after World War II."

A pea-soup East River flowed past. Raindrops pelted glassy spaces amid lacy foam circles on the river surface. In the hills huddled tight little New England houses waiting for the winter cold. The houses looked as if they were shivering behind their black windows and lace curtains. Along the river street were spots of color, where a dry cleaner and a liquor store and a check cashing place and a few other businesses advertised, colorful neon in the drabness of rain.

Catherine said: "I sometimes took the trolley down here with Tim and Sally. She was his big high school fling, Sally Levesque, nice looking redhead with pale skin and healthy lungs, if you know what I mean. Sweet girl, really, but all the other girls were jealous of her."

"Does she still live around here?"

"Sally?" Catherine shook her head and made a condolent *mmm* sound. "Poor Sally. She and Tim stopped writing to each when he was in London during the war. She ended up marrying a cop from West Haven and having a couple of kids, and last I heard she died of breast cancer in a rest home over in Branford. Isn't that right, Gino?"

"Right. Breasts," Gino said, nodding. His eyes looked sad at the irony. Instead of twitching, he sketched elegant loops in the air with his hands from his chest to his belly.

"Timmy always had something against his home town," Catherine said. "He took off when the war took him away, and I don't think he ever looked back. Me and the other kids kind of resented it, to be honest, but then he was the smart one, the educated one, and it was hard to think he wasn't looking down on us a little bit." She softened. "We were four of us girls, including my mother, and now I am the only one left. We were sworn to lifelong secrecy, and we knew exactly nothing to start with. We've kept our mouths shut all these years. I hope you find him, hon. Drop me a line if you do." A tear rolled down her cheek. "I might just want to visit him if he's still alive someplace. Tell him I won't ask any questions."

Coast of Skeletons

What a strange and beautiful world, Tim thought as he made his way along the eerie coast that might be from some other age, perhaps even some other planet.

Camels trundled majestically on a distant scrub ridge hazed with mist. Beer-yellow evening haze thickened along the coast, while fierce sun still beat down inland. The tide was going out, and beach sand glowed like molten gold.

To the left rose a wall of black night, quickly enveloping Africa as the continent spun away from the sun. In the final half hour of daylight, the sea itself seemed on fire, and the sun resembled a tomato sinking into an atmosphere of colorful vegetable juice. *Of course that is thirst talking,* Tim thought with a faint little grin.

He picked his way over sand packed around the protruding ribs of a long-dead wooden ship, maybe an old whaler from the last century, or some Arab *dhow*. A while later, he walked past an elephant's huge skull that lay alien and staring in the sand. Its magnificent tusks lay crossed like an x, and the empty eye sockets looked haunted.

Now he could see the structure toward which he'd been walking. He could see from a distance that it was a ruined tower, and there wasn't a human being in sight—a disappointment to be sure, but maybe a blessing in that he wasn't sure who owned this area. He knew vaguely that all the major European colonial powers had historic claims in this general area, but his knowledge of African geography was embarrassingly scant. Was he anywhere near the colony of former American slaves, Liberia? Or British Gambia? French Morocco or Togoland or Mauritania? Spanish Sahara? He'd give anything for a map.

Night fell as he traversed the last quarter mile. The full moon lay low on the horizon now, brighter than ever against a starry night sky. He could have enjoyed this, were it not for the grinding thirst that sandpapered his tongue and made his palate burn as if a razor blade had made fine cuts in it.

The gun dangled heavily. He felt a cold wind starting to blow from the desert as dusk neared. He made his way to the tower ruin. He heard something in the desert—a motor! It sounded as if someone was testing a motorcycle. What a strange thing to do, so far away from civilization.

The desert sent its odd smells too, and he caught a whiff of something rank.

The ruined tower stood out bone-white in the eerie moonlight.

London, 1942: Good Time Robby

Major Robert Malone, who was just having a cigar and brandy in his London office with Colonel Ivor Crane and Major General William "Wild Bill" Donovan, understood the strategic importance of rubber. He came from a family of rubber barons. As his older brother Teddy had once remarked, they were born with a rubber spoon in their mouths, the Malones of South Carolina and Arizona. What neither Donovan nor Crane could know was that Rob Malone had a serious problem, and he needed a drastic solution—fast.

Donovan had recently formed the Office of Strategic Services, which he now headed under the aegis of President Franklin Delano Roosevelt. It was the belated United States answer to the mother country's vaunted intelligence services like MI-6. Tall, graying, priestly, with a wild but melancholy look in his eyes, he was certainly eminent and gray enough to be the pope of this new spookery.

Ivor Crane was an amateur spy master, a friend of Allen Dulles and other dabblers in the new American sophistication now that the former colonies were becoming a world power while the old countries of Europe had yet another one of their senseless bloodbaths. Also tall, but younger, darker haired, a big eager child, sincere without sacrificing a certain carefully weary worldliness, he had stocked the empty oak shelves of his Lambeth offices with at least a thousand volumes of U.S., Canadian, and British as well as Continental reference books, classics, everything from Hugo and Goethe to Twain and Hawthorne, with Rabelais and Paine in-between, and of course all the dictionaries, encyclopedias, and other reference works to populate an effective spymaster's office. Crane had been badly wounded in North Africa, and now had an artificial, wooden left forearm and hand, not to mention an achy left elbow that he rarely complained about.

Robert Malone, at 30, was the youngest of the three. He had already seen service in North Africa with Montgomery in a liaison capacity at El Alamein and Tobruk, and taken a piece of shrapnel in one shoulder. Luckily the wound had healed during a month-long convalescence behind the lines in Rabat, Morocco. The experience had given him a taste for Africa that Donovan and Crane now wanted to exploit.

Besides their tailor-fitted dark olive jackets with polished cross-shoulder leathers and expensive pistol belts, the three men offering each other a toast of pre-war French Armagnac from crystal snifters, while holding the driest and most fragrant Cuban cigars, had this in common: all three had graduated from elite colleges. Their leader, Bill Donovan, was a World War I hero and Congressional Medal of Honor recipient after being gravely wounded in battle. At least one movie ("The Fighting 69th," an acclaimed 1940 production starring Pat O'Brien and Jimmy Cagney) had been made at least indirectly about him and his Irish-American regiment. Born into an Irish family of modest means, he had put himself through Columbia University and practiced law before assuming command of the 69th. Now, as FDR's premier spymaster, he was recruiting the best and brightest from the top U.S. universities. Malone, an Irish American (Yale, '35) and Crane (Princeton, '28) were no exceptions. It earned O.S.S. the soubriquet 'Oh So Social.'

This evening, aromas of cigar smoke, brandy, and prime bluish gin for later filled the bookish London rooms housing Crane's O.S.S. division. Rain dribbled down the windows. The three men turned from their laughter and conversation about New York and Boston society to rumors about some ominous work being done on a new weapon of unimaginable destructive potential.

"It's all a theory as yet," Donovan said, sitting on the corner of Crane's desk swinging his leg.

"Sounds a bit far-fetched," Crane said. "What is this thing called?"

"An energy bomb," Donovan said. "That's all I know. Uses heavy elements somehow to release the energy in the atom. Hard to believe that a piece of it the size of a coffee can could devastate a small city, but that's what I am told." He looked at Malone. "All strictly hush-hush, mind you, though the intelligent reading man could find it in the newspapers before the War."

Robert Malone felt as if he had unfinished business in Africa. He could still hear the call of the *muezzin* to prayer, and see the minarets of a mosque etched against a purple desert evening sky along with camels and palm trees. Like Richard Burton and other explorers before him, he was hooked on the magic of Africa. Donovan had read Malone's file and recruited him for the job that was about to befall him. "Rob, I need you down in black Africa. Down in the Belgian Congo, in a place called Katanga Province. That's where the world's prime uranium comes from, and I need a competent man on the ground there to keep me informed."

"Uranium," Ivor Crane said with a shudder. "Sounds ghastly, doesn't it?
"

Malone could see the image. "Dark, mysterious, ungodly." He held up the watch on his wrist to Donovan, asking: "Does it glow in the dark like this?"

Donovan shrugged patiently and honestly. "I don't know. I understand if it's concentrated enough it will. It's radioactive, that's for sure, so don't go bathing in it or anything."

Crane said: "I hear that those men who paint the watch dials are all getting lip and tongue tumors, have you heard that? They take their brushes like so, and rub them in their tongue to put a good point on them before dipping them in the uranium. Makes their mouths glow in the dark. Then they all get sick."

"Well," Donovan said, "it's nothing to mess around with, that's for sure. All we really need to know, Rob, is what the production statistics are and where the stuff is going. There has been a glut on the market for at least a decade—how many watch dials can there be? The Belgians own the Congo, and the Nazis own the Belgians. However, the Nazis are almost finished in Africa, and the Belgians tend to act on their own—we are getting ready to openly station troops down there, regardless of all the Nazi sympathizers, and I want you to keep an eye on them for us, Rob."

"Sure," Malone said self-confidently. He'd spent parts of his childhood in Malaya and other faraway rubber-producing tropical places that most people could only dream about. The idea of keeping tabs on yet another esoteric substance being gathered in a tropical locale seemed like more of the same to him. He would have no qualms being stationed there or anywhere else, as long as the women, the liquor, and the cigarettes were first-rate, along with the betting.

"You might," Donovan added, "keep an eye on our good friends the Soviets while you're at it. We need them almost as much as they need us, and there is one school of philosophy which says that after we beat the Nazis we'll have to watch our backs about Uncle Joe Stalin."

"I've heard that," Ivor Crane said with bland curiosity. "Anything to that, Sir?"

Donovan shrugged. "Hard to say. Russia is in ruins, almost one fifth of her population dead, her industry destroyed, rail capabilities gone, devastation everywhere. They'll need a century to recover from all the damage. I think we'd do well to focus on our primary adversaries right now, the Axis." He added. "Bob, you'll keep an eye on the uranium that Uncle Sam is lusting after. That may take you as far south as Capetown or as far north as the Kasbah. Do what you feel you have to do, get a solid foothold down there for us, and keep me informed through secure channels."

Crane snapped the fingers of his hale right hand and jiggled his hips. "Begin the Beguine!"

Malone laughed. A bachelor, he thought about the Belgian women stuck in the jungle. He'd done well with British girls stuck in places like Ghana just waiting for a fine young English-speaking fellow to come along with charm and breeding. "So when do I leave?" he asked Donovan.

The general's dour mien broke into a smile. "How about Monday?"

"That will be great with me, Sir." Rob Malone grinned back. What he doubted even Donovan knew was that he was awash in gambling debts more than ever in his life. Gambling was his passion and his weakness, more even than women. Women might come easy to him, but Lady Luck kept playing him bad. Maybe down there he'd find the angle he needed, that new spin on things, to pull out of the hole he was in and get himself flush again.

Mauritania, 1942: Ruined Tower Mystery

Tim thought the ruined tower looked dreary.

Twenty feet square, the tower overlooked the beach on one side and the desert on the other. The tower's whitewash, what was left of it, had long since gone dirty gray and was falling off, to reveal salt-stained brick underneath. From the tower's rear, a deserted road led into the desert. As Tim approached, dazed by his hunger and thirst and by the wild beauty of this forsaken thousand-mile beach, he drew the Webley from its holster under his shoulders. He just wished it weren't so heavy, and hoped it wouldn't explode if he had to fire.

Nearby, he heard the roaring sound again, which sounded like a motorcycle revving. He conjured images of unfriendly troops, whether German or Vichy French, or the unknowns—Spanish, Moroccan, Berber, bandits—anything was possible.

The tower might once have been several stories tall, but it was now crumbling, and truncated halfway across its second story. One window had a sill of cracked mud bricks but no top, just moonlit clouds eerily drifting in a starry sky.

Tim walked around the concrete apron, holding the gun in his right hand and feeling his way along the wall with the palm of his other hand, partially for support because he felt weak and dehydrated. His lips were cracked and bleeding, his eyelids swollen. His nose felt swollen. Its surface seemed to be running with pus or fluid and wet shreds of sunburned skin that sloughed away when he brushed a hand across his face. *Am I coming apart?* He shuddered, seeing blood and skin shreds on his hand.

The road leading into the desert was overgrown with strange lunar-looking weeds that fit the silvery light in which they basked. Nobody had driven here in a long time, he could see. There were no tracks of any kind, and no vehicles, not even a rusty wreck. Nothing. No motorcycles either.

He came back around the front, to the open doorway whose wooden door had long ago vanished. He did notice a stenciled sign on a granite slab that had been mortised into the adobe facing, along with a faded tricolor and some sandblasted symbology referring to some obscure French army engineering unit. Faded French words looked official, but about as ludicrous as pompous edicts on shattered tablets of long-gone pharaohs along the Nile.

As he stepped across the stone threshold, a scrabbling noise caught his attention. Rats? He wished he had a flashlight.

In the next instant, something brushed past him, and he caught a clear glimpse: a large tan animal with an ungainly gait, gangling, clumsy.

A second later, he understood the roaring sound nearby.

He'd stumbled into a lion's den and he'd just scared out one of the cubs.

Something else was in the dark, barren interior, lying on the concrete floor: one or two other cubs too small to move?

He didn't have time to question. Now he understood the ear-splitting roar behind him. For an instant, he stared into the enraged face of one of nature's largest predators. It was an ancient, savage face—oddly angular, a breed of lion that wasn't quite like any he'd seen in photos or at the zoo. She was female, judging by the fact she had no mane—a primordial predator whose eyes glowed yellow in the moonlight, cold as a snake's, calculating, filled with a mix of fear and calculation, didn't matter which, and utter savage hatred because he stood between her and her cub.

He fired the revolver, but it only made a popping noise. Despite, or because of, being packed in grease to withstand the sea, the gun misfired. It sent off a shower of sparks that momentarily made the lioness flinch back a step. The mechanism jammed, and the trigger wouldn't fire again.

Tim dodged aside, throwing the gun in the air to distract her.

The lioness hesitated, taking a step sideways as the heavy metal object thudded into the sand near her.

Tim made it another step.

The lioness hesitated again, making a slinking body language as she cast a glance at the tower, despairingly, toward her children.

Tim made it to the edge of the tower and had no place to go.

On a sandy ridge thirty feet away and twenty feet above his head, several other lion shapes appeared in a tactical formation. They would herd him down to the water, where he could not escape.

The lioness roared and started to lope toward him.

Tim froze in deadly icy fear.

At that moment, several shots rang out.

The lioness was in mid-jump when she was hit by heavy caliber bullets. She landed with a hollow slam that shook the ground near Tim's feet curled up, and died with a final, truncated rasp. The other lion shapes disappeared.

Tim heard excited voices, men babbling, feet scrambling.

He smelled gunpowder and realized he was still alive, but frozen in place and trembling.

Abruptly, through the drifting haze of gunpowder, he saw several shapes swaying toward him. The shapes scrambled down the sand dune where the lions had been arrayed moments earlier, and approached Tim on the beach sand. They were Berbers on camels, with turbans wrapped around their heads and antique flintlock muskets protruding as long elegant shadows.

Several black men in torn khakis and red fezzes blocked the doorway and held a net among them. They laughed, showing broad white teeth as they babbled happily, and Tim instantly got the picture that there was a market someplace for live cubs as well as dead lionesses.

So if the lions had not killed him, would these desert nomads?

The leader of the Barbary nomads opened his turban, revealing a fierce, dark face with curly beard and scarred nose. The man jabbered at Tim in Arabic, French, and at least one local dialect.

Tim raised his hands and said: "Friend! *Allah!* Friend!"

"*Allah?*" Two of the camel-mounted men consulted each other. They swept their face coverings aside and looked at each other in disbelief, then at Tim with evident anger. Had he committed some kind of blunder, a blasphemy perhaps?

"*Islam*," one man said, adding a torrent of words in Arabic while waving a small book. "*Al Qur'an*," Tim understood. *Allāhu akbar...* "God is almighty. Muhammad, Blessed Be His Holy Name, is his only Prophet. Are you a believer?"

"Whatever you say," Tim said fervently, licking dry lips and feeling faint. As he spoke, men clambered from their mounts. One wrestled with a bulky object behind his saddle, producing a hydra-like *hookah* for multiple users. Men came menacingly toward Tim with ropes, guns, leering faces. At that moment, the world went blank, and Tim collapsed into darkness.

Congo, 1942: Malone with Mistress

Major Robert Malone had little trouble integrating himself into diplomatic life in Leopoldville.

The tropical heat took getting used to, but Malone had experienced similar extremes in Malaysia and even in Florida. One had to get used to traveling everywhere with bodyguards, given years of growing popular unrest at Belgian mistreatment of their colonial subjects. The bodyguards could be inconvenient at moments when Rob found an opportunity to gamble. The card games were a way to raise cash, keep ahead of his creditors, and listen for interesting intelligence tidbits. Among the floating crap games, he could hobnob with every official of any significance in this part of Africa.

As a cover story, Rob was supposedly a journalist for some obscure news service, drifting among Allied military officers, diplomats, and bureaucrats that swarmed around the rich province. The Belgian exile government's colonial governor Pierre Ryckmans ran the Congo. Belgian rule had never been a kindly one, though nothing on the scale of the royal depredations in the late 1800s, which had created a world outcry and caused the king's personal colony to be handed over to the Belgian people as a national fiefdom.

Dozens of miners and other local laborers had recently died in uprisings in Luluabourg and Élisabethville. Relations with the locals remained testy.

Belgium was still in name and reality a Nazi possession, while the Belgian Congo was in reality already a staging area for the Allies in their drive to retake Africa from the Axis. Under cover, Rob was the eyes and ears of Wild Bill Donovan in the Congo. His concern was less with the Nazis, whose star had already badly waned in Africa, than with the incipient efforts by Stalin's Soviets to create the first atomic bomb and make the world safe for communism.

Rob's primary technical contact was a Belgian physicist, Henri Brégel, who lived with his wife and daughter in a villa in the resort town of Boma but spent much of his working time in Leopoldville where he served as a scientific advisor to various Allied governments. From Brégel, Rob learned that the United States had interned a shipload of prime Belgian uranium-235 at a dock in New York City. Initial research into using radioactive material was being conducted at a secret facility in Manhattan. That was all Henri Brégel knew, or was willing to divulge. From the importance Donovan placed on this mysterious green glowing watch-dial paint, Rob could readily surmise Brégel knew his health was at stake if he had a loose tongue.

Rob moved easily and elegantly in the frontier society in Leopoldville. He found the wives of European and American administrators were intriguing and bored, and their daughters eager and attractive. He learned who was selling what, and who needed that, while staying as squeaky clean as possible. Most people believed he was a foreign correspondent for several U.S. weekly journals, and probably nobody knew he was a U.S. Army officer, much less an O.S.S. operative.

As far as the women went, everything was "the war." *C'est la guerre.* Among the dalliances Rob cultivated was one with the neglected and beautiful wife of a Belgian mining engineer named Simon Clery—a big, brutal man who was away most of the time, usually in Katanga where rubber and coal were mined, along with uranium ore, diamonds, and the other fruits of a jungle paradise spoiled by human greed. Clery's wife was of no particular intelligence value, but she was beautiful and needy—and, like Rob Malone, had a dark and terrible secret. Rob only saw her occasionally, and he hardly thought of her when they weren't together, but each time he saw her she roiled up a lot of inner turmoil in him. Their affair was going nowhere, they both knew—among other things, she was married—which made it all the more passionate and pungent between them.

Rob found himself hovering around Brégel's 23 year old daughter Astrid—no child, certainly, and surely deflowered long since, though she radiated girlish innocence—who had been studying nursing at Louvain, but had fled with her mother and siblings to join their father not long after the German invasion in 1940. Astrid was a willowy blonde with bright blue eyes, a sweet smile, and long slender arms—she looked great holding a drink, and Rob discovered she was something of a lush. That would account for that perennial reddish blush in her creamy peach fuzz cheeks, he thought.

One day, he was invited to tea at the Brégel villa near Boma. This was 60 miles inland from the mouth of the Congo River, on the last upriver tidal beaches of the Atlantic Ocean. Rob, Brégel, Astrid, and several servants and bodyguards drove down to the beach in a white convertible Peugeot driven by a local in black uniform, white billed cap, and white gloves. There were several children along, and the party frolicked down to the tumbling river water. Brégel was a stiff, somewhat dour civil servant who insisted on wearing his suit and tie, though he made a concession by removing his dress shoes and socks. He sat in a beach chair sipping a vinegary Belgian ale and wiggling bluish veiny feet. Rob sat nearby, sipping Campari and soda, while Astrid walked down to the water with several small children. The sun filled her yellow dress, barely concealing in its glow young limbs that invited being touched.

Brégel held forth about Congo politics. A loyal bureaucrat, he assumed the Belgian Congo would return to its timeless colonial torpor as soon as the current Teutonic craziness had been resolved. Rob had been briefed by a midlevel State Department official from Katanga, a gray soul named Sylvester, who, when he passed about the fourth or fifth rum cola, became lubrifaciently detached and scholarly. According to Sylvester, local agitators like Joseph Kasavubu, Patrice Lumumba, and Moïse Tshombe were pressing for independence, at a time when black Congolese were considered primitives and not allowed to own land, purchase alcohol, or similar prerogatives of human dignity. The colonial military had attempted mutiny recently, and there were constant strikes and riots with many deaths across the province. Many black revolutionaries had strong ties to the international workers' movement centered in Moscow. Rob listened and nodded sympathetically to Sylvester's barroom conversations at The Yank downtown, but Rob kept his own counsel privately. He had no love for European colonial powers, and felt sympathetic to the blacks, but reflected that in the United States, particularly in the South, a black man could be lynched for looking at a white woman the wrong way. Rob had his doubts about how the black man's lot could be improved in the Congo if it was still so dreadful in the alleged homeland of modern democracy, the United States. Rob also felt uneasy about staying involved in another country's colonial morass, particularly when the Belgians had been so arrogant and cruel, and made such a mess of things. Why inherit a century of resentment? Then again, as the Old Man (Donovan) had made clear, it was all about the future world balance of power—a compelling reason to lay prudence aside.

Brégel seemed to feel at ease with Rob, and let slip information that might be considered sensitive. Or was he trying to divert Rob's attention from Astrid? The girl was on her way back from the water now, toying with a slim bit of driftwood and looking mischievous. Time for her to sneak another glass of sour *lambiek*.

Brégel talked about yellowcake, the refined uranium ore avidly sought by all major countries. "Down there in Katanga," he said, "uranium oxide is in the ground and you can practically dig it out by hand. We have locals down there digging day and night, now that we can be certain the Germans won't be back to take it away. Your country will want the stock that is coming out. We must be careful of the Soviets, and these local monkeys who want to sell their souls to the Communists." The wattles under his chin shook with outrage, and his bushy gray eyebrows hid glowering steel-blue eyes.

Rob sat back, squinting his eyes shut in the late afternoon sunlight and not reacting, except to swat a large, loud fly.

"How are my men doing?" Astrid said, tipping back a bottle of lambic against china teeth, and sitting down in the sand beside Rob.

"Your men are solving the world's problems," Brégel said with a brushing motion of his red and blue mottled hands.

"The men are hungering for the company of someone who walks up from the sea like a young goddess," Rob said softly.

Astrid laughed, and her father didn't hear. Madame Sylvie Brégel of course missed nothing, but appeared to aid and abet her daughter in a subversive way. Rob noticed that Sylvie rarely sat beside Henri or touched him. Rob reached languidly behind his chair and pulled a cold Alsatian beer from a cooler kept refreshed by a black valet. It would be an interesting evening, and interesting sport. After a certain amount of subtle negotiation at some telepathic level assisted by gestures and nuances, the game became clear. At the moment, Sylvie had no need of actual assistance in bed. Rather, her game was to secure a sense of approval by flaunting still attractive charms and receive signals that, if she were open, they might connect on another day. During all this, Sylvie deftly saved Astrid at the last moment, reining the girl in with the children and servants and making off to the villa. This left Rob to drive back along the river with Brégel to the capital. Madame Brégel had rewarded Rob by contacting a mutual friend that afternoon in Soyo. Rob had momentarily forgotten about Régine Clery, and looked forward to some steamy relief with her from his needs. While the limousine with Brégel and Rob rocked through the deep Congo night under rustling trees and palm fronds with the great Congo River on their left. Rob listened to Brégel's endless monologues about his home in Belgium and his ideas about white people in Africa. Rob occasionally caught glimpses of another limousine following half a kilometer behind, and he guessed that would be Madame Clery.

He was right. The parties in their two cars, separately, each caught small bumpy river planes that smelled of spicy local food. Flying via Matadi and Luozi they arrived in Leopoldville in a little over two hours. There, Brégel thanked Rob for a lovely day and had himself driven off to his hotel suite near the Belgian mining conglomerate headquarters.

Rob, on the other hand, continued on with a taxi to the small but elegant Hotel Blankenberge, not far from the airport and the Congo River.

Régine Clery was in the waiting room reading a newspaper. The hotel was quiet and subdued, since it was getting late. The concierge, a gray-haired Arab, kept busy behind his counter, and the one page, a young native lad wearing white gloves and a round hat, took his time about sweeping dust out of the corners with a half-length broom.

Rob walked up and offered his arm. Régine put her paper aside and rose. She was a slim, elegant dark-haired woman of 30, wearing a crisply cut black jacket and dark dress with small flowers. Her husband, a mining engineer, was away in the field most of the time and had a black mistress in Katanga with whom he preferred to spend his free time. Régine was a French-speaking Walloon from Chimay in Hainaut. A strong touch of the Mediterranean, perhaps even Araby, ran in her veins, and her skin had a light complexion like gold tobacco, darkening around the finger joints. She said she had an ancestor who had come from France in the 1830s, with the Foreign Legion of Charles X, and married an African woman, probably an Egyptian, but she wasn't sure—it was a dark, hushed family secret. Régine had freckles the same dark color all over the sharp, exotic lines of a body perfectly made for skimpy Art Deco-style dresses. Her color made her the object of disdain (jealousy, Rob thought). She'd had a fine education in a cloister school and spoke flawless English in addition to French, Flemish, and German. The husband was an ignoramus, Rob had long since decided, and Régine needed rescuing. Her thin figure, though, came from another source.

"Hello, Régine."

"Rob, darling."

"Did you have a nice flight?" Rob said wrapping his hand over hers as she thrust her arm through his.

"I dozed," she said with a slight laugh. "Sylvie is my closest confidante. I had no idea you were in Boma."

"Does Sylvie know everything?"

"I'm sure she does. She is very tolerant. She helps me when she can." They walked arm in arm together as if they were married, a deceptive portrait. "I wish I could be like her."

"You're still young."

"A faded flower," Régine said.

"Nonsense. You just need a fresh start, that's all."

Régine looked at him sadly. There was hunger in her eyes, and he knew the routine.

"Want me to take you home?"

She shook her head.

They stepped outside for a few moments, and Rob asked: "Do you have it?"

She nodded, held up a small white packet. "Will you help me?" She handed him a tiny metal object. "Let's have just a snort and a nice drink first." This was only for starters, they both knew. *Poor thing. Poor darling.* Such a beautiful woman, married to a tree stump.

"My pleasure, Régine." Opening the small brown earring box inside the packet, he used the spoon she'd given him to take out a small quantum of heroin, one for each nostril. She held a finger on each opposite nostril and inhaled, quickly, violently, so that her cheekbones looked like ceramic and her eyes closed as if she were dying. He put the rest away, pressing it into her hands, and she stuffed it into her purse in the same motion. Then she leaned against the wall, face up toward the moonlight, and sighed deeply. Her breathing became relaxed and easy. "*Merci.*"

They entered a tiny room overlooking the river with its lights, very romantic, and sat at a table with a candle. The proprietor, a tired looking old black man, shuffled out grumpily and informed them the restaurant was closed. After a bit of haggling, he left them two glasses and a bottle of *Elephant* palm wine. He offered to light the candle, but Rob emphatically raised his palm and shook his hand. The old man left the matches on the table and shuffled off. The wine was too sweet and too harsh and a bit warm, but they sipped it sparingly and let it wrap itself around them with its faint intoxicated aura. They held hands and laughed gently as they talked.

"Brégel was telling me about mining in Katanga," Rob said.

She laughed. "I heard enough about that when we first got here. Now I hear nothing." She shrugged. "It's just as well. After the war, *c'est tout.* We are finished. I go my way, he goes his way."

"He is a fool."

"We knew that long ago. And you, *mon cher*? You are not a fool. Will you ever marry?"

He grinned. "Probably not." Probably yes, but to a nice Virginia debutante who could fuss like a Southern lady but probably couldn't tell Angola in Africa from Angola in Louisiana. "You covered your tracks?"

She shrugged, lighting a cigarette. "I'm with Sylvie in Boma." She exhaled and he enjoyed the smells of her mouth, her tobacco, her perfume. He leaned close and kissed her. She leaned willingly, hungrily, forward. Their tongues swept silently together, in the silence of the little room where a clock ticked and out on the river a ferry whistle shrilled briefly, a steamy hiss that echoed around the hills and river bends.

"I have information for you," she said.

"Oh good. I need something to make my day interesting."

"This is good information, darling. It should get you started paying all that money you owe, and it should keep me supplied with what I need."

He held both her chill hands in his. "What, darling? Tell me."

"In the morning, sweetheart. I want to enjoy you with me tonight. In the morning, we will travel north together. You'll see." She touched his nose with the tip of her forefinger and made a naughty, promising face.

Several times, he helped her shoot up, because she did not have the courage to face the needle herself. For his part, he licked a bit of the monkey but didn't want to get any further involved in its grip. Régine needed the stuff, but managed to get by most of the time with substitutes like cocaine and hashish brought in from the north by Arabs.

As he slipped into bed with her for the third time, she dozed off. Frustrated in his desire for her, he considered going out to find a tart on the street, but he was too tired. So he contented himself with one of her cigarettes and a tall glass of Clery's red Bordeaux. He fell asleep in bed beside her, trusting that her staff would let her know if by some astronomical chance the *maitre* was coming home, which he almost never did, and when he did one could tell by the bright headlights shining up the driveway and illumining the bedroom so that venetian blind shadows swam like shark gills on the wall. As Régine snored softly beside him, Rob fell asleep with one arm around her slender waist.

There he shaved, showered, and had his maid make a solid breakfast for two, with strong black coffee. Whistling, he packed a travel bag and listened to the birds, the trees, and the street noise of Kinshasa.

Régine appeared at his house just in time as the heavyset maid—wrapped in silky white native dress, and frowning—brought their food. They ate under a large tree, at a mossy little table with two rickety wrought-iron chairs. Birds twittered loudly overhead, and every once in a while a monkey or a parrot screeched in the neighborhood.

Régine smoked a cigarette and laid her arm across the table. Rob cooked up a spoon and put a tourniquet on her. Carefully, he drew up the bubbling yellowish brown horse and injected her. She squinted and looked away, holding up fingers and cigarettes to shield herself from the view.

Rob ate heartily, while she picked at her dry toast, smoked, sipped coffee, and stared out through the hanging willow fronds. "What are you plotting, sweetheart?"

She flicked her cigarette carefully on the stones around the table. "We're going to fly up into Mauritania."

"Mauritania! That's far away!"

"Oh don't be silly. I know you go there with Willi and Walther on business."

"It's still a long way off. Why would I make the time for that?"

"To keep me company."

"I can keep you company right here."

"I know, but it will be worth it. You'll make money."

"Okay, that's interesting. How did you latch up with my old friends?"

"I watched you, darling. I was with you when you had them fly in a crate of French brandy to pay off a gambling debt. I made inquiries and found out they can hook me up with some Arabs in Mauritania who bring in my stuff from Tunisia and elsewhere. I met one of them long ago, in Belgium."

Malone considered carefully. She needed her stuff badly enough to take risks, but fortunately, he knew the two Germans well enough. They were expatriates, like so many people here. Normal Germans quickly became ex-Nazis once they got out of their toxic Hitler world. "Okay, it's a deal."

"You'll have a good time, Rob. I'll make sure of it." She puffed deeply, exhaled luxuriously as the drugs coursed through her mind. Rob, meanwhile, felt a slight sweat break out along his neck. "Régine, I wish you'd clear things like that with me first."

She sat up, looking drunk. She seemed to have trouble focusing for a second, and her lips trembled as if she wanted to speak. A minute later, she had recovered, and sat close to him. "Darling, it's the answer to all of our problems. They have a large amount of hashish and some opium that I have already agreed to buy from them, and I need you to go along to carry the cash. Plus there is supposed to be a pound of heroin and some cocaine for me. It will keep me for weeks. Bring a gun."

"How much cash exactly is that, Régine?"

"Ten thousand dollars."

He whistled. "That could get us robbed and killed along the way."

"Yes, but Willi and Walther are good men. I happen to know Willi from a sports flying club near Houffalize before the war, when the Germans still had to hide the fact that they were developing an air force. They were in thick with people from Fokker."

"Small world." Rob shook his head slowly. "You're sharp, babe."

"Intelligence, Rob. They have a connection to a Russian spy network up there. I know it because I overheard my husband talking with another Belgian last week. You can make a note of it for use in your little private business."

"Of which you must never speak," Rob said. He'd known her husband was an enthusiastic Communist, though just as much a Belgian nationalist opposed to letting the colored people steal back their own land.

"Just think," she said. "If this works out, and I'm sure it will, we can make this trip once every two months, or you could go more often. You can buy drugs from them, posing as an ex-pat. You can give me my bit, sell the rest, and pay off your debts."

"Brilliant," Rob said. It was a gamble, but he was just desperate enough to try. Besides getting some money to pay off his debts, he was developing a lead on a double agent, code-named Jaguar, playing for both Hitler and Roosevelt, which probably meant he was also in Uncle Joe's crib. That would make him a triple, but Rob was still working on that angle. He'd already hinted about it to his boss, Ivor Crane, and indications were that Donovan would look favorably on Rob if he could crack something that complicated.

Within 30 hours, they sat aboard the Märzig brothers' stolen Ju-52, headed north into Mauritania for their drug deal outside the desert city of Néma.

Mauritania, 1942: Nordhall's Ransom

Tim Nordhall awoke feeling stiff and numb.

A woman sat watching over him. She was covered from head to foot in black robes. Over her head, she wore a black hood with gilded decorations around eerie looking eyeholes. A fire crackled nearby, and he could smell the sea. He heard surf crashing faintly. Light wind keened through rock formations scoured by eons of blown grit. He smelled camel dung and the greasy smells that went along with camp life. He smelled charcoal and tea and tobacco. The woman looked up toward a knot of men around the fire and let out a low, quick yell. Then she spoke softly to him, offering him a broad shallow cup. He rose effortlessly onto one side and accepted the cup. He sipped hot tea that tasted faintly of butter, cloves, and blood. It was salty to the taste, and he drank it in quick, short, eager sips. Anything to get salt and fluids down his throat. There had to be some food value to this stuff. "Thank you," he told her, "shukran."

"Ah," she said in the shadows of her veils, echoing: "*shukran*." It was about the only Arabic word he knew. She seemed appreciative, and let forth a small torrent of praise for God and kind words on Tim's head.

A man rose by the fire and came close. He was a tall and wiry mix of Negro and Caucasian, like so many North Africans. He had quick, intelligent eyes and a sharp mercenary mien, and spoke some desert dialect. Tim couldn't understand any of it, but sensed that he was in roughly the same bargaining position as the lion cub mewling in its net cage 100 feet away, or its dead mother lying beside it. Tim made beseeching sign language with his hands, with his entire body, promising peace, offering the sky if they took him to a police station.

The Berber laughed—a knowing and dirty snort and pulled a gun out with his right hand. He bent over and in a flash had a knife at Tim's throat. He held the gun on Tim while scraping the knife's razor edge loudly through the unshaven stubble on Tim's neck. Tim felt the pressure of the blade's edge moving over his skin, just strongly enough to indent the skin without breaking it, but he could feel each tiny nick and dent on the delicate nerve endings around his carotid artery as that blade slowly moved from one side to the other. The message was clear, and he looked up into the Berber's eyes in exhaustion and submission. He had never felt so helpless in his entire life, even while nearly drowning with his shipmates a day earlier.

Two other men tied Tim's feet together at the ankles so that he could not run. They laughed as they tied a small goat-collar around his neck. Every time he moved, the unevenly shaped, hand-carved wooden balls inside those steel bells would roll around with a rattling noise. Not only was he not going anywhere, but he was noisy as a London bus every time he breathed in and out. The men laughed, and one made a bleating noise. To them, he was something of a goat. He began to get the dreadful feeling that he was about to be sold along with the lion cub. Was there still slavery in this part of the world? Would he ever see civilization again?

Stomach was full, he belched uncomfortably as he sank into an exhausted slumber. The last thing he saw was the coppery faces of the men regarding him from around the campfire. He had the twin impressions that he had been drugged, and that they were debating what price they could fetch for him.

📖

Tim awoke, retching.

His head was filled with fumes from poorly burned gasoline fuel, and his bones ached from being banged around on the steel floor of an old, tiny Citroen truck. Only a faded, worn carpet scrap separated him from the metal floor of the truck. A canvas awning over the top shielded him from the hot sun that shone through pinholes in the canvas, blinding him and searing his skin wherever the sun's rays struck. The air was dry and hot, like inside a furnace. His stomach seemed to want to jump out through his mouth. He jerked onto all fours, retching. Already, a thin watery puddle full of clotted milk bits covered the floor near him, and the smell was like rotting baby vomit baked in animal urine and old diesel spillage. At least, that was his muddled sense of what was coming out from inside him and mingling with the already not very charming contents of the truck.

The truck, in any event, had stopped moving. He'd been dimly and sickeningly conscious of movement throughout the early dawn hours and into the ever-hotter daylight as the vehicle bumped over old French military roads.

Each time he retched, the goat collar around his neck gave a series of spastic rattles, almost in a musical rhythm. It made men laugh harshly outside the truck where he couldn't see them. He didn't need to see them. He remembered their cruel faces from the night before.

His ankles were tightly bound together, and rubbed raw where they touched. Sand had gotten in the wounds, and flies buzzed mercilessly around the serum and hopped around over his vomit, annoying his eyes. The flies buzzed hungrily around the cream stuck to his cracked lips, and he made sputtering, spitting noises to blow them away.

When the men outside heard him, their tone changed from laughter to serious haggling. One threw aside the canvas flap on the back of the cargo container, letting in harsh sunlight. There was a crash as the tailgate went down, and a common roar of disgust at the sight and smell of him. A hand reached in, grabbed him by the collar, and yanked. Half-throttled, coughing, too weak to fight, he slid out over his vomit and landed on a mixture of hot sand and gravel and sharp little protruding rocks outside.

He was in a *sooq*, a market square. All around, two and three story mud buildings cast merciful shade, and he crawled out of the hot sunlight into the shade of several men's hems. A stick descended on his back, in a half-hearted whipping motion, as a white-bearded man negotiated unyieldingly with a shadowy man in a gray wool robe.

He was thirsty, and tried to get the man's attention.

The man hit him sharply on the back with the stick, making him cringe with pain. He tried to double over backwards, which was physiologically impossible, but he writhed with his hands reaching behind his back and his mouth open in pain. The goat bells rattled, and people around him laughed. Drifting in and out of delirium, he saw again the shark dismembering his fellow sailor under the water. He saw again the awkward pose of body—was the man already dead, or just numb with shock?—and then the plier-like attack of that shark—the darting, snapping grab, the floating pieces of the torso...

He found himself sobbing helplessly at the loss of all his shipmates, the realization that he hated Hitler for the first time in a flesh and blood visceral way for causing all this when he could be sitting in a miserable, damp, drafty factory by the East River in Fair Haven, toiling over a Seth Thomas engine, and listening to the alcoholic shop supervisor tormenting him about not taking a full hour for lunch...it was all jumbled together in a blender of sobs and emotions and thirst and despair...

📖

Tim hardly ever got to see his owner. He was kept in a big, dark room in chains. It was not as unpleasant as the truck ride, except for the pain where his ankle was chafed by the cold iron.

He woke up in Néma, chained to a wall. At least, the goat collar was gone. His hands were manacled. A skinny Arab with a French accent and graying hair came to see him. "I am the school teacher Selim Bey of Néma, Mauritanian city. I speak English. What is your name, Sir?"

"Timothy Nordhall, Lieutenant Junior Grade, U.S. Navy, serial number..."

"Very pretty. British?"

"American."

"Yes, very pretty, thank you." The schoolteacher sat on a wooden chair at a scratched dark oak table with a glass top and smoked a cigarette. His features half-stayed in amber shadows. He had pale, delicate hands and a bit of a nervous tic. He had big dark puffy eyes and a paunch. Evidently he lived fairly well, but had a lot of stress. "Mr. Omar Nasr Tandileh has paid to have you here. He is wealthy man who owns much property in Néma. We are deep in the desert and there is no place to run. You will stay here until your embassy calls."

"Calls or comes?" Tim said. He sat in a corner, leaning against the coolness of a whitewashed mud wall. The floor was hard packed dirt, but had some frayed old oriental rugs thrown haphazardly over it. Tim pulled together a kind of soft seat for himself. The chain on his ankle was attached to a wrought iron grating inset over a small fireplace. It was mortared firmly in place. A little probing told him it would not come loose. No matter—where could he go, in the middle of the desert near the Mali border not too far from Timbuktu? The idea of escape was laughable.

"Calls, comes, they will negotiate. Very pretty. You will stay here quietly and if you have any concerns you call for teacher Selim Bey, you understand?"

"I understand, Mr. Selim Bey. Thank you."

Selim Bey had a way of mugging his cigarette, getting half of it wet while it hung with a long ash under his nose. Tim, who rarely smoked, didn't understand how the man could tolerate the smoke drifting through his eyes. Selim Bey rose and hitched his white pants up. He tucked his shirt in and came close, bending down to run a speculative and feminine pair of fingers up Tim's spine. "Very pretty. You lucky, Mr. Nasr Tandileh does not like sleep with men. If you stay quiet, Mr. Tim, it will be easy. If you make trouble, Mr. Nasr Tandileh will cut your foot off, then your tongue. You won't run far." He made a horrified face and pointed his index fingers at his own eyes. "Or he take your eyes out. Be careful. Very pretty." Selim Bey tilted his head to one side, with big eyes and a protruding tongue. He ran his fingers up and down Tim's back, grunting, while holding his other hand over his own thigh. Tim recoiled, throwing himself against the wall and raising his manacled hands to ward off the dirty old man.

Bey looked at his fingers as if to inspect their tips for possible damage. Shivers ran up and down Tim's spine. Still with that cigarette dangling like a physical appendage, Selim Bey reached behind the desk for a walking stick Tim had not noticed before. He gave the desk a sharp whack, and Tim shrank back at the clear threat, the ominous sense of beatings and other abuse to come if he did not cooperate.

Bey walked to the door. "You be smart, Mr. Tim. Very still, wait until negotiations complete. Nothing happen if you stay smart." With that, he saw himself out. The door clapped shut, and a latch descended with a slam. Tim imagined that Bey was being cut in on whatever Tandileh hoped to get from the Embassy for his investment. Everything had its price.

Tim tried mentally to push away the aura of slime the man had left in the room. He reached for the tin dog bowl nearby and splashed water on his dirty, stubbled face. Warm droplets like thick blood dribbled off his chin and down his chest, into the hairs under the ragged tunic they'd given him to wear.

It was quiet in this empty room with its torn little carpets. Tim felt sick and exhausted. He rested against the wall until he slumped down and started to go to sleep on his rugs, like a dog. He heard layers of noise outside the quiet nucleus of this gloomy hall. Just beyond the confines, he heard the clatter of pots and dishes in a kitchen, and the laughter and conversation of women. Beyond that, he heard the noise of the city, the braying of camels and other animals—no dogs, for those were considered unclean—but he heard a cat meowing someplace. Those animals all had more freedom than he did, but then again he reflected, he was alive and all the men he'd served with were dead, gone painfully to a watery grave. He listened to the haunting song of the *muezzin* pouring like a dark and baleful river of words through the air every few hours—"God is great. There is no God but God. Mohammed is the Messenger of God. Come to prayer and be saved."

Tim dozed as much as he could, but five times a day he awoke to the nightmarish sound of that call droning away. He began to tell apart the voices of the men who made that call to prayer from the highest minaret in the city. One was a higher, brighter voice, like that of a man happy with his work; the other, a dour and gloomy voice like that of a man wanting the world to suffer under the same penances and reproaches that crushed his own heart.

Tim grew tired of waiting in his prison, and started to plot an escape. He was still shackled and chained to the wall, and his ankles had developed weeping wounds that caused him considerable pain. His legs kept growing numb, and he kept having to shift painfully around to keep them exercised. This dance of the hours coincided with the passage of shadows across the white walls like the shadows on a sundial, and kept him hypnotized.

In all of this time, he only met his owner once. Mr. Nasr Tandileh was a brown-skinned man of Egyptian origin. So said Madame Noualah, a dumpy middle-aged wife of his who came in twice a day to rub fats and oils into Tim's wounds. She spoke a little bit of English. Apparently, Selim Bey gave English lessons to Nasr Tandileh's four wives. Tandileh came in one day, wearing a khaki and brown uniform of his own design, which was a cross between that of the French Foreign Legion (Vichy) and the Spanish Foreign Legion. He wore a French-style officer's *kepi*, dark blue, with gold braid and red top. He wore a cape, evidently borrowed from the Spaniards not far up the line in Morocco's western Sahara district. And, on his arm, was an armband with a French tricolor but in the middle of that was a small red diamond with a white circle inscribed, and, within that, a black swastika. He wore highly polished brown boots, yellow puttees, jodhpur riding trousers, and a dark green-brown wool British battle jacket associated with Eisenhower.

Evidently weighing his loyalties, Mr. Nasr Tandileh no doubt understood the British and Americans were wresting Africa back from the fascists, but there was always the danger of Adolf and Benito's return. Besides, western Africa was largely a French operation, since the French were situated just across the Med. The French had staked their claim in North Africa around 1830, after the end of their Napoleonic follies, and Louis Philippe had created the FFL to do the heavy lifting in the invasion of Tunisia and Algeria. In the 1920s, Spain had followed with its own FL and, between the two nations, they'd broken the back of Barbary's Rif warlords.

Two swarthy thugs accompanied Nasr Tandileh during his inspection of his prisoner, while Tim lay moaning on the floor from an ankle infection he was developing from the shackles. Turning up his nose, Nasr Tandileh left the room after just five minutes with his bodyguards. Tim heard a powerful engine start up in a garage just on the other side of the wall. This got Tim using his hearing, like a kind of Huff Duff, to divine the layout of the sprawling house with its harem, and the world beyond.

📖

He noticed that Nasr Tandileh appeared to be a man of habit. As near as Tim understood, Nasr Tandileh owned a carpet factory and some other industries in Néma. Natural sunlight poured in through high windows during the day. There were no windows on the south side, and these houses were efficiently built of thick thermal bricks and mud, so that it stayed relatively cool inside. Much of the day, Tim rested on his carpets in semidarkness; and then there were the long, black nights during which his eyes grew sensitive to see in the dark.

Most of all, Tim began to rely on his senses of smell and hearing. He knew what time of day meals were, and what was being served, by the smells of vegetables, cabbage, *couscous*, peppers, onions, and garlic being fried in the kitchen. The routine of the house was easy to learn and was based on the comings and goings of Nasr Tandileh first, and secondly on the living patterns of his four wives. Apparently his first wife was the kind, soft-spoken gray haired woman who came twice a day to care for Tim's feet and to feed him. Then there were two younger ones with loud voices, who argued a lot. Those two had teenage children who also carried on. Finally there was another loud wife who sounded as though she might be Senegalese, from south of the border. That one sang when she worked alone in the kitchen, but yelled when the other wives were with her. Tim began to really appreciate the virtues of monogamy, of marrying a sweet girl next door and having a quiet home where a lamp glowed in the window, and the children were safe and asleep in their beds upstairs. Sometimes he felt God was punishing him for leaving Sally Levesque. He could close his eyes and run imaginary fingers over the soft skin of her pale, freckled legs, and smell lilac soap in her golden glowing red hair. *I am such a fool,* he thought, more than once.

Within Néma's sounds and smells, Tim triangulated the layout of the house. In a way, it was like Huff Duff all over again—so that he knew there was a wall about a foot thick separating him from the garage where Nasr Tandileh kept the powerful French limousine with which he left early in the morning and returned late in the evenings. There was a chauffeur who puttered in the garage for another hour, apparently cleaning the car and sometimes having assignations with a giggling young woman (Tim suspected it might be the young Senegalese, but he couldn't be sure; it was just another scrap of information he stored up for the future). Most importantly, he noticed that airplanes flew overhead, and he learned to triangulate their flight paths. He would walk around the room, at least the part where his chain would allow him, and he'd look up, rapt, with his arms spread and his fingers splayed like antennas, and he'd listen. He would follow, by body language, as a plane flew in or out. At times he was so light-headed that he almost felt like a plane himself, or a bird, flying in the darkness under the larger machine's prop wash. Once, while doing this, he fell down and banged his head, but the earthen floor there was forgiving, and he awakened sometime later when the old lady came to bring food.

A few times, while the old woman was in the room and the door was open, Tim could see into the house. He saw the gloomy corridors of packed earth, the rounded ceilings, the distant kitchen with its black oven doors and hanging pots. Once, he saw two men in the hallway on prayer rug while the *muezzin*'s call still echoed in the air, and the direction of their obeisances told him roughly which way was east, since they always prayed facing toward Mecca. From that he put together a mental map of the city. He sensed that it was a wide-open desert space with wide roads and sparsely placed mud and brick buildings. He stood under each window at various times of day, listening to the varying gradients and types of sound, and surmised that the main *sooq* was about two or three blocks east. From there, he heard the braying of camels, the shouting of hawkers, and the constant hammering of metal smiths.

One day, after the woman had come to rub his ankles in soothing balm, and after she'd left, he discovered that he had lost so much weight, and the shackles were so slippery, that he was able to slide first one foot and then the other out of his shackles. Worse, he couldn't get them back in because of the pain and swelling that followed the acrobatics of twisting his feet around.

He had no choice. He must escape that very day, his seventh or eighth, or face having a hand or foot chopped off, if not worse. Already, his captivity was making him stir crazy. He was feeling stronger, more rested, from the feeding and the inactivity. He had a fairly decent roadmap of the town in his head—and his only plan was to reach the airport. He knew that was about a mile away through twisting alleys and streets. From there, he had to hope that he could bluff his way onto a European plane, be it Allied or Axis, and make his way back to the world he had grown up in, not this primitive and alien desert existence of centuries ago. *Damn you all to your slimy, hypocritical, savage mud-brick hell!* Suddenly, he was tired of getting screwed with, and he determined to escape or die.

His evening meal, of *couscous* with rolled up flatbread and mint tea with honey and milk, came at the usual time, when the house grew still as the family ate. They were becoming more generous about feeding him, probably to have a nice fatted slave to hand over to some Western embassy in exchange for a suitcase of cash. Tim pictured how it would work. The Arabs would accept the highest bid, probably from the U.S. Consulate. They would leave a suitcase of dollars, cash, on some distant stretch of highway, where Tandileh's gangsters could watch from the hills above to make sure there was no stakeout. Having paid, the local police would find Tim drugged and sleeping in a local hotel. There would be no paper trail. And the gangsters would be sure to follow through without cheating, because Tandileh had more gangsters, smarter and better armed, to torture them to a slow, hideous death if they tried to run off with the suitcase. Sweet plan, and Tim determined they would not have him as a person on whom to practice their plan.

The old man was home, and from a quiet niche he presided over a roomful of women and children seated at their cushions elsewhere in the house. A servant usually brought Tim's food and tea in two tin dishes, left them near the door, and retreated locking the door behind her. She also changed the slop bucket, which sat in a corner with a battered wooden lid on it.

Tonight, Tim ate and drank like a camel storing up for a long journey. He must be full, and yet stay light on his feet. No swollen belly to make him sluggish. He must make every second count, and he had a desperate plan. The chauffeur finished cleaning the car, the giggling came and went, and the garage door rolled up and then down again as the man and woman left for parts unknown.

For days, Tim had been examining a crack in the wall. Using his spoon, he now gouged at it, loosening plaster and underlying sand. Every few minutes, he froze and listened to noises in the house. He had a carpet ready to put against the wall in case anyone came to check on him, but nobody did. So far, so good.

Within a few hours, he had managed to loosen a few bricks. There was no turning back now. Feverishly, with bloodied hands, he gouged and dug into the wall. Slowly, one by one, he dug out the long flat bricks embedded in the mortar. To his dismay, he discovered another layer of wall beyond this one, but he kept digging. He was going on blind faith, hoping his ears had told him truly what lay beyond. Sweat ran down his face, dribbling into the piled debris around his ankles. He took off his clothes so they would not become soiled with a mix of sweat and dust. He dug nude in near-total darkness. His ankles were swollen and achy, weeping blood, pus, and yellow plasma.

A moment of truth came when he had a hole about two feet in diameter. The brick second wall looked solid. He edged close on his buttocks, steadying himself by pressing work-raw hands on the floor by his sides. Slowly, with his heel, he began to push and tap at the wall. Every few minutes he'd stop and listen. His heart pounded in his ears. He pictured getting a foot or hand cut off in punishment.

There! He worked a section of brick loose.

Abruptly, a chunk of masonry and brick fell out and landed with a clatter in the dark room beyond.

Tim lay back, sobbing for breath, fighting his slamming heart while trying to listen for sounds of running feet, but nobody came.

Tying his clothes in a bundle, Tim crept through the opening.

📖

The doors were locked from outside. Tim softly broke a window. He threw an old blanket over the sill to climb out. He was outside, in the yard! The night air blew dry his sweat, and bathed him in the freshness of freedom. This was worth it. It was worth dying a free man.

He clambered through a bush, over a wooden fence, and stood in a dirt alley among looming houses whose windows threw light out upon the darkness. He heard radios playing Arabic music, the lilting wail of a woman singer praising God, or lamenting a lost love, or commenting on the eternity of the desert, or on the brevity of life and love. He walked toward the airport, as he had HD'd it in the darkness of his captivity. He was surprised at the smell of flowers in the air. Maybe the town must have grown up around an oasis. There were no streetlights, but here and there a corner lantern in a glass case threw light on the next turn or the next alley. Occasionally he passed other night pedestrians—an old man with a donkey, or a young boy hurrying along with a package. Someone would greet him, and he'd mumble back *salaam aleikum*, "be well, go with God." A hooded shape stepped in his path, a woman veiled from head to toe, who muttered seductively. He smelled her cloying cinnamon and *hookah* breath. He brushed past her saying his greeting, adding *shukran*, "thanks," and he heard two or three young prostitutes giggling behind him.

The airport was a long dirt strip with several buildings along the side. A windsock fluttered in the chill night wind from the desert, above what looked like a small warehouse and was probably a hangar. Next to that blazed every light on earth inside an office building that carried the French and Mauritanian flags (a tricolor, and beside that a green banner with a yellow star above an upturned yellow crescent). Inside at a desk he spied several dark-haired men in military looking uniforms, hunched over forms and engaged in conversation. He hurried past them, looking toward another building that had a sign, "New-York City Bistro." Loud music and laughter emanated from there, and he thought he heard a man's coarse voice bellow something in English.

Tim waited in the shadows with his hood up. Being dark-haired and unshaven, he looked a bit like a Moorish northerner of Caucasian stock. Many of the guest laborers were Fulani or Wolof, brown-skinned Senegalese, with occasional bluish-black-skinned tropical Africans from further south and inland. The French West African territory of Mauritania had been administered from Saint-Louis in Senegal since 1920.

Tim craned his neck, looking past the half-open blue wooden door, and into the interior of the establishment. Smoke from *hookah* pipes floated out, as did smells of strong, sweet black coffee and an occasional sour whiff of strong French cigarette smoke.

How long could he stand here like this before being challenged, discovered, thrown in jail, perhaps shot? It was all or nothing. He started walking. He kept his hands in his pockets and his hood up to keep his features in shadows.

He crossed the threshold onto the bistro's wooden floor. He smelled cooked lamb, cabbage, a dozen other pungent vegetables. It was a rich, gamy smell with a strong undertone of wood fired grilling, but he had no appetite.

A pair of men in gray clothing whose shoulder patches had been carefully razored off, and wearing gray visored caps, were just leaving with bundles of food under their arms. The bundles were wrapped in blue and white-checkered towels. Each man also carried a wooden container of drinking material (tea, probably, Tim surmised).

"Fellas, you've gotta help me," he said, confronting them in the narrow hallway.

"*Was sagt er?*" said the one to the other. "What'd he say?"

Krauts, Tim thought, *just my luck.*

The other, the older and stockier with the redder face, shrugged. "*Engländer, wahrscheinlich.*" "Probably an Englishman."

The younger man, who was the blonder of the two, said: "You speak English?"

"Yes, I'm an American. U.S. Navy. I surrender. Please take me with you."

They laughed. "We are noncombatants, *Check*," one said in good though thickly accented U.S. idiom. It took Tim a moment to realize he was saying 'Jack,' pronouncing it sounded like 'Check'."

"Make that Tim." He began to see some hope.

One of the Arabs in the place shouted a question, probably asking if some Rif baggage were bothering them.

"*Schon gut—alles klar*," the younger man said with a wave. "No problem—take it easy.*"*

"*Keine Sorge, alter Chef*," the older man told the Berber. "Not to worry, old boss."

"You didn't kill or rob anyone, did you?" the younger man asked.

"I was shipwrecked and sold into slavery."

The old man laughed. "Anywhere else, I'd say *Du spinnst Märchen*, you tell fairy tales, but not here."

They took him between them, protectively, one at each elbow, and guided him along toward the landing strip. The older man introduced himself as Walther Märzig, co-owner of a one-plane airline called *Güterspedition—Westafrika Sternlinie* (*Cargo Express—West African Star Line*). *Big name for a one-plane show,* Tim thought. The younger man, by maybe ten years, was his paternal cousin, Willi Märzig. They were originally from Kiel, but Rommel had brought them to Africa. Now Rommel had gone one way, and they had gone another, taking with them one of his cargo planes.

"You want to go to Morocco?" Walther asked Tim.

"Why Morocco?"

"There is a colony of American expatriates there. We met some of them last year, including the writer Paul Bowles and his wife Jane, a playwright. They come and go like the rest of your countrymen."

"Strange birds, many of them," Willi said.

"Artists," Walther said. "Bohemians. And she is a Jew."

"Very dangerous for them," Walther agreed. "You want to travel north on our next trip?"

"Very dangerous for me," Tim said. "No, I'd rather head deeper into Africa."

"Then the Congo," Walther said. "The Germans occupy Belgium, and so they think they own the Congo, but everyone is there now. Americans, Belgians, British…"

Willi added: "And the Soviets too. It's a fight between allies.

From his technical reading, Tim had an inkling that it had something to do with the rich radium mines in that Belgian possession. He'd read about a terrible energy bomb, made from radium, that could win the war and change history.

"Come," Willi said.

"We'll get you out of here," Walther added.

Both men slapped Tim goodnaturedly on the back. Together, like old *kumpels* (comrades), they They climbed on board a gray-green Junkers 52 whose *Luftwaffe* markings had been painted over in matte black. Mauritanian and French markings had been stenciled on in smallish white letters and numbers.

Walther pulled the steel ladder up. Willi locked the main door of the plane, while Walther climbed among the stacked crates and packages under a row of overhead lights, until he reached the highest little oblong compartment, which had a picture of a fire extinguisher on it. Using a skeleton key, he unlocked the door, which fell open to reveal what looked like a pile of bowling pins lying stacked on their sides. Walther took two of them down and slammed the door shut. He jumped down with a look of triumph on his face. "The fire must be extinguished, *ja?*"

Willi pulled out a crate marked as containing delicate glass. Walther unwrapped the checked towels from the restaurant. "Plenty here for the three of us, if you are hungry."

The bowling pins turned out to be bottles of some exotic Central African beer, wrapped in men's undergarments. Walther threw the long johns in a pile behind the pilot seats up front. "We Germans cannot breathe without our beer. These local barbarians drink nothing but coffee and tea, and they smoke hashish until their eyeballs explode, but they are very saintly about not touching the holy brew."

Corks popped in quick succession, and the interior smelled of food and beer. Tim closed his eyes with delight. "I'm suddenly developing an appetite." The two men laughed heartily and toasted him.

Willi continued their brief biography. "We saw that the Italians could not hold North Africa, and Rommel did not have enough supplies. Hitler kept pushing him to do the impossible in the wrong places with the wrong equipment, which is why Germany is losing the war, so we took our *Tante Ju* (Auntie Junkers) here and headed south instead of north. We had four paratroopers and a supply of documents on board. With half a million men and much equipment being captured or fleeing, who was going to miss us? We let the paratroopers out in Morocco, because they had dreams of defecting to the Spaniards. We dumped the documents out in mid-air over the Atlas-Chouf mountains, where nobody will ever read them. And then we headed south to start our little business."

"That's right," Walther added enthusiastically after a big swallow of beer and wiping foam from his mouth with a hairy forearm. "Now we need only a little more funding and we buy a second plane. Then we are in business for real."

"After the war, we go back to Germany and start a *Konkurrenz* with Lufthansa if they still exist, *ja*?"

Tim was just about to ask what kind of business they hoped to conduct, when there came a loud and frantic banging at the door.

"*Schnell!*" Walther said, pushing the bottles across to his cousin, who swooped around and hid them under the pile of underwear behind the seats. "Quick! If the Arabs see alcohol they will go berserk. It's their religion to hate this holy liquid."

The banging on the side door continued until Willi slid it open. "*Ja, Mensch.* What is your problem tonight, my friends?"

A squad of native gendarmes in flowing white garments sat on camels outside, brandishing swords and muskets. Nearby stood a blocky, dark-green personnel carrier with French Foreign Legion (Vichy) markings. In an open, round hatch on top, a helmeted shape loomed over a Châtellerault Model 1924/29 *calibre*-7.5x54 machine gun with its dipod folded back— mounted on the rim of the hatch, and capable of a 360 degree field of fire, using a 150-round drum magazine. Several men on foot or camel wore Spanish Foreign Legion-style khaki garrison caps with a tassel hanging from a front fold of the hat. Two military policemen in French Foreign Legion uniform (Vichy) accompanied them, brandishing German *Schmeisser* rifles. An officer in regular French (Vichy) army uniform led the group. The officer, a boyish, blond first lieutenant, looked crisp and European, his skin noticeably pale compared with the other men's. "*Bonjour, Monsieurs*," he said. "We look for a criminal who escaped from custody of Monsieur Nasr Tandileh a few hours ago. He is armed and dangerous. May I see your papers please?"

Walther grumbled. "Of course, *Mon Colonel*." He patted himself on the pockets and exchanged glances with his cousin. "*Willi, wo sind denn die Papiere?*" "Where are the papers then, Willi?"

"I have them put away already for the flight," Willi said. "Hold on, I'll get them."

The lieutenant looked at Tim and saluted, palm out, fingertips smartly touching the short black bill of his kepi. "Monsieur, you have your papers?"

"Monsieur Malone is with us," Walther said gruffly, handing three passports and three sets of oilcloth-covered documents down to the lieutenant, who stood snappily examining them.

"Who are you, Monsieur Malone?" the lieutenant said without looking up from the documents.

Willi whispered to Tim from behind: "Don't let him rattle you. He just wants to go back to his whores and his cognac."

The lieutenant looked up. "Major Malone, U.S. Army?" He waved the passport. "This is not in order. I could suspect you of spying. Why would I not?"

Tim felt his stomach sinking.

Walther sat on the edge of the door with his feet swinging down. He beckoned for the lieutenant to come closer, which the lieutenant did. Walther spoke softly in German with the lieutenant, while secretly passing across a wad of Reichmarks. "Listen, *Eugène*, don't be tedious. He's a deserter, like we are. Nobody likes the stupid war. Go buy yourself a bottle of nice *cognac*, and think only of civilization, ja?" The lieutenant nodded, glancing up at Tim. The transaction was concluded shortly, and the lieutenant said: "Major Malone, kindly get that passport updated before returning to this French colonial territory, *oui?*"

"*Oui,*" Tim said with hollow forcefulness. He returned a snappy military salute. "I sure will, Sir, and thank you very much. *Vive la France.*"

"*Vive la France,*" the lieutenant said. He told his squad. "*Allons*, let's continue looking for our felon." The mixed entourage wheeled or walked away together. As the colonial unit rumbled off into the night, Tim drew a deep shuddering gasp of relief. He wiped sweat from his forehead and asked Walther: "What were you telling him, in German yet?"

Walther nodded with a wicked grin. "It's ironic, yes? We are German deserters who should be working for the *Führer* but we aren't. He is a Frenchman but he is an Alsatian, of German descent. Did you see his name tag? *Rittermann*. He's as German as we are. Yet he is at heart a loyal Frenchman who wants to puke at having to work for the Vichy regime, and he cannot wait for the *Tapetenhänger* to lose the war."

"The what?"

"The wallpaper hanger. Hitler. The greasy little vagrant from Austria who isn't even German."

"To hell with it," Willi said, "where is my beer?"

"The important things," Walther said as he slammed the door shut.

They sat at their meal again and toasted each other with foaming glasses while they ate their *couscous*. "To a speedy victory for Churchill and Stalin and Roosevelt," Willi said.

"No politics," Willi admonished, as if afraid his cousin might say too much.

"What do you think of Stalin in the U.S.A.?" Walther asked Tim, ignoring Willi.

Tim thought for a second. "Well, officially we are allies. Then again, we've been worried about the Red Scare for a long time, or at least the wealthy people are, so maybe we'll be at each other's throats with Uncle Joe after the war."

"I believe so," Walther said, "and Uncle Joe will send his Cossacks to eat the German people alive, mark my words. This Hitler son of a bitch had to go wake up the Russian bear. Damn that idiot!"

"I do agree with you there," Willi said. "Now we've got to get some sleep. Where is Malone, do you suppose?"

"Good question."

"Yes," Tim said, "thanks for saving my skin. So who is this Malone?"

Walther belched happily and pointed his beer glass. "Robert Malone, my friend, is an American spy and a gambler. Don't tell him I told you so, but we know. In your American idiom, he is a crook, but a nice one. "

Willi added: "We run our freight routes, and we see a lot. Malone is definitely working for the Allies. He is even more crooked than we are. We salute him. We help him."

"That's right," Walther said. "Malone comes and goes on missions very secret that we do not ask about. He likes us. Well, maybe he likes our beer, which we bring from Leopoldville and Lomé. You know, Belgian beer can be good, but there is nothing like good German brew made by folk who know how."

Tim saw a map lying nearby and pulled it close. It was a compact navigational map in a plastic sheath, with faint black china-marker lines on it from a host of previous flights. Lomé, he saw, was the capital of formerly German-owned (now British) Togoland, while Leopoldville was the capital of the Belgian Congo.

"Very conveniently," Willi said, "we have Malone's papers, and those of his beautiful lady friend. He had to run an errand on the other side of town a few days ago and did not want to be caught with the wrong papers. We flew off to Nouakhchott and back, and now we have to pick them up to take them back to Leopoldville."

"That's where you are going?" Tim asked. He was shocked at the distance.

"It will get you far from here, fast," Walther said soberly. Tim had to agree. About Malone, Willi continued: "I believe he is checking on movements of the Vichy Legionnaire regiments in this area, what's left of them after they were misused in Finland and Tunisia and God knows where else."

"The Balkans," Walther said authoritatively. He turned to his cousin. "Can we get moving?"

"Yes." Willi glanced at his watch. "About four hours to daylight and we must take off. Where can he be? He was supposed to meet us here, he and his woman, Régine Clery."

"Another man's woman, borrowed for a few days. Nice one, too. Sort of Anita Berber with at least some clothes on." Walther referred to a notorious 1920s Weimar Berlin socialite drug addict, cabaret dancer, bisexual, alcoholic, androgyne, and tragic beauty notorious for going about naked, who'd died very young. "A lost world," Willi said wistfully as if speaking of something a thousand years ago, a thousand kilometers away.

Walther nodded. "Before Hitler. We were eating from trash cans, but we still had it better than this." He scratched his stubbled cheek, as if to poke himself back to reality. "I do want to get my sleep. I'll pilot the first leg. You want to go look for Malone?" He explained to Tim: "Malone runs all sorts of errands. Tonight he is here with a dazzling Belgian woman who loves her drugs. Heroin, cocaine, you name it, she drowns her misery when

Malone isn't *schtupp*ing her. We need to pick them and the drugs up and take them with us."

"Where to?"

"The Belgian Congo."

"Yes," Willi said. "If we leave him here he will be mad at us. We need his business." Willi strapped on a holster with a Wehrmacht Luger. "You want to come with me, Tim?"

Tim did not want to leave the safety of the plane. His ankles were swollen and they hurt. Walther saw them and gasped. "You're in bad shape." He dug out a First Aid kit with Nazi marking and rubbed a sulfa ointment into the wounds. He then wrapped them in white gauze. "Go with Willi. I'll stay here to guard the plane. We'll nurture your ankles back from the dead, don't worry."

"That feels better already," Tim said as he clambered barefoot to the ground. "Just get us out of this country as fast as possible."

"*Ja-ja*," Walther said. "We do this every few hours. Meanwhile, about Malone, you'll be back in an hour, and I will have the engine running."

"I'll drive," Willi said to Tim. "You have Malone's papers and the lieutenant is the gendarme in charge tonight. You have nothing to worry about." He offered a second Luger, which Tim assumed was Walther's. "Please."

"Okay," Tim said, strapping the heavy gun on with its canvas waist belt. "You do all the talking if *Monsieur le General* stops us again."

"I'll go get the truck," Willi said as he trotted off toward the restaurant.

Walther said in the cockpit above: "I promoted him to Colonel. You make him a general. He should be Charlie Chaplin. " Both Germans laughed.

The truck rode high on its rear springs, looking oddly insectlike. The front smelled of spilled gasoline and balled up oily rags on the floor. The floor mats were gone. Tim spotted a hand-sized hole under which the roadway spun past.

"Keep your feet away from there. It's rusted through," Willi said. "These French. Why can't they be like Germans and fix things? I'd never fly on a French airline. I'd be afraid to fall through with my seat."

They raced over dark roads among shadowy houses from which occasional small patches of lantern light flickered, or now and then an open hearth gone into embers for the night.

Several clustered, broken columns flew past. "French?" Tim asked.

"Roman," Willi said. "Two thousand years old. They used to send expeditions into the interior from here to hunt exotic animals for the *Colosseum*."

"I had a run-in with some lions on the coast."

"Ah yes, the old Barbary lions. Thought to be extinct, but a few have come back with all the confusion of war. They aren't pure breeds, but mixed with various other subtypes."

"You are a hunter?"

"I was a Classics student," Willi said simply. "I had aims of going into the pulpit as a Lutheran pastor, but the war changed everything for us." He trailed off, grinding gears loudly on a hill as he downshifted before descending into an outlying village.

The desert was bright with moonlight as far as Tim could see. What a beautiful country, he thought. The beer was going through his system, and he had to relieve himself. Soon, Willi pulled up with a screech of brakes at an isolated farmhouse made of wedges of same-size stone neatly fitted together under a roof of corrugated tin scrounged from some old French mine in the area, probably.

Tim found a stand of small palm trees and let the beer flow back out of him while Willi went around the dark house knocking on doors and windows. "Malone!" he called out. "Malone!"

Tim finished and sauntered over. Willi had a strange look on his face. "You hear something?"

Tim listened intently. He heard a distant buzzing sound. "Airplane?" He rumpled his nose as a dreadful smell reached him on the clean alkaline desert night air.

"I think not," Willi said, holding his nose with one hand. In the other hand he held the Luger, aimed ahead, as he kicked the door open.

"My God," Tim said, as the stench wafted out.

Willi flicked on a single overhead bulb, using a large white ceramic switch beside the inside of the door.

On the floor, subject to the buzzing of a thousand flies, was a bloated green corpse with a large knife sticking in his back. Nearby lay the smaller, thinner corpse of a dark-haired young woman who must have been very attractive before the green bloat set in. She might have been European and Arab or some similar exotic cross.

"Malone?" Tim mumbled holding his nose.

Willi nodded. "I recognize the ring on his finger. Whoever did it wasn't robbing him. It was a bit more thoughtful of a crime. And the woman. They were up here to buy drugs. *Christus*, now what?"

"Let's run," Tim offered helpfully.

"Not that simple," Willi said. "Not sure what happened here, but we can't have our Alsatian police hound find this. Not when we had you playing Malone on our plane and now Malone is dead." Willi scratched his head. "Can't carry him in the car, or we'll get a mess all over Osman's boot and he does need to carry food out to the workmen on the roads when the French are paying men to work. What to do?"

"Maybe Malone smokes in bed," Tim said.

Willi looked confused for a second, then brightened. "Say, that's good. How do we get him to walk over there?"

"Good question," Tim said, looking at the bloated greenish-black mass that would surely fall apart in ripe chunks if they tried to help Malone walk to the bed by picking him up. "Maybe he is drunk. He is wrapped up in a sheet."

"Good," Willi said, "I like it." He started ransacking cupboards. "This was Malone's little local hideaway. I know from flying with him that he liked to drink nice American-style whiskey from South Africa, which we fly up here sometimes to the local *Mahdi* for his intimate male get-togethers." Bottles, cups, plates, forks, spoons, all clattered down onto the kitchen counters. "While I am doing this," Willi said, "Pick out what you want from his clothing. The two of you are about the same size and build. Grab some shoes and socks."

Feeling macabre, Tim poked through dressers and closets. He found the man's suitcase and put on an ensemble—khakis, boots, baseball cap, everything for the well-dressed American. He took the suitcase with suit, shirts, ties, socks, dress shoes.

"Aha!" Willi said. "Look at this, how subtle!" Behind the spice rack was a false door and there, lined up like soldiers, were bottles of Johnny Walker Black. "American stuff. Good quality. Shame to waste it, but this is more important." He tossed a pair of bottles through the air, and Tim caught them expertly. In a few moments, Tim and Willi had uncorked four bottles.

Holding his nose, Willi leaned over the body and pulled the knife from its back. He went to the back door and threw the knife as far as he could into a mass of brush and thorns where nobody would ever find it. He came back, clapping his hands clean of dust. "It will look as if he and his girlfriend died smoking in bed while dead drunk."

They got a sheet from the bedroom, laid it beside the corpse, and used rolled-up towels as a pushbar to roll the corpse over onto the sheets. The flies buzzed more loudly, and a new stench rose as foul smelling liquids burst through the blackened, greenish skin and soiled clothes in which Malone had died.

Now it was quick work: roll him up, carry him to the bed, unroll him dumping him onto the bed, soak the bed with scotch, and leave a mass of lighted cigarettes lying around.

Régine Clery went the same way, though it was easier because she was smaller and lighter. Her blackened skin burst open in various places as they moved her. Her eyes, her nostrils, her mouth divested shiny greenish-black puddles of liquids, including cadaverine and putrescine, along with knots of wriggling white maggots. *Poor thing,* Tim thought, *she must have been quite beautiful.*

The interior of the place had a lot of bone-dry wood in it, including furniture and stacked newspapers, and other combustibles. From a single dropped match, the bed caught with a loud *woosh!* before Tim and Willi were out of the living room.

As Tim and Willi raced to the car, Tim became aware of a shadowy presence. It was a spooky feeling for a moment, and his hackles stood on end though he had no idea why. Willi threw him the car keys, and they got into the car. Tim pulled his door shut and turned the key in the ignition.

As Willi's door slammed, there was a popping noise. Willi twitched in his seat. Tim looked over, puzzled, as several more popping noises rang out. Willi was arched over backwards with his eyes glazing over and blood running from one temple. Someone was shooting at them! Tim cranked the engine, wishing it would turn over. Glass shattered around him. Another shot. Two men, shadowy figures, stood by the house. Tim pulled out his Luger and let go a few rounds at them. They scattered. Tim got the engine going, fishtailed the car, and raced away down the road leaving a cloud of dust. Through the dust, he saw the two men coming at either side. He shot at them until the Luger was empty. A few more bullets whizzed by his head, and some more glass shattered, as he raced away. The house became a blazing ball of yellow-blue light, miles back. Tim reached over to check for a pulse, but there was none. Willi's body grew cold long before Tim drove into the mud-walled outskirts of Néma.

Katanga: Tim Nordhall Signs On to OSS

Walther was distraught at the arrival of the blood-soaked car, with his cousin's corpse in it.

Together, Tim and Walther pulled the corpse from the car and laid it on the tarmac. Walther cried and sobbed over Willi's stretched out form, while Tim looked anxiously about for signs of pursuit. "Hurry," Tim muttered. At the same time, he patted the German understandingly on the shoulder, feeling the other's strength and sweat, and the rage there at the way this war seemed to reach down like a fist from the clouds and destroy individual lives with heartless randomness.

They pushed the car out of the way, into the shadows beside a wall, where it would not be found soon enough. Walther took a few minutes to torch it. He crawled underneath and severed the fuel line with his *Luftwaffe*-issue bayonet. The air filled with a gasoline smell as gallons emptied out in a puddle. Walther jumped back.

Tim, hearing the throaty roar of a motor, said: "Hurry up, man!"

Walther fiddled with matches. "Get Willi on the plane." He struck a match and tossed it. Within a minute, the little truck was ablaze.

The engine sound drew near. Tim heard shouts.

Walther jumped up into the plane, pulled the door shut, and cranked up the motor. Tim sat in the passenger seat, feeling helpless. He had left the gun in the truck. Now he pulled Walther's Luger from under the seats.

"What are you doing?" Walther cried as the engine reluctantly fired and then sputtered out. "You can't shoot at them. It would be suicide."

"Just in case," Tim said as he held the gun in his lap. "I'll go down shooting if I have to go down at all."

Walther shrugged, a battle-hardened man. Then the engine rattled into life, just as machine gun bullets flew overhead. There was a hedge between the plane and the French armored personnel carrier.

"Go!" Time yelled as Walther swung the plane around and raced down the runway, past the restaurant, while the APC lurched onto the far end of the runway and opened full throttle in pursuit. Bullets flew past, audible as the cockpit windows were still open. "All right you persistent son of a bitch," Tim yelled. He took careful aim and shot the man in the turret. No more machine gun bullets, at least for a few minutes.

"Oh Jesus, now we're in for it," Walther yelled. "It will be a long time before I can land here again." A bullet tore through the sheet metal of the portside wing, leaving a dangling strut. "Here we go!"

Strangling on its over-tasked engine, the plane heaved up and made for the darkness amid southern constellations. The French below stopped firing.

Tim stowed the gun away. "I'm very sorry about your cousin," Tim said. "Thanks for saving my life."

"Our lives," Walther corrected. "Go back there and wrap him in a tarp." The Junkers-52 droned south-southeast at one-mile altitude, doing 135 knots. Capable of carrying 17 passengers or about three tons of cargo, old Auntie *Ju* was still a workhorse of the *Luftwaffe*, of the same generation as her look-alike, the Ford Tri-Motor.

Walther gently pounded the steering yoke with both hands, fighting back tears. Willi's body lay wrapped in a paint-stained canvas on the steel floor, where Tim had respectfully placed it before returning to the co-pilot's seat.

Walther washed his face with canteen water and uncorked a beer. "He will begin to smell tomorrow in the heat," shouted over the engine din. "We'll have to lay him to rest, but I can't land to bury him. We'll throw him overboard in the desert tonight and pray for his soul."

About two hours later, having located a wide river, Walther piloted the Ju-52 swooping in low over a broad stretch of sand dunes. Tim thought of lions as he sent Willi's body sailing out into the night, like a package, with one corner of the canvas flapping. Then Walther throttled up and slowly brought the plane to cruising altitude heading southeast toward the Congo. "I can't believe he is gone," he said in a wailing voice. He wiped his tears with a towel and splashed more canteen water over his face. He drank some more holy beer.

Tim found a cot on an aft bulkhead. It was made, with dusty white sheets and an old green blanket. The sheets and the blanket both had eagle and swastika markings on them. Tim didn't care. He finished a bit of cool, fresh tasting *Bambari* beer. The stuff was brewed by a Germanic sounding house, with Ubangi River water, in French Equatorial Africa just north of the Belgian Congo. Then he lay down. Everything rattled, and the plane sounded like the interior of a giant chain saw, but the aircraft was solid as a tree. Soon, Tim was fast asleep.

"How long?" he asked, sitting casually in the co-pilot seat, rubbing salve on his still angry looking ankles. He felt rested, though spiritually exhausted from the struggles in his dreams. He stepped forward amid the clamor of the engines and the rattling of metal surfaces. A mile below, Tim saw tawny desert stretching from horizon to horizon. The dawn sky was aflame with colors, and Tim was glad to be escaping from the hell in which he'd spent the past two weeks. "How much longer?"

"About twenty hours," Walther said. He wore a headset and looked relaxed and comfortable at the controls of the plane. His eyes were dark with shadows, but other than that he betrayed no sign of his loss yesterday. "We make a stopover for fuel and to trade goods at Lomé, Togo. Without

Willi, I don't have a second pilot, so I have to sleep. Then we travel on from there one more stop in Douala, French Cameroon, and then the last leg directly to the Belgian Congo."

"Will you carry on alone?"

Walther shrugged. "What choice do I have? I cannot go back to Germany. You want to fly this Afrika route with me?"

Tim shook his head. "Thanks, but I need to connect with an American Embassy as soon as possible."

"You stay with me until Leopoldville, is my advice. Togo might be tricky. Next door are Ghana on the left, and Nigeria on the right, both British, but we don't go there."

"You can't stop in Accra?" Tim asked looking at the map.

"Sticky for me," Walther said. "Nazi plane. You understand."

"Ah yes" Tim said. "Why can't things be simple here?"

"They just were for poor Willi," Walther said.

Tim nodded. "I'm sorry."

"Not your fault," Walther said. He pointed down at a smallish city of mud buildings baking in the desert. "Timbuktu," he said. "Famous center of Islamic learning. Terminus of caravans from all Africa."

Tim let his gaze linger on the fabled city until it had passed beyond the horizon. Then he went back to sack out again in the Wehrmacht ambulance stretcher, for lack of anything else to do. The desert heat reached even this high, and made his eyes sore and dry with a sandy wind that smelled almost of mummy dust. But he was a free man.

📖

By evening, Walther was up. He stretched, bent, did pushups and other exercises. He made coffee and brought out the last bread, and chilled vegetable-mutton, from the Néma airstrip. As dusk fell, amid a still-thick dry heat, the plane leisurely took off in a long, slow glide. No bullets, no rush.

Walther looked refreshed, though his expression and the darkness around his eyes testified to his grief. He said little, and Tim respectfully stayed quiet in his co-pilot seat.

Walther touched down twice during the night to rest and refuel. On the first stop, the air smelled of aviation fuel and spicy African food. The sand still emanated that mummy-smell of heat and dust and dead, dehumidified organic matter.

On the second stop, there was more of a fetid jungle smell, and the atmosphere seemed more humid. Tim sensed a change as they flew into Equatorial Africa. He slept exhaustedly in fits and snatches.

Tim awoke from a deep, sound sleep many hours later, as the plane's engine pitch changed noticeably. "We are landing soon!" Walther said.

Tim sat up rubbing his eyes. He yawned and stretched.

"Good morning!" Walther said. "You have been asleep since yesterday."

"My God, I was in another world. Are we in the Congo yet?" He walked forward and sat in the co-pilot's seat. Below was a solid canopy of jungle as far as the eye could see. A tropical haze enveloped the horizon on all sides. Flashes of light blinked occasionally below as they flew over some wide river, perhaps a tributary of the great Congo River.

Walther pointed to a thermos. "There is fresh hot coffee in there, black." He pointed to a package wrapped in a blanket. "That is cold *saucisse* and *baguette* from Douala. You must be hungry."

"Starving," Tim said. He found a knife with SS markings and made himself a butter sandwich with the fresh bread, adding Alsatian style hard salami and a kind of Gouda-like cheese. He washed big chewy mouthfuls down with hot black coffee.

"About three hours we land in Leopoldville," Walther said. "You have to understand that nominally it's German controlled but the Belgian exile government runs the place, and there are Americans and other Allies swarming all over the place. Must be strategically very important, but all of that is beyond me."

"What will you do now without your cousin?"

Walther shrugged. "What choice do I have? He was my helper and my good friend. I miss him terribly, but what I dread most is writing to his mother to tell her the news." He sighed. "I lost many friends in this war." He pulled the navigation board close and raised his aviator sunglasses to stare at the map. "This is the Dja, my friend. Very big river. Flows together with the Sangha and the Likouala and then into the Congo, which empties into the Atlantic Ocean between Boma and Soyo."

It was an enormous land, Tim saw, staring down from a mile high as the continuous strip of jungle stretched from horizon to horizon.

Walther said, "Meanwhile, I will continue to haul bananas, typewriters, auto parts, whatever I can, to get by."

In the early afternoon, the Ju-52 dropped down, slowing, and landed at a large macadam airfield on the outskirts of the Belgian Congo capital. Tropical heat rose from the concrete apron at the edge of a peripheral commercial hangar where Walther parked the Ju-52.

Tim stepped from the plane into the blinding tropical heat, which was like a steam bath, and looked across the runway to a small circle of U.S., British, Belgian, Soviet, and Free French flags fluttering in a small breeze.

"Good luck!" Walther called, waving from the cockpit window.

📖

A sign said *Leopoldville * Provence de Kinshasa * Le Congo Belge.* The airport and the city had a frantic, businesslike air. Military operations and commerce mingled, and judging from the rapt looks of men in business suits hurrying here and there, plenty of opportunity for the right person in the right place to make a hefty franc—or buck. Most of the businessmen were white. A small number looked like well-heeled local officials, representatives of tribal chiefs, the small number of Congolese natives allowed into the restrictive and paternal Belgian administrative bureaucracy.

Tim carried Malone's suitcase. He had his shirt collar open and was mopping his neck with a large handkerchief by the time he arrived at the grassy half circle where the flags of the main Allied nations flew. The sun beat down with hammers. He pushed through a glass, aluminum-framed door into a gloomy, cooler lobby where several large fans blew the turgid air around, but it was noticeably cooler than outside. Tim walked up to a reception counter, where one black Congolese woman and two white Belgian women were busy answering phones and being secretarial.

"Hello," he said, "I'd like to see the American consul."

A Belgian woman, a pretty young blue-eyed blonde, looked up. "*Bonjour, Monsieur.* You are *Anglais?*"

"American," he said.

"*Bien.* I will send you in." She depressed an intercom switch and spoke in French. Then she nodded to him. She twisted in her seat and pointed down a dark tiled hallway. "You go there, *s'il vous plait.*"

"Thanks." He headed down the pleasantly gloomy corridor that smelled of cigarettes and coffee. He passed doors with tiny flags on them, until he came to one with a stars and stripes and the legend: "U.S. Affairs."

He knocked, heard a man's voice, and found himself in a cluttered office with four desks, three women busily typing, and a middle-aged man in shirtsleeves practicing a golf stroke on the red carpeting. The man hardly looked up. "You American?"

"Yessir." He gave his name, rank, and serial number. "I was shipwrecked off Mauritania and escaped from slavers by air. I want to be repatriated."

The man laughed. "You're shitting me."

"Why do you think that?" Tim was beginning to think he'd look cute with the golf club sticking out of his rear end.

"Slavers? I've heard some stories, but that's original." He putted and his ball rolled unevenly across the carpet to make a small *pok* sound going into an empty soup can lying on its side. "Yeah! Damn, am I good." He wiped his brow and set his putter aside. "What's your name again?"

"Tim Nordhall, Lieutenant (j.g.), U.S. Navy."

"Got papers?"

"Not my own."

The man frowned. "What does that mean?"

Tim felt a prickling of concern on his neck. Reluctantly, he waved the dead Malone's papers. "Took these off a dead man to help me escape Vichy cops."

The man looked at him with mean laughter in his eyes, but snatched the papers. As he arrogantly flicked the papers open, he said: "What's your game, pal? What's your racket?"

Tim didn't bother answering. Why get into a scene with this paper pusher?

The man, whose name plate on his desk read *Edward Bouvard, GS-7,* said in a slightly louder tone: "I am asking you, what's your game?"

Tim put one foot up on his suitcase and folded his hands on his knee. "I guess, Mr. Bouvard, you need to see your audiologist. I've already told you my story."

"All right," Bouvard said. "Be an asshole. Sit down outside in the waiting room. I'll hang on to these." He waved the papers, as if he'd fight Tim for them if Tim were to lunge for them.

Tim picked up his suitcase. "Don't make me wait, Mr. Bouvard, or I'll come in and ruin your day for you."

"What's that supposed to mean?" Bouvard said with outthrust chin.

"You figure it out, Eddy boy."

Tim went outside, down the hall, back to the reception area. He found a bench and a stack of old Life magazines, and sat back to kill time reading while keeping an eye on the occasional attractive secretary wandering past on high heels and with padded shoulders. Tim breathed in deeply— perfume, attitude, beauty—oh it was good to be back in civilization.

A quarter hour, a half hour, an hour went by. Tim put his magazine down and strode down the hall carrying his suitcase. If Mr. Bouvard, or Eddy boy, was making him wait just to bust balls, he'd have a word or two with him. He thrust the door open so that it slammed against the wall. The three women stopped typing and looked up.

"Where is my friend Eddy?" Tim said. "Mr. Golf."

The women looked at each other. One said: "He was making some phone calls about you and suddenly got called away."

Another woman said: "You wait. They are anxious to see you."

"Who?" Tim asked.

The women looked at each other again. "The men in Building 405."

Tim set his suitcase down. "What men are those?"

"Why," the oldest of the three women said, "the mystery boys. We have no idea what they do in there, but there are guards all over the place."

Tim went back to the lobby and cooled his heels some more. He felt agitated, as the day waned and he was getting hungry again. A water cooler with New Jersey nomenclature and little paper cone cups offered some comfort and solace. The bathroom was a wooden shack outside that smelled to high heaven and offered warning notices about checking for snakes before sitting down on its dark, whispering secrets. There were even pictures of the offending vipers, including the deadly green mamba.

When he returned to the front of the building, a dark blue sedan was parked in the drive, surrounded by three big guys in suits and hats. The license plate was Belgian, with palm trees and a crown. The shoes on one of the men were distinctly American white-walls of the golfing variety. A fourth man, spectacled, slick-haired, graying, came out of the building looking very worried and trailed by a much-humbled Edward Bouvard.

"Major Malone!" said Spectacles.

"Nordhall," Tim said, "but we're getting close. Did dumb-nuts here forget my name, rank, and serial number?"

Bouvard looked like a different fellow, utterly meek, but Tim grasped the top of his ear to shake it. Bouvard feebly resisted. Tim said: "I told this stupid bastard who I really am." He let go of Bouvard and repeated his name, rank, and serial number.

The three heavies had a rear door open, and their *Führer* took Tim by the elbow. "Major Malone, I apologize for what you have been through. I was away on business and just debarked from the airplane. Bouvard assures me that it would never happen again." He pushed gently, persuasively, and Tim crawled into the ample backseat that smelled of leather and cloth. The four men piled in, the doors slammed, and the car pulled away leaving a glowering Bouvard at the curb. Tim sat jammed between two men in the back, while two were in front including the driver. Tim reached behind his head, as if to scratch the back of his neck, and surreptitiously gave Bouvard the finger.

"My name is Crane," the spectacled man said offering a soft white hand with severely trimmed pink nails. The other hand, upon closer inspection, was a pink prosthesis. He smelled of starch, stamp pad ink, and gun oil. "Ivor Crane. I'm sort of a loose intelligence wheel rolling around here. I'll be in charge of helping you."

"Nice to meet you," Tim said cautiously.

"It's all very hush-hush. And your name again?"

"Nordhall. Not Malone."

"Ah yes." Crane lit a cigarette and placed it in a green onyx holder. "*H.M.S. Sturmer.*"

"Oh my God," Tim said, "you know."

Smoke wrinkled around Crane's unperturbed face. "Of course. We thought the entire crew was lost, but here you are. You were testing a variation of Huff/Duff—High Frequency Direction Finder. The Navy will want to brief you about that, but I have other plans for you. You just happened to get stuck in a bureaucratic bottleneck with Mr. Bouvard. Let me apologize again for Eddy. He's rather dense, but useful. He filters out the frequent diamond smuggler or other unsavory character we get."

"Why did you call me Malone back there?"

"You'll figure it out soon enough, Lieutenant Nordhall. By the way, I'm a colonel in the U.S. Army, extremely high level intelligence operations. I'm not pulling rank on you. I just want you to feel comfortable knowing this is a very high-level show. You're in good hands. No more run-around."

"Yessir," Tim said. He did feel reassured, though still mystified.

"The Navy will want to debrief you about the sinking of your ship," Crane repeated, "but I have other plans for you."

Tim laughed. "Are you transferring me between services, Sir?"

"Sort of. Actually, you'll be two people, in two different services, with a security clearance so high you'll have to kill yourself just for knowing." Crane winked.

"Nice joke, Sir."

Crane made a wry face. "I never joke unless I'm holding a glass of scotch in one hand and a cigar in the other."

The car sped through city streets, slowing for pedestrian crowds, treating red lights as suggestions rather than commands. Tim glimpsed dark-skinned men in business suits carrying newspapers, women in colorful garb with bundles on their heads, white school children in cute uniforms, all the trappings of modern Belgian governance, overlaying a resentful native culture.

"The situation with Major Malone was very unfortunate," Crane said. "Good family, good breeding, lots of money, all the right jokes, and he has to ruin himself by gambling. I learned just yesterday that he had died. That creates inconveniences, but also an opportunity."

"Oh?" Tim felt sorry for the dead man, but he was tired and had no stomach for intrigue. He was too tired to ask how Crane knew about Malone, and how much he knew. That was a mystery in itself. "I really would like to get back to my engineering duties in a regular U.S. Navy capacity."

"I understand," Crane said, holding up his cigarette holder and letting smoke dribble from his lips while they waited in the middle of a throng of people and two large white cows. "You are a clockmaker at heart, are you?"

Tim wrinkled his lip. "Hardly."

"You left New Haven because your country called you, but also because you are looking for something more out of life. Is that correct?"

Tim nodded.

"What's the name of your best girlfriend, Lieutenant?"

"Huh?" He had to think...back to summer nights at Lighthouse Point or Morris Cove, football games, the marching band playing, and people enjoying themselves as best they could. Prohibition was over, but the Depression was still on, and even buying a cola and a hot dog was a bit of an expenditure. But taking a girl to the Yale Bowl, treating her just right, appreciating that she'd gone out and bought a new gray sweater just for the occasion...

"In high school," Crane said helpfully.

"Sally," Tim said. "Sally Levesque." He could picture her, green-eyed, red-head, with dimpled cheeks and a smile that sort of lit up her whole face. She had soft, thick thighs like creamery butter, just asking to be touched. She liked that, in the back of the old Chevy, breathing faster...

"Very good," Crane said. "And what street does your mother live on?"

"Orange Street." Elm trees all around, green, leisurely waiting for the mailman on endless summer afternoons, cool glass of orange juice... "Why?"

"Just some questions I need to ask. To make sure you are who you say you are." Crane flicked ashes out a partially cracked window, and said patiently as if explaining gravity to a child: "Major Malone was not only starting to deal drugs to pay his gambling debt—he was working both sides of the fence. That's what got him killed."

"Meaning?"

"Malone was a good officer and a good soldier. He hated the Nazis and the Communists as much as you do. It's just that he compromised himself."

"And the woman with him?"

Crane made a disagreeable face. "Wife of a prominent Belgian mining official named Clery. It's caused quite a flap, and we've had to cover it up. It's one of these social things. The husband is in Katanga, having affairs, and she's bored and stepping out up here. The simple solution is to say they were on a plane together with several others and went down over the jungle." Crane grinned. "Convenient, having one of the world's largest primordial rainforests all around us. Don't you think?"

"Yessir." Something about Crane didn't sit right with Tim, but he wrote it off to the fact that the colonel was in the intelligence business. That seemed to speak for itself. *Unsavory, but necessary.*

"We'll put you up in a nice hotel room for a few days," Crane said. "I want to show you what we are into here. Very important stuff. I hope you will help us out."

"We, Sir?"

"O.S.S., Tim. Office of Strategic Services. We don't like to advertise, except when we are recruiting a guy, like I'm doing here, now, with you."

"I'll think about it. I'll do my best, sir. Not my cup of tea, I'll be honest."

"I appreciate your honesty, Lieutenant."

"I am so damned glad to be safely back in American hands that I'll be happy to help my country in any way I can. I just hope..."

"Yes?"

"I'd like to get back stateside soon, Sir. I've been away for a long time."

"I understand. A lot of good men and women have been serving in dreadful little corners all over the world."

"Of course." And the poor guy with a wooden hand, yet! Putting it that way shamed Tim into thinking he ought to square his shoulders and accept whatever he could do for his country.

It was a long ride, and as they talked, Crane sometimes scribbled in a small notebook with a tiny pencil. Sometimes he rubbed his prosthesis absently with his other hand, as if the artificial limb ached. Outside, plantations passed in the afternoon sun, and everywhere black people were on the move, walking, carrying bales, hanging wash out before blue or green houses, children running in alleys, policemen on bicycles, Belgian officials in big cars...

They came to a group of two story cinderblock office buildings in the austere modern style, lots of glass, flags in front, very official, very colonial, with black men looking subservient in ill-fitting suits opening and closing the doors of cars that pulled into the front arcade.

The car drove past all that, around the side of the buildings. All but Tim, Crane, and the driver got out. Crane put a finger on his lip to signal Tim to be quiet. The car went around the back, into a garage, up to a set of indoor gasoline pumps where men in Marine Corps fatigues stood wearing .45s.

"We get out here," Crane said.

A Marine Corps corporal opened the door and stood at attention, saluting.

Tim and the colonel got out. Crane casually returned the corporal's salute. The driver of the car handed off the keys to a private and left by another way as Tim and Crane walked across the indoor parking lot to a small doorway. In a small lobby. The lobby was refreshingly cool, dark, and paneled in polished marble swirling with tomato and white veins. They took an elevator up two flights and emerged in a solarium with its own receptionist, a man in a white shirt wearing a gun in a shoulder strap. He had a crew cut and looked very Bouvardish as he pushed a clipboard across the counter for Crane and his companions to sign in. Crane ordered coffee and pastries from a small canteen in passing—just poking his head in, speaking French to a heavyset black woman in a gray smock, who nodded and turned to relay his order back into the tiled kitchen.

They sat together in Crane's spacious office, which had carpeting, walnut furniture, big glass windows, and cool air coming out of a wall duct. "Air conditioning," Crane said noticing Tim's stare at the ceiling. "Really helps us to concentrate here." Crane sat behind the desk while Tim sat in a plush leather chair before the desk. It was a client-manager kind of arrangement and felt comforting to Tim, as if he were now in safe and competent hands.

"I am sorry you've been through all that," Crane said.

Coffee and pastries arrived, served by two young Congolese whose skin was so black it seemed to glow with bluish highlights. A white-haired Congolese man named Pierre supervised. His left hand had been cut off at the wrist.

"*Merci*," Crane said patiently. With a few friendly nods, the men left. The old man closed the door loudly and turned the handle with a noticeable click to indicate they'd have privacy in the office.

"Bad old days," Crane said quietly. "The Belgians are going to lose the Congo, sooner rather than later. All the colonial powers are going to have to leave, it's clear. And that opens up a huge can of worms." Crane smiled gravely. "Humor me for a few moments, Tim. The old man, his name is Pierre. That's not his real name, it's a name the Belgians forced on him. He was given a real Congolese name by his parents, who belonged to the Zande people, when he was born in the 1880s. The Congo had been the personal property of the Belgian king, who exploited it mercilessly. Their favorite games included cutting children's hands off if the parents didn't work hard enough. Or they'd hold a man's wife and children hostage, and cut their limbs off if the man didn't bring enough rubber out of the bush. The Belgians were the cruelest of all the colonial rulers in the world. It got so bad that the world became outraged, and Brussels forced the king to relinquish the Congo, which became the property of the Belgian people. You'll see pictures of Congolese men in chains, with nets over their heads, waiting to be deported to work camps for the slightest crimes real or imagined. Oh, yes, Pierre, he was nine years old when an overseer with a machete whacked off his hand, because the overseer happened to be having a bad day. Well, I could go on. The point is, you see, whites aren't too popular here. The European powers have bled each other dry in two wars, have beaten each other to the brink of death, and cannot hold on to old colonial possessions. That means there will be a power vacuum. We're still fighting this world war, Tim, but the Axis is already beaten here in Africa. It's just a matter of time until the rest follows, and then, with fascism in the trash, the world will become a fighting ground between capitalism and communism."

Tim sipped his coffee, munched sweet almond-chocolate pastries, and listened in silence.

Crane sipped black coffee and lit another of his endless cigarettes. "Tim, we are headed for a huge showdown with the Soviets."

"We?"

"The United States. Capitalism. Free enterprise against state-control. I'd like you to work for me in London. Work for Donovan, O.S.S., for your country. What do you say?"

Tim thought about it. He liked the Navy, but didn't want to serve at sea again—at least for a long while. "If it will help my country, I'm in." The fan spun slowly, steadily, casting its shadows rhythmically over the desk and the carpet.

"Excellent. I thought you'd say that. Rest up for a day or two, and then I'll fly you down into Katanga Province and show you a thing or two."

They drove out of the downtown area and along a broad boulevard, through an area of sidewalk vegetable markets, along a short stretch of highway, and into a wealthy European settlement with parks, mansions, and palm trees lining the street.

"Welcome to Gombe," Crane said, flicking a cigarette out the window into the steamy air. "Nearby is Mbala Park. Very scenic."

They came to a small house on a side street, and the driver helped Tim in the front door. Black servant women in gilded, colorful silk turbans clucked worriedly and helped Tim into a back bedroom. It was a small, pleasant, sunny ranch style house with large, leafy trees in the back yard and a swimming pool with a small waterfall. Coconut palms graced the background. Black gardeners worked at a steady but unhurried pace. Tim found himself fading quickly as someone closed heavy yellow drapes, shrouding the room in darkness.

📖

Crane was not married, but appeared to have at least one live-in black woman, a voluptuous young Kongo with short, thick hair and bluish-black skin. She had a bruised, worldly-wise humor that suggested she was a survivor who knew how to keep her mouth shut and serve. Or service. But she was exclusively Crane's. He could not, of course, parade her about, but he sent her shopping several times a week in a red Mercedes that he kept for her in an apart garage in nearby Matele. Tim learned this because their driver, Moise, liked to combine his chores into a complicated itinerary that served everyone's purposes, including Crane's. Moise was a young Congolese with a cocky, wise attitude but no apparent rancor against whites. Rather, he regarded himself as a kind of homme-fixer who made things happen, whether it was bringing Giselle (the mistress) to a fashion show downtown, or the delivery of used clothing to an orphanage in Brazzaville across the river, or running Tim by the improvised U.S. Legation commissary/PX in Kinshasa to pick up favorite items like his green Colgate soap, Burma-Shave, Juicy Fruit gum, Maxwell House coffee, just about anything one could buy in the good old U.S.A.

Crane and Tim sat in the rear, sheltered by a carpeted half-wall. Crane said: "We're going to send you back to London, Tim, and you'll be promoted a grade in the Navy. That's your life as Timothy Nordhall. At the same time, secretly, you'll be Major Robert Malone. That's part of the plan. We'll be watching you while you'll trade secrets with a man we tell you to watch. No strong-arm stuff, nothing dangerous. Brains over brawn."

"No gunplay?"

"None," Crane said with sureness. "It's a game. We feed you misinformation to pass along to him. He thinks it's valuable intel. He'll give you equally worthless information, thinking you'll believe it's real. We follow him, map out his network, and eventually clean out a whole nest of Stalinist spies. The man's code name is Jaguar. He is an ice-cold killer, but it won't do for him to leave bodies all over London, which he is quite capable of doing."

They set down on a jungle strip on the edge of Élisabethville, capital of Katanga Province. The surrounding countryside was lush, with plenty of activity showing agricultural wealth. Mines and refineries belched forth smoke as men from the region found work. In particular, copper and diamonds from Katanga were prized. But Crane had something quite different to show Tim.

They rode in a private car owned by a local black official, whose female chauffeur drove. They rode along narrow asphalt roads, following a railroad line into the highlands. There, among the low mountain ranges, entire hillsides were being gouged out. "The mineral wealth of this area is staggering," Crane said. "The Belgians have been sitting on a strategic goldmine, and it's more valuable than ever now that uranium is about to get a new boost."

"You mean that stuff that makes watch dial numbers glow at night?"

Crane grinned darkly. "It makes more than watch dials glow." He drew a circle in pencil on a napkin on the little dinner tray that folded out from the seat back before Tim. He drew a mass of dots in the circle. "You can read this in any good newspaper, but it's little more than fantasy as yet." Crane tapped his pencil on the paper. "This is a uranium atom. It's a very heavy element, with lots of protons and neutrons in the nucleus. In fact, we are interested in two kinds of uranium—U235 and U239. Those are isotopes." He drew a plus sign and a minus sign. "Basic physics. Protons live in the nucleus of an atom and have a plus charge. Electrons whiz around the outside of the nucleus and have a minus charge. Every atom has exactly the same number of protons and electrons, starting with hydrogen, which has one of each, and helium, which has two of each." He drew several circles around the first one. "Know anything about quantum mechanics?"

"Just a little bit from my general physics and chemistry classes. Niels Bohr has lately dreamed up the idea that electrons aren't exactly just particles, but packets of energy that zoom around at certain predictable levels or orbits."

"Close," Crane said, pausing over his rough sketch. "Or quantum jackets, or orbitals. Whatever you want to call them. Then there are those electrically neutral particles called neutrons, which sit in the nucleus. They look a lot like protons, except the neutrons have no charge. If you add up the number of protons, electrons, and neutrons, you get the mass number of a given isotope. Uranium-235 has a total of 235 of these major subatomic particles. Uranium-239 has 239. And so forth." He paused for a moment, trying to succinctly capture the next step. "These very huge atoms don't stick together long. They decay. They give off those extra isotope neutrons, which whiz away. That's called radioactivity, and it's measurable with a Geiger counter. If you get exposed to too much radioactivity, you get sick and possibly die." He drew an arrow pointing away from an atom. "When you put a lot of uranium together in one place, the atoms smash into each other and lose their neutrons. If you get a whole lot of uranium in one pile, doing that, it's called critical mass. When you have critical mass, the chain reaction multiplies in split seconds, so the mass explodes. That's the theory, anyway. It explodes with a big bang, so it would make a dandy super-bomb." He put the pencil down. "The world's best uranium is right here in Katanga."

"Ah!" Tim said. "And gives the place new strategic value."

"Right. When the Krauts invaded Belgium, the Brussels government transferred its stocks of uranium to the Americans. The Germans, however, captured some of the Belgian stocks and took them inside Germany. That tells you, my friend, they are working on the same thing we are. The Japanese, the Soviets, the British—they all have research going. We all have the same problem: it's not hard to understand how the critical mass leads to the explosion. What's devilishly hard, Tim, is figuring out how to filter the raw oxide so you get 98% of better near-pure uranium-235. One of the things we're going to need you to do in London is help us find out how far along the Germans are, and British for that matter. There are no friends in international politics—only alliances of convenience."

Toward nightfall, they arrived at a smaller lake, tributary to Lake Tanganyika in the east. They drove along deserted hilly roads above jungle level, until they arrived at a sheltered cove. There, they drove about a mile down into the shore area. A narrow gauge railway ran to the lake shore, where Congolese men were busy loading piles of uraninite, or uranium oxide, into small cars for transport to a main rail line and thence mysteriously to Europe or America.

Crane lit a cigarette and stood with one foot up on a boulder, smoking quietly in the evening air. The men below sang as they worked. "I can practically see that stuff glowing from here," he said softly. "We'll never need to touch the stuff. Poor bastards, they'll all die of radiation sickness. Nobody will warn them, neither we nor these Belgian bastards. They'll never know what made them sick. Just bad *ju-ju*. And do you know they'll be right about that.

Canterbury, 1991: Marianne Searches

With each small leg in her journey, Marianne, Countess Didier was getting a little bit closer to the secrets of her father. She could scarcely imagine what it would be like to see him. Would he hold her? Would he call her his good girl, like her mother had, his *Umnitsa*? Would she be whole again? It had to be the other half, the lost half, torn from the golden mantle of her mother's love, so long ago lost. Her parents had been united once, god and goddess, at the creation of her life and her world. She had barely known her mother—a dark but nurturing force—and never met her father.

Finding Tim Nordhall was the Holy Grail of her life. So much lost, so long ago, so far away. Broken. Her soul was a poor thing lying in pieces. Beyond her wealth, beyond the love of the darlings who had raised her and given her all that they had, made her who she was—beyond all that, her mother's love was like an unreachable but deep, true fog horn, guiding, urging, booming, breathing that word over and over without rest, without respite, without cease, to shudder across the distant sea: *Umnitsa*. My dear little girl. My good little girl. Winking on and off like a faithful lighthouse, courageous in storms, loving like a lioness, with the rhythm of a lifetime's heartbeats. Marianne would not be complete until she held his hands and gazed into his eyes and said the word: *Daddy*.

Somehow, despite being married to a playboy and taking half a life time to grow up, she had only praise for her three boys. They had raised themselves, and kept a reserved distance from their mother. She must convince them, as well, that she had become a different person—after she finished this primordial quest in search of her own parents. Her ultimate dream was to find the long-ago, handsome Tim Nordhall—and to return to the soil of her birth near Anadyr in Siberia. She felt as if she could not start living life truly until she finished being born. Auntie Dora had nurtured her in Anadyr before the French couple came to adopt her. And grand-mère, bless her, had orchestrated Troisroses-Didier wealth to ensure that her the three boys were properly raised.

📖

During the evening in London, she called Paris as she often did, to speak with her sons and their wives. They were all at the grande maison in Passy for a celebration. Her daughter-in-law Estelle, the youngest, was pregnant and it had just been learned it was to be a girl. The name Marie-Dora had been chosen, since there already was a two year old grandchild named Marianne. The countess spoke with each of them at length, by turns laughing or biting her lip to hold back a sob. "I miss you all so much," she said. She promised: "Soon, I can be with you for good. It's this—wanderlust—you know…" She papered over the urgency of her journey. They were good children, all of them. At times, her sons had seemed almost like older brothers to their wayward mother, during her wild years. How shameful it all had been. She must put it all behind her. Thank God they were so supportive. She spent half an hour on the telephone with them—they were, after all, only an hour's plane trip or less away from her. After ringing off, she took a hot bath and slipped into bed in her Kensington hotel room for a long, sound sleep. Her dreams were troubled, but not about her children or grandchildren. A beach in Siberia…

In the morning, a hired limousine took Marianne from London south, through the Kentish countryside with its red clays and rich green woods, and into Canterbury. When she arrived, it was noon, and she was hungry. The elderly American, Jack Haywarden, had told her on the telephone that morning he would meet her, with his wife, in a shopping mall near Canterbury Cathedral.

Marianne gave the driver a generous tip for his journey back to Gatwick. Then she set out to find the retired U.S. Army colonel. She had little trouble, for he stood out even among the many tourists marching from their buses to the medieval town center.

"Madame Didier?" he said, a tall old man in a light blue sweater, who still carried himself with a certain stiffly flowing grace. With him was a small, undistinguished woman, in her 80s as he must be. The minute she opened her mouth to say hello, Marianne could put two and two together. The Haywardens were delighted at her detective work. "Yes," Haywarden said, taking the women in arm, one on each side as if they were old friends, "I stayed here after the war. There was a lot to do in Europe, putting it all back together after the mess the fascists made. I met Andrea and never looked back."

"I was a radio operator during the war," Andrea said. She had dyed her hair so that it was a mild sort of shoe-polish rusty color, but silver wisps trailed over her delicate white embroidered blouse collar. The Haywardens were a playful couple, and they seemed to forever be tugging at each other, giggling, so that Marianne laughed as she found herself being rattled about. "He looked so tall and handsome in his colonel's uniform," Andrea said, "and of course he had more ration cards than Churchill himself."

"I settled in Boughton-under-Blean—a village near here—and raised our kids here. Good place to be. Have you spent much time in the States?"

"I'm afraid not enough," Marianne said. "I was sent away to a girls' schools in Switzerland. My ex-husband and I lived for ten years in Paris, where I work as a curator in the Louvre. I recently took leave to look for my father."

Haywarden asked delicately: "Is there a present Mr. Didier?"

"Past tense," she said. "Oh, don't look pained—it's old history. I was rebelling, I'm afraid. It was the late sixties. We all hated our parents. Especially we spoiled rotten rich brats who'd been sent away. I married a wealthy Austrian insurance exec and we had three lovely sons, all French citizens and grown up now, but we divorced. Didn't affect the title I inherited from my stepfather."

"Oh yes," Mrs. Haywarden said. "Old Bourbon nobility or what?"

"Bourbon, Habsburg," Marianne said, "de Rothschild bankers."

Haywarden nodded. "Yes. It's like studying a lost world. Doesn't hurt to have it hanging on your name though, does it?"

"It can hurt, Mr. Haywarden. Attracts paparazzi, unwanted notice, tabloids." She corrected herself. "Colonel Haywarden, sorry."

"More old history," he said, clapping a liver-spotted hand gently over hers. "Yes, I have to confess, We've seen photos of you in the paper. Never dreamed we'd meet you one day. Never dreamed there might be a connection with our old friend Mr. Nordhall." They came to a touristy pub, took one look at the long queues, and decided not to eat there. "Come," Mrs. Haywarden said, "I have an idea." They marched through a maze of shops and plate glass walls to a large supermarket, and there was a clean, bright, modern delicatessen section with a few red plastic chairs and tables in a corner. "Not your rustic pub," Mrs. Haywarden said, "but they have good things to eat." Haywarden added as they walked up to the barely busy glass windows looking over the serving trays: "Comes right over from France several times a day on the ferries."

His wife laughed. "There is also Dover sole, imported from America."

"Dover is not far down the coast from here," Marianne marveled. "What a strange world. Was Mr. Nordhall a nice man?" It seemed strange to be talking about her father in so third-person a manner, but then he was a stranger to her.

Haywarden shrugged. "It was long ago, but I seem to remember he was a nice enough guy. Came bursting in one night to tell me he was being framed for espionage. I thought he was crazy, but he turned out to be dead right. I kept an eye on him after that. We lunched with Allen Dulles one day near Westminster. Nordhall was reassigned and disappeared into the war, like so many fellows."

Andrea put her arm around Marianne and said: "I do hope it turns out he was the fellow your mother—well, it just sounds like he was a nice fellow, that's all. Now tell us about your chateau, ski trips, the Riviera and all."

"Dear," Haywarden chided his wife gently.

Part Two: London, 1943-1945

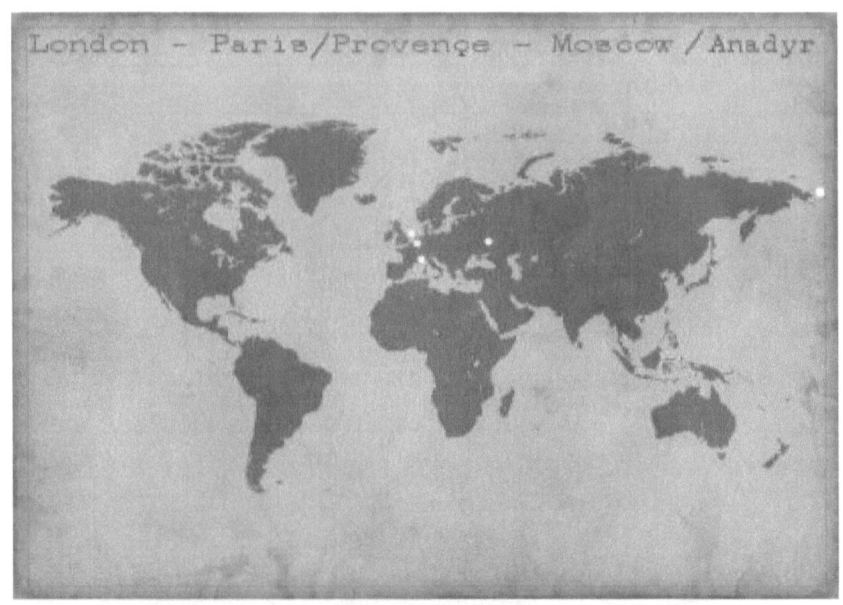

London, 1943-1945: Tim Nordhall Deep Under

Tim Nordhall flew on a Sabena DC-3 from the Congo to the Canary Islands. From there, he flew to London on a Pan Am DC-4. London was to be his home for the next two years. He loved the city's atmosphere and antiquity, as with Big Ben (in St. Stephen's Tower near Westminster Bridge and the Houses of Parliament) shuddering the hour-strokes through fog so thick neither German bomber nor American tourist could navigate—leave it to Cockney taxi jockeys.

Tim underwent several months of general training as an O.S.S. operative. He dabbled in many disciplines, from cryptography to parachuting, from secret radio transmission to elements of spy craft like dead drops and shadowing. In early 1943 he began living a double life.

On the Navy side, as Lt. Tim Nordhall, he worked for Commander Jack Stone, a friendly enough bureaucrat with a Reserve commission and a University of Chicago engineering degree. Jack Stone was 45—a tall, graying, jovial man with crisp blue eyes and a wry little grin. He served in a tangled chain of command that ultimately led to the Allied High Command.

On the O.S.S. side, as Major Robert Malone, things were kept purposely murkier. Officially, he was attached for pay and records to an office in Whitehall, in a back street, behind closed doors and in utter secrecy. It was a place he was never meant to see—save things going haywire one night in autumn 1944.

Tim's primary contact on the O.S.S. side, as 1943 wore on, was a shadowy figure code-named Jaguar, whose real name Tim did not know. Jaguar was a civil servant someplace in the City of London, or at least pretended to be. They met for the first time a month after Tim's arrival in London. This was the double or triple agent of whom Ivor Crane had spoken.

Tim spent most of his workweek on the Navy side, as if the O.S.S. side did not exist. He worked with a Naval Intelligence branch that analyzed captured enemy munitions and equipment. Their working location was a village outside London—Tining Mallow to its British workers; Marshmallow Heights to its American work force. Every morning at dawn, a train would come in from the southeast, from London, disgorging about 2,000 men and women in a variety of military and civilian garb, speaking a variety of languages from English to French to Polish and beyond. Some of the work was highly top secret, but most of it had the standard Government nod of Secret. Much of it was carried on in a maze of converted railroad repair workshops belonging to the London tube system, which had sent cars and locos out this way for servicing before the war. In the middle of the sooty little town was the ruin of a glass and iron Victorian structure that had been bombed to rubble early in the Blitz. Inside that hulked a half dozen or more rusting steam locomotives amid piles of debris and coal. The yard had been slated for obsolescence, but now no resources could be spared to clean it up. Like so many other things in a world on hold, that would have to wait for the future after the war, when and if that ever came. The beast of war dragged on and on, year after year, swallowing entire childhoods and youthful years in its bizarre and hideous maw.

Tim and his section, which worked for Jack Stone, were tasked with examining salvaged Axis maritime equipment. Tim shared a small office with two female petty officers who specialized in radio equipment. They were plain young women from the Prairies, who brought with them a small town, white-bread, no-nonsense dedication. They were smart and liked to joke in innocent little ways that Tim found pleasant but frustratingly inhibited.

Tim had a tall, narrow window overlooking a flowerbed bounded by remnant gravel ballast from the town's fading rail factory days. Tining Mallow was slowly becoming a suburb of London. Before the war, people of the middle manager class had started buying little homes on tidy streets and commuting to the capital to work in its banks and administrative departments. Now the town was swollen with American and British military personnel. Marshmallow Heights had a booming little American Main Street with jazz and bebop joints that swung all night. The pubs might close and open at bizarre hours by American tastes, but soft drinks were on sale at any time, and shifts were forever coming and going at staggered hours, so Main Street glittered with activity around the clock.

There was a large bomber command base not far away, and it was not uncommon to see young women in uniform pouring outside suddenly to watch overhead as a hundred machines droned home— some often with an engine out, or an engine burning and trailing a long smoke plume. Once or twice, Tim watched a hapless B-17 or B-24—quietly engulfed in flames and ugly black roiling gray-black smoke—disappear with a loud clapping echo into the hillsides. Men who had fought to hang on to life, sometimes missing limbs or holding dying comrades, would make it all the way from Dresden or Berlin, only to perish in an Anglo-Saxon hillside. For hours, smoke would mingle with ashen air. There were usually no survivors. The lone little box of a fire engine from the airfield could be seen trundling on its obligatory inspection, far away along stone-walled country lanes, looking ineffectual and out of place, taking its time to get there with flashing blue lights but mute siren.

📖

It was larger, and he shared it with a roommate—another young U.S. Navy officer named Stan Kehoe. Stan was a well-intentioned guy who often managed to say the wrong thing, or speak at the wrong time. He worked in ONI with Tim and held a Secret clearance. He knew nothing of Tim's work with O.S.S. Stan was a good-natured, freckled young man with short sandy hair, who tended to talk out of the side of his mouth, faster than his brain could follow. He was honest and easy-going, and Tim felt he couldn't ask for a better fellow to room with, if room one must. Stan had a girlfriend, English girl he'd met in Tining Mallow, by the name of Connie Brace or Branch or something, whom he took the train to see each weekend and it appeared they were pretty serious. Good for them, Tim thought. Good, too, to have the place to himself on weekends.

Jaguar, a slim Englishman in the ubiquitous work uniform of the London middle manager—black suit, umbrella, briefcase, bowler—met Tim for the first time on a quiet side street near the bombed out church of St. Dunstan in the East on St Dunstan's Hill, between Lower Thames Street and Great Tower Street in the City of London. This was within a stone's throw of the ancient Roman wall across the river from the Tower of London. London life flowed on around these landmarks and their ruins, as it had for thousands of years, and would no doubt continue for thousands more.

A telegram arrived, slipped under Tim's apartment door when he arrived tired from work and a few touts at the pub up the street. "Robert," it read, "Jaguar has the stamps you ordered. The 1913 Philatelic was not available but..." and so on, the coded nonsense, which Crane had shown him how to decipher.

At their first meeting, they exchanged no materials. As Crane had explained, Tim was to pass along slightly wrong information, under the guise that Major Malone was a U.S. Army officer gone bad. Some of the information was to come from the Maps Service, some from Tim's Navy section, and some from other sources, all carefully doctored to seem real. The Allied side knew Jaguar was passing bogus information, expecting good. The Allies wanted to track Jaguar's network and take them down. Jaguar, in the flesh, seemed dramatic and ageless, tall, maybe 35 to Tim's 27, with watery blue eyes, thin brown hair with the first speckles of gray, and a bland sort of pleasant Everyman face. He wore the dark suit, with bowler and umbrella, of a million London bureaucrats. He could have been ten years younger or ten years older. Anything would have worked. Tim felt relaxed and in control of himself, knowing he was only a blind in a larger hunt. He only needed to go through his motions. Jaguar, who saw Tim likewise as only a conduit, said: "This will be our meeting place when I summon you." Jaguar sat on an age-blackened wall overlooking the rubble-strewn green area under the ruined walls of the church. The church tower, still intact, was a minor Wren masterpiece. The church dated back to Medieval times, and had received a Christopher Wren tower after the massive fire of 1666 that destroyed much of London. During the Blitz of 1941, London had been covered in smoke and flames every night. This ancient church was a victim. Luckily, the Luftwaffe failed to demolish the great Cathedral of St. Paul, whose original structure dated back almost to Roman times. Every morning, it was said, Prime Minister Winston Churchill's first words were, to his aides: "Is St. Paul's still standing?" And it would remain standing, though a single bomb had cut through its nave and splintered a section behind the main altar. That would be replaced by a stained glass window and the American Memorial Chapel, in thanks for the sacrifices of U.S. forces in defense of Great Britain.

Now only some of its window arches remained intact of St. Dunstan in the East, aside from the Wren tower. Jaguar sat looking away with his umbrella and briefcase stiffly on his lap. Tim stood between two ogive arches, amid ivy that had splashed out like green blood from the dying house of God. He finished the last slices of an orange from his lunch. His fingers were sticky, and he washed them in rainwater captured in tulip and crocus cups. "This will be our only mode and time of contact. I will have further instructions for you as time goes on." With that, Jaguar rose and walked briskly away leaving Tim standing at the edge of the rubble. Jaguar strode off, whistling, and twirling his umbrella.

📖

He dated English, Canadian, and American women, nothing too serious. His American girlfriends typically completed their tours and returned home, one of them to a fiancée she had not mentioned. He sometimes woke up screaming in the middle of the night, dreaming of the faces of large-eyed drowning men just under the waves, their arms waving at him for help. He remembered their names—Jerry Harris whose wife Edna had the finches in Manchester; Ben Meyer whose Shula probably cried daily over her carpets right here in London; red-haired Harvey Kinnan, whom he'd watched torn in pieces by sharks, whose wife Nuala was a nurse right here in London; and of course dour Jerry Harris with the dark staring eyes. It was material for many a nightmare, many a strangled scream, suddenly sitting up choking and unable to go back to sleep.

There was an *H.M.S. Sturmer* mothers' league centered in Canterbury. Tim first learned of this organization from Jaguar, who instructed him on firm orders from Crane not to go, not to contact any of the bereaved parents. The official British line was that the ship had gone down with a total loss of life.

One day, in Spring 1944, Tim returned home from work to find his friend getting quietly drunk in the backyard. Rain fell on the grass, while Stan sat still in uniform, tie loose, with a bottle of gin in one hand and a toothpaste glass in the other. Stan was already leaning to one side in the white wrought-iron lawn set—four chairs, and a table covered by a torn multi-hued umbrella. Tim was just in time to rescue him from a fall on the flagstone walk. "Connie Bruce," Stan managed to mumble, "she's run off with a freckled guy from the U.S. Army, damned infantryman, gonna get killed and see there we are, whatcha get, she'll eternally regret..." It was the familiar scenario of many a British training film, warning the wives of absent soldiers not to break up their marriages over the intoxicating and wild new presence of American G.I.s stationed in England by the tens of thousands. On that dire note, Stan passed out in Tim's arms. Tim had a hell of a time dragging the body upstairs to its bed.

In the next few weeks, Tim almost welcomed Stan's morbid state because it distracted from Tim's own bleak horizons. A British attaché with the Logistics office invited Tim and a Limey navy nurse named Anna Stokowska to join them at a tea. The American liaison officer was a Billy Seward, who'd lost an eye in the Battle of Britain flying a Spit for the Brits, and now did desk duty in the espionage circus. Anna was a tall, willowy blonde, a classic Polish beauty with blue eyes, pink cheeks, and dimpled snowy skin. Something clicked between her and Tim from the first. She hung on Tim's arm, while Stan Kehoe's eyes snagged on her. He took Tim aside to ask: "Where did you find her? Do they have any more of her?" and Tim told him most likely in Warsaw.

They would lie together, for hours, much as they liked reading hip to hip, shoulder to shoulder in the bookstore window nooks, but naked and touching each other and it almost seemed to Tim they were in love. But there was someone else, he knew, without being told. He wanted to enjoy this for whatever it was, and not ask questions and ruin everything before its time to be ruined. She never spoke of love, but showed him with her eyes, her hands, her sex, that he could have anything he wanted, except there was that someone or something at the end of a long dark corridor in her soul where she would not let him follow her. He tried to avoid talking about love, except that he had never felt about a woman as he did about her. But he was still not done with his own freedom. It wasn't just other women. He wasn't ready just then for a commitment, which was what love seemed to mean once you got past that heady starting gate. He wondered—had it not been for the crazy war, maybe they could have enjoyed each other, let each other sow wild oats or whatever it was each secretly needed to do or not do. That wasn't it, as it turned out. As it was, the war brought urgency and brevity and shattered time where there should have been long, slow movement like the silky, mossy glow of a New England mountain stream behind sunny ferns.

She taught him something she liked him to do. It was a simple thing she admitted she had taught one other man do, back in Poland. If it was the other man, Tim did not ask. He accepted the little treasure of her secret. She would lie still beside him, as rain trickled down the window in a pale half-light. They were both naked, and he gazed over the geometries of her long pale body. It filled his eyes with nourishment. She had him lightly, softly, rub the little fur on her Venus mound while she turned her lips to nuzzle against his neck. She would like very motionless, eyes closed, with her hands limp and motionless on his forearms. Once in a while, she would emit the tiniest whimper. His fingertips, together, all four, would make circling motions in that hair that was drying out after their sex. At first she had to teach him, just once, with one hand, taking his fingertips and showing him. He would make those circles and then increase the pressure on her soft mound just a bit, just a teeny bit. This went on for a quarter hour until she raised a hand and tightly grasped the wrist of the four fingers. At first he thought she wanted him to stop. She pushed his hand down and dipped it briefly, and he saw how wet she was. She held his wrist, pulling his hand tightly to her, and the fingertips kept up their walking in circles. Until. Until. She would start doubling up in fits, in shudders, silent at first. Then the earthquake would come—three or four rolling cries, before she doubled over on the bed as if in pain. Funny thing was, she'd then roll over on her belly and pass out, snoring, leaving him to look at her long back, her rear end, the space between her thighs—all of that being, as the expression went, easy on the eyes, and never boring. Sometimes her little secret aroused him so much he'd take her just once more, softly, from behind like that, and she'd mewl gently and shift her pale orbs to make room for him to get in easily while she slumbered on. She was a good woman, willing to please, never a problem. Except that nothing was perfect, nobody was perfect. Everyone had a Thing in their life at some time, and Anna Stokowska did indeed have a Thing in her life, as Tim would learn.

Acting on Billy Seward's invitation—about a week later late on a Saturday afternoon as they were closing shop—Tim and Stan wandered to the Joint Command side, through sunken courtyards, amid long-dead lanterns in which birds nested ever since blackouts had become a way of life. It was an office tea and cookie munch sponsored by the American A.G. in this hybrid North American-European command of British, French, Polish, Canadian, and U.S. staffers. In a somber library, whose walls were studded with trophies and stag heads, Stan and Tim each politely hoisted a bracing dark porter while wind howled outside. Leaves blew against darkened windows. Window glass rattled in its frames. One was almost tempted to pull up the blinds because no Kraut would be out flying on such an afternoon. But rules were rules.

"Your friend looks so bleak," Billy Seward said to Tim, with a glance at Stan Kehoe. Seward held a cup of tea laced with vodka, and a cigarette on which he puffed voraciously.

"His love life just went down the drain."

"Ah. Poor guy. How's the Polish beauty, what's her—?

"Anna Stokowska."

Seward shuddered, making his one eye tremble. "Even her name is gorgeous. D'jever notice how these Germans and Polacks and Russians have these horsy names like something that's tough to chew, full of syllables like *charf* and *shrauf* and *rowf-rowf* and stuff, and they are all the more beautiful, like they want to go nuts and bite you while you make love to them?" Seward looked distressed, despite the humor.

Tim laughed. "She's on duty at the hospital. Poor kid works hard."

"You'll ease her pain, I'm sure." For a moment, Tim wondered if he were the Thing in Anna's life, but decided not. They talked about other things.

The British were good hosts, amid their canvas-draped filing cabinets and locked library vitrines. Tim had a vague idea that they were in the same game, picking apart lost screws and radios and machine gun parts. In fact, Billy Seward introduced Tim to a senior colonel, saying "This is Lt.

Commander Nordhall, Sir. He wrote the fascinating white-paper about assaying hardware to determine the enemy's lot as we bomb them into the ground."

Colonel Grimsby was a pale man with bushy gray eyebrows. He looked like a schoolmaster who smoked so much there were hints of yellow in his brows. Grimsby said: " I read your paper, Nordhall. Nice work. Picking out clues from the purity of the alloys and so forth. We found traces of contaminants, using your method, suggesting the Krauts are mining inferior ores on their own land, which sets them back a good bit. Good sort of hip-pocket information to wow the top cigars at the weekly report luncheon."

"Thank you, Sir."

"Tim is a clockmaker and an engineer," Seward said with easy social grace.

"Indeed." The elderly man effused: "You should love London then. All we have here is clocks, if the damned Hun would stop bombing our churches."

"I'm enjoying London very much," Tim said.

A loose knot of happily glowing, gin-soaked faces were beginning to form around their elderly baron.

The old man noticed the ribbons on Tim's chest. "Been through some shooting, have you?"

"Took a torpedo in the North Atlantic a while ago, Sir." It was a standard story Crane had made up for him, at MI5 or MI6's request.

"Oh? What ship?"

"Not allowed to say, Sir."

"Of course. Of course. Top secret. Everything is top secret these days. A wonder we all remember the way home at night if that isn't also secret." Grimsby continued: "Too much of that these days. Too many fine lads. Took mine in the leg during the Great War." He clapped himself on the left hip. "I walk funny when it's cold. You and Seward here. Damn shame. Young men and all. You should be out squiring, not firing." He burst into laughter, echoed by the barks of young officers around them.

"You are a poet, Sir," Tim said.

The old man reddened. "Oh, what. Sunday school rhymes. I teach Latin when we aren't living between sandbags. Small private school for boys in Devonshire. You ought to come up and visit some time, when you tire of London. But then, wasn't it Boswell who said, if a man..."

"...Tires of London," Seward said, "he is tired of living, for London offers all that life has to afford."

More laughter. The party drifted hither and yon, as parties did. Stan tugged anxiously on Tim's sleeve, and pointed to a particularly attractive young woman. "I'm in love, buddy."

Tim used both hands, gripping Stan's dark blue dress uniform by the padded shoulders, to position Stan in the line of vision so he could look from behind Stan, just past his ear, to examine the lady in question. "She is an angel indeed," Tim said. "But she seems to be hovering around that guy with the gold ropes swinging from his uniform, or is that a detail you prefer to ignore?"

"Just look at her," Stan whispered as if they were in a church looking at stained glass. "Her name is Claire Denby. *Lef*tenant Clair Denby." He said the woman's name and rank as if lingering over a favorite dessert.

Tim looked, and sucked back a breath. The dark uniform, the white blouse, the tightly wrapped bun of dark reddish-brown hair, added that certain crispness. She had pale skin and a softly angular face that looked as though someone with great talent had carefully brushed her features in, making it look easy, making it look careless as her clean white smile, her lively dark eyes in pure white settings, like fine bone china. Whoever she was, she had a polished, perfect sort of insouciant grace that brightened the entire room. She was the woman for whom the WREN uniform had been designed. She was a lieutenant, with cute little cords and bangles of rank and decoration, and young officers hovered about like sullen magnets, like little planets soaking in the glow of her sunlight. They all knew she was Admiral Todd's assistant in Naval Engineering. Tim wished Stan would figure that out. For a moment, Tim thought she must be American. Maybe a visiting movie star. Stan, for his part, seemed to think so too, and was having trouble swallowing. Then Tim heard, quite distinctly, her charming and well-tooled upper class British dialect. Immediately, he was conscious of the entire divide. Perhaps the Gilbert and Sullivan admiral standing nearby was her father, or her lover, or for that matter Jupiter to her Io. In any case, it was immediately clear that they were equestrians while the rest of the crowd were an array representing the plebs.

"Give it up," Tim told Stan.

"I can't," Stan said. "I've fallen in love."

"You've fallen out of your mind." He was secretly glad, at least, that Stan was getting over the disaster with Connie Bruce or whatever it had been.

In the ensuing weeks, Stan's infatuation for Claire Denby became a source of comment, amusement, and pity between Anna and Tim. They took Stan with them on the early halves of dates, just so he wouldn't be alone. Eventually he'd drift off to go bar-hopping with some guys, apparently oblivious to the great city chock full of unattached young women away from home and looking for a kindly squeeze. Stan, who had seemed so happy with his Bruce or Bryce woman, had taken a hard fall. Anna leaned close, one evening. She and Tim sat in plush blood-leather chairs in a restaurant near Pall Mall. Stan had just spotted two of his drinking cronies and rushed off to be with them. Through the smoke and gloom, Anna told Tim in Polish-accented English: "He will find a woman for himself. But I don't believe it will be Claire Denby."

As they usually did, Tim and Anna went for a walk, for some air, along a foggy dock or down a drizzly street. They huddled arm in arm and shivered as they made small talk. The questions tumbled out, unbidden, as they eventually must. "You are suddenly quiet," Anna said.

"Oh, I'm just thinking about Stan. He's like a teenager in love."

She laughed. "Lucky boy."

"Aw come on, Anna, we're a strange item."

"Honey..." There was a kindly little warning in her tone.

They walked along in silence for a time, with the Thames on their right, and barges quietly shoving along at a steady clattering pace. Occasionally, a whistle would pipe, and a response would come booming over the black waters.

"Are you growing tired of me, darling?" She clung tighter, arm in arm, as if telling him in body language she was afraid of losing him.

"No." He thought about it. "Not sure what I'm trying to say here. I guess we speak different languages."

"Yes, I speak Polski and you English. The sausage and the hamburger. We need to find a bun that fits the both."

"I'm a little scared that I might just decide to give you the whole bun, Anna."

"And what does that mean, my heroic chef?"

He steeled his courage to say what he had to. "Okay, I hope I don't ruin everything. I think about you a lot."

"Oh my poor darling." She stopped and put her hands on his shoulders. Her eyes looked into his, full of worry.

"What?" he asked, taking her hands in his as if he could take charge of a life he knew, then and there—suddenly, definitively, at that moment, for the first time in a new understanding—was not his to have.

She looked worried, and had this expression as if she was about to blurt out something shocking. She played with the buttons on his coat. He waited. He hoped she would say she loved him, but when she looked up, he knew with a sinking heart that she was not thinking of saying that to him.

"Don't—" she said.

He was too dry mouthed to ask what *don't* meant. He was mindful of a play he'd seen, in the new existential, minimalist style. He pictured himself as a man adrift in the universe. He remembered his lost friends on HMS Sturmer, and those conversations about minimalist theater.

He walks onto a stage. It is pitch dark, except for one light directly above that sheds a small puddle of dim, achy light. The invisible audience watches. The man finds only a chair, a stand, and a typewriter. He sits down—

In a very careful, small, measured voice, she said: "Tim."

Put sheet in typewriter. Clear throat. Begin memo.

"Yes, Anna."

"Tim, if we talk now, everything will change between us. And yet, nothing will change for me, for you, for the whole world. Sometimes, darling, it's like the war. *C'est la guerre.* Some things we cannot talk about, and other things we should not talk about."

He grew angry. "I don't know what that all means."

"I know. And I can't tell you, Tim. We have had moments together that I have never shared with another man. You are so very special."

"Is that like—I love you?"

She gave him a hurt, vulnerable look. "If I say I love you, what will happen? You want me to say that, Tim, knowing that I am going to be reassigned soon. We will never see each other again."

"You knew this?" He stepped back, almost stamping his foot in anger.

"Yes. I could have told you, and—well, now I can say it. I love you, Tim. I can't have you, and you can't have me."

"This is nuts, Anna."

"Okay." She put her hands in her pockets. They resumed walking.

Yank sheet from typewriter. Sign in black ink. Mail memo. Nothing will ever be the same again from this moment forward.

"I was a very innocent girl who lived a very sheltered life. Very Catholic girl from a fine and wealthy family. Mass every Sunday."

Tim walked beside her, aching and in love with her. They walked with their hands in their pockets and the river flowed ceaselessly without comment.

"I fell in love with my cousin Erek. He is five years older, very tall and handsome, university graduate, artillery officer, great hero. Beautiful looking boy. I was in love with him from the time I was a little girl. I was always so happy when his family came to visit, or we went to their palace. They are titled. I was just turning 20 when the Germans came, and I had never gone all the way with a boy. I was saving myself, you know. What can I tell you? A silly girl. I cried when he went off in his beautiful uniform. He wore his family's great regalia as a Reserve Colonel, though only 25. He fought when the Nazis invaded my country. He escaped to France, and fought with the French in 1940 until the Germans defeated them too. He could have escaped to Spain or to England, but what did he do? He returned to Warsaw, in secret, to propose marriage to me. I said yes. I didn't even know until then, so innocent was I, that he had been in love with me all those years but was afraid to hurt me because we are second cousins, and there would be scandal and so forth. He is very proper. We told our parents, who were shocked, of course, but it's the war, the crazy terrible war, and they gave us their blessing. We were married secretly in his house, which is a large old palace. There were jealous servants even in our little dinner party, who betrayed him. We were supposed to secretly leave from Gdansk to Kaliningrad by night boat and then cross the Baltic Sea to Sweden, where we would be safe. He and I had five nights and five days together. It was like it is between me and you. I have never been with another man in that way, except you. We stayed under false names in a little hotel in Wislinka, and on the fifth day, we stood on the dock at Olowianka waiting for night to fall and the ferry to come from Helsingborg to take us to Lithuania and then across the Baltic Sea. A car pulled up, Gestapo got out, and we were taken away. He managed to create a diversion downtown when we were stuck in traffic, told me to run, and I did as I was told, screaming. A crowd closed around me to protect me from the Germans, and I have never seen Erek since. But I have word from him."

Tim was too stunned at the whole story to speak.

"Erek my husband is in a prison camp near . The Germans are holding him so that I will work for them here in London. Or they threaten to kill him. He sent word to me that he is willing to die rather than let me compromise my honor, as he puts it. I, instead, went to your friend—"

"Oh no." Tim was thinking Stan Kehoe.

"Billy Seward, the One-eye. I work for him now." The way she said it, Tim knew she had no feelings for Seward. Was she telling the truth? Was this all some giant con game? She stopped. "Tim."

Put sheet in typewriter. Stare at blank. Tear from typewriter and throw away.

Tim stood transfixed by the ever flowing river, loving her, loving Erek for her, loving Poland, wishing this all wasn't so.

"Tim, I have told you something that people could die for knowing. I told you because I am in love with you. Do you understand now? It is sometimes harder to say I am in love than it is to just be silent and be in love."

"I love you, Anna."

She stepped close and rested her forehead against his chest. "I know you do, darling. And I—am a married woman and there is something more."

"What?"

"I have to think about it, telling you I mean. I have to consider the life of Erek, what they will do to him back home if they learn I am seeing a man. They will know they cannot rely on me anymore for using my love of Erek. And so they may kill him."

"I don't want that."

"I know you don't, darling, because you are a very kind, principled man. That is one of the things I love about you." She put her arm through his. "So you see. I was right. I can tell you I love you or I don't love you, and it makes no change in the equation. Now you see why I don't want the Poles to see us together. It was a mistake that first time, with Gostomski. I was careless."

They walked arm in arm, almost—but never again—as they had been before.

📖

"Is there a game?" Tim was disappointed at that verdict, almost annoyed with Anna. How unworthy that such enchanting and lively beauty should be so easily written off.

"There usually is." Anna betrayed a Byzantine side at that moment. She expressed no kindness toward Claire. To drive her point home, Anna said: "She is like broken rocks inside. A woman can tell a lot about another woman. She is hard, but something hurts."

Tim could almost get a crush on Claire Denby himself. It seemed many of the Americans in particular did, though the Brits for some almost botanical reason seemed to shy away from her. They knew in their genes she was not of their class. He found himself fantasizing about her until one night, while walking an unfamiliar route on an errand to fetch medicine from a chemist shop that was open late, he saw the two of them come staggering out of a private home. She looked delectable in a tan and white outfit with high heels. Tim stood fascinated, capturing the near-erotic intensity of the moment. They were quite inebriated, and her skirt was hiked up in the back. Lord Humhaw had one hand up her behind and the other on his fly as they bounced from wall to wall on their way to his car. Apparently he was trying to urinate while walking, and at the same time clumsily fondle her, while she laughed like a braying horse. Tim glimpsed pale skin and gorgeous curvature, but her hat was crooked, and she laughed too loudly. She stopped abruptly and fire-hosed a gallon of dirty fluid from the mouth, several seconds of turbid high pressure discharge that momentarily hung like a sheet in the air before her, then loudly spattered down her front and all over the sidewalk. Her outfit had a large wet cone shape on its front. Tim turned away in distaste. She seemed cheap, her companion an incomprehensible match of old age and grossness.

A few evenings later, Stan had had a few drinks too many to drive safely. It was a rainy evening, and the Germans were momentarily quiet on their side of the Channel. War raged across Europe, and buzz bombs dropped randomly on Britain, but at the moment it was nothing like the nightly horror of the 1940 Blitz that people talked about. Britain was full of Americans, Free French, Free Poles, anyone who hated the Nazis, and there was a growing confidence now that the Krauts were getting a bloody nose. In that relaxed, almost excited atmosphere, Stan demanded that Tim drive him to a small village about forty miles north of London. Tim was tired and tried to demur, but Anna was working and Stan was insistent. So rather than stay home and catch up on his sleep, Tim found himself driving Stan along narrow country roads, trying to dodge among military convoys that tied up traffic everywhere.

"Would you mind explaining what this is all about?"

"Sorry," Stan said, "maybe a bit later." He looked about with an air of conspiracy. "The walls have ears."

They rode in silence a while, Tim driving, Stan behaving rather smugly with an air of someone who has been desperate for so long that the most harebrained scheme begins to seem logical. "I'm telling you," Stan said nursing a cigarette and a small bottle of whiskey in the passenger seat, "I am finally going to strike while the iron is hot."

"Claire Denby?"

"Yes."

"You're still not on first base, and you never will be."

"I am in love, Tim."

"Don't you get it?" He'd seen enough of the beautiful Claire to agree with Anna's instant assessment. "You are American. She's some sort of British snob. They look down on their own people. To people like her we are the colonial riffraff that come back to do our duty and help them out of a jam. Then they'll want me and you to go back to our farms or wherever we came from, and they'll want to get on with their empire."

Stan shook his head. "Tim, my boy, you are getting cynical in your old age. Open your eyes, in the beauty of youth, and live what short span is our destiny before the snows close our petals softly and without pity or remorse, forever."

"What's that—John Donne? Shelley? Keats?"

"Stan Kehoe."

"You're kidding."

"She drives me to poetry. Isn't that insane?" Stan lounged dreamily back in his seat, forgetting his cigarette until it burned his fingertips and he threw it out the window, fumbling. "I've been spying on her. Hard act she is to follow. She's got some kind of dark and unfortunate thing going with old Brigadier Brigadoon there, who is old enough to be her father. I can't figure it out. But she has smiled at me more than once."

"She hopes you'll take a hint and go away," Tim said.

"She wishes I would come and rescue her. And that I shall."

"I have to save you from yourself," Tim said. "That's the only reasonable explanation for why I am driving you across England in the middle of a squalid night like this."

"The rain has let up," Stan said.

"But the fog is setting in, you dumb bastard." Tim had to start rubbing the condensation off the inside of the windshield with an old rag, because the heater was out.

"We could stop for a dram or two," Stan said, pointing to a tavern.

"Closed. They look up the liquor at all sorts of strange hours to keep the working people productive."

"Too bad. Well, we'll scare something up in Ledding Lyme. I can't tell you how much I appreciate this, pal. You will forever be a hero to me."

Tim shook his head. "Remind me to stay home and get drunk instead."

"Now don't be harsh. You've got Anna. She's a beautiful young woman. You can afford to be patronizing."

"I'm sorry. Don't mean to be patronizing." Tim pulled over and took a leak in a foggy field while thunder growled and lightning flashed someplace far away. What a mad night. When he got back in, he said: "Now either you explain, or I head back home."

"Spoilsport. Okay." Once he'd made sure Tim was headed to the town of Ledding Lyme, a crossroads in the middle of nowhere, Stan launched forth: "This babe, Claire, is a spy."

"No."

"Yeah. I'm sure of it. I was eavesdropping on her and Lord Haw Haw in a dark and dank murky cellar under the armorium where we toil, along the banks where once flowed the River Fleet. I kind of know where they meet, and I have been looking for an opening."

"You are sick."

"I know. Love makes one ill. Love makes one puke. Love makes one, well, crazy, so here I am. I'm not the only one. Half the building is in love with her. You know that guy with the pirate eye patch, Billy Sewage? He actually warned me off. He's in love with her too! So I'm listening in on this argument she and Lord Scrimshaw are having. She is demanding some kind of document, and he is saying he can't fork it over because ships will sink and planes will fall from the sky. England will be forever lost. He pleads with her to run away with him. They will settle in the Bahamas or some other faraway nook of the Empire, to raise roses and fuck night and day so she'll forget he has a paunch. He's got a couple of bluish jowls, older than she is, pickled in forty years of Bombay blue."

"I can't imagine what she sees in that guy."

"Yeah, well you know how it is. Host country nationals." That was the old byword from a hundred training films—*never raise an eyebrow no matter what the Host Country Nationals do or say. If they offer you a drink of something that smells like shoe polish mixed with goat urine, kindly thank them and demur, saying you are of a religious denomination that prohibits*...well, all sorts of rubbish like that. Tim and Stan both laughed.

"Seriously," Stan said, "I've got it figured out. She's a spy. She's been letting this geek violate her in return for some information that she needs."

"To sink our ships," Tim said thickly, not liking where the conversation was heading.

"To shink our sips, but there has to be a reason," the lovelorn Stanley mooned. "Don't you get it, Tim? See what I mean? Here is my chance to tell Lord Humbug to fuck off and go tend his tulips and be thankful I didn't turn him in, and at the same time I tell her I can save her if she'll only let me."

"How?"

"I don't know yet. I'll figure that out as I go along."

"Stan, you are insane."

"I am Napoleon, leading my armies. I trust my fate. I will prevail."

"He died on an island halfway to the South Pole."

"I'm a lot younger. I have a long time left."

"You go on the wagon tomorrow, you hear?" Tim couldn't help laughing. "I swear, unrequited love has turned your brain to porridge." He added: "So why does she have to betray her country?"

"I don't know. Figure it out. She needs money to save the family castle."

"And you can help her more than he can."

"Just get me there, Tim. I'll figure out what to do. First, I need her love and cooperation. Love conquers all. She'll see the logic immediately and surrender to my charms."

They came to a crossroads in the middle of nowhere, just as Tim had expected. Two narrow roads—flanked on either side by hedges, which contained fragments of ancient walls—met at a little turnabout. On a metal post were several enameled signs: Lyme Canter, Lyme Wendell, Less Lyme, Upper Lyme, but no Ledding Lyme. "Now what?"

"We find a cop and ask directions."

"Okay; it's nearly ten thirty. I think all cops are in bed by ten in this country."

"An old Civil Warden then. They are always on duty."

"Right. Here we go." Off they sped, Tim picking the most likely target, which happened to be Less Lyme. His worst fear was that they'd be sent back and forth from one Lyme to another, always by some well-meaning soul who insisted that the correct Lyme was 'just that way over that hill there.'

Not only did they not find anyone to ask for directions, but Tim found they were driving in large circles and getting low on gas. The same landmarks began to whirl past with tiresome regularity: a certain large tree, a hedge with a hole in it, a small tan car parked at an odd angle before a stone church, a village in which several shop lights still burned behind locked doors. Fog rolled silently through the opaque air. They passed the unhelpful crossroads several times. Stan was out of liquor and beginning to sober up, though he complained of a low, nagging headache.

The fog was really starting to roll in now, bringing an eerie silence. The men had the windows down, and the echoes of the motor rattled back and forth through pastures and orchards.

"That church back there," Tim said. He tortured the car through a six-point turn on the narrow road and drove back.

"We've been by it a dozen times," Stan agreed. He half hung out the window, head, shoulders, one arm. "We've got to find her!"

Tim was on the verge of calling a halt to the adventure and driving home, when they rolled up the gravel path before the Church of England parish church of Ledding Lyme.

Tim cut the engine and they sat in silence.

In the silence, the little car parked nearby was making eerie clicking and popping sounds. "Cooling down," Tim said. "Been driven recently."

"Damn," Stan said. "I could have sworn I heard her say to meet him in a town called Ledding Lyme."

"Well, it's not a town, and it's not Ledding Lyme," Tim said, "but we found it. No Claire."

"Yes, but what is that in the car over there?" Stan asked, pointing. He still hung half out the window.

Tim looked at the oddly parked little tan car, which seemed to have exceptionally smeared windows. "Let's get out and stretch our legs." With Tim in the lead, they stepped out on the gravel. Tim left the parking lights on.

Footsteps crunching, they walked across the front portal, to the edge of a little copse of trees, where the car sat with its windshield glinting with reflected amber light in the darkness. The car was a rather plebeian Leyland.

"What's that inside?" Stan asked. He'd begun trembling.

Tim felt a knot in his stomach. He leaned in close and rubbed water off the window. "Stan!" he said, seeing a twisted shape inside.

Stan came running around the front of the car. "There's a man inside!"

"It's them," Tim said. He tried to pull the door open, but it was locked. Inside were two bodies, and they weren't moving.

"Oh God!" Stan shrieked. "It's him! Admiral Todd! Then that must be her!"

The windows were smeared with gore, and there was a smell of gunpowder in the air. The older man's face peered out, fish-like, as if he'd been caught in a net and dredged from the lightless void at the bottom of the ocean, where his skin was white and his eyes were pale blue dots swimming in egg white. His face was tilted up, his mouth open in a gaping motion. His pale hand, and the heavy black service revolver it loosely held, were plainly visible. Tim kept pulled on the door handle, but it was locked. "Stan, what the hell is going on?"

"Oh good Jesus," Stan said holding his hands over his ears. He appeared to be fully sober now. He fumbled with a cigarette, but dropped it in the wet gravel at his feet. Then he dropped the whole pack. Small white cylinders, cigarettes, dropped everywhere and got wet.

"Gentlemen," a voice said.

Tim and Stan whirled and looked at several men in hats and raincoats who had appeared on the church steps. With them were several constables, including two British military policemen in red caps. Tim noticed infantry-like figures hovering in the mist holding rifles.

Billy Seward stepped down and walked across toward Tim and Stan, who stood frozen. Tim's heart was pounding in his neck, causing him to have trouble breathing. Anna's handler.

Seward lit a cigarette and stuck it in Stan's mouth, slapping him lightly on the cheek, audibly so, humiliatingly so.

Tim said: "Are we going before a firing squad? Got a blindfold?"

"Funny guy, eh?" Seward stepped close to Tim. "You too?"

"I really have no idea what is going on," Tim said.

Another, older man stepped down. He was gray-haired and chubby, with thick glasses. "Dammit, Seward, this has really become a mess."

Seward seemed rigid, but tried to regain his usual comedic composure. "Sorry, Inspector. The last thing I ever expected was this fool to come rolling along, much less our friend Nordhall. Quite a combination."

"Never mind the comedy," the Inspector said. "You know these fellows?"

"I'll take full responsibility for them, Sir."

"Then run them over to the station and keep them there until I can deal with this. Hurry."

A powerful dark-green sedan pulled in with only its parking lights on. It was an American made Ford, olive-drab, with British plates. Its motor thrummed in the night. "Get in if you know what's good for you," Seward said. "Hurry."

Tim and Stan sat in the back seat. Seward sat in the passenger seat beside a young red-haired man with a steely face, who wore a plain black suit and coat. As they pulled out, another man followed closely, driving Tim's car. They left the tiny country church and its grisly scene behind.

"You boys may have blown a major operation for us," Seward said, lazily popping a stick of American spearmint gum in his mouth. He didn't offer to share from his pack. He sat with one elbow over the neck rest, looking toward the backseat while the driver focused on the road ahead.

"Sorry," Tim said. "We were out for a drive. I had no idea."

Seward shook his head, grinning sardonically at Stan, then addressing Tim again. "Sorry, won't wash. Too much of a coincidence, your working in the same area in London, and then showing up less than twenty minutes after Admiral Todd kills himself."

Stan whispered: "Was that Claire in the car with him?"

Seward stared at him as if Stan were an insect. "No, that was Mrs. Todd. I imagine he had just explained to her why he must blow their brains out. She was totally innocent and never saw any of it coming."

Stan was pale and silent. Tim explained as briefly as possible, from his friend's infatuation to their joy ride out here. Seward chewed his gum pensively, looking from one to the other. "This is your roommate?"

"Yes," Tim said.

"You have some explaining to do, both of you."

Tim could imagine the consternation, the need for explanations, the possible reprimands, Article 15s, who knew what, when he did not show up for work in the morning. It would be at least as devastating for Stan. "Tell them the whole story, Stan."

Stan nodded. "I was hoping to help Lieutenant Denby. I had no idea the situation was so grave."

"Really?" Seward chewed. The car smelled of spearmint overlaid upon damp wool and dusty upholstery. "How grave did you think it was?"

"I don't know," Stan said, getting more rattled. "I just thought...I overheard them talking. Her and Admiral Todd. I thought she was a spy."

"Uh-huh. Keep talking."

"You knew." Stan's eyes widened. "You knew all along. You were watching her. Waiting to catch her." Stan's mind seemed to be churning out ideas that spilled over the wheel of his tongue as fast as they came into being. "You had a stakeout going. You were waiting to catch her accomplices, and then we blundered along."

"Very close," Seward said. He looked at Stan with much contemplation. "You have it a little backwards. He was the spy. She was working for the Crown."

Stan looked as if he'd been struck by lightning. The effect was amplified by the fact that the car pulled into the back parking lot of a brick building. The East Lyme Police Depot, according to a sign looming out of some bushes in the fog.

"Let's get out," Seward said. They all stepped out onto crunching gravel. Seward sent the driver away into the building. "You men stay here a moment and we'll talk." He stood staring at them. Stan gave Tim a look of apology and Tim stared back in annoyance. Fog rolled by thickly, and the air smelled damp and woodsy.

Tim's car drove in and was parked. The driver got out, exchanged a few words with Seward, threw him the keys, and went into the station.

Seward threw the keys to Tim, who was relieved to get them back. "The question before us is, what to do with you two." Seward took out his gum, slowly rolled it into a ball, and tossed it far away into the woods. "Things are back to where they were before you rolled in, and we may still catch our Germans if you two didn't warn them off."

"I'm so sorry," Stan said. "I got him into this."

"You guys want this to be over with, forever?"

"Yes!" Tim and Stan said in one voice.

"You both have high clearances, which is one reason you do not now disappear to some destroyer escort guarding ice floes south of Australia. I know where to come find you if either of you opens your mouth."

Tim cleared his throat. "Billy, okay, we get the message. So what's the poop here? How do we get on with our lives?" He had not let on about his relationship with Jaguar and O.S.S., and was a bit nervous about that secret.

"Very carefully, my friend. You guys are young, so it's not surprising you'd be chasing this bitch. " Billy grabbed his trousers between the legs and hopped comically up and down. "Get the hell out of here, both of you. Hope I never lay eyes on you again, unless it's over tea at Colonel Haw-haw's office."

Stan Kehoe was transferred to California not long after. A late night bash over beers with a few fellow officers sealed the deal, and Tim drove him to his standby hop on an elderly B-17 heading for retirement from RAF Lakenheath. An attractive young female ferrying pilot looked out from the cockpit.

There was, however, an upshot to the recent affair, about which he would not tell Stan until long after—the following year, in San Francisco.

📖

He had to admit: "I've tried thinking it through, Anna. Much as I love you, and I think you love me, I think maybe you're a bit confused. How can a person be in love with two people?"

She burst into a patronizing little laugh. "You haven't experienced it, my love. I hope you never do. It's like being torn apart down the middle."

"I still love you."

"And I love you, my darling. Tell you what. Let's make a deal. I see how you look at the beautiful girls, single, free, looking for love, all around us in this wonderful city. Let's see each other once a week, let's say Sunday. The rest of the week, you do whatever you want."

At first, Tim fought the idea. Then he saw her logic. He had already lost her. Or he had never had her. Whom was he kidding? What was he to her? A crutch in a tight spot. She would stay married to Erek, who hopefully would be free soon. He wished Erek only the best. From then on, for the rest of her time in London, they made passionate love at his place on

Sundays. She told him: "Sundays with you is all I need to keep me happy. I want one other thing."

"What's that?"

"I've decided I want you to take me to lunch once a week also."

"You drive a hard bargain."

"None of it makes sense, does it? It's the war."

📖

Tim and Ginny took a train from London's Waterloo Station to Winchester, about 50 miles southwest. They wore raincoats and carried umbrellas, because it was a cold summer day in 1944. Ginny was one of those women who forever had a program of every scheduled event for miles around, and Tim could always count on her to have a pair of free or cheap tickets (when they weren't available through the USO or its British sister agency), and they walked arm in arm. The concert was scheduled for 2 p.m., and they arrived at noon, in time to eat a leisurely lunch of fish and chips (the fish fresh from Portsmouth on the Channel). They strolled through the ancient city, enjoying the park, the museums, the medieval guild hall, High Street with its market and shops, and then of course the famous cathedral.

Winchester Cathedral had the longest nave of any medieval cathedral. It had a spectacular 12th Century Bible in the original Latin of St. Jerome's Vulgate, lavishly illustrated with gold and jewels, and representing the life's work of a band of master craftsmen. As Tim and Ginny wandered from exhibit to exhibit in the sprawling complex, there were plenty of visitors and tourists despite the war. As at St. Paul's in London, parts of the stained glass windows had been packed away for safe keeping.

As they passed through the galleries, the main organ emitted a blast of sound. Ginny gripped Tim's arm and whispered: "They're staring early. We'd better hurry." As they rushed toward the chapel where the concert was to be, they heard the piping voices of boy choristers at practice. Organ music stunned the echoing and incense-smoky space with exquisite ribbons of sound. "It's not our concert," Ginny whispered, "it's something else." As they passed another side altar, they heard the stentorian voice of a priest. Two men in bishops' miters and gold-crusted copes or cloaks stood waiting. Their white-gloved hands held gold crosiers like question marks. A crowd of well-dressed persons stood around a baptismal font, including men in military uniforms glittering with gold, a few of them with old-fashioned tricornered hats with white plumage. "Friends," said one of the bishops, attended by several priests, "we are gathered here for the solemn and joyful christening the newest child of Sir Peter and Lady Jane DeLory." He raised his arms, draped with the lacy edges of an alb or white tunic, and in his hands was a smiling baby girl exquisitely swaddled in expensive linen and lace, with pink bows in her thin blonde hair. The bishop's voice echoed among the burial stones of British gentry going back to the Middle Ages: "We are honored to celebrate with one of England's most ancient families the birth and christening of Lady Elspeth Marie Jane Beatrice Anne Victoria DeLory. Please, let the parents and siblings step forth."

A row of small children in immaculate suits paraded forth. Behind them on crutches came a slender young dark-haired army officer wearing a sword and fancy uniform; he was missing one leg but carried himself with strength and dignity on crutches. At his arm, demurely dressed in a somberly joyous mauve dress complete with pillbox hat and eye-net, was the beautiful spy briefly known as *Lef*tenant Claire Denby. Her thin, tastefully red-glossed lips, dark hair, white teeth, crisp facial features, were unmistakable, along with the humorous and self-possessed eyes. Having done her duty for God and Crown, she had earned some sort of female knighthood or damedom or something in addition to being hereditary aristocrats. She must have cracked quite a spy ring and saved many lives. Tim intuited that Dame Commander (DBE) DeLory had risked her life cracking a sophisticated German spy ring stealing vital engineering secrets from Marshmallow Hills.

Ginny tugged at Tim's sleeve. "Tim darling, you are gaping. What ever is the matter with you today?" She jokingly brought a finger up under his chin, and sardonically pressed his jaw shut.

From the replies he occasionally received, he learned that the letters were posted for him from Tining Mallow or a neighboring town. His superiors were not letting him let his family know that he was openly working in London for the Office of Naval Intelligence (O.N.I.), covertly for O.S.S.. The strategy was to sow seeds of doubt that perhaps he was really Robert Malone working under cover of the late Tim Nordhall, deceased in the sinking of H.M.S. Sturmer.

Jaguar called him to their *rendez-vouz* point on a drizzly day. As water dribbled down from the broken ogives, and wet ivy splattered in windy gusts, Jaguar huddled under his umbrella. Tim stood nearby, hunched in his poncho, with his hands in his pockets. Jaguar said: "There is a weekly courier pouch that goes from a technical section of your headquarters to a courier division across town at Home Army Division One. Starting next week, Robert Malone will start carrying that pouch."

Props to support the Malone deception arrived via a package left at his apartment door. The packet contained I.D. card, ration cards, dog tags, and other items ostensibly part of Major Robert Malone's life. Tim sat on his bed in a gray half-light, while rain dribbled outside the window, and read a brief about Malone. The guy had been quite a gambler and a ladies' man, but with some heart. Apparently he had demonstrated some tenderness toward the Belgian woman who had died with him. The gambling must have been a burden in itself, Tim thought. It felt ghostly, eerie, to carry forward a dead man's life.

Tim changed into civilian clothing at three p.m. on Thursday, and walked a quarter mile across town to a factory facility on Womble Road. There, as instructed, he signed in at a front desk as Major Robert Malone. He showed the Malone I.D. card and was ushered through a series of heavy, locked gates and down echoing semi-lit hallways to a U.S. Army secure technical facility. There, a technical sergeant had him sign a log book and handed him a canvas bag with a heavy lock built into the zipper. The sergeant seemed to feel his work was done, and he respectfully wished Major Malone a good day.

Feeling downright creepy, Tim marched with his bag, out through the gates, wished the pretty young female English petty officer a good day, and took a taxi across town. He walked through St. Dunstan's in the East, where Jaguar came the opposite way and traded him for an identical looking pouch. Jaguar walked away toward the Thames, lost in fog with his umbrella and dark suit. Tim took the bag to Home Army Divisional HQ, where a British NCO signed for it with a snappy, respectful "Thank you Sir!" and the exchange was done.

It was after 5 p.m. now, and he stopped at a pub for dinner, taking the rest of the day off. This would be his routine for the next few months. Every Thursday at 3 p.m. he would become Major Malone and deliver his courier pouch to Jaguar in the ruins of St. Dunstan's in the East. When meeting Ivor Crane's courier, Tim always privately had a feeling of suspicion, but he never had anyone to whom to voice it directly. He carried out his duties as Major Robert Malone, just as much a semi-conscious ghost of the dead man moving in a gloomy, blurry landscape, as he was an alter-ego of his own living self. The signal came, the pouch appeared, he met Jaguar, and the elusive traitor would walk briskly away in his Bowler, holding the pouch under one arm, and twirling his umbrella as if he owned London with its fog and drizzle.

📖

Tim was still very fond of Anna, and he now feared she might be more smitten with him than was good for her. They went to movies and concerts, and spent their steamy Sunday afternoons together at his apartment. Anna was warm and loving, and Tim was in that awkward limbo. The Thing in her life was out of his control, and out of her reach. He had carved new spaces for himself with other women, friends like Ginny Bell, none with the fire he'd felt for Anna. He still found Anna irresistible but could not fire the extra piston or two to fire up love with her and force the issue of Erek. She never spoke of Erek, and Tim did not ask. He felt like a caretaker lover. He was a placeholder. He knew, therefore, that she would not be the woman in his life, and the affair was slowly unraveling. Its impossibility added a frantic passion and spice that made them still hot together, but when he drove her home every Sunday evening, it was with a damaged, empty feeling. Not against her. He loved her. It was the crazy war, grinding away at the normalcy of natural things. Anna's English was exceptional, since she was of aristocratic background and educated at a finishing school. She'd returned to England after escaping from the Germans in Danzig. She'd studied nursing—she said to help the English or anyone else who needed help, so she could be of practical use in case someone, somewhere, decided to come to her nation's aid...which nobody did, Germany being the big bully across the continent, France gone, England on her knees, but Anna soldiered on. Tim couldn't tell her about his Malone side, but she quietly sensed there was more to his story than he could tell. Theirs became one of those friendships with the spark of sex but not quite the flame of love. They were deeply affectionate, and it might have flowered into love, given a chance. They enjoyed their passion as much as it served them in the loneliness of being far from home. He thought about these things over and over, always coming to the same conclusion. It was a dead end affair. Enjoy it while it lasted. He would never forget her.

"My brother had a new camera," she explained. "This roll of film contains the only pictures I have of us together."

"How precious they must be, these pictures."

"Yes," she breathed, leaning her chin on her clasped hands on her knees, and staring lovingly into the past. Tim put his arm around her, and she leaned her forehead against him with a martyred look in her eyes.

It was now six p.m. and the main iron gate was closed as the taxi let Tim out. Still wearing his naval uniform, he dashed through the small side gate. He returned a snappy salute rendered by a fatigue-clad Royal Marine standing stiffly at ease against a granite wall covered with gilded inscriptions, boots apart, toting a Bren machine pistol. He made his way through a complicated set of diversions, including sandbagged corridors full of whispers, under high ceilings, between blacked out windows, under the watchful eyes of several U.S. Marine Corps NCOs. He came to the night desk. There, a Royal Marines corporal checked his I.D. and questioned his reason for coming in.

"I normally come and go by the main entrance, Corporal. Today, I left my wallet in the office and had to double back. Anxious to get to a dinner date."

He showed his I.D. badge and the man nodded. "I understand fully, Sir. Please sign in and we'll have you right on your way."

Tim picked up a pen and started to fill in his information: name, rank, service, nationality, I.D. number, the works...as he scribbled furiously, his eye roved up a few lines, and his hand froze in mid-signature. A Major Robert Malone, U.S. Army, had signed in just twenty minutes earlier. The service I.D. was the same one as on the Malone card in Tim's pocket.

Shivers ran up and down Tim's back as he glanced at the signer's destination: the top secret map room on the third floor.

Tim stopped and stared at the corporal, a bony man with a large Adam's apple, who stared back with blue eyes that radiated a desire to be helpful.

Tim looked around. The corridors were busy, even at this hour, with night shift and round the clock signals people, mostly in Marine Corps and Army uniforms.

"Is everything all right, Sir?"

"I'm just thinking." Absently, he began to doodle over his name and signature to make them illegible without making them stand out too much. Hopefully, the impostor would not notice while signing out. Nor, hopefully, would the guard as Tim scribbled.

"Hot date, remember, Sir?" The Corporal winked.

"Yes." Tim laid the pen down. "Thanks." He calculated. It would take him about 15 minutes to get his wallet and make it back here. Dinner with Anna was out, that was for sure. He'd call her later at the restaurant. She'd have to be understanding. Maybe they could still link up later. At the moment, however, he had a mystery to solve.

As he strode down the zigzag corridors with their caged-in overhead lights casting a ghastly gleam on men and women carrying gas masks at their sides, and the occasional grunt clomping along in hobnails, Tim thought furiously. Was there a chance of some mistake? He kept coming up with *no*. Somehow, the impostor had to have shown an I.D. badge similar or identical to the one Tim was carrying.

Tim entered the locked office where he'd labored all day. He flicked on the lights and marched past empty desks to his own. With trembling fingers he unlocked the desk and took out his wallet, pocketing it. He locked the desk, turned out the lights, and let himself out. Trying to seem nonchalant— what if the impostor spotted him? What if he didn't recognize the impostor?—he strode back to the night entrance. As he signed out in the book, he noticed that "Malone" was still in the building. How to handle this?

"Corporal, I'll wait over there by the statue if you don't mind." He pointed with his chin to a beautifully carved honey and white marble of some 18ᵗʰ Century aristocrat in pigtail and breeches, waving a book in one hand and holding a thin, elegant sword erect with the other hand. The niche was in a dark corner with a window overlooking the path outside.

"Not at all, Sir. Do you need me to call you a taxi?"

"Not quite yet. I'm hoping a friend of mine will come by."

"If you need—"

"No, really, thanks!"

The man brightened. "Quite, Sir. I understand."

Tim stepped into the shadows and pretended to be looking outside, but kept the corners of his eyes on the desk. He tried to position himself so he could tell at a distance who had signed which line as individuals left.

The corporal's desk was located under a broad arch. A dim lantern glowed in the central ceiling, amber glass trapped in iron cage. Footsteps echoed as men and women came and went, each quickly and casually signing in and out.

Tim sweated. Would he miss the impostor? He craned his neck to see who was signing where. Finally, unable to stand the suspense any longer, he walked up to the desk and said: "Is there a drinking fountain?"

"Right over there, Sir," the corporal said without fuss. He had *The Times* furtively at his side.

"Right. Thanks." Tim glanced down. The impostor had not yet signed out. Tim went for a sip of lukewarm water that tasted of gravel and chlorine. He just realized how dry his mouth was. As he turned, he almost came face to face with Jaguar, who tromped along in a U.S. Army major's uniform, carrying a stiff cardboard tube. The tube was olive drab, with a cover and a strap at one end. Jaguar walked right past Tim, but apparently didn't notice him. Tim froze. He could have reached out and touched the other man's lapel without extending his arm fully.

Tim turned quickly and had another drink, watching through the corner of his eye. Jaguar signed out, exchanged a cool formal pleasantry with the corporal and a private who had arrived, and left.

Tim sauntered after him, nodding to the sentries in the sandbagged entrance.

Jaguar strode confidently along, cool as a pickle, and emerged on the broad sidewalk outside. Tim tailed him, staying just far enough back so he did not have to seem furtive.

Jaguar hailed a taxi in the front circle.

Tim hailed the next cab and had the Cockney tail the other taxi. Tim slipped him a five-dollar bill. "No questions," he said.

"No questions, Sir. Right." The driver never missed a beat, looking thoroughly bored and in control. He was a slight man, in a light blue sweater, balding early in life, and combing the dun-colored remnants of his long-ago mane over a bony skull that shone like refrigerated cheese. They cruised easily along the north bank of the river, until they came to Cheyne Walk, then Chelsea Embankment, and turned onto Albert Bridge Road. Still following the other cab, they rode down past Battersea Park and the Boating Lake. Then they crossed over toward Kennington Oval, back up Clapham Road, and finally stopped at Cleaver Street.

Jaguar got out of the cab.

Tim was a half a block back, tucked in at the curb behind a blue delivery truck. When he stood half out of the rear door, he could see past the delivery truck that a man walked up and accepted the tube. Jaguar's taxi roared off, and Tim made a quick decision. He threw a five-pound note in, thanked the cabbie, and hurried up the sidewalk.

The man carrying the tube was a slender little man in a broad-brimmed brown hat. He wore a long dark woolen overcoat and solid walking shoes. He carried an umbrella tucked under one arm and the tube under the other.

Tim followed at a discreet distance, as the man walked toward Kennington Lane in the general direction of Lambeth.

Suddenly, the man stepped into the street and hailed a black taxi, which stopped briefly. The man climbed in and slammed the door. The taxi took off in a screech of rubber. Tim had only time enough to see the white license plate with its black lettering as the taxi drove off into a gathering fog.

What now? Tim stood helplessly on a curb in the middle of a side area of London. There were shops around, several of them open. He walked into a well-lit, warm little newspaper shop and asked directions to a phone.

First, Tim called the restaurant where Anna was waiting for him. She sounded patient, if a bit disappointed. She seemed happy when he asked her to meet him later at the hotel. Then he hailed a taxi and rode it to the only place he thought he should sensibly turn right now: his Navy chain of command. Jack Stone had recently made captain, and lived with his wife and three children in a tidy little Tudor style second-floor apartment in Alderney Street. As the taxi drove him along rain-slicked streets, Tim could picture himself having a soulful conversation with his bland and friendly Navy-side boss, whose reaction, as Tim thought about it, would have to be increasingly veiled and furtive. After all, Stone gave Tim top ratings. He winked an eye shut each Thursday afternoon as Tim absented himself for Special Operations duties. Throwing himself under Stone's protection would serve to blow what was left of his own cover, Tim began to see, and he told the driver to change course. "Union Street near Blackfriars Road in Southwark," he told the driver, who nodded at the sight of an extra pound coin and swung sharply right onto a side street.

Tim stepped from the taxi, paid the man, and put his collar up. The rain had spent itself a bit, but a sharp wind drove cold stinging slivers of water against his cheeks as he hurried down several townhouses, up a flight of steps, and tried to look into a dark hallway through a door whose glass was criss-crossed with wires. Gold lettering arching over a gold bird with a scepter in its claws and a fish in its mouth on a black background advertised a victualer company called King's Point & Pelican Purveyors To The Crown. He pressed a doorbell and waited. A dim red light winked on, and he looked into a wall nook with little marble columns on either side. A small square of onyx-black plate glass reflected his face. Tim held up his service card, pressing it against the glass. The door buzzed, and he pushed inside. Letting the door shut behind him, he opened his coat and shook water from it. He stepped into a dimly lit, narrow hallway with offices on either side, and stairs leading to a second floor.

The inside was bustling—anything but a civilian supply company asleep for the night. Young women carrying cable printouts strode by, wearing U.S. Army uniforms. Soldiers and sailors with headsets ran from office to office with dispatches. Officers rushed like foot soldiers through the smoky corridors.

At the reception desk, a heavyset, older sergeant with three chevrons and one rocker, and a T between them, looked up and saw his I.D. card. "Lieutenant Commander Nordhall, Sir. What can we do for you tonight?"

"I need to see the Staff Duty Officer, M.I."

"That won't be possible, sorry."

"It's urgent."

"What about, Sir?"

"Can't tell you. I need to see the Old Man."

"You'll have to go up the chain first."

"Let's do it—fast!"

"Yessir. Please hold." The tech sergeant turned and spoke into his huge telephone switchboard. Then he said: "Down the hall, Sir. Room 101."

Tim strode down the hall, cap in hand and coat over arm. In Room 101, the duty officer, an Army lieutenant, briefly reviewed the cryptic bits of his situation that Tim could tell him. After some cajoling, Tim reached the assistant Staff Duty Officer, a major, who seemed more interested in an upcoming Saturday football game between an Army and a Navy command near Brixton. Tim and the major were approximately equal in rank, and the conversation became forceful.

"What, you want to keep secrets from me?" the major said, putting his feet up and playing with a leather football.

"It's a matter of—it's important."

A side door opened and a gray-haired colonel stuck his head out. "What's the commotion?"

The major rose and with a red angry face explained, in effect, that this Nordhall had disturbed his betting pool reveries and should be shot, although he did not express it in quite those words.

"Come in and close the door," the colonel told Tim.

Conscious of the major's venomous eyes on his back, Tim followed the colonel into a large office with plenty of bookshelves and oak furniture. The wallpaper was ghastly mustard and yellow stripes, with large bright spots where some family portraits, no doubt a century or more old, had been removed for safe keeping from Yank cigarettes and other depredations. The colonel was a slender, aging tennis player type. He strode about with his tie loose and his collar open. One hand in his pocket, he held a cigarette with the other and smoked incessantly. The room had layers of smoke that looked almost solid. "Lieutenant," the colonel said, "I'm the S.D.O. My name is Jack Haywarden. You're one of Donovan's boys, I take it?"

Tim wanted to speak, but couldn't bring himself to.

"Bill and I play poker on Friday evenings. He and I go way back. Columbia, Class of 1905." Seeing the look of mistrust on Tim's face, he dialed through to Donovan's headquarters. Moments later, the familiar voice of one of Donovan's assistant adjutants was on the line, and he assured Tim it was okay to spill the beans to Haywarden.

"You can square with me," Haywarden said, hanging up the phone.

Tim took a deep breath. "Thank you! I'm in over my head, Colonel. I think my contact has framed me. I'm not sure what's going on, but I need to tap the mat. I have no idea what's going on."

"Tell me what you feel you can."

Tim had his own metaphor. "I've been a blind, like in duck hunting."

The colonel grinned. "Long as you're not a dead duck."

"Not yet, Colonel. I supposedly hold a commission as a major in your service branch, strictly an O.S.S. creation. I'm supposedly a Major Robert Malone who was actually killed in Africa. Tonight I happened to go back to my office because I'd forgotten my wallet, and there was my opposite, posing as Major Robert Malone and walking out with a tube full of who knows what from the Top Secret Engineering Review Division."

"Did you follow him?"

"Sure did. He passed the tube off to another fellow, and I had to make a split second decision."

"You're not a seasoned operative, are you?"

"More like a piece of meat for bait, Sir."

Haywarden nodded. He picked a piece of tobacco off the tip of his tongue. "Offhand, I'd say you went for his bluff. Whatever he was carrying, it was probably in his pocket. The tube act would have been to throw off any potential followers."

Tim's heart sank. "You mean, I was had?"

"That's my guess, Nordhall. Don't worry, it happens. Who signed you up for this espionage racket?"

"Man named Crane, in the Congo, in 1942."

The phone rang and Haywarden picked up. "Yes? Yes. Yes. Yes..." After saying yes a bunch more times, he hung up. "Well, that's interesting. The license plate you gave...that particular cab made a stop near the Soviet embassy. The fare was a man with a document tube, who got out and walked toward the embassy. The driver remembers seeing a door open, and two embassy guards let him in."

The room was silent for a moment.

Haywarden said: "You've delivered another important piece of information without meaning to."

"What's that, Sir?"

"This reaffirms that we can't trust the Soviets, no matter how close an ally they may be at the moment."

Tim rose. He was tired of shadowy games.

Haywarden seemed mildly nonplused. "Are you going somewhere?"

"Sorry. Effective right now, I'm resigning from my position as Major Robert Malone, since I've become redundant. If you'll excuse me, I have a dinner date waiting."

📖

Bleary as he felt, he let Donovan's people talk him into assisting them yet a short while longer in their spy craft. "Follow-through!" they heartily called it, and Tim could see the sense in it. A few days later, as expected, Jaguar did not show up at their assignation. Tim walked slowly through the ruins of St. Dunstan-in-the-East and then down toward Tower Bridge.

A call from Haywarden the next day confirmed: Keep delivering the Thursday pouch, even if Jaguar doesn't show up, but otherwise sit tight. It was important to signal Stalin's boys the Allies were dumber than their actual capabilities.

Early the following week, late one morning, a yeoman dropped off a little note. Tim was to call the number circled in purple pencil. He went to a secure phone and returned the call. It was Haywarden. "Nordhall, can't discuss details just now. Stop by on Thursday. Good work."

Tim met Haywarden as ordered at a pub in East London, but it wasn't Haywarden doing the talking today. They sat in a back room that was sealed off. Two radios played simultaneously at an otherwise dark and shuttered bar—one, the BBC symphony orchestra laying down cover in the form of Mozart's Symphony No. 42, the other a football game between Leeds and Manchester with over 50,000 fans screaming themselves hoarse. This was during closed hours, and they couldn't order beer, but they were served a decent meal of bangers and mash with hot tea.

With Haywarden were two other high officials. One introduced himself as Allen Dulles, working out of Bern in Switzerland. The other was a younger man who was his assistant. Tim and his three companions were all in unassuming civilian clothes, including hats and overcoats soaked with rain. It was what one called a working lunch. "I wanted to meet you," Dulles said, beaming. "Heard about your exploits and wanted to shake your hand."

"I'm quite honored," Tim said softly and guardedly as he shook the men's hands. "I feel like it didn't go so well the other day."

While water dribbled down the picture window at his side—shade half drawn, window embellished with painted pub name—Dulles ate fastidiously holding his knife and fork in the European manner. He spoke softly, in an aristocratic version of an upstate New York twang that seemed heavily tinged with a variety of subtle accentual shadings from his many years of service across Europe and the Middle East. "Good of you to meet with us on such short notice, Nordhall."

"My pleasure," Tim said.

"I understand your reasons for wanting to leave our service," Dulles said. "The last thing we want is an unhappy trooper on board. However, I hope I can prevail upon you to think about something."

"I'll think about anything you prevail upon, Sir," Tim said carefully. Dulles conveyed an air of such stratospheric importance, sophistication, and competence that it was hard not to think about whatever he said. Though nothing was said, Tim suspected Dulles probably held at least brigadier general rank. In any case, he handled himself like a very senior flag officer.

"Simply," Dulles said, dabbing at his lips with the corner of a linen napkin, "we seem to have lost your handler. You knew him as Jaguar, I believe." Dulles had matter-of-fact, lordly attitude.

"Yes, that's right."

Dulles quaffed at his beer and sighed, wiping foam from his mustache with the back of his hand. "If we take it on face value, always a dangerous thing to do, but we have no choice at the moment—that our Jaguar is a double agent, then most likely he is working for our Soviet allies. A less likely scenario is that he was working for our enemies over in Germany. We have been able to determine that he made alcohol prints of some maps, and those are what went out in the tube. We know that at least one of the maps was of a German physics research site near Joachimsthal, so it looks increasingly dubious that he is working for the Germans. The fact that he entered the Soviet embassy would seem to clinch it."

"I'm not done then?" Tim asked.

"Commander, the Soviets are of course our rightful allies, and we understand how desperately they grab whatever they can. At the same time, there are some things we simply cannot afford to give away to anyone. We must guard our intimate secrets at all costs. I am here personally today to beg you—please keep a hand in the game a while longer."

Tim finished eating and pushed his plate away. He sat back, and with his napkin stifled a belch. Reluctantly, he nodded. "Of course, Mr. Dulles, if you feel it is in the national interest."

"I do feel that, or I would not presume to ask."

"Very well then."

"Thank you, young man." Dulles looked visibly relieved.

"All I ask is that you keep me from being framed again."

"I assure you," Dulles said, "I will personally review your records and see that you are duly promoted, decorated, and whatever else is due to you."

"That's all I ask," Tim said.

"Good. Here's what I'd like you to do. We're going to suspend the courier runs. We want to send a vague signal that you are in fact somehow no longer in our trust. You won't take this personally, of course."

"Oh no," Tim said, "I'm getting used to it."

The other men laughed.

Just then, Ivor Crane apologetically rushed in and apologized for being late.

Dulles nodded to Tim, grinning. "Good sense of humor. I like that. Nordhall, you are in our dearest favor, never mistake it. You are going to be a sleeper, after a fashion. You go right on doing what you are doing, but we are going to transfer you to the West Coast of the U.S.A. early next year. With the invasion of Germany under way, it looks as if it's only a matter of time until they break. Meanwhile we'll want to focus on the Pacific war, and we'll be shifting people in that direction. Until then, I want you to remain aware of the Malone persona but stop going to that church to meet Jaguar. That's all finished. He's gone back to his people, whoever they are. If he's a Kraut, he'll turn up in Germany. If he's a Soviet, we'll never see him again—except maybe in the U.S., come to think of it."

"Sounds like something I can handle."

"We'll check in with you about once a month or so," Crane said as he ordered tea and tapped water from his bowler and umbrella. "Nothing to it, Nordhall. Oh, and I'm authorized to inform you that you'll be receiving a number of decorations when you depart command, with false citations, but you'll know it's in regard to the *H.M.S. Sturmer* sinking, including the Navy Cross, the Purple Heart, a Navy Commendation Medal, and several British decorations. The citations can perhaps be updated in a few years to show your uncommon what not and so forth."

"What he means," Dulles said, "is that we won't tip our hand too much. We want to leave that faint scent in the air, as if we're not entirely certain what to do with you, when in fact we love you dearly and recognize Uncle Joe has kicked us in the nuts. We just don't want the Commies to see our pain."

"Understood, Sir," Tim said with a grin.

"Don't call us, we'll call you," one of the men joked.

"It's a pleasant way to ease you out," Haywarden said with a happy, toothy grin. "You're good on the technical analysis side, and we'll get you a plum job in San Francisco. I believe your friend Stan Kehoe is already on his way there."

"Yes, he is." Tim felt jazzed. He was ready for a major change in his life. He was contemplating the departure of Anna Stokowska, and it hurt. She was the best woman friend he'd ever had, and he'd had many women. If one had to get married, it should be to Anna or someone like her, if such a woman existed.

"I did ask to be transferred," she admitted as they stood on the sand, looking out at the sea and holding hands.

He squeezed her hand. "I understand. Any word?"

"Erek is alive in a prison near Warsaw for interned Polish officers."

"Hopefully he will be safe for you."

"Thank you, Tim."

He put his arm around her waist, and she laid her head on his shoulder. He had just let her go, and she had thanked him. It was over. They walked slowly to the car together.

"You come and visit us in Warsaw after the war, yes? My family live in Praga, which is an elegant area. I miss home very much."

"Sure," he told her as he gallantly helped her into the car, "and I will bring you home to New Haven." Even as he said it, he knew that these were all just words now. None of it would ever happen. He thought of his hometown—the little city would ever be big enough for him anymore, with its old brick university buildings and quietly rainy green streets in spring, hot and muggy in the summer, snowy in winter, radiant as an umber lantern in fall. There had to be something more for him, but he had no idea yet what that might be.

📖

V-1 buzz bombs hit London within days, starting June 12, and killed thousands. For the first time since the Blitz and the Battle of Britain years earlier, sirens sounded regularly across London. The V stood for Vergeltung, Revenge, for the horrific firebombing of German cities, which was in turn a result of Goering and Hitler's vicious assaults during the Battle of Britain and so many other atrocities. The V-1 carried a one-ton warhead and was powered by a pulsejet motor. It cruised at 350mph at 4,000 ft with a range of 150 miles (240km). It was a small plane 25 feet long with a 20-foot wingspan. Germany launched over 9,500 V-1's against England in late 1944, causing over a million people to flee London in panic, though most residents showed great bravery and stayed put in their homes and jobs. Half of the buzz bombs were destroyed by anti-aircraft fire or by RAF fighters including the new Gloster Meteor turbojet fighter. Some 6,184 people were killed in the attacks. By late 1944, fewer and fewer of the buzz bombs were getting through to their targets.

Tim's room had a skylight overlooking a little rampart. At one lucky moment—or unlucky, depending on one's point of view—he lay on his bed resting, glanced out, the window, and saw a buzz bomb or V-1 go cruising by. This diabolical German invention was a kind of super bomb or unmanned aircraft that came sailing in with a loud buzzing noise. Often the RAF sent up a Spit or two to knock one down. The scary part, the thing people stopped and listened to with bated breath, was the silence. When the V-1 was ready to do its dirty work, its engine would cut out. The V-1 would come buzzing in like a hornet, sputter once or twice, and go silent. Then it would heel over and drop like a stone, and seconds later one would hear a loud explosion. Sometimes it would land in a field and kill a sheep or two;

at other times it would destroy some thousand year old church with lovely stained glass windows that might have survived the great fire of 1666.

It was all part of wartime life in London. American GIs crowded the streets and defined the new nightlife. British girls, like their American counterparts, made do with scarcity and painted mascara lines down the middle of the backs of their legs to fake the seams of good silk or nylon stockings. People made new clothing out of old. A smart new Eisenhower jacket on a pretty woman might be grandpa's moth-eaten army blanket from the ironically named War To End All Wars. Here and there, one saw an automobile whose front half had been sawed off, to be replaced by a horse in harness as if the centuries were rolling backwards.

On July 21, the Democrats announced that FDR would seek an unprecedented fourth term, with Harry S. Truman as his running mate.

In the Pacific, the Japanese continued opposing U.S. advances. On Europe's Eastern Front, the Soviets were advancing broadly across the Ukraine and into Poland, bombing Warsaw. Hitler razed Warsaw to the ground, but the Russians took the city. Tim imagined poor Erek shifting from Nazi hands to Soviet hands, and thought about what that might mean for Anna in so many different ways.

To further indicate the shaky position of Hitler, a bomb plot by some of his top generals just barely failed on July 20th. The Allies were beginning to plan for the world after the war. At Bretton Woods in New Hampshire, representatives of 44 nations met to hammer out future world monetary policy, establishing the International Monetary Fund (IMF) and creating agencies for reconstruction. On August 25, General Charles deGaulle marched into Paris at the head of a Free French Army, signaling the effective liberation of France. Right behind him were many Allied units, including elements of a special O.S.S. team scouting out German atomic bomb sites, with an eye toward measuring Nazi progress toward the ultimate weapon of mass destruction.

In September, the first U.S. forces pushed into western Germany. By late 1944, the V-1's had ceased to buzz across the sky and drop silently. Instead, a devastating new weapon started dropping silently from the edge of space. Sometimes there was a whistle or a contrail, but most often nothing because the V-2 rockets reached the outer limits of the atmosphere and dropped back in at enormous speeds. Like the V-1, it carried a one-ton warhead. Where the V-1 had essentially been an unmanned bomber whose engine would sputter out so it dropped and exploded, the V-2 was an actual rocket that shot to the edge of space, and arced down to strike its target. Hundreds of V-2s were reaching England by the time Tim boarded a B-29 for a new posting in San Francisco. The dreaded new V-2 rockets were causing new panic and thousands more deaths. The Royal Air Force had been able to intercept and shoot down some V-1s, but the V-2 came in too high and too fast to be visible. For a moment, Allied commanders feared there could be atomic warheads coming across the Channel atop those V-2s. But the V-2s were simply faster, higher carriers of the same high explosives payload as the V-1. The new rockets would kill 7,000 souls in Britain, ironically for some 5,200 V-2s launched, and 20,000 slave laborers would die at the secret Peenemünde plant making the rockets.

In October, MacArthur liberated the Philippines, clearly signaling that Japanese power was on the wane.

Also in October, the Soviets entered the eastern German province of Prussia, home of the modern Germanic military heritage of the Junkers and the Kaisers.

At Christmas, when the Allies thought they had it wrapped up, Hitler threw forth a tremendous offensive in the Ardennes, the Battle of the Bulge. For several weeks, Eisenhower's forces were shaken, until they destroyed the German counter-attack and punched back into Germany with renewed fury under the leadership of men like Patton.

Meanwhile, at Yalta in the Crimea, representatives of four great nations met to plan how the world would be divided after the war. An ailing FDR, a struggling Churchill who was about to be thrown out of office by thankless voters in Britain, an ineffectual and corrupt Chinese warlord named Chiang Kai Shek, and a wily Joseph Stalin sat down together. It was one of those moments of history when, as with the almost casual British division of the Near East after World War I, a few pencil marks on a map, or an offhand dinnertime phone call, would spell the division of millions of people, the lives and deaths of future generations in the resulting civil wars, and the fate of the world.

📖

Ivor Crane returned the salute and stared for a moment, then brightened. "Tim Nordhall! Well, I'll be. Looking good—I didn't expect to see you again."

They shook hands, and Tim said: "What a surprise."

Crane grinned. "You're telling me. I was just over here to drop off some paperwork. They have me working over at a British location." He rolled his eyes up in the general direction of the upriver skyline some blocks away inland. He put a fingertip on his lips. "You know how it is."

Tim nodded. Half the people in London were on secret business, so why not Crane? "Quickly therefore changing the subject, are you in town for long?"

"I'll be moving to the Pentagon soon if this war ever ends." He held up his arm, with the raincoat half draped over his prosthesis. "Time to chew grass in the back forty." Both laughed. "Look, Nordhall, can I buy you a drink?"

"I'd be delighted, Sir." Tim felt genuinely flattered, though puzzled.

"Great! In the City then, some bangers and mash with a stout to wash it down." An olive drab Ford with Colonel pennants rolled around. They got in and Crane said: "You're looking mighty fit." A young black sergeant drove, expertly and fluidly navigating the heavy traffic.

"Thanks. I've been walking a lot. Seeing the sights."

"Women?"

"Oh, a few. London is filled with pretty girls." He didn't mention his loss of Anna, and the dearth of really interesting women since. If you could call losing someone you never had a loss. He had written to her twice, and received a brief, vague post card from her from a vacation trip on Capri. It was signed simply A.S., without any emotional close.

Leave typewriter empty. Rise and walk away. Audience too stunned to applaud. In the silence, close door as you leave. Finished.

"It sure is," Crane said sitting back comfortably in the plush interior. Crane had the driver leave them near Piccadilly Circus and told him to return in an hour. Tim took his former boss to a pub he liked on Friday Street, off Cannon, near the badly bombed out Wren church of St. Christopher Cole. As they climbed over rubble and wound through home defense barricades, Crane commented: "Seems like a million years ago that we were in Africa. Did you ever actually meet Malone, that poor fellow who wound up in Mauritania with a knife in his back?"

Tim shook his head. "Not in this life. It was pure coincidence that the German fellow and I stumbled on him and his girlfriend."

"Oh yes, the Belgian woman. Régine Clery. Poor thing. Your luck was with you throughout that African ordeal, from *H.M.S. Sturmer* forward."

"Yessir."

"I never did bother reading the whole crime report. Must have been a ghastly scene." They sat in a smoky Victorian pub with its clutter and mirrors and hard wooden benches. The first ale tasted good, and a rather heavy but hearty smell of fried fish and potatoes filled the air. Tim agreed things had turned out reasonably well. They lifted their mugs and clicked them together in a toast so flecks of foam spattered on the tabletop. "Here's to your continued success, my friend," Crane said warmly.

"Good luck to you too, Sir."

Tim dashed off a reply to her, just as he received a visit from his boss, U.S. Navy Captain Jack Stone. "Tim, my lad! The war's winding down, and we are going back to the States! Are you ready? Pack your belongings and be ready in two days. I have billets for us on board a B-29 on military orders. We'll fly by way of Paris. Two weeks TDY with SHAEF, just strolling around, and then you're being reassigned to San Francisco. You get to take a month off in New Haven along the way."

A last postcard finally arrived from Anna Stokowska, who had been promoted to Major in the Nurse Corps of the Polish Army, and was now stationed at a British Army rear casualty hospital in Athens. She wrote to wish him well—she had fallen in love, and was about to marry a Greek industrialist. Tim sat and stared at the postcard for a long while—wondering about Erek, about himself—and then filed it away with his private papers. They were finished for good, then. He would move on, feeling rather empty and crushed. *We get over things like this*, he thought, *she's only one woman.* He called some male friends to see who was up for getting drunk with Guinness Stout on a walking ramble through the City.

Canterbury, 1991: The Haywardens Remember

Marianne sat at the lunch counter in Canterbury with the Haywardens and had a last cup of tea. Outside, the weather turned blustery. A mix of rain and wind peppered the broad store windows. Dim grayish light filled the interior, making the trundling shoppers and the colorful little neon displays all the more wan looking.

"Was there a Major Malone, or was it an impostor playing multiple roles?" Marianne asked.

Haywarden looked at her with a mix of sheepishness and belated insight, while his wife patted his hand and leaned against his shoulder as though they were reminiscing about some long-ago bobbysocks dance at a high school. "Western powers are just beginning to get access some of the old NKGB records. It will take years to sort it all out—half a century or more of Soviet espionage—if we ever manage to shed light in all the little nooks and crannies. I do have a contact for you, a man in Moscow who worked for the NKGB back during the war and later the KGB. His name is Viktor Mutsev, and I have a feeling he is the fellow we knew as Jaguar before he defected. Or rather, a triple agent who returned to his own people after his mission became too hot to continue." Jack Haywarden slipped a piece of paper across the counter with a name, address, and number written in willowy ballpoint letters. "Try this," he said softly. "Mutsev may be your man. You may find him in Moscow, if he is still alive."

"He would know of my father?"

Haywarden said: "If your father is still alive somewhere. You have to understand that he became a hunted man after 1945. Being hunted by Stalin and his minions was no trivial matter, not even within the United States."

"But my father had help?" Tears blurred her vision.

"Yes. That much I can tell you," Haywarden said. "Your father was—is, if he is still alive somewhere—a fine man. He was young, searching for his place in life, well-intentioned, a good engineer (that's all that clock-making, and who should know better than the New Englanders?). He was quiet and unassuming, sort of an iceberg if you see what I mean, but he was a deep searcher. His courage was exemplary, as proven in Africa." Haywarden paused to choke back his own emotions a bit. "He was an accidental spy. Really more of a solid technical intelligence officer who liked to study machinery and blue prints. He found a few useful tidbits that helped the war effort, but his major contribution was in this Jaguar matter."

"During which he met my mother?" she asked.

"Oh yes. She was a stunning woman, both for her courage and her loyalty, as well as her brash…well, almost craziness the way she threw herself recklessly...but then again, she must have felt she had no choice, playing one side against the other. That's what OSS learned to do professionally, and here were these amateurs, these accidental players, going head to head with the Nazis, the Soviets, the Americans...it was quite breathtaking. Your father was one of those national heroes we never hear about, or think about. For every force pursuing him after the war, there was an equal and opposite force out to protect him."

Mrs. Haywarden added in the bemused tone, of a spy master's wife, who had seen much in her day: "And his women."

Part Three: San Francisco, March-April 1945

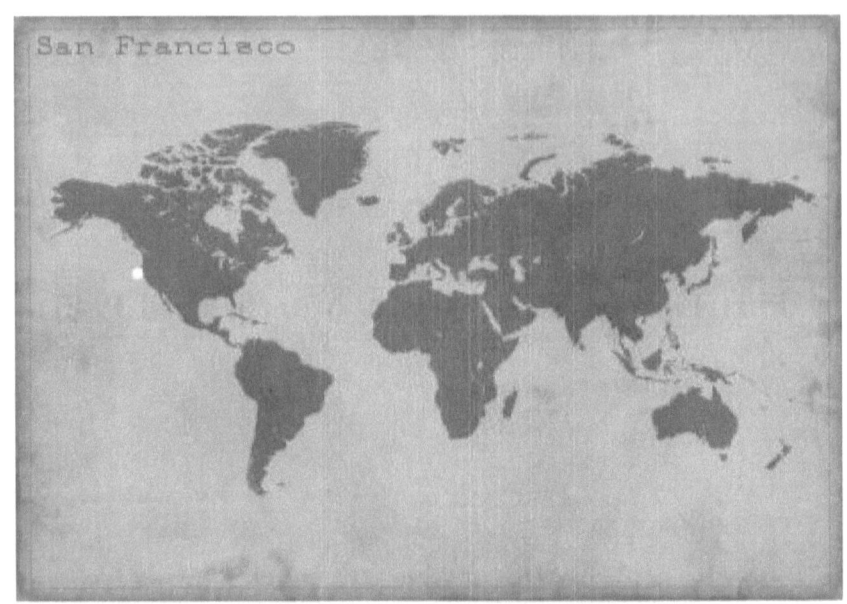

San Francisco

Tim's Arrival: San Francisco

On a rainy evening, in a time when gas rationing still kept most cars off the streets of San Francisco, a lone trolley car rumbled along Clement Street in the Presidio. Tim Nordhall was glad to be back in the U.S.A., and looked forward to exploring the West Coast for the first time. Already, he had a whiff of San Francisco's unique flavoring, as different from anything he'd known as London was from Katanga or New Haven—an exotic cocktail of Asian and European cultures at times garish, at other times subdued, thriving day and night. It might mean a Japanese fish market or an alley right out of Canton, an Italian spaghetti restaurant or a Oaxaca taco shop, an Alabama Negro gospel hall or an all-White Southern-style boarding school, a Zen meditation center or an Episcopalian church perched on hills ages ago inhabited by Shellmound Ohlone. Overlaying it all was a comfortable American feeling of home, complete with neon, jazz, Sinatra, bobbysocks, and lots of cars.

Tim had arrived just that afternoon on the train from back East, and now the city seemed to slumber. In the stillness, shreds of fog drifted among glistening sidewalks and shuttered buildings. Fog horns whispered in from ships far out at sea on the Pacific Ocean. Smoky clouds winked as they fled past a full lemon-pie moon, which, had it been outfitted with clock hands, might have shown a jazzy and exotic Pacific Time.

The world was at war, but just now all the warriors seemed to be asleep behind blacked-out windows in the sprawling Presidio military complex. Like a mobile island of sanity and reassurance, the White Front trolley of the Market Street Line hummed along Route 31 on a journey that brought its passengers west across the peninsula from the *Embarcadero* on the east docks. Behind thick shades drawn for safety from possible air attack, the car was dimly lit inside. Sitting at his controls behind the front window was a white-haired man in rumpled conductor's uniform.

The loud hum, metal on metal, dissipated like a bow wake on all sides into the shadows of large Canary Island date palms and inky lawns among darkened official buildings. Five young soldiers in khaki Class B uniform sat smoking near the front. They smelled heavily of beer consumed in the Barbary Coast nightlife district. Cigarette smoke drifted thickly in the yellowish, almost orange light under colored print ads for such patriotic American commodities as Lucky Strike cigarettes with their green circle package, Wrigley's Chewing Gum, and Maxwell House Coffee.

Seated alone in the back was a handsome, dark-haired Navy officer of 30 with a sea bag on the floor under his polished black shoes: Tim Nordhall. His white saucer cap lay on the seat beside him. He hunched in his night-blue knee-length coat betraying the fatigue and beard shadow of a man who had traveled far and alone.

Letting the muted noises of the trolley and his fellow passengers fade into an aching haze, Tim rested his head to one side against the cold window and dozed. In his fragmented dreams, he thought of himself as a tiny dot on a vast landscape of war. Up came distant flashes of his ship being torpedoed and sunk in the South Atlantic, then more flashes as London succumbed to V-1 and V-2 bombings. He'd spent a few heady days in Paris and Versailles as a tourist, then flown back to CONUS via Reykjavik, Greenland, Gander, and Westover; then had a week's nostalgic leave with family in New Haven, Connecticut. He could still see his sisters' faces—warm, cheering, wistful in the ache of his departure. Then came the long journey behind a chuffing coal locomotive across the vastness of the U.S.A. as one of myriad warriors being pulled toward the still-raging war with Japan. All this, in a blender of image fragments and emotional puzzle chips, until he jerked awake as the trolley stopped.

The trolley's hum deepened an octave or two and grew silent as the car stopped before a row of partially lit enlisted barracks from which emanated the click of pool balls, the echoes of dozens of shouted conversation fragments, and a steady swing beat from a radio turned up loud on a window sill. The young men and the NCO got off in a drumbeat of shoe leather. The trolley ground on several more blocks before its next stop. "Visiting Officer Quarters," the driver intoned tiredly with a glance over his shoulder. "VOQ."

Tim heaved himself erect in a powerful motion, gripping the shining steel handle atop the seat before him. He slipped the cap onto his head with the bill riding low over his dark eyes. Grabbing the sea bag off the floor, he strode down the wood slat floor, nodded to the driver, and stepped out onto the sidewalk. A wood sign in black lettering on white background stood in the grass, advertising the Visiting and Bachelor Officer Quarters (V/BOQ).

As the trolley hummed away on its last few blocks before turning around, Tim adjusted his white scarf and tucked it securely under his lapel collars.

Two Shore Patrol enlisted men in white puttees, white helmets, and white belts over dark blue Class A uniforms strode lazily toward him. Their helmets and white armbands bore, in large lettering, the legend *SP*, for Shore Patrol. They walked almost in step, looking bored but alert. Their nightsticks swung ominously on each man's left hip and their holstered, lanyarded pistols looked huge on the right hip. They saluted.

Tim returned their salutes. "You fellows got the time?"

"Yessir," said the older, a grizzled looking petty officer, snapping his wrist up under his chin to look at a silvery watch. "2230 hours, Sir."

Tim nodded. "Thanks." He put his collar up against the damp night wind that smelled of grass and kelp and the sea. Distant lights winked on and off, blood-red, on the towering, cloud-shrouded concrete piers of the Golden Gate Bridge.

"You doing okay, Sir?" said the petty officer with some concern.

"Oh yes," Tim said. "Just catching a few breaths of night air before I go in to sleep."

The two men fumbled in their pockets and produced cigarettes. They offered, but the officer shook his head. A lighter clicked, casting up a weak orange light that flickered on the men's cavernous cheeks and veiled eyes. For a moment they were all one with the world and the war, and the petty officer nodded as though someone had said something. The clouds loomed up over the screaming moon as if Japanese bombers were about to pour out by the thousands any minute, like in those war propaganda cartoons, obliterating men and ships and buildings. That was how people lived these days. The memory of Pearl Harbor was acute, painful, and scary. No telling when an innocent evening with parlor lights could turn into an inferno under a wave of enemy bombers. It wasn't clear if the Fascists really did have Fortress Germany and Fortress Japan. The nuts were on the run these days, but everyone assume they'd have to be cracked on their home turf.

As Tim spoke with the sailors, men crossed paths in the night without speaking, nodded at each other's secrets without asking any questions, and passed on just as quietly to their separate fates. Everyone figured there would be a day, someday, in the dark and dangerous and looming future nobody could read, when there would be peace again. It was the same helpless patience that had seen people through the Depression a decade earlier, when poverty and starvation had endlessly danced with fear and despair. If nothing else, this was an enemy you could shoot at. Then again, it was an enemy who had shot first and would be happy to shoot back. And the scariest part was that one could not imagine what new horrible weapons the enemy was about to throw at the free and democratic world. The two

SPs drifted on down the quiet, glittering sidewalk under a weak street light kept as dim as possible.

Tim picked up his sea bag and walked into the building. He stepped up to the grill of the reception desk, where an Army sergeant sat by a galvanized-steel olive-drab saucer lamp as Charge of Quarters. "Evening, Sir. Signing in?"

"Yep. Here are my orders." Tim took a thin sheaf of folded papers from an inside breast pocket and smoothed them over the battered wooden counter. The place smelled of laundry soap, the cheap paper used in religious tracts strewn on the tables in the waiting area, and stale cigarette ashes in overflowing old coffee cans on the linoleum floors.

"Lieutenant Commander Timothy Nordhall," the sergeant said, savoring the name as he read it to himself full of speculation. "Will you be staying with us long?"

Tim sighed and made a face. "Is there a good hotel nearby anywhere?"

The sergeant grinned, showing a gold tooth. "It's San Francisco, Sir. They have anything you need here, from the Top of the Mark on down. All you need is the cash." The sergeant rose and lightly tossed up and down a key on his palm. He was a squat little man needing a shave. As he bent to open the steel linen locker, he said: "Looks like you came a long way, Sir."

Tim was too tired for small talk, and did not answer. The sergeant carefully—as if linen were his career—laid sheets, a blanket, a pillowcase, and a tiny blue-white pinstriped pillow on the counter. He smoothed the linens with a gnarled hand as he spoke. "Need you to sign in and leave one copy of your orders, Sir."

Tim produced a fountain pen and signed the logbook.

"Oh, I just realized—this came for you." The sergeant produced an official looking Kraft envelope with War Department seal and a bunch of administrative hieroglyphics in the upper left corner. It was addressed to Lt. Cdr. Nordhall.

Tim took out a small pocketknife and slit open the envelope. Inside was a letter on official stationery, signed by the executive officer of his new station. They'd known each other while serving at Admiralty Headquarters near St. James's Park in London. Scrawled under the signature block was a note in pencil: "Call me right away—Stan" followed by a phone number and a wild zigzag.

"Got a phone?"

"There is a booth in the corner," the sergeant said.

"Thanks." He dialed Stan Kehoe's number and waited while it rang on the other end. Tim stepped into the wooden booth and closed the windowed door behind him. The booth inside smelled of old phone books, of ashes and gum and stale coffee. An endless procession of uncaring callers had dropped their cigarettes or gum on the floor while speaking, and forgot half-empty coffee cups.

Stan Kehoe, his former roommate in London, now stationed in San Francisco at the same command where Tim was to work, answered with a muffled voice that sounded as if he'd had a few drinks too many. "Hey, good to hear from you. I was afraid my note wouldn't get to you in time."

"Thanks. Are you sending someone to rescue me from this flea hotel?"

Stan laughed. "There's a duty driver at the Coast Guard barracks up the road. He'll drive you to a spot we reserved for you. I pulled some strings."

"I'm in your debt, old pal. I hope it's good."

"The best, my friend. Wait till you see the place."

"I can't wait. Tomorrow at work, eh?"

"See you." Tim stepped from the booth, unbuttoning his coat and loosening his tie. "Sarge, call the Coast Guard duty car for me, will you?"

Fifteen minutes later, Tim sat in the back of a grayish panel truck with military numbers stenciled on the doors along with the legend U.S.C.G. The driver, a lanky young Japanese-American yeoman, with a cigarette over one ear and a pencil over the other, drove as if the truck were on fire. "Nob Hill, Sir. Nice address." He grinned.

"Let's get there alive," Tim growled, holding on to the door handle.

The young Coast Guardsman slammed the stick shift from gear to gear, and swung the big wheel in wide turns as the car sizzled on slick roads, around turns, ever uphill. Fog lay wrapped around the empty houses in Japantown, whose denizens had been taken away to some snowy freezing hell on the Prairies. Neon signs gleamed in their reflections on the sidewalks as the truck labored up the grade on California Street. Here and there, men and women spirited past in the night from doorway to doorway, standing on corners talking under their umbrellas, or catching a cab, or stepping in twos into one of the many cozy looking little bars for a little relief from the rationing. Everything was in short supply—metals, meat, fat, rubber, flour, anything one could think of. If you had the cash and needed x, there was a thriving black market operator who either had x or knew where to get x, always just around the corner or down in a basement or pool hall nearby, in return for cash or y, whatever y might be—silk stockings, coffee, whiskey, gasoline, anything.

They drove past neo-Gothic Grace Cathedral, whose spectacular windows were blacked out. The city was pleasant and cosmopolitan, even in wartime with its minimal lighting. It was a great place for walking, congregating, conversing—if one had time. The car passed Huntington Park with its trees and fountain. They crawled along ever-narrower streets, around corners, and came to a quiet, tree-lined back street. "Here you are," the driver said. Tim thanked him and got out, hefting the sea bag onto the sidewalk. The truck sped off.

It was nearly midnight now, and the street was quiet. A strange, lovely magic descended that Tim would remember always, recalling a special time that was about to unfold in his life. It would be a short but wonderful, if dangerous and crazy little block of time, like all things topsy-turvy in a world war. It seemed the laws of logic and convention were suspended. It was okay for a stranger in uniform to be dropped off at an unknown address in the dark of night, carrying only a satchel and a scrap of paper with an address scrawled in pencil.

The houses were decorous old wooden Victorians, with high, narrow fronts that reminded Tim of places in London, though those were stone. Same wrought iron fences, ornate trim, and warmly glowing, barely blacked out windows. These were the few that had survived the terrible 1906 quake.

Just as was so typical in London, a rain squall broke loose. Cool, fresh, silvery raindrops dropped at an angle, shattered on the sidewalk, and bounced up. Tim pushed up his collar and pinched it together over his chin. Gathering up his bag with his free hand, he walked down the sidewalk until he spotted the white on blue enamel number sign, 56 that signaled his new residence. His hair was plastered down, and water ran freely down his face so that when he sputtered his lips, spray flew. He huddled in a rounded doorway and knocked on the door. Sheltered from the worst of the rain, but chilled by a wind that blew up from below and whipped trees and his coat tails about, he waited by the door. After several knocks, he heard movement somewhere back in the house. A dim light snapped on. A voice muttered, and slippers shuffled on wood floors and carpeting.

"—is it?" an elderly man's voice called out, query truncated.

"Tim Nordhall, USN."

A latch snapped, and an elderly, balding Asian man in a nightshirt peered out. After a solid glance, a chain rattled and the door swung open. The man took Tim's bag, towed him inside, and closed the door.

📖

He was young, and jaunty, with a nice collection of ribbons, and he attracted his share of attention from passing women. A lot of those were in uniform themselves, particularly the nurses from Letterman Army Hospital and other duty stations overflowing with distaff military. San Francisco had a reputation as the Paris of the West, a City of Love. He felt more comfortable in his own country with its more generous living space, soap, baths, all the little extras of life that had been missing in Europe and nonexistent in Africa. Whistling, he carried his personnel folder and medical records around to various sun drenched, whitewashed offices set on well-sprinkled green lawns. He sent a telegram home to New Haven, announcing that he'd arrived in good shape.

His duty station was at the Presidio in a two-story stucco building that itself was an annex to the rambling Navy Quartermaster Corps facilities all around the Bay area. He had a small office overlooking a sunless courtyard. One of the many cute young enlisted women who did administrative tasks like typing and filing told him, while chewing gum and patting her brown hair, that the sun did penetrate down to the second floor during the mornings on clear days, but generally she was always happy to get out. He thanked her, getting his own coffee rather than asking her to do, it, and began the process of settling in.

He met his immediate supervisor, Captain Martin Teague, in a large office with a round conference table overlooking a sunny, breezy intersection below. Teague was a tall, white-mustached man with a dignified mien and a somewhat sardonic, dry sense of humor. Sitting in was Lt. Cdr. Stan Kehoe, Tim's friend—a freckled, sandy-haired young man, athletic and brash.

"I hear you went for a swim in the North Atlantic," Martin Teague said without making light of the tragedy. He had been fed a half-true story. Nobody would know the truth about *H.M.S. Sturmer* for years, to prevent the Nazis from knowing how superior their submarine technology had been at that moment, in that place. Stan Kehoe as usual was forward. He'd say just one thing too many, or say not quite the right thing considering the company, but he was so good-natured that most people overlooked his eager quality. He usually had his tie slightly loose, as if he needed air while he bounced about in his seat and gesticulated as he spoke. "Yeah, Tim and I hit all the hot spots around London. I'll vouch for him."

"Glad to hear it," Teague said quietly, raising both hands over Tim's personnel field file as if in blessing. "Everything in here looks first rate. I feel very lucky that we have a good solid staff officer on board, and I'm sure Admiral Lemney will feel the same way as he gets to know of you from our weekly briefings."

Hiram L. Lemney was the two star flag officer in charge of Procurement 5549, which specialized in turning specific small captured exotic enemy weapons over to the maw of the vast U.S. industrial machine, and receiving back production versions that could be shot back at the enemy.

Later that evening, sitting over a red checkered tablecloth in a smoky bar in the commercial district of Union Square, Tim and Stan reviewed the day's meeting. "Teague likes you. I can tell."

"Glad to hear it." Tim had begun thinking about home.

"You'll do just fine. Say, I thought you were going to be the life of the party. You look a little under the weather."

"Still a little bushed from the long trip." Tim sat back in the corner and propped one leg up on the dark red plastic bench. "That meeting today got me thinking about clocks."

Stan laughed, sucking ice from his empty glass and letting the cubes tinkle back in while his gaze roved after young women in military hats parading by outside on the neon-lit avenue. "Clocks? You feeling okay?"

Tim shrugged, pushing an ice cube around so it left soggy little trails in the table cloth amid the bread crumbs from the Italian sandwiches they had just eaten. "I begin to wonder, you know. Do I really want to go back to Connecticut and design escapements in a little town. You know, marry the girl next door, have children, live out the whole conventional life style."

"Hmmm. Do you miss London?"

"A bit. Not the plumbing."

Stan laughed. "I know what you mean. And not the buzz bombs."

"I'm sure they won't have those after the war."

"And the V-2s."

"Not since the Germans surrendered."

Stan waved to a pair of young women who waved back. They were Army nurses in Class B uniforms. They'd traded their starched caps for rakish khaki garrison caps, but still wore their dark green sweaters. They carried their regulation leather purses as well as hat bags with them, and wore their *caduceus* brass on their rounded blouse lapels. Lieutenants fresh out of some nearby state college, it turned out. Before long, Tim and Stan were having beers with Lorraine and Susie and getting more and more tight. They did a lot of laughing and shoulder-hugging, told a lot of off-color jokes, and rolled from one bar to the next while the air smelled of drizzle and smoke and French fries. At some point, Susie left but was replaced by a darker skinned nursing aide named Myrna or something—Tim never quite got it straight and didn't really care. They all went dancing in a hall near Chinatown, and by now Tim felt thoroughly anaesthetized. Before long he had trouble standing. Then they were singing in a bar while across the street the Shore Patrol arrived in several gray jeeps. A squad of Marines and one of sailors had decided to exchange opinions by knuckle telegraph. The girls vanished. Men in white cracker jacks and helmet liners piled from trucks, waving night sticks. A row of Black Marias arrived to haul off handcuffed, hatless young men with shiners and torn shirts.

Tim walked with Stan under glaring industrial lights, along endless blocks of dockyards. It had gotten cold, and damp, and fog rolled in. Tim stopped by a lamp post and barfed his eyeballs out into a black void filled with crawling yellow-green lights, or were those inside his skull?

Stan patted him on the back. "Got it all out of your system, eh?"

Tim nodded, feebly spitting out the last remnants, particle by acidic particle, of the evening's pizza.

"Here," Stan said, offering a drink."

"Get away," Tim said spitting some more.

"Just a soda. It's a little warm, but it will clean out your bilges."

In reply, Tim barfed up another slice or so. "That's it for me. Get away with that." He dug around in his pocket and found some gum. He popped four sticks in his mouth, one after another, and welcomed their mint taste.

They walked another block or so. It started raining lightly again.

A yellow taxi cruised by. Stan waved, and the cab pulled over. "Thank God," they both said getting in.

"Good evening," the driver said. He was a Mexican-American wearing an old, stripped police cap with no strap or hardware.

"Nob Hill," Tim said with a groan.

"That, and then Lafayette Park where I live," Stan instructed.

The rain came down hard for a few minutes and then eased off. The driver put on the wipers. The inside was warm, and smelled of upholstery cleaner. It almost made Tim want to gag again.

Stan nudged Tim. "You still alive?"

"Barely," Tim said, slumped in the seat with his chin buried in his chest. He dozed most of the way back to the hotel, catching flashes of passing lights, snippets of laughter from people still partying away the craziness of the war where nothing was what anyone used to assume to be normal.

"See you at work tomorrow," Stan said yawning.

Tim stepped from the cab waving a five dollar bill. "Pay the man."

"Oh, *amigo*, no," Stan said, fumbling for his own wallet.

"Treat's on me," Tim said as he pushed the door shut. "Thanks for showing me around."

Tim waited a moment, standing in the quiet street. The taxi hove off with a receding motor sound, putting out puffs of vapor on the streets. It was just drizzling now, and Tim welcomed the fresh wind, the sobering calming effect of being away from the frenetic bars and women and the swing music pouring out of every window and dive. He took a deep breath, staggered a bit, and turned to enter the hotel grounds. Okay, that was it. He'd had his little blast. He felt a bit old to party like a kid. He wanted something that he found hard to define—something more, somehow, a bigger meaning in life. He wanted to read important books and think weighty thoughts. Being alive was too precious to waste on trivialities. Thus, over the next few days and weeks, he would settle down to a normal working routine punctuated by dinners alone in this restaurant or that followed by evenings sitting by a lamp, reading Aristotle or Steinbeck or Dos Passos or Fitzgerald before turning in early. Nothing exciting, he thought as he fumbled for his room key.

The front entrance was locked for the night, and he'd been instructed to enter by a smaller secure entrance in the courtyard. He walked around the building, his shoes crackling on the asphalt and gravel of the driveway running alongside, and entered the little maze of flagstones leading through grape bowers, ivy, bougainvillea, and night jasmin. This brought him onto the glistening and moss-edged courtyard of Spanish pavers surrounding a concrete fountain. The fountain barely trickled from its age-dark copper mouth, but it had a picturesque old poured-concrete Classical-style statue set against one ivied wall of the courtyard. The statue was of a female goddess representing a bountiful and happy city. She had a dimpled smile and one breast bare as she poured rainwater from a horn of plenty into the cupped palms of an aroused looking satyr with tiny horns and a mass of tight curls caught in a stone band.

As Tim walked unsteadily into the courtyard, he stopped for a moment to admire the details of the fountain. He noticed a light out of the corner of his eyes and looked up. Two lights, actually. One was the full moon, which had just swum out from behind a bank of rain clouds and shone like dripping liquid down the gilded piles and wrinkles of cloud and bounced off several windows. The other light came from the window where the brunette had fed the birds. For a moment, Tim glimpsed the silhouettes, through the curtains, of two women holding drinks and talking earnestly. One laughed—probably the brunette—and, next instant, the light went out. This left the window dark, smoldering with moonlight, like the other windows.

Duty, Skirts, City of Love

It was good to be out in the fresh air of San Francisco, wearing a slightly rumpled but clean uniform that his sister Catherine had ironed for him and carefully folded up in the sea bag.

He was young, and jaunty, with a nice collection of ribbons, and he attracted his share of attention from passing women. A lot of those were in uniform themselves, particularly the nurses from Letterman Army Hospital and other duty stations overflowing with distaff military. San Francisco had a reputation as the Paris of the West, a City of Love. He felt more comfortable in his own country with its more generous living space, soap, baths, all the little extras of life that had been missing in Europe and nonexistent in Africa. Whistling, he carried his personnel folder and medical records around to various sun drenched, whitewashed offices set on well-sprinkled green lawns. He sent a telegram home to New Haven, announcing that he'd arrived in good shape.

His duty station was at the Presidio in a two-story stucco building that itself was an annex to the rambling Navy Quartermaster Corps facilities all around the Bay area. He had a small office overlooking a sunless courtyard. One of the many cute young enlisted women who did administrative tasks like typing and filing told him, while chewing gum and patting her brown hair, that the sun did penetrate down to the second floor during the mornings on clear days, but generally she was always happy to get out. He thanked her, getting his own coffee rather than asking her to do, it, and began the process of settling in.

He met his immediate supervisor, Captain Martin Teague, in a large office with a round conference table overlooking a sunny, breezy intersection below. Teague was a tall, white-mustached man with a dignified mien and a somewhat sardonic, dry sense of humor. Sitting in was Lt. Cdr. Stan Kehoe, Tim's friend—a freckled, sandy-haired young man, athletic and brash.

"I hear you went for a swim in the North Atlantic," Martin Teague said without making light of the tragedy. He had been fed a half-true story. Nobody would know the truth about *H.M.S. Sturmer* for years, to prevent the Nazis from knowing how superior their submarine technology had been at that moment, in that place. Stan Kehoe as usual was forward. He'd say just one thing too many, or say not quite the right thing considering the company, but he was so good-natured that most people overlooked his eager quality. He usually had his tie slightly loose, as if he needed air while he bounced about in his seat and gesticulated as he spoke. "Yeah, Tim and I hit all the hot spots around London. I'll vouch for him."

"Glad to hear it," Teague said quietly, raising both hands over Tim's personnel field file as if in blessing. "Everything in here looks first rate. I feel very lucky that we have a good solid staff officer on board, and I'm sure Admiral Lemney will feel the same way as he gets to know of you from our weekly briefings."

Hiram L. Lemney was the two star flag officer in charge of Procurement 5549, which specialized in turning specific small captured exotic enemy weapons over to the maw of the vast U.S. industrial machine, and receiving back production versions that could be shot back at the enemy.

Later that evening, sitting over a red checkered tablecloth in a smoky bar in the commercial district of Union Square, Tim and Stan reviewed the day's meeting. "Teague likes you. I can tell."

"Glad to hear it." Tim had begun thinking about home.

"You'll do just fine. Say, I thought you were going to be the life of the party. You look a little under the weather."

"Still a little bushed from the long trip." Tim sat back in the corner and propped one leg up on the dark red plastic bench. "That meeting today got me thinking about clocks."

Stan laughed, sucking ice from his empty glass and letting the cubes tinkle back in while his gaze roved after young women in military hats parading by outside on the neon-lit avenue. "Clocks? You feeling okay?"

Tim shrugged, pushing an ice cube around so it left soggy little trails in the table cloth amid the bread crumbs from the Italian sandwiches they had just eaten. "I begin to wonder, you know. Do I really want to go back to Connecticut and design escapements in a little town. You know, marry the girl next door, have children, live out the whole conventional life style."

"Hmmm. Do you miss London?"

"A bit. Not the plumbing."

Stan laughed. "I know what you mean. And not the buzz bombs."

"I'm sure they won't have those after the war."

"And the V-2s."

"Not since the Germans surrendered."

Stan waved to a pair of young women who waved back. They were Army nurses in Class B uniforms. They'd traded their starched caps for rakish khaki garrison caps, but still wore their dark green sweaters. They carried their regulation leather purses as well as hat bags with them, and wore their *caduceus* brass on their rounded blouse lapels. Lieutenants fresh out of some nearby state college, it turned out. Before long, Tim and Stan were having beers with Lorraine and Susie and getting more and more tight. They did a lot of laughing and shoulder-hugging, told a lot of off-color jokes, and rolled from one bar to the next while the air smelled of drizzle and smoke and French fries. At some point, Susie left but was replaced by a darker skinned nursing aide named Myrna or something—Tim never quite got it straight and didn't really care. They all went dancing in a hall near Chinatown, and by now Tim felt thoroughly anaesthetized. Before long he had trouble standing. Then they were singing in a bar while across the street the Shore Patrol arrived in several gray jeeps. A squad of Marines and one of sailors had decided to exchange opinions by knuckle telegraph. The girls vanished. Men in white cracker jacks and helmet liners piled from trucks, waving night sticks. A row of Black Marias arrived to haul off handcuffed, hatless young men with shiners and torn shirts.

Tim walked with Stan under glaring industrial lights, along endless blocks of dockyards. It had gotten cold, and damp, and fog rolled in. Tim stopped by a lamp post and barfed his eyeballs out into a black void filled with crawling yellow-green lights, or were those inside his skull?

Stan patted him on the back. "Got it all out of your system, eh?"

Tim nodded, feebly spitting out the last remnants, particle by acidic particle, of the evening's pizza.

"Here," Stan said, offering a drink."

"Get away," Tim said spitting some more.

"Just a soda. It's a little warm, but it will clean out your bilges."

In reply, Tim barfed up another slice or so. "That's it for me. Get away with that." He dug around in his pocket and found some gum. He popped four sticks in his mouth, one after another, and welcomed their mint taste.

They walked another block or so. It started raining lightly again.

A yellow taxi cruised by. Stan waved, and the cab pulled over. "Thank God," they both said getting in.

"Good evening," the driver said. He was a Mexican-American wearing an old, stripped police cap with no strap or hardware.

"Nob Hill," Tim said with a groan.

"That, and then Lafayette Park where I live," Stan instructed.

The rain came down hard for a few minutes and then eased off. The driver put on the wipers. The inside was warm, and smelled of upholstery cleaner. It almost made Tim want to gag again.

Stan nudged Tim. "You still alive?"

"Barely," Tim said, slumped in the seat with his chin buried in his chest. He dozed most of the way back to the hotel, catching flashes of passing lights, snippets of laughter from people still partying away the craziness of the war where nothing was what anyone used to assume to be normal.

"See you at work tomorrow," Stan said yawning.

Tim stepped from the cab and handed him a five dollar bill. "Pay the man."

"Oh, *amigo*, no," Stan said, fumbling for his own wallet in his back pocket.

"Treat's on me," Tim said as he pushed the door shut. "Thanks for showing me around."

Tim waited a moment, standing in the quiet street. The taxi hove off with a receding motor sound, putting out puffs of vapor on the streets. It was just drizzling now, and Tim welcomed the fresh wind, the sobering calming effect of being away from the frenetic bars and women and the swing music pouring out of every window and dive. He took a deep breath, staggered a bit, and turned to enter the hotel grounds. Okay, that was it. He'd had his little blast. He felt a bit old to party like a kid. He wanted something that he found hard to define—something more, somehow, a bigger meaning in life. He wanted to read important books and think weighty thoughts. Being alive was too precious to waste on trivialities. Thus, over the next few days and weeks, he would settle down to a normal working routine punctuated by dinners alone in this restaurant or that followed by evenings sitting by a lamp, reading Aristotle or Steinbeck or Dos Passos or Fitzgerald before turning in early. Nothing exciting, he thought as he fumbled for his room key.

The front entrance was locked for the night, and he'd been instructed to enter by a smaller secure entrance in the courtyard. He walked around the building, his shoes crackling on the asphalt and gravel of the driveway running alongside, and entered the little maze of flagstones leading through grape bowers, ivy, bougainvillea, and night jasmin. This brought him onto the glistening and moss-edged courtyard of Spanish pavers surrounding a concrete fountain. The fountain barely trickled from its age-dark copper mouth, but it had a picturesque old poured-concrete Classical-style statue set against one ivied wall of the courtyard. The statue was of a female goddess representing a bountiful and happy city. She had a dimpled smile and one breast bare as she poured rainwater from a horn of plenty into the cupped palms of an aroused looking satyr with tiny horns and a mass of tight curls caught in a stone band.

As Tim walked unsteadily into the courtyard, he stopped for a moment to admire the details of the fountain. He noticed a light out of the corner of his eyes and looked up.

Two lights, actually. One was the full moon, which had just swum out from behind a bank of rain clouds and shone like dripping liquid down the gilded piles and wrinkles of cloud and bounced off several windows. The other light came from the window where the brunette had fed the birds.

For a moment, Tim glimpsed the silhouettes, through the curtains, of two women holding drinks and talking earnestly. One laughed—probably the brunette—and, next instant, the light went out. This left the window dark, smoldering with moonlight, like the other windows.

Clock Maker at Work and Play

At first, Tim's new life in San Francisco was governed by pleasant routines.

By day, he worked in the G-2 section, processing intelligence information. It was interesting work, not earth-shaking, but enough to keep his intellect stimulated. Unlike London, he wasn't shadow boxing or playing dirty spy games. The job was more engineering than intelligence work, though it was intellectually challenging at times and involved both disciplines. Most often each dossier came with a dark pasteboard container resembling a shoebox, both bearing related part numbers and logged in and out by indefatigable young WAVES. At times he had to evaluate huge folders of information on given items of enemy hardware salvaged from sunken ships or downed airplanes. Other materials might be recovered from a dead enemy soldier on some snowy battlefield or from a mummified Luftwaffe corpse at a desert crash site. Sometimes it was a washer or a petcock or a threaded pipe or a detonator. At other times it might be something more personal, like a military issue wristwatch or eyeglasses or a helmet liner or a wool glove. Every item contained some element of information that went into the hopper of a national intelligence network that had until recently been a lackluster imitation of big-mama British intelligence.

All the while, Tim ate his lunches with Teague and Kehoe, washing burgers down with beers, watching the skirts of San Francisco breeze by.

In the evenings, Tim preferred to sit alone in his room and read. He'd discovered a fine USO lending library nearby, and soon a stack of cheap, wartime, paperbound Victory books sat teetering next to empty coffee cups, crumpled napkins, stained cardboard donut boxes, and empty soda cans, all on the morning's breakfast tray.

Mrs. Auger's fine facility provided breakfast either *a la carte* or, more inexpensively, by the week. If there was one thing Tim liked, it was having some predictability, a routine. He was a bit lonely. Sometimes he thought of Anna, but pushed the impossible away. He sometimes wondered: *Will I ever make love to another woman? Will I remember how? Will it be anywhere near as good...?* He was a practical man, and decided he wanted to live in the present. Leaving London had been just what he needed. Who knew what new adventures might befall him here? He was in no danger of getting shipped out. He could sit out the war here, puttering with his petcocks and machine screws. He'd write cute little engineering reports and leave it all behind him when he went home in the evening.

He loved traveling and he enjoyed faraway cities, along with the kind of insular world of its own that the military offered. You could be in the most distant place on earth but it could attain a certain bizarre imitation of American hominess if you could just get colas and grilled cheese sandwiches, and listen to the music of Tommy Dorsey and Glenn Miller thumping from a juke box or let the crooning of Frank Sinatra wrap around a person. Tim enjoyed the pounding of Gene Krupa, the peppy ditties of the Andrews Sisters, and all the hopping stuff from boogie to jitterbug. How could you be young and not groove to such alive and happy noise?

Sometimes he went for walks up and down the long hills, like down to the cable car turnaround at Powell and Market Streets, for a drink at the Pig 'n Whistle or a sandwich at the Cafeteria with its stainless steel Art Deco sign across the street.

Sometimes he sat at his desk and wrote letters to his family in New England. He never discussed his ordeal in Africa with anyone. In London, he'd made some visits to the chaplain at his BOQ off Buckingham Road to talk about why he was still alive and the others weren't. The answer of course had been the usual nostrums about God's will and all that, but Tim had concluded that either there was such a will or there wasn't, but either way it just played out the way it was meant to be. The only worthwhile thing he'd ever heard on the subject, as far as he was concerned, came during a brief conversation over chips and beer in a Brompton Road pub with an Anglican padre who wore a yellow and blue checkered scarf and had an ugly blue smash on one side of his head from a bit of flying tile some time earlier during a V-2 explosion. The good man, whom Tim had never seen before nor ever saw after, had said: "Life is too short feeling guilty or for that matter becoming cynical. The lads wouldn't want you to waste your precious time, my boy." He'd patted Tim on the hand and growled in a low, urgent voice. "Live your life, lad. You have to live it for those poor broken boys out there drowning in the cold water, crying for their mothers. You have to go on, for them, boy. Do you understand? You owe it to them, and to yourself."

There was another time he'd split up with some friends and taken a cab home early after a few dark, sweet porters. He'd wound up in the same taxi with a tipsy hooker who smelled of gin and cheap perfume, on her way back from *shomeplace* to *shomewheres-elshe*, and she'd babbled on and on. Tim had ignored her until she'd segued into the serious part of her conversation about 'ow 'er mum and 'er sistah had perished in the Blitz a few years earlier, and the boy she'd been engaged to marry had been shot down by some ruddy foakin' Hun and either burned to death or drowned in the Channel. She'd said: "I miss me 'Enry, I do, every day, but I live me life to the fullest, knowin' 'ey's smoilin' down a' me. We all go there soon enough, don' yer think, Sir? Eh?" With that she'd gently wompused Tim on the shoulder with her purse. He'd stared at her, waiting for any more wisdom to pour from her lipstick-streaked mouth, but she'd sat back silent as a stone and watched with unsteady head and watery eyes as the blur of street lights flew by.

Now he sat in his slightly chilly room nine thousand miles and nine time zones away, almost on the other side of the world, and wrote letters or read books and slept alone.

One thing about the war: you always heard some distant swing music, night or day, as if life was being lived too fast, too hard, too desperately because as the woman in the London cab had said, it all ends too quickly.

Things bugged Tim and he couldn't sleep well some nights. Sometimes it wasn't the swing music or the boogey-woogie. Sometimes it was remembering the endless rustle of surf on the West African coast, the steady buildup and then dumping of water crashing down in a white foam among the rocks a quarter mile out in the moonlight. Tim realized one day he had yet to visit the beach here. The thunder of surf crashing down reminded him of Africa, of *H.M.S. Sturmer,* which he wanted to forget. And the lions. He could still see the poor lioness, desperately looking toward her babies in the tower, moments before her death and the capture of her cubs.

Funny part was, Tim wasn't bothered by the part about mortality too much, now that he understood it was there. He'd wandered in and out of Europe's cold stone churches more than once, alone of an evening, with their mysterious scent of incense dating back centuries, an oil ground into the stone walls. He'd always felt somewhere in the shadows among fluted pillars or in the ogives of stained glass windows, where it was never either night nor day, there was some spirit, some higher thing, something parental, that did care about a person. He might now be a thin string of bleached bones crumbling away on a beach in the Western Sahel, with the eternal sea breaking in white foam on sand under a pure azure sky, but he wasn't. He still had precious hours ahead of him, assuming he didn't get hit by some beer truck or fall into a sausage vat—days, years, even decades and generations—a wealth of time greater than that of any aging millionaire.

Still, there was a gnawing something. Was he doing enough? Was he living those hours usefully enough? The walls creaked now and then as the building adjusted to the cycle of cold and hot from day to night. The floor boards might emit a loud crack. A window might make a popping noise as it resettled itself in its hardened putty. Sometimes the wind would kick up and send a wet leaf to cling to the window. Sometimes a tree branch somewhere outside would bang against the wall, briefly waking Tim before he nodded back to sleep. Faraway cathedral bells tumbled slowly in their rafters, tinkling forth drifty notes.

There was the steady glow of the tiny uranium strips indicating the hours on his travel clock. There was the steady *tick, tick, tick* of the ratchet wheels, the faint twang of the escapements, the snick of ruby on ruby inside the little clock, and then the magnification of those sounds inside the thick brown and white marble night table top, and the echoes of those sounds bouncing back and forth underneath among hard wooden table legs and on the shelf with its books, as Tim dozed the nights away with one eye sometimes opening a bit, then closing again. Until he met Corinthia, the brunette neighbor, and from there on nothing was ever the same again.

U-234 Sails to Japan—Hitler's Final Weapon

As Fortress Germany began to crumble, the Nazi war machine churned on in surviving cities like Kiel and Kristiansand on the North Sea. Nuremberg in the east had just fallen into Soviet hands. Italy, Austria, the Balkans, Poland, France—the litany of lost empire was a mile long, and now Germany was like an insect on its back being plucked apart one leg at a time. In the west, the Allies had crossed the Rhine at Remagen and roared into the ancient cathedral cities of Cologne and Speyer, cutting supply lines and decapitating command centers as they went.

In the Pacific, Japan was fighting her way backward to the homeland, leaving a trail of bitterly contested blood on every tiny atoll and island, but her cause seemed doomed. Tokyo was being firebombed night and day, as were most major cities across the Land of the Rising Sun. Still, on both sides of the world, the victorious Allies were leery of marching into some unknown death trap. There were ominous legends of an impregnable redoubt in the Alps of Europe from which Hitler's legions could continue the war for years, and there was every indication the mainland of Japan would fight to the last man, woman, and child rather than surrender.

The dark romance of Fascism and Nazism seemed to have everlasting life, and fanatics everywhere were prepared to continue the fight at all costs. In Germany, specially trained teenagers, perhaps the ultimate in a series of vengeance weapons starting with the V-1 and the V-2, roamed about at night as 'werewolves,' assassinating Allied occupiers and their German sympathizers. Across Europe and the Pacific, millions still died as the war raged on. And in the surviving pockets of Nazi power, plots were still hatched to save the Third Reich from Doom, whose necrotic breath blew down the Germans' backs.

In the midst of this chaos, where often the most basic rules of law and order were breaking down day by day, many pragmatic individuals could see the coming doom of the Nazi order and sought practical ways to ensure their survival. One such individual was the handsome and rugged captain-lieutenant of a giant sub, the *U-234*, named Johann Heinrich Fehler.

In the badly damaged concrete redoubts of the harbor in Kiel, one of Germany's preeminent seafaring cities, several surviving submarines were being hastily outfitted for desperate, last-minute missions on behalf of the *Führer* and the Reich.

The Germans had been developing a dizzying array of so-called *Wunderwaffen*, wonder weapons, during the last year of the war to stave off the growingly inevitable defeat. They were launching rocket ships with explosive warheads hundreds of miles downrange from Northern Germany into England. They were perfecting early jet fighter and bomber aircraft like the Messerschmitt 262 and the Arado 310 *Blitz*. When their runways were bombed out, they invented the Jet Assisted Take-Off (JATO) rocket which helped lift propeller-driven cargo planes off the ground in a golden shower of light. Their ingenuity was boundless, although they were in fact behind the allies in certain critical technologies. Two of these technologies, whose development by Britain and the United States was shadowed at every turn by Nazi and Soviet spies, were RADAR and the atomic bomb.

Captain Fehler himself had no real idea, and only half-heartedly cared, what top secret cargo was being loaded into his gigantic submarine in the desperate days of April 1945.

U-234 was a 1600-ton boat, 270 feet long, one of the two largest submarines ever built in Europe (the Japanese had some twenty even larger I-Class subs, 356.5 feet long, all but one sunk by late 1944 after putting nearly sixty Allied merchant ships on the bottom). By comparison, at 882.5 feet (269 meters) and a beam 92 feet (28 meters), the late *R.M.S. Titanic* was just over three times *U-234*'s length. *U-234* had been designed as a minelayer of the XB Class but circumstance and strategy had changed her to a long-range heavy underwater transport, meaning she would now be used to ferry up to 250 tons of cargo halfway around the world between Germany and Asia. She could make 20 knots on the surface, or 12 knots submerged, and could dive to 300 meters (over 900 feet). She was a *Wunderwaffe* in her own right.

Johann Fehler needed to make no excuses to anyone. Now 34, he was a much-decorated war hero who had sunk 22 Allied vessels in his first major wartime assignment as mines and explosives officer on the raider *Atlantis*, rescuing scores of sailors from death in the icy Atlantic after the *Atlantis* was sunk. In its own way, the journey might be classified as one of the minor epics of seafaring, since he'd ordered his men to tie their rubber life rafts together in a chain, which was then towed surreptitiously by a German submarine, *U-126*, over 1,000 miles to a safe German port through high seas patrolled by powerful Allied sea and air forces. His brilliance and heroism had earned him an Iron Cross and command of the huge new submarine. However, Allied air raids had destroyed many of the subs in the Kiel pens, severely damaging *U-234* so that she required months of repair.

She'd sailed surreptitiously from Kiel to Kristiansand, Norway, where she now lay in a secure bunker with a row of other boats awaiting their cargo and orders. A collision with another sub, shortly after arrival, had left her damaged. She had a leaking outer hull and a cracked fuel tank, but those repairs had been completed by now at round the clock, breakneck speed.

As heroic but practical men like Fehler watched the war grinding to an ignoble end, they had to gauge the best course of action for themselves and their sailors while Germany's ruthless leaders continued to exercise their last mad plans.

Fehler had a lot to think about as he stood with his hands in the pockets of his leather coat on a windy spring day in Kristiansand, Norway. While overseeing the preparations for *U-234*'s long journey to Japan, he had to fight the imperatives of his deeply ingrained German *Pflicht*, or sense of duty. He avoided speaking about his dark ruminations with the other skippers—Schness of the *U-2511*, Preuss of *U-874*, Petersen of *U-875*, and others—who were taking on mysterious cargoes and passengers. Fehler understood the desperation of the Reich's logisticians and strategists, and nothing surprised him—not the advanced Messerschmitt ME-262 twin-jet fighter plane being loaded disassembled into his cargo holds along with schematic plans for mass manufacture by the Japanese; not the 74 tons of lead, 26 tons of mercury, twelve tons of special steel, and seven tons of optical glass; as well as aircraft support parts, ammunition, and plans; not the routine medical supplies and mail including diplomatic pouches; not even the 1,232 pounds of weapons-grade uranium 235 in heavy gold-lined containers, capable of making at least a half dozen atomic bombs. There were also special proximity fuses and other exotic scientific toys whose criticality Fehler understood, along with the danger of carrying them on his boat. Fehler had no doubt that these were *Wunderwaffen*. They would not save Hitler and his regime.

Fehler did not have control over the nature or the loading of the cargo. That was in the hands of a Commander Becker of the *Marinesonderdienst Ausland*, or Special Naval Service-Foreign. Fehler normally had the final say as to whether the boat was seaworthy or not, and that included the method of cargo storage, lashing, and so forth. Here this support organization conducted the loading of the highly sensitive cargo while Fehler was expected to twiddle his thumbs. And twiddle Fehler did, but with a purpose and no small amount of humor. There was always a deep, irrational loyalty between a larger than life skipper and his hand-picked crew. Fehler could safely order his officers to have his men conduct a clandestine loading program of their own. There had always been, in the German soul, a thirst for adventure in faraway places. For generations, the average German had been enamored of the fanciful stories of the writer Karl May, who created the mythical North American Indian hero *Lederstrumpf* ("Leatherstocking") and his exploits. Every German boy was at heart both a cowboy and an Indian, and just well familiar with the exploits of Robinson Crusoe. The trouble was, today North America was a hostile land, and Fehler and his officers had to look a bit farther for their plans. Like so many things about wartime, their plans and actions would have been unthinkable in peacetime. In wartime, however, the improbable and the impossible happened every day and nobody questioned much. Their plot was as exotic and crazy as the times in which they found themselves. In the remaining 75 tons or so of empty cargo space, Fehler ordered his men to secretly store enough food rations to support the complement of six officers and 44 enlisted men. He also ordered brought on board hunting rifles, ammunition, fishing poles, and other survival equipment, in addition to 900 bottles of whiskey. Fehler's plan was to follow through on any good German boy's childhood adventure plans. After delivering cargo and passengers to Japan, Fehler would take his boat by force, if necessary, and sail on to some remote, uninhabited island in the South Seas, where they would hide their vessel and then live on coconuts, fish, wild pigs, and whiskey until the war was safely over. A lark! It was the only dream that kept Fehler going as he grimly surveyed the loading activities on this misty, drizzly North Sea dock.

And what a crew of mystery guests came aboard! Along with the ME-262 and the other wonder weapons came a *Luftwaffe* general, Ulrich Kessler, who made no secret of his disdain for the likes of Hitler and Goering while maintaining his profound loyalty to the Fatherland. Along with Kessler came his own staff, to serve him while he helped set the Japanese up as jet-flying atomic powers capable of annihilating Los Angeles, San Francisco, and other major U.S. cities in mushroom cloud blasts. As Fehler understood the stratagem, Germany was now putting her remaining eggs in the Japanese basket, hoping Japan could still defeat the Allies and then restore the Third Reich. Aside from Kessler, Fehler's 'guests' included two Japanese Imperial Navy officers; three *Luftwaffe* officers of Kessler's staff; four German Navy officers who were technical experts (whom Fehler well understood, with his background in naval artillery and ordnance); two civilians from Messerschmitt to go along with the plane and its manufacturing plans; and a naval judge on a separate diplomatic mission.

While Fehler's low opinion of the regime stayed in his innermost thoughts, Kessler was a much more political and outspoken individual than the quietly competent Fehler. Both men were fiercely loyal to the Fatherland. Kessler set the tone aboard the sub by his open tirades against Hitler, Goering, and the rest of the criminal gang. In previous years, Kessler might have been shot; in today's desperate times he was a necessary evil, simply being shuffled as far from Berlin as possible, at the same time to help bolster Japan's defenses against her common enemies with Germany.

U-234 steamed from Kristiansand on 25April under cover of night. Given Allied air supremacy, the once-proud Kriegsmarine now had to run subs at slow speed underwater. *U-234* had just been modified to use a new snorkel technology. Atop her hull lay a long mast, or *Schnorchel,* which would let her travel weeks at a time without surfacing for air or to recharge batteries. As a trade-off, she must plod along at 12 knots with her periscope ready to pop up any minute in a nervous search for enemy antisubmarine hunter-killer planes or depth charge-ready destroyers. Standing grimly in his control room, Johann Fehler planned to discharge his final duties to the Third Reich and then hijack his crew on a glorious South Seas adventure.

Then came sudden, stark news out of Berlin: Hitler was dead.

Part Four: Nob Hill, April-May 1945

Coast to Coast

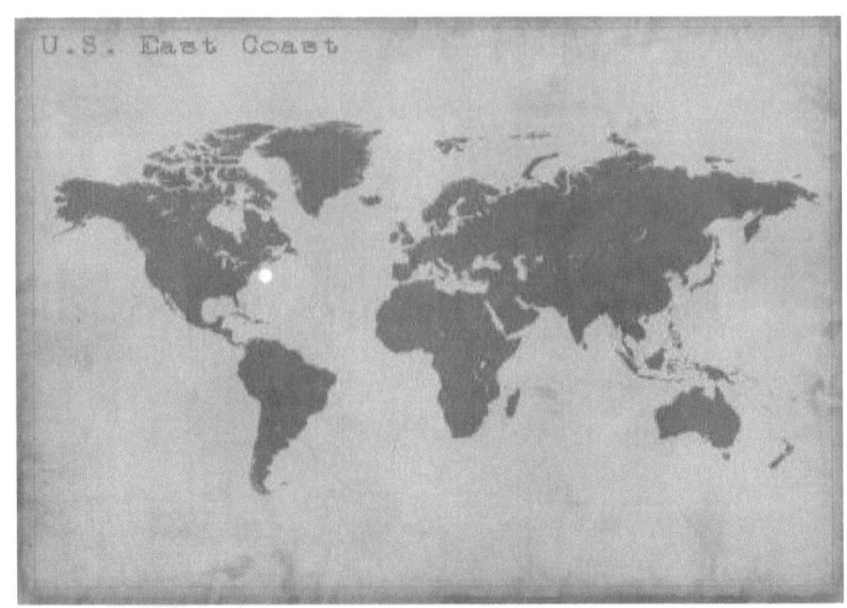

Courtyard, with Wind & Leaves

Tim read The San Francisco Chronicle in the hotel every morning with his coffee and muffin. He tried to keep up with the vast and mysterious ocean of human events. At the same time he had to keep an eye on the chrome Art Deco clock on the cafeteria wall to avoid being late for work.

Most importantly, the City of San Francisco was readying herself to become the scene of one of history's turning points, a hinge of new hope, as representatives of at least 50 nations gathered for a two month conference for founding the United Nations that June.

On April 12, 1945, shocking news spread. The President of the United States had died during the night. San Francisco quieted under a pall of grief and shock. Those who had ceaselessly denounced FDR, feeling he had done too much, as well as those who felt he had not done enough, for once remained silent. People at Tim's office couldn't get any work done in this climate.

FDR, 63 and long ailing from the after-effects and side-effects of childhood polio, suffered a massive cerebral hemorrhage in the afternoon at his favorite resort at Warm Spring, Georgia, and died that evening. The new President, Harry S. Truman of Missouri, was sworn in and waiting as the funeral train made its way to the nation's capital. The train traveled with excruciating, numbed slowness, along tracks lined for miles and miles by tearful citizens. Often, the train would slow to a stop as crowds overwhelmed the tracks to lay flowers or touch the passing car. The common people had given him enormous landslide victories in his unprecedented four terms. Everyday working people of all races and religions now came to say their goodbyes, and nobody needed to restrain them or lay a hand on them in this great democracy—they were dignified and restrained of their own spirit. Arthur Godfrey narrated the long, slow journey to Hyde Park, and his voice was broadcast over every radio in every town and city across the nation. The funeral train took FDR to Washington, where FDR lay in state, and then on to New York. Life got on under the administration of Harry S. Truman, the bespectacled and plain-spoken Missouri haberdasher who seemed like an odd choice to follow in FDR's footsteps.

The nation was in mourning. The majority of people felt a genuine sense of loss. They felt they had been rescued from the dark, cold jaws of modern history's worst financial ruination by this aristocratic, wheelchair-bound dandy who had told them "There is nothing to fear but fear itself," at a time when a deep and unspeakable terror gripped those who had been out of work and hungry and unable to feed their families for so many years that it really seemed as if a Biblical end of time had arrived. Then, against the rabid screeching of the German tyrant, and the obscene posturing by Italy's bully, and the cruel strutting of the Japanese throughout Asia, Roosevelt had presented an urbane, civilized, charming counterpoint. The news of FDR's passing was in the air, a single voice, a single radio broadcast emanating everywhere from windows, doorways, in bus stations and train terminals, on the streets. Even the newsboy did not need to shout, but silently passed out papers and collected his pennies as fast as his grimy fingers could fly. The voice was everywhere: Arthur Godfrey, recounting the final bittersweet journey down those broad boulevards in the nation's capital to the train station—not for burial in Robert E. Lee's onetime backyard at Arlington, but to the President's home town of Hyde Park, New York. With each tolling drumbeat, there was a sense that this young nation, which appeared to be weathering yet another crisis, was gathering about itself the heavy folds of history's mantle. It was one of those moments when people felt in their marrow that this was an important turning point of history. Even Hitler, hiding in his bunker and about to blow his brains out, rejoiced that his own grim fate had befallen his key enemy eighteen days earlier.

A week after Hitler's death, the mangled bodies of Benito Mussolini, his mistress Clara Petacci, and their closest aides hung upside down, by their heels, like pigs, on slaughterhouse hooks in a Milan gas station. Her skirt was modestly tied around her bloodied legs. A rifle butt propped up *Il Duce*'s battered face for photographers' flashing bulbs. The bodies' arms spread stiffly in a final, morbid offer to embrace a people they had led into pointless disaster.

Two days later, Hitler shot himself in the mouth after giving poison to his dogs and to his new bride Eva Brown. The rubble-choked, fetid, stinking bunker in the heart of Berlin was a ruin filled with the corpses of some of the Third Reich's leaders and their children. Cossacks swarmed through the city raping, burning, and looting. Many German men killed their families and then committed suicide rather than suffer at the hands of the Russians. In the last frenzied days of the Reich, when its leaders were either committing suicide or looking for Americans to surrender to rather than be captured by the Soviets, *Grossadmiral* Doenitz took over the helm of the crippled state, at Kiel on the North Sea, for less than three days, just long enough to surrender. During those chaotic days, a frantic barrage of orders crisscrossed in the dying machinery of Hitler's military services, and all of it was too fast and too confused and often too secret for the news media to keep up with. Europe was enveloped in the greatest humanitarian crisis in history, the wandering of over twenty million displaced Germanic civilians—most from Slavic nations, many of them innocent children—through lands in which they were hated for what their countrymen had done, or for who they were, or both. In many cases, babies were simply taken from their mothers and thrown down wells or into latrines to drown. Starving people who could hardly walk anymore were bayoneted or stomped to death. Some were dragged from their death march on muddy and cold roads and forced to labor without sustenance until they dropped dead. Meanwhile, the Allies were opening up the hundreds of crusted-over sores of Hitler's mass extermination program. Photos and stories coming out of concentration camps were too ghastly for comprehension. Still, as always, the cold, cynical, calculating machinery of human events ground on. Where one suffered, the other rejoiced. Where one cried, the other laughed at his pain. Stalin could well do a little victory dance of his own, in the manner of the dead Adolf, at the thought of having wrested half of Europe into the Communist darkness. And so it went. Would the world be any different now that nationalist socialism had been exterminated? Would a world suffocated by international communism be any kinder? These were the questions being asked by readers and editorialists in the newspapers, on radio, in movie newsreels.

In October 1944, FDR had met with Papa Joe, Churchill, and China's Chiang Kai-Shek at the Georgetown residence of the heirs of a vast laxatives fortune, the Blisses, to hammer out a proposed world future. Hopefully, this would create a stable world order and a sound money and banking system within a framework of mutual security. The enterprise that was about to spring forth from this, as Tim read in his papers, would be called the United Nations. The hope was that the victors had learned from the mistakes of their predecessors in places like Vienna (1815) and Versailles (1919). The sundered enemy would not be humiliated and chained to devastating reparations, which had led to renewed warfare; but fed, clothed, housed, governed, rehabilitated, and ultimately set loose as a democratized ally rather than a liability. That was the hope. A few editorial writers had misgivings about Stalin's long history of deceit, violence, and treachery in the service of international communism. They pointed, for example, to the genocide of Kulaks in the 1930s and the mass murder of the

Polish officer corps at Katyn, but a pretense had to be made that one was dealing with civilized folk—how else to create a new world order?—and thus the partition of Europe proceeded apace, as did the daydream, as some called it, of a United Nations.

In February 1945, two months before his death, the ailing FDR had met with Stalin and Churchill at the Crimean resort of Yalta to lay out the groundwork for the world's future alignments. Churchill and Stalin concentrated on the division of Europe, while FDR focused more on the ongoing world war with Japan in the Pacific. There had been other meetings, but at Yalta Stalin brought with him concessions he'd wangled from Churchill—for example, the West would get Greece and Austria, while Stalin could take Bulgaria, Romania, and Hungary. Similar considerations would apply to Poland, to the Soviet-occupied eastern zone of Germany, and to other old Russian hegemonies. Marshal Tito, a Communist maverick, firmly controlled the hybrid nation of Yugoslavia. The losers of Yalta were men like DeGaulle and Chiang Kai Shek, who were excluded while their national interests were pawned like second-hand goods.

Men like Tim were being shifted from the Atlantic front to the Pacific front as the endgame of the Asian war started to play itself out. Tokyo was being bombed night and day. The Japanese had lost most of their navy, their air power, their army. They yielded their entrenched positions in the Pacific one island at a time, one atoll at a time, one ditch at a time, every inch exacting a bloody toll in lives. The Allies applied the lessons learned over Germany and brought the new technology of fire storming to the paper and wood cities of Japan. The very air over some cities caught fire and burned for hours in huge fireballs as incendiaries created cyclonic updrafts of superheated air that sucked in more cool, oxygen-rich air, continuing the plasma cycle. Humans were mummified alive in underground shelters as they had been in Dresden. In all of it, Tim felt a vague uplifting sense of hope that the future would be brighter with this vast war behind. A world at peace must perforce be a happier place than a world in which nearly a hundred million lives were shed in a grisly manner in just five years.

The City of San Francisco, in particular, took great pride in announcing to the world that it would be the mother, the founding womb, of an organization that would cause men to beat their swords into ploughshares: the United Nations.

This April 1945, the city cleaned and preened itself as it prepared to receive dignitaries from some 50 nations who would sign their names and commit their nations to a new way of running world affairs. Already, the city's hotels were filling up with foreign dignitaries like arrays of exotic birds in their turbans, dashikis, tunics, uniforms, suits, and colorful wrappings. Flags snapped crisply in balmy spring breezes atop the city's hills. It meant much tighter housing for a city swollen with troops and officers marshaling to finish the war against Japan; consequently, many a colonel or Navy captain found himself unceremoniously doubled up in on-post housing instead of sitting in the city's best hotels. Tim thanked his lucky stars that the Hotel Auger was not on the primary requisition lists, and he kept his fingers crossed that nobody would remember him and evict him in favor of some beribboned South American colonel.

📖

The Hotel Auger had certain rules. You brought down yesterday's tray, if you had taken it with you to eat in your room. You left the tray on a window counter at the kitchen. Then you picked up a clean, empty tray and went to another window where a pair of Mexican cooks filled your plate to order. Then you paid the person at the cash register, usually the old Chinese man or one of his family. Then you went to your seat. People tended to sit in the same seats day after day.

Tim just happened to bumble down glancing through the newspaper, so he was surprised when he lowered the paper to see a sullenly handsome, glinty-eyed man in black dress uniform half rise, extending a hand in apology. There was no apology in the eyes, but icy calculation. Tim gathered he was shaking hands with a logistics officer. The man had a deep voice and strong beard shadow, and exuded an odd feeling as if he went about requisitioning bits of power here and there and yet seemed hungry for any kind of human contact. "Hello," said the man, "I'm Dick Nixon. Did I take your place here?"

"No, no," Tim said as they shook hands. He felt the strength in the other's grip, almost as if the man wanted to pull him down and make him sit with him. He pulled his hand back. "Excuse me."

Nixon pointed to the chairs on either side of him. "Please, help yourself. Keep me company."

Tim nodded. "Sure, thanks. I'll get my food first."

As Tim picked up a fresh tray, he heard a woman's voice: "Looks like you lost your spot." He turned and saw the brunette. "Yes," he said, "Thank you."

She pointed to the long empty table beside her. "Well, if you need a parking spot, you're welcome to drive up here."

"Thanks. That's very kind of you. I'd like to." *How lame am I?*

She seemed poised and sure of herself as she pointed brightly to the empty spot opposite her. He did not give Nixon another glance, and he never did see Nixon again in person, but was grateful for the inadvertent introduction.

"How are you?" he asked as he unfolded his napkin on his lap.

She was buttering a scone, and looked up with mischief in her eyes. "I'm not sure. You're not going to scold me for throwing crumbs out my window, are you?" It was the silly kind of thing men and women said to one another when flirting. He shrugged, knowing it didn't matter what he said as long as the unspoken message conveyed pleasantness and poise. "Were they contraband crumbs?"

"Are you the crumb police?"

"Yes, but I won't issue a citation this time—"

"But next time?"

"Next time, we will have to have a serious talk."

She laughed. "I'll see if I have any more crumbs. This might get interesting."

"I am prepared at all times to check your crumbs." And so it went, back and forth, and quickly they were smiling, leaning toward each other, wrapped up in each other's aura. He checked her out while babbling happily. She wore an odd uniform, kind of an Army officer's khakis with baggy pants, and lumpy looking, scuffed work boots. It was almost a jump suit of sorts, and she had flight wings on her lapels. She had a rakish little garrison cap tucked through her shoulder epaulet on one side. Her hands were long and feminine. Her features were pretty, and she wore light makeup. Overall, an intriguing mix of feminine and gamine. He was about to ask about her job when she held up both hands and looked startled.

"Oh wow," she said as she glanced at her little wristwatch. "I've got to run, run, run! I had no idea I am so late!"

"Look what I made you do."

"You are a very bad man." She rose and threw things on her tray. "Will you have breakfast with me again? This was fun."

"Every day if you'd like."

"Deal," she breathed and was gone. She left a mysterious little lipsticky smile and a coy afterglance in her wake. He caught a glimpse of her leaving: athletic, medium height, with short-cropped hair. Her hair was brown underneath, and unruly reddish-gold on top where it caught the sun by day. His last glimpse was of her slim figure walking gracefully and unaffectedly away.

Work was routine, and he kept busy. Stan Kehoe joined him for lunch. They each drank a beer with their sandwiches in a little deli on lower Sacramento Street not far from the Ferry Building. Stan kept talking, as he always did, and Tim's mind kept wandering. After work, Tim begged off from bar-hopping.

"What's the matter with you?" Stan said. "You used to be a blast back in London. Are you getting old?"

"Must be," Tim said with a grin, clapping him on the back. "You go ahead. Have fun."

"Fella..." Stan said, shaking his head grimly. "Whoah. Last time you got like this, you were heavy with that Polish movie star nurse."

"Next week we'll paint the town just slightly russet, not red," Tim promised, clapping his friend once more on the back. "I'm just not ready for another bender any time soon." He left Stan standing in the doorway of the office building, and headed for the cable car that would take him up to Nob Hill.

Once he arrived at the Hotel Auger, he stood in the courtyard, looking up. *No sight of the brunette.* Her window was shuttered, and the gray curtains were tightly drawn. The afternoon mist had rolled in, coating everything with a gray damp perspiration that made Tim shudder and put his hands in the pockets of his pea coat. So who was "they?" He assumed it was one of those common roommate situations that young military people got into when housing was tight and housing allowances were skimpy. The gray light reflecting from the closed window gave him a faintly disturbing, chilly sense, almost of abandonment. How silly. He shook his head. As he stood there, he heard the noises of the city around him—the rustle of people hurrying by on the sidewalk outside on their way home, the slam of car doors, the starting of engines, the twitter of birds who sounded uneasy at some coming weather. He heard, as always, the distant sound of swing music, and someone's too-loud laughter.

Then, on the wind, he thought he recognized a tinkling laugh—*hers*. But from where?

Quickly, and feeling foolish about it a second later, he stepped aside into the shadows of the grape arbor. Staring at the gray, desiccating wood among the stripped vines, he frowned and focused on hearing every tiny sound that the city offered up from its mysterious corners. Instead of sound, he got a fresh, healthy blast, a smell of damp loam, strong like animal musk but sweeter, and mixed with a Tantalus of herbs—anise, verbena, lavender—and blossoms—lemon, jasmine, apple. It reminded him of the backyard in Hamden, Connecticut when he was small. It made him a tiny bit homesick. Nearby a lantern glowed in its windowed rectangles, a small electric light made to look like a flame inside, casting ember-like glow spots on mute windows around the bottom floor.

He wandered inside, and took the lift upstairs. When he got to the hallway near his room, he thought he heard a faint giggle someplace. Curious, he tiptoed down the softly lit hallway toward the bathroom at the end, and the window looking west toward the harbor. For the first time, he noticed a door open just a crack, opposite the bathroom. It was a heavy wooden door, dark, with a little rectangular white enamel sign printed in plain blue letters: *Private. No Entry.*

Curiosity got the better of him, and he pushed the door open a bit. He leaned inside, ready to be chased out, but saw only more hallways, more carpeting and soft lights and wall pictures under glimmering glass. He saw a maid's cart in the hall, with towels draped over it, and a vacuum cleaner beside it. He heard the giggle again, and understood: it came from an open room in which two Mexican-American maids were cleaning. As they worked, the young women joked about their boyfriends and one man's offer to take his girl on a drive to visit a relative in Petaluma. Whatever it was all about, Tim didn't care to probe. He was usually quick with languages, and remembered a lot from his brief high school encounter with Spanish years ago, but he did not want to intrude on their privacy. What got his interest was the fact that the door to that other apartment was slightly ajar. Did he dare walk over and knock? Did he dare...No, better not. Hearing the sound of a man's approaching footsteps, he pulled his head out of that private hallway and went quickly to his own room, where he let himself in, took off his coat and threw it across a chair, and then sat on the bed feeling a mixture of embarrassment and curiosity.

She beamed. "I was hoping you would."

"No sign of our friend," Tim said, sliding his tray down and sitting opposite her as he had yesterday.

"Who, Nixon?" She laughed that quicksilver little laugh again, and he was sure now he'd heard a trace of it in the garden last night. "He's gone back east wherever he's stationed. I was talking with him yesterday, and he was bending my ear about how he's from Yorba Linda and he's going to run for Congress when he gets out."

"Well, we don't need him anymore, do we?"

She shook her head, blushing a tiny bit. They ate in silence for a few moments.

"Have you been here long?" Tim asked, sipping orange juice. "In San Francisco, I mean."

"About two weeks."

"I forgot to ask your name."

"Corinthia Johnson." She folded her arms behind her tray, leaving half her breakfast untouched. She didn't look like a heavy eater. "You can call me Corie if you'd like."

"Okay..." He wasn't quite sure whether he liked the nickname or her real name better.

"We hung some short handles on each other in a rush." She added, "In England."

"You were stationed there?"

"No, I was flying bombers to there."

It began to dawn on him. "Oh, you're—"(He noticed the garrison cap stuck jauntily in her epaulet under twin silver captain's bars.)"—a WAFS." It was the acronym for the Women's Auxiliary Ferrying Service.

"That's right, Doughboy. So what's your handle?"

"Make that sailor, kiddo. I'm Tim."

"Okay, Tim." She rolled his name around on her tongue and seemed to like it. "Tim, Tim, Tim..."

"Are you grounded here permanently, WAFS?"

"The shorter the better, sailor." She sucked orange juice through a straw.

"What do you fly?"

She said self-confidently: "Big ones. B-17s, B-24s, you name it."

"You're kidding."

"Nah. In fact, if you're interested, I'll take you up. I bet you're scared to fly."

He laughed. "I'm more scared of sinking on a ship."

She whistled with new respect. "Did that happen to you?"

"Oh yeah. North Atlantic, on a DE. Nazi sub. I was the only survivor. Saw a bunch of good men die."

"Aw geez." She slapped his forearm. "Then I owe ya, pal. For real. I'm going to be test-driving a giant soon—really big plane. Want to play?"

"You're scaring me."

"I am not. I see lust in your eyes."

"You are obviously mistaking terror for passion."

She grinned around her straw. "Hey, come on."

"Oh okay, you're twisting my arm." He put his hand on her wrist, and she leaned closer with an expectant look. He had not realized how blue her eyes were. "I wouldn't miss it for the world."

"I thought so." She winked. "I wasn't misreading anything."

He folded his hands between his knees and looked plaintive. "I was thinking also...well, along simpler lines...that maybe you'd like to do something like, well, take a walk along the water some time, or take in a movie, or an art gallery..."

"Art gallery," she said speculatively.

"I dabble."

"You have a few surprises of your own, sailor boy."

"You like art?"

"I love it. Spent many hours in the British Museum when it wasn't being splintered by Gerry bombs."

"Me too."

They talked on, exchanging pleasantries, and again suddenly she looked at her watch. "You do this to me all the time, Tim."

"I'm sorry. If I could, I'd say let's run away together."

"We can do that. Just not right now." She rose, gathering her purse and tray. "Want to call me?"

"I can holler from my window to yours."

"No you can't. That's one thing you can't do—get involved on that side."

"Okay." He was an iota taken back. "I can't have visitors either. I'm actually thinking of moving totally out of the Navy's reach."

"Good idea."

They rose and walked together to the tray disposal window.

"I don't have a lot of time," she said, earnestly. They pushed their trays in, and walked out of the dining room. "I'm going to be ferrying planes again soon, and that means I'm always in the air, in Europe, or now maybe Hawaii, the Philippines, who knows what. So if you want to show me the sights, better hurry." She touched his nose with the tip of her index finger and walked away down the main call. He watched her slender figure retreating on the wine-red Oriental carpet strip with its royal blue and other vivid colors, cast over a gleaming marble floor the color of tan taffy. She turned and said her phone number, and he waved.

Later that day, he called the number from his office. The sun shone, and a breeze through the half-open windows blew yellowed draw-shades around, floating beer-colored shapes of light over the paperwork on his desk. He tapped his fountain pen nervously on the wood desktop. A woman answered. Some air squadron with a long number and an odd acronym. He asked to speak with Corinthia Johnson, and a moment later she answered in a bright voice.

He said: "Hey, it's Tim."

"Hey."

"I was wondering if you would care to join me for a very ordinary American hamburger, French fries, and a cola. Maybe a pickle."

"Let me check with my stomach." She rustled. "Yep. She says let's do it. We have the what, the how, and the why covered. Just tell me where and when."

"Let me handle the details. You just show up."

"Sounds like a deal. You're flying?"

"I'm flying the 59 cent special. You fly the planes. We'll get along."

"You sweep me off my feet, sailor."

Then he remembered: "I don't have wheels."

"It's okay. I'll meet you..." She named a corner about three blocks from where he worked. "See you at lunchtime."

Intrigued, he went there in the thick of the lunchtime throng. Stomach growling, he craned his neck to look over the heads of men and women milling around him. Traffic was heavy, the air smelled of cigarette smoke and perfume and sweat, the street lights did their dance of colors, and the noise was deafening.

He heard the horn two or three times before turning to look at the large black 1944 Chevrolet with white-walled tires that had pulled up alongside him, drawing stares. Though there was no chrome, which was severely rationed for war purposes, the bumpers and grill and everything about the car glowed with newness. She beeped again, creeping forward as the light changed and someone else honked behind her. He got in as fast as he could, and let the door fall shut as she accelerated. "Wow, some chariot." He had to speak loudly to be heard over the noise of traffic and the roar of the engine. She had a boogie-woogie tune chugging from the ample radio speaker in the middle of the dash.

"I travel in style." Her aviator sunglasses glittered. A long, thin Pall Mall burned in the ashtray. Bluish smoke curled up over the dark brown wood-inlaid dashboard. She wore her khaki jumpsuit. That rakish little garrison cap tilted forward down one side of her forehead, right down to her sunglasses. The short brunette hair stuck out where she didn't have it pinned down, the way her mother probably had pinned it when she was small. "Honestly, Tim, it's my boss' car. I get to borrow all kinds of things with wings and wheels. You have no idea. I could have flown here in an autogyro for all that anyone cares."

"I'm just your average guy, sis." He held on as she accelerated through an orange light while a policeman glared after her and blew his whistle but did not wave her down.

"Sis! I have five brothers who call me that. You want a date or a handshake?" She had a wad of pink gum hidden in one cheek, and blew a bubble at him.

He pointed at her, one-up. "I have three sisters, and I'll take the date, Corie."

She pursed her lips and for a second he thought she was going to yell at him. The pink bubble popped, and she sucked its remnants off her upper lip. She yanked the gear shift lever around by the steering wheel and the car sank into fourth gear, cruising smooth as a battleship inland along Market Street toward Buena Vista Park. "That's sweet."

"What?"

"I like the way you call me Corie."

"That's your name, right?"

"A lot of people seem to think I'm some kind of grease monkey. You remind me that I'm a woman." Her sunglasses gleamed. She blew a bubble toward him. It popped, and he caught a breath of berries. "It's how you say it, sailor."

"I like Corinthia too."

"Too formal." She popped a bubble, and sucked the pink gum off her upper lip. "The Brits all seem to have names like that. Martina, Cornelia, Augusta."

He mouthed the old Gershwin tune: "I say tomato, you say tomah-to..."

She laughed and sang along: "I say potato, you say potah-to. Potato, potahto, tomato, tomahto!" They sang their way along several blocks, until they came to the line *If we ever part, Then that might break my heart!* She made a mournful face and whispered: "But we only just met!" and they continued singing about wearing pajamas, pah-yamas, and calling the calling off off. It seemed an oddly appropriate choice of songs. Her messages hit him broadcast strength. No dodging or evading. She was the real magoo. He felt sunshine inside. He said: "I'll bet they liked you over there."

"I think I disgruntled most of them. Though they have their BATs."

"Bats?"

"BATA. British Air Transport Auxiliaries. My flying cousins. We used to go drinking together in Sloan Square. Nice gals." She blew another large pink bubble and they pulled into the parking lot of a little restaurant. She handled the big wheel and shift lever with ease, parking. She had graceful hands, with long, trim fingers. Her nails were painted light pink, matching her lipstick.

She locked the car, and they walked toward the restaurant.

"It's quieter here," she said. "Less crowded."

His arm slipped easily around her waist, and her arm slipped around his, just for a minute or two. It was a court-martial offense for two officers to be seen this way. Arms back to their own torsos, they walked to a takeout window on the side of the building. They sat on the grass under a large eucalyptus tree, eating in the shade.

"Do you figure you'll be stationed here long?" she asked.

They sat side by side, and he liked the way her thigh touched his a few times when she bent forward to get a napkin or a pickle or a sip of cola.

"For the duration, probably." She sat close to him, hip to hip as if they were old friends, or lovers. He looked around casually, to see if there was a private moment when he could lean close and brush his lips against hers, and see what she was like when she got aroused. But no such moment availed itself. "I spent two years at the Admiralty in London, and now they're moving us all west to keep adding pressure on the Japanese. So, if things go badly, they may move a lot of us to Hawai'i. If the war keeps going well, they won't bother. Who knows, we might all be going home in a year or so." He winked at her. "What do you do then?"

"The thought kind of scares me." She dabbed her mouth with a paper napkin. "The girls think they'll scrap the WAFS and send us back to be homemakers."

"You'd make a cute nurse."

"I don't want to stick thermometers up people's arseholes. I like flying four engine bombers."

"I don't like tinkering with clocks, but that's what I'm likely to go do in Connecticut unless I can think of something better."

"You could go to Paris and paint."

"I spent a short vacation there." He smiled at vague memories of red wine, cheese, and good bread. No time to meet any interesting women on that trip.

She looked wistfully into her own past. "I went to Paris with a girlfriend from Kansas. We spent three cold, dreary wet days without a shower running from one museum to another, didn't understand a word, and I caught a cold, but we had great food and the people seemed really nice."

"They were damned glad to have the Germans gone," Tim said.

"Funny. We're from these little towns across the USA. Like I'm from St. Louis and you're from New Haven. With all the ugliness, we did get to see the world a bit. Maybe we can start a company or something, huh?"

"Sure. I could sell clocks and you could fly them to their new owners."

"Think positive."

"I am. I'm glad we're friends."

"Me too." She winked. "Good business idea, though. Kind of like making time fly, eh?"

"So what were you saying about the why this morning?" he asked.

"Huh?"

"Now that we've covered the who, what, when, where, and how. You left the why up in the air."

She propped her chin on her palm and regarded him coyly. "That, my friend, is a delicate matter that will require considerable thought."

"Is it something I can help you with?"

"Oh, I think we'll have to do it together. Cost you extra though."

"You mean like postage and handling."

"Naw. A strawberry shake, you lug."

"Oh baby, talk to me like that all day."

She slipped her arm around his. He patted her hand. "You have no idea how nice it feels to be holding hands with a real, hundred percent American girl. It's good to be home." He looked at her in amazement, for it had not occurred to him until that very moment.

She said softly: "If I can help the war effort, I'll be glad to do my part." She sat really close to him, and gave his hand a squeeze under the table. They couldn't hold hands in public, being in uniform, but they did manage to squeeze each other's hands furtively several times. After lunch, she rocketed the car down an alley framed in bougainvillea, and pulled under the shade of a big, leafy tree. She kept the engine idling. "We have a minute or two," she said. "How creative can you be?"

He put his arm around her, and pulled her close. "Depends on how you appreciate your art." She furtively stuck her bubblegum under the dashboard, and slid very willingly toward his embrace. He pulled her softness and warmth close. They kissed passionately. He felt her hand on his ribs, caressing, while their tongues hungrily wriggled together. He caressed her downy cheek as they kissed. The moment ended when rowdy men's voice sounded in the alley, drawing near, laborers back from lunch. She whisked a last kiss on his mouth, with a brief flick of the tongue between his lips, and sprang to the wheel. "Tim, I have a thing for you, honey."

He clapped a fist to his chest. "You make my clock strike every minute on the minute."

When she was within a few blocks of the corner where she'd picked him up, and the light turned red, she stopped the car as throngs of pedestrians passed before the hood. She turned to him and said with a measure of urgency in her voice: "Tim... don't take this the wrong way. I really hope you will take me out a bit. I don't know how long I'll be here, and you seem like such a swell guy."

"I was just thinking the same thing," he said. "Not that you're a swell guy, but that you are...you make...well, you make me feel warm all over."

She regarded him pensively. He peeled her bubblegum off and handed it to her. She didn't put it in her mouth, but sat looking at it, rolling it between her fingertips. "Tim, I am involved in something that I cannot tell you about."

"Me too. We all have our secret duties. I'm prepared for anything."

She looked away into some darkness. "I want to play straight with you, and I can't. That bothers me." Her eyes looked troubled. "I wish things were simple."

"Oh no," he said. "Do you have a Thing in your life?"

She looked him straight in the eye. "Yes."

"Another man." His heart was falling like an Empire State Building elevator.

She had to pause a second before answering. "Hm—no."

"You're married. You have a husband who is a prisoner of the Nazis. Unless you spy for them, they'll kill him."

"Tim, be serious."

"I am serious. That's what happened to me in London."

She looked at him long and hard, running a fingertip down his chest. "You're kidding. Well, this is nothing like that. At the risk of making myself seem cheap and easy, you don't have any competition in this ride at the moment."

"I want the ride."

"Will you always be nice to me like this?"

"Yeah. Let's make a deal," he said. "You don't break my heart, and I don't break yours."

"I'll do my very best. You do the same, sailor." She threw herself against him, hands on his chest, and planted a warm, wet kiss tongue to tongue, intense and full of puppy eagerness. He closed his eyes, wrapped his right arm around her so that he cupped her delicate shoulder blade in his palm and felt the long, smooth rille of her spine all pinched up receiving the intensity of his returning kiss. She held his face in her palms and looked at him, around the ceiling, and at him again. "Is it just me, or is it springtime in this car?"

Corinthia Johnson

Over the next several days, Tim and Corie saw a lot of each other.

She warned him again, on another occasion. They met in the lobby of the Hotel Auger one afternoon, having changed into civvies after work: "I have some ugly stuff to do for a while, and I can't wait for it to be over." When he looked at her, puzzled, she made an exasperated face. "Have you ever had a splinter in your finger, and you keep forgetting it's there? And every time you touch something, it hurts?"

"You got a splinter?"

"Yeah."

"Anything I can help with?"

"Absolutely not. I have to live a double life for a while longer, and it's killing me. I am so happy to be with you, and then I feel the splinter. Every time I let myself go."

"Is it another man? A woman? A person." To each, she said "Mm—no."

He tried to put on a casual air, but some alarm was going off inside. "This damn war. Damn, crazy war. Now I seem to be getting a splinter too."

"We can't." She looked sad, hugging her purse to herself. "Fall in love right this moment."

"You gotta level with me, kid. Is there a husband? A guy?"

She shook her head. "No husband, no fiancé, nothing like that. It's more complicated than that. And I can't tell you."

"I'm puzzled, because you're telling me there's something you can't tell me."

"Oh I know, you think I'm nuts. I don't blame you. The trouble is, Tim, I'm so bad at lying or being deceitful." She pressed the tip of her index finger against the softness of the bow of his upper lip. "Tell you what. I'll do my best to try and fool you. How's that? Don't snoop, don't ask. It will go away before the end of the year, at the latest."

He had a flash of insight. "Uncle Sam?"

She shrugged, letting him believe what he wanted to. "Yes." She turned away, wrapped in self-loathing.

He glimpsed a dark corridor of the soul, like the one Anna Stokowska had not let him in, and when she did, it ruined everything. "I'm not going to pry," he said. "I've been around this block before."

She stared up at him, her eyes looking haunted. "I do like you a whole lot. It's just—I may have to go away for a while now and then. Official stuff."

"Gotcha. I dabble in necromancy myself. Mum's the word both ways. Can we just enjoy being together?"

"I do so, so want that, so very much," she breathed in relief.

Crank sheet into typewriter. Stare at blank paper. Rest head on fists, shake head. What is the script here?

They walked together, arm in arm, into the late afternoon sunshine and strolled down Powell Street toward Union Square. She wore browns and tans today, coffee and cream: dark loafers, fine sand-colored wool knee socks, a dark pleated skirt; a brown wool blazer with a little dark green trim on the lapels; a silk kerchief from Paris thrown around her neck; and a small chocolate colored beret. He wore a gray wool suit, blue shirt, and red tie loose at the neck. He felt slightly embarrassed because he had not bothered to buy a fresh hat, but he hadn't felt like dressing up since his arrival—until now. A man without a hat was like a man without shoes and pants.

They walked downhill, with the tall Art Deco style tower of the Francis Drake Hotel on their left. A yellow-paneled cable car ratcheted past going uphill on the twin tracks, while another hummed on its way down over the cobblestones, farther up. Cars and roadsters were tightly parked at the curb. The streets looked well kept and not much like those of a city at war— except for the men and women in uniform everywhere. San Francisco was, after all, one of the great debarkation points for military personnel and ships heading west into the war that continued to rage with exceptional and increasing savagery, as the stakes grew higher for the Japanese, and the battles came closer to their home turf.

He squeezed her arm against his ribs, and she huddled against him as if they'd been lovers for a long time, when in fact they had only kissed once or twice. He pointed to the neon-lined star atop the Drake. "See that up there? The top floors, that's the swankiest dance place in Frisco. Want to go there sometime?"

"How about tonight?"

"Not sure we're dressed enough. We can stop and ask."

She squeezed. "Mm." She breathed: "Let's." She laid her head on his shoulder so that her chin pressed into his chest. "Let's go buy you a hat."

The doorman directed them to the reception desk, and a short, dark-skinned man with a mustache, who could have machinegun-sandbagged at any desk in Paris or London, examined their I.D. cards. He threw his airs aside and spread his arms. "Military officers...by all means. Floor show is at eight, and you might want to freshen the tie a little, young man, but you both look just great."

"Thanks," they said beaming. She towed him along to the bar on the first floor, which was dark and smelled of steaks and smokes and whiskey. They stepped down into the darkness and almost had to feel their way along. Tim let the dim glow of the brass bar rail guide him. They nosed through a crowd of enviously watching older men, many nursing long slow beers and sucking on cigars. They found one bar stool free, next to a sign "No Ladies At the Bar." All the tables were taken, so Tim sat on the barstool. She stood between his knees with her arms around his waist and her chin resting on his shoulder.

The bar manager, a harried man in a sweaty white shirt with rolled up sleeves and loose green tie, stepped up. "Sir..."

"She's not at the bar. We'll grab a table as soon as one is free."

The man started to turn and point to the sign, but Tim laid two bucks on the bar and held his military ID between index finger and forefinger. He said: "We're both tired from defending America all day."

"Since you put it that way," the man said, "What's your poison?"

Tim and Corie had a brief eyeball consultation. "Couple of short ones," Tim said over his shoulder, as she pressed close. They really did hit it off so well, Tim thought. What was the catch? Why the underlying *yes, but...*?

"On the house," the manager said curtly, slapping down a pair of small beers that slid for a second or two in a wake of their own overflowing foam. The manager pushed the two dollars back at Tim and strode off to supervise his busy bar. "Wish I'd known you in London," she said into his chest.

"Me too."

"I'll bet you were the hit of the town. All the girls thought you were suave."

"I refuse to answer your inflammatory question on grounds that I may incinerate myself." Tim impulsively did what any red-blooded G.I. was likely to do in this setting—he put his palms against the small of her back, pulled her to him, and tilted her head back to plant a long, oscillating kiss on her, to which she responded by hanging from his neck and giving back as good as he gave. Their tongues wiggled hungrily together. Couples at a nearby table applauded.

The manager called from the middle of the room, where he stood guarding a small table. He tapped a pair of menus onto his palm like hatchets to ward off potential table pirates. Tim and Corie carried their glasses as they sidled through the crowd to their table. They shuffled over the hard wood floors, among coats and hats that smelled vaguely stale, catching the occasional whiff of a man's spicy pomade or a woman's alluring fragrance.

"I've forgotten what it's like," he told her as they sat huddled close, holding hands, waiting for their chops and fries. They were surrounded by a wall of sounds: a din of words and laughter, punctuated by scraping chair legs, clattering dinner ware, clinking glasses, and of course the distant sound of music pouring from a jukebox smooth as toothpaste: Duke Ellington and Harry James (*I'm Beginning To See The Light*); Johnny Mercer (*Accentuate the Positive*); Buddy Kaye (*Till The End of Time*); and more.

"Oh come on, I'll bet you were out every night in London." She seemed a little jealous, and he liked that.

"It got old."

"No steady flame?" Speaking of flames, little candles of worry guttered in her eyes. She gripped him and wasn't letting go.

"Lots of candles, no flame." He held her to him as if she were his girl.

"That's what I suspected, with a sailor like you." She relaxed and regained her cocky composure.

"And you?"

She looked down. He'd forgotten—it was complicated, whatever it was. But she smacked her bubble gum in his face and said: "I'm picky."

He said: "Honey, I almost fell in love back in London. I mean...I probably was halfway in the soup, and I still feel a little watery around the scuppers about her. There was another man buried deep down in her background, and I may never really understand—" *How a woman can love a man who is out of reach, and yet love a man who is right there with her in another place, and just have everyone dangling out to the wind without going backward or forward, just stuck on the tracks going nowhere. Anna!*

"The Nazis?"

He stared at her bubble. "Oh yeah, I told you."

"Nothing like that, sailor. I can give you one honest answer. There's nobody special in my life. Nobody. You can bank on that, sweetheart. I'm true blue, a straight shooter. That's why—" She seemed to bite her tongue.

"I believe you, and I appreciate that. Before I met you, all I had to hold at night was my book." He could still make out something in the shadows of her psyche, something hidden, something secret. Why did the women he met all have these hidden Things? But she brightened and lifted that brunette head in a smile. "Romance is a scary thing, sailor." She smacked her gum. "We have to be very brave." The way she said it, he got the feeling she'd been badly burned somewhere by someone. Who hadn't been?

"Will it be easier if we hold hands in the dark?"

"Maybe I'll be lucky and get to hang out with you for a month or two. I might get to be a real nuisance."

Start typing: "Love, a brief, one-act play starring Nordhall and Johnston." Brief run of a few days only.

"Somehow I doubt that, and you know it."

She sat back, smoothing her skirt. as if crafting just a few molecules of separation between them. "I'm going to try not to make it a painful parting when it comes, Tim. You understand it does have to come."

"You keep telling me that."

She frowned. "Tim."

"Stop Timming me. I take your word for it. Hey, it's war and we live from one minute to the next. When you go, you go. When I go, I go. It's simple."

She clutched his hand in both of hers. "You're not going to be grouchy about it, are you?" She reached up and stroked his hair.

"No. Time's too valuable to waste on negativity." He wanted to take her in his arms. They'd just met and he had no right to go getting googoo about her. Better to do as she'd suggested and just enjoy things while they lasted. Remembering the boys in the surf off Mauritania reinforced his conviction that he must take life a day at a time, sometimes an hour a time, or even minute by minute. Nothing was certain. Armed with that bitter crutch, that astringent medicine, he took her hands in his and turned them this way and that, admiring her boyishly trimmed square nails with their plain pink polish. They were hard-used hands with faint scars and one or two ink stains, but they were soft and electric when they lovingly brushed over his skin. "I'm going to enjoy every minute we have together," he said looking into her worried, waiting face.

"Oh, I think I might just cry," she said suddenly, fumbling in her purse for a hankie. Out came a dainty folded square smelling of cologne. She dabbed her eyes a bit. He worried about her just then. What could make her seem so trapped and so sad?

Dinner came, and they ate quietly. She made a *gamine* face and pushed her broccoli over onto his plate, looking about as if she hoped nobody would see.

"Don't like broccoli?" he asked.

"Makes me think about throwing up."

"These are the nice little things about you that I soak up like sunshine."

"Oh you are such a Sinatra radio."

"I would croon for you, but the other cats would toss me off the fence."

"You don't need to croon, sailor. I hear your sweet voice and I swoon."

"Poetry, huh? You know what I can't wait to do?"

"What's that?"

"I want to have a little privacy to sit with you, hold your hands, and gaze into your eyes—for hours. Just for whatever short time we have."

"Aw, gee. Well, maybe that can be arranged." She rubbed her ankle against his leg under the table.

They ate their dinner and then drifted to the lobby, where she waited with a cluster of women while Tim lined up with other men to buy tickets. The floorshow was just starting when they were ushered into the drafty dance hall. They found seats near a table full of high ranking U.S. military brass and their wives, just as the backlit red curtains rose and the 18-member band started its opening number, and exotic female dancers in tight little blue outfits and tall-plumed headgear came running out of the wings. Everyone clapped happily and the show was on. Across the world, Tim knew, the master race were sitting in their smoking ruins wondering what had gone wrong, as were the rest of the self-proclaimed superior beings around the world. The steaks and the beer were gone, as was the stage show, and America was on top of the universe. America had been kicked around, sprung upon in a vicious surprise attack by wild-eyed murderers, and now they were vanquished while she rose triumphant, a power like no other the world had ever seen. Liberty waved her torch over New York Harbor, a light to the world, and on the West Coast the recently completed Golden Gate Bridge held out its lights like a jeweled necklace for the Orient to behold. Everyone in the room was aware of it, and nobody had to say it. And everyone was aware there were plenty of good souls who had left their lives in graves, marked or unmarked, around the world to make it possible, but even that would soon become memory as time marched on. As the good padre in the London blitz had said, "Live your life for their sake, lad." So Tim held hands under the table with Corie, and they both knew well enough to enjoy every moment for what it was worth. *C'est la guerre.*

Secret Heart—Meg

Corie worked at a secret installation somewhere in the vast tangle of Navy facilities along the coastline. Sometimes she was gone for days at a time. At other times, she had time off to go shopping or lie around her apartment doing her nails and listening to show tunes while sipping cold juleps; or, lately, to go out on dates with Tim.

Tim worked regular hours, starting at seven and ending at four-thirty, with an hour off for lunch. His time was regulated by the blare of production whistles in the shipyards along the harbor line and the repair facilities near the Presidio. San Francisco had become the war, and the war had become San Francisco. It wasn't like that for those fighting and dying on remote, sun-baked atolls in the Pacific. Same went for the Allied occupiers mopping up the ruins of Germany with its Werewolf teenagers, its fanatical Nazi sympathizers, and its secret Alpine redoubts. Tim had seen enough of war and was content to now be part of this city that daily grew a little more assured of victory. Already the flags of peace flew as the city girded herself for the founding of the United Nations.

Then there was the roommate, who was intriguing in her own right.

Holding hands one evening, Tim and Corie wandered into the mausoleal halls of the Hotel Auger. They walked up the stairs, through the French doors, and into the upper lobby where the concierge desk dominated the landscape. At the moment the lobby was dim, the concierge desk empty, and only a green-shaded banker's lamp lit by the switchboard to indicate that someone was on duty and available if needed—probably Li Wong, the enigmatic functionary whose family had served Josephine Auger since the 1800s. The Hotel Auger had a private wing that was off limits to all military residents using the facility as a BOQ. The private wing, in whose top story the rarely seen Josephine Auger herself still resided, housed longstanding residents, most of them elderly and wealthy with Auger connections dating back into the previous century. Their privacy was sacred, as was their right to quiet and respect.

Corie put a finger over her lips to shush Tim. She towed him along down a hall to the left. This had thus far been forbidden territory to Tim. "It's like wonderland," he whispered. She giggled. Somehow, Corie had become insinuated into this private world in which hospital equipment sat in shadowy hallway corners, and private duty nurses came and went at all hours. "We have to be very quiet," Corie whispered as she towed him up a back stairway. The stairs were wood, the walls white, the Fire Department markings very institutional. "Mrs. Auger lives here. She took in some nursing home patients to free up hospital rooms. They're all old and confined to their beds," she whispered. "It's great. Nobody bothers us."

Us? He wondered. She had a key, with which she unlocked one of the heavy double doors with frosted glass that overlooked each floor. He caught a glimpse outside, through the hall window, and recognized his own window nearby.

She pulled him into the hallway on her floor and locked the heavy door behind her. She strode out with her arms spread as if drawing a picture. "It's a cross shape. There are twelve apartments—three to each arm of the cross. We got lucky and wound up in an end unit. They each have an extra room."

Before he could ask any questions, she shushed him again with a finger on her lips. "Not supposed to be here with you," she whispered. She knocked softly on a door and then put her palms and one ear against the door to listen. Delicately, she knocked again and listened. "I think she's home," she said, and unlocked the door. "My roommate." Shushing him yet again, she pushed the door open, sidled inside, and beckoned for him to follow.

Once he was in and she closed the door, she wiped imaginary sweat from her forehead with her wrist. "Whew!" She pressed her hands against his shoulders to suggest he stay by the door. "Meg!" she called out. "Meg?"

An attractive young dark-haired woman appeared. She strode toward them down a long hallway. She held a cigarette in one hand and wore a thick dark blue bathrobe. She had a bath towel wrapped around her head, with frizzy stray wisps of black hair visible where the towel folds crossed over her damp forehead. She clearly had just taken a bath or shower. With her free hand, she flicked open a pair of pink-rimmed glasses and put them on. She stared at Tim through round lenses with frank, penetrating curiosity, then at Corie. "Friend?"

For a second, it seemed to Tim that time stood still as the two women regarded each other with telegrams of information flickering between their eyes, a hooded semaphore of past conversations and agreements, while traffic noise drifted easily up through an open window along with a timeless breeze of citrus blossoms.

"Not foe, for sure," Corie said.

"I'm Meg," the woman said, shifting the cigarette to her left hand and sticking out her right. She had smaller hands than Corie, but Meg's fingers were heavier. She wore dark-red, richly glossy nail polish. Meg had a slight foreign accent that Tim couldn't place. "Tim," he said, shaking her hand.

"Mind if I show Tim around?" Corie asked.

"Honey, next time give me some warning so I don't look like this." Meg turned regally, holding up her cigarette with two fingers so the smoke would trail behind her. "You see, Mr. Nordhall, that we do not entertain often."

Corie laughed. "We're very virtuous."

Meg made a face. "Not exactly overflowing with boyfriends, are we? Go right ahead, kids. Make yourselves at home. You can show him my room while I finish my nails in the bathroom."

"Thanks," Corie said. She took Tim's hand. "Come on, I'll take you on the grand tour. It's free and lasts all of two seconds." The two-bedroom apartment had a small entrance hallway with closets at either end. Slightly off to one side was the entrance into the kitchen, a small crow's nest affair with a pair of windows overlooking the city and the harbor in a spectacular view. The bathroom was on the right, where Meg sat in steamy isolation. She looked up like a towel-clad polar bear disturbed in its ruminations. "If you have to go—" Corie said, and just as quickly she pulled the bathroom door shut. "It's awkward," she whispered. She led Tim to the other side of the kitchen, where a hallway led down to a window facing into a tree crown. On either side of the hallway were two doors. Corie opened the first door and let him look into a shadowy world of old heavy ornate oak furniture, glass buffet windows behind which pewter and china gleamed with borrowed light. "Meg's room," she said, pulling the door closed. She pushed him gently on. "My room," she said, pulling the next door open. Tim glimpsed a lighter, airier room—a curious mix in which baby blue bed clothes, fluffy pillows, and stuffed animals mingled with bomber ornaments on the walls, a helmet and a pistol in its web holster, combat boots sagging in the middle of the floor, and a collection of award plaques with military signature blocks. That door was pulled closed just as quickly in his face, and she guided him to the living room at the end of the hall, a small enclosure that made a kidney-shaped turn to the right with two more windows, all three windows losing their views in tree crowns through which street lamps from the next block dimly cast their glow. "Our little home," she said "Ain't it divine?"

He nodded appreciatively, looking up and around while she took his jacket. "It beats my little cell."

"I was going to make a cocktail for myself," she said. "Want to join me?"

"Then I'll have one too." He waited alone, sitting on a couch over a coffee table, while she went to the kitchen. He heard a mixer whir. He heard the bathroom door open, and a long whispered conversation ensue in serious tones with many exclamation marks in it. Each woman took her turn at remarking at some unidentifiable outrage with a slight yelp. Then, after about five minutes, he heard them laugh, and he heard the snick of a long-handled cocktail spoon in a glass, and the rattle of tumbling ice cubes. He sat uncomfortably, not wanting to listen in to their conversation, so he diverted his attentions to vague sounds of wind, plumbing, and echoes of the night through open windows.

"Here we go," Corie said brightly, bringing a pair of cocktails professionally mixed, with tiny lemon curls on each rim. "I didn't tell you that I helped out in the family bar back home in Kansas."

He was glad not to have to sit waiting any longer and laughed. "No." He took the glass. "Thanks. Hmm, feels nice and cold."

"We have ice cubes," she said. Not everyone did. She sat down on the couch, a discreet distance away—just far enough, if he became so bold later, to put a hand around her back and pull her close. It was her show, he felt, and he let her define the program for the evening. He was taking it day by day as they'd agreed, flowing with it, accepting whatever came next even if that included the end of the friendship.

"Thanks," Meg said, holding a martini with a lemon twist. Meg was a bit more solid than the wiry Corie. Meg still wore the turban and robe, and was barefoot. She sat in a stuffed chair opposite them. Both women were about the same height—about 5'6 to Tim's six feet tall. Corie sat on the edge of the couch for some time, while Meg sat back, modestly pushing the heavy robe down to cover as much of her legs as she could, down to her ankles. Meg looked directly into Tim's eyes and said: "You'll have to forgive me, but I've taken off my makeup for the day."

"I don't mind a bit," Tim assured her. "You look just fine to me." She looked Mexican but then maybe not, yet faintly exotic, and attractive.

They all laughed, and the atmosphere mellowed even more as they raised their glasses in a toast. Corie rose and turned down the light, so that the room was dim and cozy. Meg lit a cigarette and with the same match lit a candle that lay flickering in an apricot-colored dish on the coffee table. Some time later, after much small talk, Corie mixed another set of martinis. Tim began to feel warm and loosened his collar. Corie leaned over and undid his tie. As she did so, she diddled his stomach with little-kid fingers, tickling him. When he looked down, she brought her finger up to gently brush his nose. "Gotcha."

Meg sat enthroned in her turban and blew smoke to one side. "My roommate needs constant supervision."

"That's why you're here," Tim said.

"That's right. You better watch out, Tim, because we know you live over there and we are going to supervise you too."

"I need two supervisors, huh?"

"Two attractive young women," Meg said, "you should be so lucky."

"That's right," Corie said, "we could be two fat old sergeants with beard shadow and big sticks." She held her hands up like bear claws and made grunting noises.

Meg laughed. "Corie, sweetheart, you are too much." She flicked her cigarette ash into the candle. "I worry about you in those giant planes. It's a wonder you can reach the controls."

Corie squared her shoulders. "They do what I tell them."

Tim broke the ice a little more with the roommate. "Meg, are you Navy?"

Meg shook her head and picked a speck of tobacco from the tip of her tongue. "Civilian," she answered, "State Department." She seemed a strong, self-assured dynamo. Her eyes, though, had a veiled, calculating look that suggested everything was far more complicated than anyone could guess. *Does she have a Thing?* Tim wondered. *All my women lately seem to.*

Meg seemed clairvoyant. She said in a low, nurturing voice: "You don't smoke and my cigarette is bothering you." She pushed two windows open, stretching from her seat. That let in a night breeze, cross-current. He heard again the soothing sounds of traffic, the faint chuckle of a radio playing boogie-woogie music, distant ships' horns—high piping, then low booming, then a blast of sound, then more piping—as they conversed with each other in fog off the coast. Sensing his curiosity, she added to her explanation: "We're getting ready for the President and a lot of dignitaries to come out here for the opening of the U.N., and I have certain things to do in helping out with that." Sensing his further question, she added: "Corie and I happen to be friends and this was a good opportunity to set up shop together. I'm sorry it's so small and we're all jammed in on top of each other. As a Navy man you're used to close quarters."

"This looks quite nice," he said. "This is a lovely city. It's a wonder they can jam so many people and ships in here. We're sardines everywhere we turn."

"One gets used to it," Meg said with a sigh. "I'm going to turn in, Corie honey. Treat our friend nice and don't embarrass me, huh?"

"I'll do my best," Corie said folding her hands piously on her knees and looking utterly insincere. "See you in the morning."

Meg gave Tim a friendly little wave. "Nice meeting you." The two women adjourned for ten minutes in the kitchen, in the bathroom, and in Meg's bedroom for whispering. He felt tired now with the cocktails in him, and was actually beginning to think about heading home. That meant sneaking back down the stairs, maybe out in to the courtyard, and then pretending to have come in from outside somewhere. Back to his cold, lone room where moonlight gleamed on floor boards and the steam heater sighed under the window.

Corie came back in about fifteen minutes and sat down by him. "We're alone!" She looked at him closely. "Are you still awake?"

"Sorry. I was lost in thought. Everything is always complicated."

She looked into her glass. "Oh-oh. I think it's time for another."

"I don't think I can."

"Oh come on. Join me. You can just sip a little." She giggled. "I can usually drink men under the table. I must have an extra-big liver." She filled her cheeks with air and raised her hands as if holding an enormous gut ten times her actual girth. Her eyes rolled and she made along *phhhhht* noise with pursed lips.

He reached out toward her, and she was ready, leaning toward him. They had been brushing their bodies close together for several days now at every opportunity, courting, hinting, insinuating.

"At last, we are alone," she whispered.

It was awkward sitting on the couch but they managed to kiss and hold each other. Gradually, they eased into more comfortable positions. She curled up beside him, he sprawling toward her with his legs scissored half under the coffee table. She lay with her back against the cushions and welcomed his hand as it roamed along the flat of her belly. Dutifully, she pushed his hand away several times in the dance that said she was a good girl. As her breath grew more rapid, her hand failed in its defensive measures and lay guardingly on his wrist as he explored more territory: the smooth skin along her back, the silky scoops of a brassiere capturing small breasts, the bony hollows of her neck bones. He pulled her down on him, and she lay on top, tongue against tongue, slender body draped over his while he clutched her shoulder blades in his palms. He became more and more aroused. The third drinks were forgotten as they embraced and kissed long and passionately. He heard a clock ticking, wind sighing, trees rustling, light rain falling and rattling on leaves. He heard her breath coming in hungry gasps, heard his own aroused wheezing, heard their faint moaning as they worked one another's pent-up desires.

"Oh my God," she said, holding her hair. "Stop!"

He lay back weakly and looked up at her. "I can't stop and I can't go on."

They spoke in soft tones and stopped once or twice to listen in case Meg scolded.

"I'll have to help you," she said, planting a controlling little kiss on the tip of his nose. "You are a very skillful kisser."

"I'm just a modest little fellow with no special talent." He cupped her firm little behind in both hands and patted her buttocks noisily so she rocked forward and backward.

"Liar." She smothered him in a wet kiss while breathing hard.

"Either I have been out of it too long, or you are too seductive for words."

"Swell my head, go ahead." She kissed his cheeks, first one, then the other.

They lay looking at each other. Her eyes were blue and filled with stray starlight or streetlight, whatever it was. Her lips had a wry quality, but her eyes were earnest. It was a confusing message. He wanted to fall in love with her, but she had warned him off. What could he do if not fall in love with her? If he could not say "I am in love with you" (and certainly it was premature for such serious talk) then what? "I am in adoration with you"? "I am in lust with you"? "I am in desire with you"? "I am in attraction with you"? "I am the seriously blue-balled guy-next-door nuts about you"?

"I had better weigh anchor and shove off," he instead said, struggling to get up. At the same time his hands explored the long, slender curve of her belly and waist, and her soft, strong thighs.

She pushed him down. "Not so fast." She giggled. "I got you up here, and now I'm not letting you go. Seriously, they have a private security guard who patrols every hour below. You're going to have to spend the night here on the couch and I'll help you sneak out in the morning." She planted one more kiss on his lips, a dry one, and sat up. She stretched and yawned. "I think I'm going to sleep very soundly."

And they both did, he on the couch, she in her bedroom.

Meeting Howard Lemon

Disaster struck in the form of a notice, unceremoniously delivered to Tim at work from the Naval Housing Office.

It was hard to find living space anywhere in the small, crowded city. Foreign diplomats were everywhere—men in turbans; and women with strange accents, practically falling out of the walls. Tim read with bulging eyes and throbbing temple arteries that he was instructed to immediately vacate his quarters in the Hotel Auger and report to the V/BOQ at the Presidio for a room. He stepped into Teague's office and closed the door, waving the sheet of paper. "I'm being bounced out of my quarters."

Teague looked up with a cold grin. "You look pale."

Tim sat down heavily, thinking to himself, *you sacred cow, you can sit there with that hideous little grin while you live with your wife and kids in a nice home on Navy property.* "I was hoping you could help somehow."

"I understand you're being bounced out in favor of some Charlie Chan types. The Housing Office routinely copied me and your chain of command."

"What a let-down," Tim said thickly.

"This United Nations comedy will be over in two months or so," Teague said, calmly working on. He was one of those gray bureaucrats who had ice water in their veins. He sat with his hands on a large open ledger, pencil in one hand and eraser in the other, checking for errors in the petty cash accounting of some WREN. He wasn't mean about it, though. Good man to work for, just cold and annoying in the service of his chain of command.

"Nothing you can do to help?"

"Sorry." Teague put his pencil and eraser down and rubbed his eyes.

Tim thought glumly that by then, perhaps, Corie would be gone, or he might be transplanted elsewhere. Anything was possible, as this forcefully reminded him.

"These foreign honchos will be gone in a month or two and we can all get back to normal," Teague said. He added, in a slightly different perspective on the same galaxy of uncertainties that everyone lived with: "Who knows, the war might be over in a half a year or a year, and we can all go home." The unspoken question was if there really was a Fortress Japan that must be taken inch by bleeding inch.

"Thank you," Tim said angrily, getting up and leaving the room.

Stan Kehoe wasn't much help either, though he tried. "Jeez, Tim, if only I'd known. It's all so sudden. Say, you want to double up with me? I can toss a sleeping bag on the floor for you."

Tim laughed, clapping his friend on the shoulder. "Thanks, bud, that's very kind of you. If I wanted to be in the submarine service I would have signed up for the extra pay. No, I'll just take my medicine and check in at the flea hotel and then look for something a little better."

"We could have some dandy parties," Stan said.

"That's one of the things I'm afraid of."

📖

Three men in overalls were busy in his room. A fourth man in a business suit was with them, a civilian who had cop written all over him. "You the owner of this room?" the man asked from behind glittering little round lenses.

"The former owner, I guess," Tim said, dusting off the gold-braided sleeves of his dark navy-blue uniform jacket.

The plump cop, who looked as though he couldn't run a block without falling down unconscious, wiped sweat from his forehead with a large white handkerchief. "I'm going to give you a piece of advice, admiral."

"Lieutenant Commander," Tim said.

"Napoleon, for all I care. You are not to speak to anyone about our being here today, do you understand?" He waved a billfold that identified him as Howard Lemon, FBI. He stepped close and shook the billfold offensively in Tim's face. "I said, do you understand, or do I need to treat you to some listening lessons?"

Tim must have looked as if he were about to belt Howard Lemon.

Howard Lemon, for his turn, pulled back one side of his ugly gray-green flannel suit jacket to expose his rumpled pinstriped shirt, with a sweat-stained armpit and below that a deadly looking .38 revolver. "Don't fuck with me, crackerjack. I don't have time."

"I'll come back when you're gone, and remove my things."

"No." Howard Lemon stuck a tobacco-stained finger in his face. "Get your stuff out of here right now and don't come back." He softened a bit: "I don't like this any more than you do."

Tim thought about thumping him, but decided to remain prudent if he ever hoped to move back into the Hotel Auger. He packed his sea bag, slamming in his shoes, his books, the whole bit. Already he'd picked up more than he could get in the bag, so he threw the bag unceremoniously out onto the carpeted hallway. As he stormed about, stumbling over the three men in overalls who measured, who drilled holes, who strung wire that they pulled off a roll in a leather bag filled with electrical equipment, he noticed that Corie's window was dark as if nobody was home. Tim gathered the rest of his things including the stack of library books in a cardboard grocery box. As he walked out with the box under his arm, it was all he could do to restrain himself from saying something more to Lemon. Why bother? He could only let his mouth get him in trouble at this point. If Lemney would come to his rescue, he might even wangle an apology from this flatfoot. But what he most wanted was his room back because it put him next to Corie.

He put the sea bag and the cardboard box by the lift and pressed the button. The stodgy, slow metal box was in service elsewhere in the bowels of the Hotel Auger and would predictably be a few minutes in coming. Impulsively, he walked down the hall and tried the door marked *Private*. It was locked. Dispirited, he returned to the lift just in time to open the door, push his bag and the box inside with his foot, and leave his little world behind. Before doing so, he left a note for Corie with Li Wong, who bowed and clucked sympathetically.

Back to the BOQ

"Welcome, Sir," said the sergeant in the V/BOQ at the Presidio. "Have we met before?"

Tim had recovered somewhat from his shock and displeasure by now. He'd begun looking at all that could go right. For one thing, maybe Lemney and Teague could get him his room back after the politicians had all left. For another thing, maybe it was the incentive to spur him into looking for something slightly farther out of town, totally on the economy, and so what if he had to pay a little extra beyond the housing allowance the Navy paid. Perhaps, even, it might be a place Corie would enjoy visiting. The possibilities were intriguing. But for tonight he was just angry and miserable. It was worst because he'd been unable to reach Corie at her office, and she wasn't home at the hotel.

The sergeant smiled innocently, elderly man that he was, rubbing gnarled fingers over the linen that smelled of soap and cigarette ashes.

"Yeah," Tim said reluctantly, "I checked in here a few weeks ago when I first got into town."

The sergeant leaned forward with a big grin that Tim at first took for insolence, but it was a gesture of sympathy. The sergeant whispered: "We're getting lots in here like yourself, Sir. Don't feel bad. Them foreigners is taking all the good spots from here to Berkeley. If you ask me, they should put them all up at Alcatraz." He laughed, a series of snorts and snuffles through congested sinuses, and Tim managed to smile darkly as he signed the register again.

What a miserable place. He trudged up a flight of polished concrete stairs, down echoing hallways with rusting lockers on either side. The place smelled of old mops and institutional cleansers, and a flock of black housekeeping yeomen sang and talked loudly while enduring their work shift under glaring yellow overhead light bulbs. The place was smelly, noisy, drafty, and depressing. Tim was not much more cheered when he opened the door of his room and found himself in a slant-ceiling enclosure under the roof pitch. It had two small windows you could open by standing on a chair under the roof. It had a sink with working hot and cold water tap—he tested it—and a little mirror with one corner missing. There was a small desk, a chair, a night table with Quartermaster storage labels stuck to one side, and a regulation steel-spring cot with a rolled up mattress at one end. Tim yanked the neatly folded, starchy sheet loose that bound the mattress like a seaweed sushi wrapper, and the mattress limply flopped open. Inside were a too-thin pillow with a lump in one corner, and a meager square of starchy linen. There were two scratchy blue-gray Navy blankets, and a cheery little booklet titled "Keep This Room Tidy and Let's Win That War!"

Tim sat on the edge of the bed, reading the booklet. He held his head in his hands, and started to laugh. The laughter pealed from him loudly, like crying, and he shook his head repeatedly. "No, no, no...this can't be!"

Corie Captains the Airborne Palace

"Aw, don't make a big deal of it," Corie said next day over lunch at a diner in Union Square. "We'll figure something out. You left a note for me with Mr. Li, huh?"

"Yeah, I didn't know how else to get a signal to you."

"That was sweet. It shows you care." She beamed within herself, looking down into her scrambled eggs. They were jammed together at a crowded Kresge counter where waitresses with little pointed paper crowns bustled about refilling coffees, taking orders, delivering armfuls of plates. Tim and Corie's waitress listened to complaints with the supercilious and dismissive air of one who heard the same song day in, day out. "Yeah, yeah, tell it to the WPA. Maybe you'll get a little badge or something." A sign over the trash can read *Complaint Department* with an arrow pointing down into the trash.

Tim put his hand over Corie's, and she stopped buttering her muffin. He said: "I enjoyed your couch."

She briefly bumped her head against his shoulder, and wrapped both arms around his waist. "Wanna do that again?"

"How soon?"

She sputtered with laughter, back to her plate. "Funny funny man. I want to take you up in an airplane if you're game."

He sat sideways with his legs dangling and his hands lightly folded, looking at her in amazement. "I'm game. What do you do, stow me away with the baggage?"

"No, silly," she said finishing her coconut custard pie. "I can get orders cut for you. Do you have overalls?"

"Me?" He looked down at himself in his black dress uniform. "I have khakis, if that helps any."

She frowned. "Yeah, maybe we can pretend you are some kind of visiting hob-nob. You know, a nabob."

"U-huh. A nabob hob-nobbing on Nob Hill. That's a sob story and a half."

"You've been reading too many dictionaries," she said. "At least one of us isn't named Bob or you'd say that too." She punched him lightly.

"I bet you don't even know what a nabob is."

"Opposite of a yes-bob?" She folded her hands in mock-sullenness. "Okay, I do do the crossword puzzle nearly every day. And I do own a dictionary."

"I'm sure you do," he said, rubbing her back. "Okay, kid. Say when."

"When."

"What, now?"

"Tomorrow. Meet me at the Embarcadero, six sharp. Wear a warm jacket."

Mystified, he said: "Okay, boss, if you say so."

📖

Tim had requested the day off, since he had some leave time saved up, and Teague had been happy to comply. "Get your mind off your misery," Teague had said. "Big plans?"

"Just a little outing on the bay."

"Ah..." Teague had said, "great fishing. Just watch for mines and submarines."

"Thanks, Sir." He added on the way out: "Marty, if your humor gets any drier, there will be no water left in the Bay."

"I hope you catch a big tuna."

Next morning, Tim arrived at the designated Navy docks. A marine layer rolled in thickly. Gray clouds and drizzle peppered the sickly-white seeming hulls of gray warships anchored all around. Tim wore his khakis, a brown leather bomber jacket, and a garrison cap. As a lieutenant commander (the equivalent of a major in the Army and Marine Corps), his insignia of rank were gold oak leaves. "Glad you could make it," she said grinning.

"I wouldn't miss it for the world."

"I think you'll have fun." She handed him a set of folded papers. "Your orders. Don't lose them."

He glanced at them, reading the formal gobbledygook signed by some adjutant at some unidentifiable place that was not a unit and not a place of duty but an acronym floating in space. He held the papers under one arm.

A motorized launch, with a U.S. flag fluttering off its stern, pulled up alongside the dock. A coil of heavy rope sailed through the air from the boat and landed on the dock. A petty officer raised a saucer-capped head. He peered over the dock to see where his passengers were. Two sailors in denims climbed up and fastened the line to a mooring post, and then raised a ladder from on deck to the dock. They climbed in. The launch soon heeled about and speeded along Pier 45, hooking right and traveling about several miles along the shore east and then south to the docks near the Oakland Bay Bridge in San Francisco Bay. There, Tim saw a huge silvery shape at anchor, along with several smaller seaplanes. "What is that?" Tim shouted over the noise of the motor and the waves while wind whipped their hair and made them squint. The object seemed big as a zeppelin.

"That's what we're going up for a ride in," she shouted back. "Don't worry. It's too big to make you air sick or sea sick."

He stared in amazement. "That's a Pan Am Clipper!" The silvery plane was so huge that it seemed to come with its own clouds around it. Sitting on the water, the Boeing 314 Flying ship's softly curving balloon edges were softened by fog. Tim had to crane his neck to see the top, where the propellers and engines sat on the leading edge of wings the size of streets.

"Yes," she said as the launch slowed and glided in to a dock. "I thought you might be surprised."

"You constantly surprise me," he said as they clambered up onto a wooden pier. "What next?"

As they walked along, they returned the salutes of passing enlisted members and junior officers. The place was crawling with civilian technicians and people in suits. Corie said: "Just stick close to me and keep your mouth shut, okay? I'll make up for the rudeness later when we are alone."

They spoke under their breath, while looking dignified:

"You will?"

"You bet. Wanna take a bath together?"

"You mean—nude?"

"Unless you bathe with your clothes on, sailor."

"Er, no, and yes I'd love to."

"Great. Me too."

"You will? You mean I get to see your—?"

"I'll show you mine if you show me yours."

"I can't wait. Let's do the Clipper thing first."

"Agreed. So look wise and follow me."

He followed her but said under his breath: "How do I look wise?"

"Look like you know a lot but never say anything."

"Oh."

"However," she added, "speak if spoken to. Nod if that will do."

She signed in at an office, delivering a copy of her orders, and picked up a flight plan in an oilcloth folder. Tim tagged along, staying close. She handed him the folder to carry. "Makes you look important." Nobody questioned his presence, even as they walked toward the gangway to the enormous plane.

Inside, technicians with clipboards and gauges were still doing tests in the cockpit. Corie waited on the dock. "Truthfully," she said, "this thing is going to be a relic before long. I can feel it. Some guy is building a big spruce plane down near Los Angeles, biggest ever made, but I think it's all going to be history soon. You wait and see."

Tim shrugged. "I don't know much about aviation. This has to be the most glamorous airplane that ever flew, if you ask me."

"Stiff competition from the DC-4."

"Maybe. But this thing can take off and land on the ocean, and it's got enough engines so that I don't need to worry if one goes out."

"Honey," she said. "You fly from A to Z. You don't need to land on water in-between. You land in a city, at an airport."

"If you say so."

"What makes me fry," she said, "is that I know after the war they are going to tell women like me to pack our bags and go home, cook, and raise babies."

"Nothing wrong with babies."

"Why, you want to have one?" she asked threateningly. She leaned into him, fists on her hips. She attacked him with a pink bubble. He made staggering motions as if he'd been shot. She laughed. She threw her hands in the air and dropped them to her thighs with slapping sounds. "We women get to test these blasted things to make sure they are safe for the men to fly, and then the guys get all the glory. One of these planes actually flew President Roosevelt around for secret meetings with Churchill."

A technician shouted from the small, high windows of the cockpit, and Corie waved back. She said to Tim: "Okay, here we go." As they walked up the gangway, she told him: "I don't know what they're testing, and I don't care. Neither do you, Tim. Just enjoy the ride. They tell me to go left, I go left. They tell me to go right, I go right. Up, down, whatever the script calls for."

"No parachutes?" he asked.

"We won't be flying high enough for it to matter," she said. "Just hang on to your seat and enjoy the ride. If we go in the drink, strap down and we'll swim home. Unless we hit a reef or something, and then we die instead."

"I'm only going because you are. I could have stayed in bed—"

"Don't worry, there isn't a reef for hundreds of miles."

"I'll try to be brave."

As the climbed up a ladder and were alone in a gloomy, carpeted corridor, she whispered: "Honey, you're very brave. You're my hero." Escaping any response, she sprang up into the plane and took charge. "Good morning all!"

"Good morning, Ma'am," came a cheerful chorus of male and female voices.

Tim sat on a small fold-out stool in a corner of the cockpit, cross-corners from the left forward cockpit seat, where Corie as flight commander sat. Several civilian technicians sat at various navigational controls, and a rather plain, very good-natured red-haired woman of about 40, a reserve WAFS captain, shook hands with Corie and then took the co-pilot's seat. Meanwhile, in an area blocked off with plywood sheeting in the converted passenger decks, Tim heard conversation and laughter but that was another world. He was too enthralled being part of the flight crew to even think about whatever secret War Department research the plane might be up to. Maybe something involving the mine fields offshore, he thought; or submarine detection; whatever it was, his interest was in Corie who looked competent and in charge as she waved to the dock crew. The co-pilot and technicians got the four huge engines revving near takeoff speed. Soon, although Tim didn't feel a thing, the dock seemed to be moving away. The engine noise was deafening, until Corie slammed her side window shut and the co-pilot did the same.

Tim found a commercial brochure in a door pocket, touting the plane's characteristics. The Boeing 314, nicknamed the Airborne Palace, was the largest passenger plane built to date, with a wingspan of 152 feet or 46.3

meters. The world's first manned flight by the Wright Brothers at Kitty Hawk in 1903, by comparison, had lasted 12 seconds and covered 120 feet, and could have been made in one hop across the China Clipper's wings with room to spare. The plane was 28 feet high and over 100 feet long, could carry over 40 tons at about 183 miles per hour for a distance of 3500 miles / 5635 km cruising at 13,400 feet / 4085 m, with a passenger load of up to 74 and a crew of six to ten. Pictures in the brochure showed luxurious interiors with attractive women in jaunty uniforms serving coffee or offering pillows to smiling passengers. For a moment, Tim realized how much the world had lost in the Axis rampage. The brochure was yellowing with age, probably printed in the late 1930s, and pictured a lost world. Maybe not an entirely true world, since it had been ravaged by the Great Depression, but there had been that wonderful world of the imagination— Art Deco buildings, China Clippers, Zeppelins, air mail, radio dispatched police cars, automats for the futuristic service of food—all changed forever in the grinder of the war effort. Then again, he might never have met this intriguing woman.

He stared with admiration at Corie, who wore a broad grin as she sat relaxed, holding the controls. She looked thoroughly at home among the galaxy of blinking lights, toggles and other switches, gauges, dials, and other gadgets right out of Buck Rogers. Even wearing cool aviator glasses, garrison cap with twin silver bars, and black earphones wrapped around her head, she had a gleam in her eyes and joy in her features.

He sat back and relaxed as she flew several miles out over the sea. He looked out over the tiny waves a half mile below as the great plane described a long, slow loop over the Pacific Ocean. One almost had the sensation that the earth was moving, rather than the plane. Two hours and many turns later, it was getting boring—even though one of the technicians had made coffee and someone else had brought donuts, so nobody was starving. Tim kept thinking about being alone with the woman whose hands controlled this airborne colossus. He had kissed those hands. They had stroked his naked ribs. He wanted to press them to his cheeks, close his yes, and draw in a deep breath to inhale her magic.

The Golden Gate Bridge glided by far below, and Corie banked south to descend toward the docks across the bay from Oakland.

📖

"I'm still speechless. One of the smoothest rides I've ever had. Like mom's pumpkin pie."

"I do make a decent pie, in case you ever wonder."

"I don't doubt it. Is there anything you don't do first rate?"

"If there is, I'm not telling. If I told you, I'd have to tie you up in the basement." She waited in the car while he ran in and changed out of his uniform into a casual dark suit and coat with a nice gray hat and tie and black shoes. She ignored several ogling young Marines, who scattered when he approached the car.

"Don't you look the flash," she said as he settled in. She looked at her watch. "Five o'clock. Want to grab some dinner?"

"Sure. How about a nice steak and the works. I'll buy a bottle of champagne."

"What for?"

"To tell you you're special."

"Aw, you're just a swell guy," she said visibly touched. She wasn't hard to please. A little went a long way, and that made it easy to do little things to make her happy. He liked that—though letting her in his life was going to be a wild ride, he thought as they drove up to Nob Hill. *The unknown. The Thing.* It was his turn to wait in the car while she changed into civvies. She came out soon after, skipping along in something resembling a toned-down bobbysocks outfit with mid-calf denim dress, wool socks, and loafers. She wore a dark blue cloth overcoat with high shoulders, and a lighter blue cap with a jaunty little feather in one side. She'd put on a bit of red lipstick, blush, and white-gold earrings, and she looked lovely. He praised her heartily. "Want to drive?" she asked in turn.

"If you'd like me to."

"I would. I'm a little tired. And you're the man on this flight."

"Do you get tired driving one of those football fields around in the sky?"

"Not while I do it. I'm so hepped up I can't stand it. I have electricity running through me from my fingers to my toes. Afterwards, I could just curl up and sleep by the fireplace."

"If you had a fireplace."

"One of these days," she said with a sigh. She buried her face in his jacket and added: "Sailor."

He drove out toward Half Moon Bay as darkness fell. It was a quiet, comfortable ride. Impulsively, she curled up against him. He noticed her arms slinking around his right arm, and her head nestling against his shoulder. She pulled her knees up so that her feet were under her, and didn't say a word. She didn't need to.

He didn't need to either, and didn't. For a while he thought she was asleep. Coming down Route 1, with beautiful city lights on the left and ships at sea on their right, and stars from one end to the other, he whispered: "See all that?"

"M-hm," she said, nodding so that he felt her chin move on his forearm.

"You've been awake the whole time."

"M-hm," she said again, nodding so he felt her chin again.

"I thought you were asleep."

She shook her head. "Uh-um." Maybe this would go on for the rest of their lives, or maybe it was just a brief interlude. He resolved not to say anything more. The worst thing to do in the face of magic was to say anything. Just run with it, he thought. That was what the padre with the bump on his noggin in the London Tube would have said. *Don't break the spell.*

They went for a long walk on the beach, holding hands. They made small talk as if there were no large concerns in the world. The moon rose, and they laughed—the moon in Half Moon Bay tonight was a full moon, and it left its quicksilver in myriad rocking waves that quietly came and went, at Tim and Corie's feet, over underwater pillows of kelp. This same sea had come and gone in places like this around the world for eons. Tim told her about a telescope that was being built for a mountain called Palomar down the coast, which would let astronomers look millions of light years into the deepest seas of stars.

"And what do they expect to see there?" she asked.

"You and me, holding hands, walking on the beach of some ocean while the moonlight is rippling around in the tide."

"That's nice. And then what will they know?"

"Nothing more than if they came here and looked at us right now."

She stopped and stepped close to him so that her chin was near his heart. "Do we know anything more than they do?"

He put his hands on her shoulders, feeling the soft skin under those cushioning pads. He pulled her close. "It's all rather secret," he told her.

"Like Government work?" She pressed a cheek against his chest.

"Yes. It's all a secret language that's spoken like this."

She said softly: "I can feel your heart beating. Like the sea."

"You make my heart beat really hard, like it wants to go to meet your heart."

"I think they've already met."

He bent down and parted her lapels a bit to put an ear against the fragrant softness of her chest. She wrapped her arms around his head and pulled it to her like a football—hard, desiring. He felt or heard—he wasn't sure, maybe both—the pounding of her heart. It had the strong, steady beat of a lighthouse signal, signaling true bearings to lost sailors. It was true and steady, like the coming and going of waves on the sand. "I hear it speaking. Sounds like it really wants company." He pulled her close, circling his arms around her. She stood on her toes, braced her hands on his shoulders, and thrust her mouth hard against his. They kissed for a long time, while the waves moved in and out with a steady sloshing sound like two hearts beating in unison.

"Is that how it's spoken?" she asked when they stopped for air. She still had one arm hooked around his neck. He ran his hand down her side, outward with the curve of her waist, inward and down along the firmness of her thigh, then back upward. He cupped her behind in his hands. He pulled her to him, and she pressed her Venus mound against his erect sex. They each groaned with desire.

"You do everything very well," he told her.

Eyes closed, she ran her fingertips over his face like a blind person trying to feel what she could not see with her eyes, maybe the landscape of his soul or the inner gardens of his mind. Her eyes opened wide—

vulnerable, and a little scared, and a lot desirous. "I'm jazzed up when I fly," she said in an airy voice while her eyes nakedly showed innermost truths and enigmas for him to sort through. *All but that Thing.* "I get so jazzed up that I feel it in my fingertips and in my toes." She ran her fingertips over his lips, slowing in the wetness of his mouth, then around the strong line of his jaw testing him as if he were a work of art, as if there were no part of him that she didn't want to touch and savor. "I get tired after, but I'm crazy while I fly. That's why I want you to drive, Tim."

"I'll be happy to drive." He held her close, knowing they were going down to a long, smooth landing that would take all night and end in a shower of sparks, a wheel of stars, a long moan, a holding of hands, a twining of fingers, a language of looks, an alphabet of silences and touches punctuated by sighs. "And about that bath," he said.

"Oh yes, I promised."

"I earned it."

"You did."

For the rest of the night, they never let go of each other after that. They walked to a little place near the beach and had beers and Mexican food. They strolled along the boardwalk and had ice cream—she a vanilla stick with chocolate coating, he a cone studded with chopped walnuts. They fed ice cream to each other and sat on the low wall looking at the Big Dipper wheeling across the heavens as if someone had flung it, while fishing schooners with furled sails and winking stern lights bobbed slowly a quarter mile offshore.

They walked silently, with linked arms, back to the car. He drove all the way back to Nob Hill. She curled up against him and fell asleep until they got into the city. She sat up, yawning and stretching and looking around.

She blew into his face. "Is my breath bad?"

"I don't smell a thing. My nose is still full of sea air. I think I smell fish, but it's probably not you."

She sat up and looked into the mirror behind the passenger side visor. Licking the tip of her pinkie, she touched up her eyebrows.

"Going someplace?"

"Home. Gotta date with a sailor."

"Thank God. I'm so tired I could roll over right now. I was afraid you were going to ask me to go dancing."

"Not tonight, Tim."

"Sure."

"I want you to come up and sleep with me."

In the pause that followed, they pondered her assertiveness.

Tim asked: "What about this land cruiser?"

"The owner's an old fart of an admiral. I happen to know he is in Hawaii with his mistress on a so-called inspection tour. He won't be looking for it tonight."

"You mean you—?"

"Yeah, I swiped it."

Tim gasped. "Even I wouldn't have that kind of nerve."

She shrugged. "A girl does what a girl's gotta do."

Tim parked on a side street near the Hotel Auger, and they walked to the hotel arm in arm. They walked down a shadowy sidewalk under great sprawling eucalyptus trees. He was barely aware of the buildings looming beyond the tree shadows, until she gave a sharp tug to the left. "Come on," she said. "We have to sneak in. You remember the drill."

"Wish I still had my place. I could catch breadcrumbs and pull you across."

She hugged his arm and led him down a bushy walk, through a gateway lit on either side by large copper-banded lanterns holding milky orange Art Deco bowls, and into the courtyard. He saw that they were near an annex of the Hotel Auger that he hadn't realized existed. She moved with practiced ease. She led him along a curving cloister walk covered with masonry arches overhead. In the peak of each arch, a round lamp glowed amber. Ivy throttled stone with anaconda strength. On one side was a building—presumably another hotel—and on the outside of the C-shaped walk were arches that were largely blocked with criss-cross lattices and bougainvillea. The place smelled of night: moss, water, loam, and jasmine. Broad-leaf ivy rattled around wall sconces, around old bronze lanterns in hybrid Japanese and Art Deco patterns. Coming around a corner, they stepped through a narrow opening and emerged in the familiar courtyard of his former residence, the Hotel Auger.

"Ya gotta know the ropes, sailor," she said as she unlocked the stairwell entrance of the private wing. Peering cautiously left and right, she took his hand and towed him up the stairs. They sneaked through the *étage* door, and quickly around the corner into her apartment. Only a dim bulb glowed in the hall; otherwise, the apartment was lit from outside.

"Made it," she said, wiping her forehead again with her wrist as last time. Then she turned. "Meg?"

No answer.

She looked across the kitchen, swallowed as if surprised at something, and said: "She's not home. Must be out for the night."

The sink, the ice box door, the cabinets, all glimmered mutely in moonlight. "What, did she leave a note I don't see?"

"I know her," Corie said. "Don't worry." She looked abashed. "Do you mind?"

"Mind what?"

"That I asked you up?"

He shook his head. "I want to be here with you."

She became business like for a moment. "You can use my toothbrush if you'd like. Want a nightie?"

"Oh please."

"Just kidding." She took him to the bathroom. "You go first. Use my toothbrush." She pulled on his arm. "Want that bath?"

"Can I have a rain check? I'm all in."

"Me too. All I want is you."

Ten minutes later, he lay in her bed wearing only his shorts and T-shirt. She came into the bedroom, turned off the light, and puttered around the room a minute longer. He watched as she put her earrings and jewelry away.

"My feet get cold," she said giggling as she crawled into bed. She wore a filmy gown and wool socks.

He put his arm out and pulled her close. She wasn't quite so passionate just then, but had a serious edge. He lay back. "I sense a speech."

She rubbed his chest. "Now don't make fun of me."

"I'm not. I'm helping you warm up for our special moment."

"Tim." Her head floated above his in the gloom. "I want you to be happy with me while we are here in this place the way things are with us right now."

"That's a long preamble."

"I care very deeply about you. I'm all yours for as long as can be."

"I won't kid around. I'm like a spring lamb around you."

"Not yet."

"Why?"

"Why what?"

"What yets can there be?"

"Fifth Amendment." She stood up on the mattress. "I am offering myself to you here, as-is, with a warning label on my ass. See?" She turned, lifted her night gown, and pulled down her flimsy underpants to reveal two pale half-moons separated by a shadowy rille.

"I don't see the label, but I'll take your word for it. Nice behind, pilot." He pulled her to him by both of her wrists. "Do like Simon says. Copy me." He put his hands over his eyes. "See no evil." She repeated after him as he ordered. They covered their ears and said in unison, as in a goodnight prayer. "Hear no evil." They covered their mouths. "Speak no evil." They laughed, and it broke the tension. She lifted her gown off, and slipped out of her panties. He touched her breasts, but she pushed his hands down. She wanted to do it her way. Her passion was surprising as she threw herself on him. She squirmed, and nuzzled, and pawed him with emphatic grunts. She reached down into his pants with both hands, sitting on top of him, straddling his thighs. She cupped his sex in the warmth of her palms. She wriggled to his side and kissed him, still grasping him. With deep hard breaths, she worked her tongue around in his mouth. He grasped those small, firm buttocks in his hands and pulled her back onto him. She pulled his shirt up and kissed him on the middle of the chest, then on both nipples, then under his nipples. She worked her mouth upward along his neck to his mouth. She slid down alongside him on the bed, while he touched the softness of her breasts.

They kicked the bed sheets and blankets away. She sat on his belly and bent down face to face. They kissed wildly, intimately, wetly. In this position, she could not reach his sex, but slid her hands, palms down, along the flat of his abdomen. She palmed his abdomen as if absorbing his sexuality into her hands. He pushed her legs down so they were between his. He wrapped his legs around her waist and rolled over so he was on top. She moaned and stretched out under him, arms around his neck. "I like it when you drive, sailor."

"Rest from all that flying, pilot." He stroked her thighs and buttocks as her knees spread under him. They weren't ready yet, so they lay side by side. She said: "Mm-mm. I'm going to turn over the controls to you." She jiggled his sex. He shuddered with pleasure. She licked his nipples steadily like waves churning in moonlight. She hugged him. "Please drive me, all the way home and into the garage. Do whatever you want with me. I will enjoy the ride so much." He pushed her over onto her back, and she whispered: "That's it. You know what I want. Take me." He bent his head down to kiss her nipples, and she held her breasts so he could do with them what he wanted. They played with them together." Take me," she said forcefully, eyes closed. His hand strayed down, over her outward belly button, over the silken plain of her belly. He reached down to her wetly dissolving cove. She pushed with both hands to urge his hand along. "Go on, I'm waiting for you." She set her heels wider apart. When his car reached her garage, she grasped it in both hands to help him drive inside. "It's so nice and big," she whispered. "Stay in me while I suck on you." Puzzled, he cried out in pleasure as he crossed the threshold. She whimpered a bit. He could fell her vaginal muscles rippling as she stroked him inside of her. Must be what she meant. He felt her legs tighten and loosen, her heels digging into his back, as she operated those wonderful muscles inside all the way from her heels and with the muscles of both legs. He knelt more erect and pulled her closer, so that her buttocks were under his balls, which pressed against her pucker. He raised each of her legs before him, by turns, kissing the bottoms of her feet—it made her whimper with pleasure, presaging her first sobbing orgasm. He licked and sucked on the heels driving that tidal action rippling his keel.

That same full moon, from the earlier romance they'd enjoyed at Half Moon Bay, rose outside the window and brazed them in warm silver-yellow light. Corie giggled. "Look, the man in the moon is watching us."

"He looks astonished."

"Aren't you? I am. I had no idea this would be so nice." She half sat up, raising her head to look down at where they were connected. She spread her open palms on the moonlit bed sheets to watch while Tim rocked inside her.

Outside, wind rustled in trees like the tides rolling massively over Pacific kelp beds under the moon's astonished gaze.

He and she swam tumbling through lubricants, sea things, crystal shining moonlit splashes. He mounted into position like a sea god, and she reached toward him with yearning hands and mouth, spreading her pale cove for his lordly intrusion. She pulled him down on her, as they began the penultimate, mutual dance amid rhythmic, broken sobs of total assault. The headboard banged about, and the bed's feet scraped in short, rapid thrusts across the floor, in that echoing building, as he thrust powerfully, and her softness made slapping noises as she lay back, holding her breasts and overcome, her mouth wide open, her eyes closed in ecstasy.

They lay side by side—after the full moon had floated away, leaving only a lemon afterglow—brushing each other's lips with a fingertip, murmuring endearments, touching each other, until they grew aroused again and he mounted for a second rising tide, the first of several more. They made sweet jazz late into the night, until overpowered by exhausted and welcome sleep.

Corie and Tim—Meg Makes Three

Tim and Corie were an item, but there was some odd, almost surreal undercurrent Tim could not put his finger on yet. He shrugged like a swimmer grown tired of fighting a rip current. He let himself spin away into a whirlpool of sweet cloying warm love too delicious to deny. And she had plenty for him, every chance they had to be alone together.

One sunny, warm afternoon, he lay beside her in her bed, with the window open and the scent of blossoms filling the air. He regarded the slender curves of her pale body as she slept. He felt utterly at ease, imprisoned and happy in this little bubble of time on a Sunday afternoon. For the first time, he was free of that vague and ominous danger that he might be shipped out to some dangerous new front if the war went sour again. There just didn't seem to be any need now. It was just a matter of waiting, of letting the clock run out. It was a wonderful capsule of time to be in. He did not worry about what he would do once he returned to Connecticut—or why go home at all? Maybe he would relocate somewhere new, like Vancouver Island. Maybe he'd stay here in Frisco. Maybe he'd move back to Europe and start some kind of import-export business. Anything was possible, and the future was like a giant candy jar of opportunities, but one just did not yet need to exert any energy on it yet. And what better place to be than in a passionate love affair that was as fleeting and sweet as the scent of blossoms on a balmy day?

Corie stirred in her sleep, groaned happily, and reached for him. She put her hands around his neck and pulled him down for a long, energetic Mommsen Lung kiss. Like a diver, he plunged into the dark green sea and wrapped himself around her anemones. They writhed and bubbled happily together until they felt spent and lay side by side breathing hard.

There was a knock on the door. "Anyone alive in there?" It was Meg.

Corie pulled the sheets up to cover herself and Tim. "Come on in."

Meg knew better. She opened the door just a crack, without looking directly in, and said: "I just stopped by for my book. Thought I'd say hello." Then she pressed the door open a bit wider and looked in. "You heard the news, right?"

"No?" Corie said holding the sheet up with both hands.

"Hitler shot himself."

"What? No!" Both Tim and Corie sat up, the sheet spilling off. Meg came in, her eyes made up with mascara, her lips red, so that she looked Mediterranean or something. She poured out the story, and while Tim felt a wave of joy—almost a reprieve, given that he'd already almost lost his life once in the war, and knew plenty of others who had. He also detected an odd wavelength of communication going on between Corie and Meg. Was there a faint edge of competition or jealousy? There was something edgy under the surface, and he couldn't put his finger quite on it. Meg finished her breathless recitation and pulled away, shutting the door.

"Why don't you go out and celebrate with us?" Corie called after her.

Meg yelled something back in her mellifluous, almost musical voice; Tim didn't understand.

"Relax," Corie said with a laugh, pushing Tim lightly so he lay back and accepted whatever was in the air. Couldn't be anything bad, not on a perfect day like this.

Corie draped the sheet around herself, and left the room to chase after Meg. She left Tim to enjoy the sunny quiet of her bed, and he felt very much at home there. She had made the threat of impermanence about this situation clear more than once, and now as he lay here enjoying her intimacy he kept coming back to a Zen-like state of acceptance.

Meanwhile, a distant but ocean-like chorus of shouts and whistles and cheers was rising over the city. Cars, trucks, buses were honking their horns in a constant wave of celebration.

Corie burst back into the room. "Okay, it's settled, the three of us are going to go out on the town."

Across the civilized world, particularly in San Francisco, a delicious sigh of relief rose up, and a party started that showed no signs of letting up. The Depression-weary and then war-weary United States was beginning to feel the balmy springtime of wealth, power, and victory.

As the savage fighting close to the Japanese islands attested, the war was still far from over, but the cards were utterly stacked against those whose savage doctrines had started the war. It seemed like just a matter of time now—and how many more lost American lives? How many more lives of Asian civilians, not to mention hordes of imprisoned Americans and Europeans, before Tojo's war machine collapsed?

In San Francisco, a feverish end-of-war fatigue spread like a forest fire. A party began somewhere in the city, and quickly spread block by block until the entire city was in a state of near-riot. People were having sex in taxis, blowing horns, running red lights, yelling obscenities and laughing uncontrollably. People rode around, packed into convertibles, and waving champagne bottles to toast anything that moved. The police were out in full force. Even special Highway Patrol units and out of town sheriff's deputies arrived in buses to try and keep a lid on. It was an exhilarating time.

Tim strode down the streets with a woman on each arm—Corie on one side, Meg on the other. The two women clung to him, as if they both were his girlfriends. He took it lightly, holding each around the waist. He did his best to treat each with equal respect and consideration. He caught little flashes of insight that could be even more puzzling. Those little moments went as fast as they came. For example, Corie and Meg left him at a café to shop for ladies' hats on a brief excursion to a shop in Union Square. As he sat sipping coffee and reading a newspaper, he watched them coming back. They seemed linked in some manner, like sisters or co-conspirators. The two women took him arm in arm between them and they strode again as a threesome by the Chinatown Gate. That evening, as they sat together in a small booth in a bar that was jammed with both men and women, Tim felt a bit tipsy and aroused. He had Corie on his left and Meg on his right. Their thighs pressed against his under the table. Meg's hand wandered briefly down and rested on her own left thigh, as the air was full of cheering and excitement. Her hand jumped to his right thigh, clenching down on his muscles while she turned her face and kissed him full on the mouth. He tasted her tongue, her lips, cigarette smoke, and was too dazed to react, because it was so unexpected. She seemed suddenly excited and exposed and hungry. If Corie noticed, Corie never let on. Tim was sure Corie had noticed. Or had she? It was almost as if she wanted to share him with her, like a kindness. She seemed protective of Meg. But why? Meg's tongue had briefly flicked into his mouth, pressing hot moist spittle against his tongue, tasting of beer and lipstick, and since he already had his arm around both women's waists, he automatically pulled her against him with his right palm. And she yielded. He wasn't sure if she was drunk or aroused—but it was just another of those lightning brief moments. Someone took Corie by the hand and pulled her onto the dance floor, and she in turn pulled Tim along. He reached in vain for Meg's hand. Meg was just leaning across the table to answer an almanac question about how many people lived in San Francisco in peacetime.

Later that night, they three drifted through one or two last nightclubs, and Tim slow danced with each woman. Corie blended against him with her self-assured coolness, her flushed face and blue eyes a cipher. Her hands alone seemed to have voice, roving over his shoulders, the neat square tips of her fingers exploring in the hollows of his collarbones and up his neck, behind his ears, across his eyebrows. She seemed so happy-go-lucky, wiry, slim, cool, a joy; and he danced fast dances with her until they were both out of breath and laughing. She kept softly urging: "Pay more attention to Meg. Dance with Meg. Pay her a compliment now and then."

Meg was a little bigger, more solid, than Corie, with smooth skin and slightly exotic features. As Tim slow danced with her, she was a bit stiffer and slower and just had a different feel. She was more delicate than he'd expected, and now he began to think she was more sensitive, maybe a bit less self-reliant, than Corie who could fly bombers with that radiant look on her face. Yet, Meg had a hard edge, Tim thought, as he held her and guided her gently around a dimly lit dance floor. Amber and red lights twirled while the soft, full big band sound of a 15-piece orchestra wafted sensuously around them. It scared, almost dismayed, him a bit that he got the feeling he could have really held Meg close and kissed her again, full on the mouth, and where would that leave him and Corie? There was something Meg said, too, in a low voice, in passing, as they three walked elbow by elbow among throngs of people. "Things aren't what they seem, but relax and enjoy the *mumble mumble*." She seemed to be trying to tell him something. "I'm not competing over Corie, if you understand what I *mumble mumble* and don't play in both courts," or something like that; he wasn't sure what words she had actually used, or what they meant. Was she telling him not to do something? Or to do something? Or just not to worry? She mumbled several things like this during a short walk between night clubs, while they waited for Corie outside a restaurant where she'd run in to use the ladies' room. Then Meg added in a louder, clearer voice: "We're not queer or anything, don't misunderstand. We both just like you a lot. We're good friends, and we're not going to fight over you. Maybe we'll just both adopt you as our *Monsieur Sweet Daddy*." At the same time, she giggled and gave him a light shove with her palm, so he wasn't sure how much of it was kidding and if any was serious. He wasn't sure if he had dreamed this, or if he was standing outside a conversation she was trying to have with him. Of course, he'd had a few drinks and was feeling mellow. Maybe that was why she shook her head and laughed fondly toward him. She rubbed his back briefly with her palm, then stood aside with folded arms and clutched purse, awaiting Corie's return.

"I don't want to come between your friendship, if that's what you—" he said, but she had already turned away and was ignoring him as she smoked a cigarette and looked around the corner for Corie. *Not queer*, she'd said. He had not thought of them that way at all, and now he wondered if he was supposed to have that suspicion but not entertain it. Was this part of Corie's *Thing*? He was sure he would eventually stumble upon it, and he hoped it would not be a piano falling on him as Anna Stokowska's revelations had been.

At one point, late in the evening when they were tipsy and tired, they danced together, the three of them. An old fashioned ball of little mirror tiles twirled slowly above, throwing twinkles around the room. The band members were all sitting down, some with their chairs reversed and cigarettes burning near them, as Tim and Meg and Corie danced slowly with their arms around each other. It was innocent fun, with nobody feeling left out. Afterward, they walked to the cable car stop together, not holding hands, just each to their personal thoughts, each tired, and that was how they rode up the hill. The two women sneaked Tim into the Hotel Auger for the night, and he slept on the couch alone in the living room. He didn't mind. He was so tired he fell asleep as his head touched the pillow that Corie slipped on the armrest just in time, and Meg fluffed out a blanket for him with a big poof of cool fresh air and the blanket descended on him like sleep itself. The last he remembered was one of them patting him on the buttocks (lingeringly) while the other patted him on the head—he had no idea which did which.

Hitler Plans to Atom-Bomb the U.S.A.

In late April 1945, the giant Nazi submarine U-234 cruised slowly south through the Atlantic Ocean, subject to constant tension and bickering among the factions on board.

Her commander was *Kapitän-Leutnant*—Captain-Lieutenant: *Ka-Leu*, or *KL* in common *U-boot* etiquette—Johann Fehler. He was a brave, adventuresome sailor in the best Germanic tradition. He loved the service, cared for his men, and only nodded to the ruling Nazi elite as a necessary evil. He had a plan, which was well known to the enlisted members of the crew who were fiercely loyal to him. While the Nazi quartermaster service had filled the cargo holds and mine shafts (the tubes used for storing and ejecting sea mines, for which the XB type boats were originally built) with a frightening cargo designed to help Japan win the war, Fehler (whose name in German ironically meant "error") had his own crew load a three year supply of whisky, food, hunting rifles, and fishing poles. Fehler's plan was to follow through on his final orders—deliver the jet parts, uranium, and other strategic materials to Japan, and then seize the *U-234*—by force, if necessary—and flee thousands of miles away to some uninhabited South Pacific paradise, some uninhabited island or atoll. There, they could wait out the end of Hitler's mad war and the return of the world to sanity.

By contrast, the devout Nazis on board—including a naval judge sent to clean up a nest of German war profiteers in wartime Tokyo—and several of the junior officers, alternated between hysteria over Germany's desperate situation, and a kind of fanatical faith that somehow the *Führer* would make it all right again.

Sitting on the sidelines were several other fanatics, like the two Japanese military officers accompanying the boat's deadly cargo of mass destruction.

The XB boats were designed in the late 1930s and early 40s as ocean-going submersible mine-layers. They could carry up to 66 mines in thirty mine shafts, as well as fifteen torpedoes in two stern tubes. Now, to facilitate the long voyage around the world, the aft torpedo rooms had been sealed off and turned into diesel fuel tanks, with compensating saltwater ballast tanks added to the bow area. Redesignated as Japan transports, the XB class carried cargo in special containers fitted to the mine shafts. At 2,710 tons submerged and fully loaded, the biggest German *U-boot*s ever built, they were slow and cumbersome. In the waning months of German power, they had been converted to the new snorkel technology, which allowed them to stay submerged for days or even weeks at a time. This had become important since Allied air and naval power had achieved near total domination of surface and air. *U-234* had an enormous snorkel boom mounted on a swivel behind her sail, or conning tower. The snorkel, which was round and had a circumference about like a man's waist, folded down into a special notch that ran along the upper central deck from the sail toward the stern. When vertical, the snorkel stood slightly higher than the sail itself, or about periscope height. While the boat had a respectable surface speed (up to twenty knots), she had to crawl at about eight knots when submerged with only the snorkel raised. At night, she could travel on the surface while blowing out her atmosphere and recharging her diesel batteries. By day, she inched along under the surface. Thus, it took her more than two weeks to reach the South Atlantic, and it might take her another month to reach Japan.

From the outset, there was conflict in the officers' mess. Fehler, a strong-willed officer exemplary of the best combat pilots and *U-boot* commanders, took it in stride. Possessing a fiery wit and a zest for life, he quickly tired of the rigid posturing of some of his guests, and in fact of one or two of his own officers. This wasn't anything new. German military units often did have politically oriented officers who spouted the usual Hitler drivel while everyone else circumspectly kept their mouths shut. Fehler relieved the officer of the first watch, replacing him with one of the passengers. The passenger, KL Richard Bulla, was an old friend from Fehler's earlier navy days, and a regular Navy officer rather than a *doctrinaire* party hack.

There was a constant antagonism between Lieutenant Colonel Kai Nieschling, a military judge and loyal Nazi, and the senior guest officer on board, Major General Ulrich Kessler, a more traditional Prussian Junker complete with monocle and riding boots. Kessler, a *Luftwaffe* general, was an expert in antiaircraft and anti-ship missiles. In more flush times, he might have been cashiered for his unorthodox views. In today's desperate climate, he was merely being shifted as far from the ruling party's horizon of view as possible—to Tokyo, as the new German air attaché. Kessler never had a good word to say about either Hitler, the government, or the management of the *Luftwaffe* starting with Goering at the top and working down. Day after day, these officers argued at the captain's mess. Nieschling and some of the junior officers would invariable side against Kessler, while nobody but Fehler dared to open his mouth. Fehler, for his part, couldn't tell Kessler to keep his mouth shut, though it aggravated Fehler that the bickering was inevitably going to affect morale among the NCOs and junior enlisted men. Then again, Fehler had already provisioned the ship for its hoped for cowboy escape, and he knew the men weren't dumb. They knew the war was lost and it was just a matter of time to try and survive while the remaining Nazis lived in dream fantasies.

Meanwhile, Fehler had some heated private conversations with Kessler in Fehler's private cabin. The two men were, to begin with, genuine military officers rather than party functionaries. Fehler was a native Berliner who had distinguished himself from the ground up. Raised in a middle class household of no particular social distinction, he had enlisted in the merchant marine as a deckhand on a sailing vessel. From there, he'd worked his way up on merit alone to the merchant marine academy. He'd joined the Nazi party more as a matter of swimming with the tide. He personally had no hatred for anyone, Russian, Jew, or otherwise, and had moderate political views. By 1936 he was an officer cadet and well on his way to being the commanding officer of a minesweeper surface vessel when World War II began with the invasion of Poland in 1939. During the early years of the war, he distinguished himself as a technical expert—mines and explosives officer—on the raider *Atlantis*, which sank at least 22 Allied vessels during his tenure.

Kessler, on the other hand, was a born and raised Prussian *Junker*, a member of the old imperial aristocracy. He was older than Fehler, having seen service in World War I. Kessler was a hard, stony individual—tall, arrogant, utterly sure of himself. He'd been *Kriegsmarine*, Navy at first and then switched to *Luftwaffe*, Air Force during the 1930s, immediately sparking dislike between himself and Goering. Like so many career military officers, Kessler hated the upstarts who had brought Germany to ruin. In this, he and the other aristocratic military officers took their cue from none other than the deceased World War I hero and former President, Field Marshal Paul von Hindenburg. Hitler was not elected in 1933, and von Hindenburg was deeply mistrustful of him. However, a coalition of bankers, industrialists, and Prussian (Junker) militarists had pressured the president to simply appoint Hitler as chancellor. The Nazis had only received 37.4% of the popular vote, and the Weimar constitution should have triggered a new election. But the oligarchs, smarting from their loss in the Great War, disliking the democracy of Weimar, and fearful of Communist inroads, thought they could control the Austrian. Hindenburg, who was growing feeble, accededto that pressure for the sake of national unity after a generation of civil war and economic disaster. Von Hindenburg died shortly afterward, and *Reichskanzler* (National Chancellor) Hitler quickly maneuvered to consolidate power into himself. Terminating the unpopular Weimar Republic, Hitler kept the office to which he'd been elected—*Reichskanzler*—and added Von Hindenburg's old post as President to his own totem. In the new Third Reich, however, Hitler created a new office for himself—supreme leader, or *Führer* (Leader). The *Junkers*, while serving Hitler to preserve what was left of their imperial power base (the Emperor had abdicated under revolutionary pressure in 1918, and the empire was finished forever), hated and resented Hitler and the *coterie* of drunks, drug addicts, perverts, and sadists he brought to power: Röhm, a sadistic pedophile; Goering, a drug addict and hedonist; Goebbels, a drug-addicted megalomaniac; Ley, a violent drunk who liked to tear his beautiful blonde wife's clothes off in public to demonstrate what a prize she was—"beautiful as *Germania* herself," he liked to say—until she committed suicide to escape her dreadful marriage to this beast; and a whole host of other freaks and misfits. Kessler's utter contempt was, to Fehler, understandable by mid-1945 when the two men found themselves on a fool's errand like this.

Kessler, however, was more than a stiff-necked throwback. Kessler had the general scientific and engineering training of a good officer in the modern service, and he was politically useful at a high level because he cut a dashing figure in his long leather coat, peaked cap, white gloves, polished leather boots, and frequently a monocle—the embodiment of the Prussian aristocracy and officer corps that had been decimated again in yet another national mistake.

Whatever class and age distinctions survived between the two men, they shared more in common. Both had won the Iron Cross for valor. Both had distinguished themselves in many ways. Both were essentially honest, fair, clear thinkers within the limited sphere of such concepts in the Third Reich. Both were pragmatists who saw the handwriting on the wall. As captain of the boat, Fehler was the officer in charge, while Kessler was by far the most senior man on board, the only flag officer, so there was a considerable stalemate of the wills, of protocols, of military courtesies. Fehler was impressed with Kessler.

As Fehler shared a few glasses of schnapps and smoked a cigar or two with his guest, he learned that Kessler had an escape plan of his own, which he confided to Fehler. Fehler also learned of a top level plan from Berlin that left Fehler's head spinning with its audacity and fantastic scope. Aboard, Kessler told him, was material to make the most devastating weapon of all time.

Fehler laughed.

"No, no," Kessler said soberly, "this is not one of their crazy delusions."

Fehler felt a chill as he poured each of them another small snifter of brandy. "*Herr General*, I'm a simple *U-boot* commander. Perhaps you can enlighten me under the bond of secrecy?"

Kessler nodded grimly. "*Ka-Leu*, it is essential that I share this information with you." He raised his tiny glass in a toast, and Fehler was bound by courtesy to follow suit. "*Ka-Leu*, we have talked about your Pacific island, your wild pigs, your hunting rifles..."

"Are you sure you don't want to join us, *Herr General*?" Fehler said feeling the warmth of the alcohol and a touch of delirium—after years of war, deprivation, seeing warriors and civilians die horribly—for what?

Kessler raised a palm. "No, no, that is not for me." In his own cold, grim way, he radiated a supreme sense of biting and brilliant humor. "I have a special request to make, *Ka-Leu*. I want you to set me down on the Argentine coast."

Fehler felt a knot in his stomach. "That would mean a considerable diversion from our course, General. At least a week if you wanted me to set you out near Buenos Aires, let us say."

"I understand fully well the risks to you and your crew," Kessler said with a hint of that sharpness that reminded a duty-bound German, Fehler, of his *Pflicht*.

"Think of it this way," Kessler said. "My situation is a bit more precarious than yours. If I am captured in Japan at war's end, as military attaché I become a war criminal. If I intern myself in Argentina, I become a tango dancer. In the former case, I may be hanged. Who knows what vengeance the Allies will visit on all of our heads for the horrors we perpetrated on the world in Hitler's name. On the other hand, if I depart the scene quietly in the middle of this mission, I may well be able to convince the world that I was against Hitler. That would be the truth, at least."

Fehler nodded. "I understand, Sir. I will plot a diversionary course for you."

"Thank you, *Ka-Leu*." Kessler was almost warm as he said it, though he was essentially giving an order to an underling of the commoner class.

He did seem sincere, Fehler thought, calculating how much the diversion would cost him in fuel, time, and risk from enemy action. "To be honest, Sir, I am in no hurry to reach Japan."

"You are a wise man," Kessler said. "I had that opinion of you."

"Thank you, General."

"Think of it this way, Fehler. There are plenty of us who have long been wise to Hitler. He never did have any lost love for us Prussians." This was a blatant attempt to curry a bit of false camaraderie, Fehler recognized, but the condescension didn't annoy him. Both men were products of the same system, just different rungs in the same ladder. "Think of it this way. There is a network of good Germans around the world, and by helping me you help yourself. Understood?"

"Yessir."

The topic of conversation switched, coming to rest on Kessler's final responsibilities. "I understand the nature of our cargo, Fehler. If we are to carry on with our plan, you should understand what it is you bring to our yellow-skinned friends *Im Lande der Aufgehenden Sonne* ('In the Land of the Rising Sun')."

"And what is that, Sir?"

Kessler leaned forward at the small table in the small cabin. He looked over his shoulder, though the door was locked and nobody could be listening. "Imagine," he whispered, "imagine, Fehler, if you will. The Japanese have been getting pushed back almost to their own homeland. It is only a matter of time before the Americans and their Allies have to think about invading Fortress Japan. But turn the tables around. Suddenly, one day, boom! First Los Angeles, then San Francisco, and that is only the beginning." His face lit up. "Chicago, land of the gangsters. Then Dallas, in the land of the cowboys and Indians!"

"What, Sir?" Fehler frowned. What could his guest be talking about?

"A bomb, Fehler, a gigantic bomb, the likes of which the world has never before seen or dreamed. Or heard."

"I don't quite follow, Sir." He'd heard stories, rumors, about work being done on splitting the atom. A German scientist had accomplished that.

"An atomic bomb, *Ka-Leu*. A single bomb contains enough energy to blow up a city the size of Berlin or New York. Can you imagine? Blow up a city and kill more human beings in ten seconds than the entire fire bombing and the weeks of fire storms that the British caused in Dresden or the Americans are causing in Tokyo."

"Such a bomb, Sir, is it not a century in the future?"

"No, no, my dear fellow, we carry the uranium right here in this submarine, along with the jet airplanes to deliver them."

"No!" The war might yet drag on for more years. He'd been so looking forward to his idyll on the Pacific atolls, but beyond that to the eventual return of Germany to some sort of peacetime normalcy. Would such a thing ever be possible again?

"Come," Kessler said one evening, "let me show you." He led Fehler from the captain's cabin and through a maze of narrow corridors surrounded on all sides by thumping machinery and dim lights. They walked along rattling catwalks and up narrow ladders until they reached the wide cargo areas of the boat's original design. Here, in rack after rack of vertical shafts reaching toward hatches on the upper deck, were the shafts in which mines were to be stowed until they were launched into the sea. Now the hatches were welded shut and the shafts had become important cargo holds.

Kessler unlocked one of the compartments and pulled the door open. "Look inside, *Ka-Leu*."

Fehler leaned into the spacious compartment, which had been designed so two loaders could push a barrel-shaped mine sideways into place on top of a launching mechanism. There sat a wooden crate smelling of linseed oil; several cardboard tubes; a stack of manuals bound in blue cardstock covers; and other odds and ends. On top sat a row of metal boxes, each about 25 mm to a side.

"Those boxes are gold-lined. They were packed in special laboratories, Fehler. They are filled with high-grade uranium oxide ore. Open one of those, and you are soon dead from the radiation inside."

"Radium," Fehler whispered with a pang.

"Not technically correct, but close," Kessler said condescendingly. "There are ten of these boxes. They will change the fate of mankind, these little boxes, unless they wind up at the bottom of the sea. And that we must not allow to happen." He slammed the door shut and locked it. "You see your duty is clear, Fehler. You must get these into the hands of the Japanese, and our loyal German compatriots will ensure that you are amply rewarded in the years after the war."

The two Japanese officers were quiet and diffident, but resolutely respectful of their hosts. They remained stoic in the face of insults Kessler hurled at them and their cherished emperor before storming out of festively bedecked mess.

Another ten days went by, punctuated by either bitter silence or violent arguments at meals.

Meanwhile, the radio dispatcher kept receiving messages by short-wave radio from around the world, particularly in German from the Atlantic naval headquarters in Kiel.

Suddenly, on May 1, the dispatcher rose, threw down his headphone, and ran with a face pale as snow to fetch the skipper.

Johann-Heinrich Fehler's voice quietly rang through the boat shortly thereafter, ordering all hands to stand by for a message. An electrified silence pervaded the vessel as he calmly spoke. Except for a few muffled shouts of anguish, and the continued throbbing of the diesels as they sucked air through the snorkel and turned the screws that pushed *U-234* further south, all was still as at a Sunday morning service.

Heavy-hearted, with mixed feelings, Fehler took the microphone and spoke. He felt tears streaming down his face, not out of any love of Hitler, but for the millions of brave men who had died—for what?—and the flower of German women and children who had been horribly sacrificed, to the bleak end that now lay at hand. With the habits learned from a dozen years of life under the Nazi regime with its Gestapo and its propaganda, with its knock on the door at 3 a.m., and with the habits of military discipline, his mouth spoke the usual formulaic words while his heart drowned in entirely different feelings: "My fellow German sailors, I have the duty to report to you that the *Führer* died yesterday while at his duty station in the defense of Berlin. The honor of leading the *Reich* now befalls one of our own, Grand Admiral Doenitz, who continues to direct the defense of the Fatherland from his headquarters in Kiel. At this time, our orders remain operative and we proceed with our mission." Groping for more words in the stunned silence, and finding none, he replaced the microphone in its cradle. The loud click of its hook engaging its eyelet echoed through the ghostly corridors of the boat as she churned on, serviced by silent sailors with shocked faces.

U-234 was snorkeling south two weeks after departing Norway. She was in the mid-Atlantic, south of the Equator, when a storm rose and he was forced to surface to recharge his batteries and the air inside the wave-tossed boat.

By prearranged plan—for they remained under strict radio silence—*U-234* made a *rendez-vous* with another German sub, *U-530*, an aging boat of 33rd Flotilla, half the size of *U-234*, that had been cruising on various missions from the Baltic to the South Atlantic since the loss of French seaports in 1944. Under cover of darkness, on a cloudy night when the air was filled with drizzle, the two boats lay rocking within a hundred meters of one another, and there was an exchange of rubber dinghies. This in itself was not unusual, given that subs passed mail, courier pouches, and all kinds of technological gadgets routinely among each other.

This time, the commander of *U-530* came on board. He was the young (24) and relatively inexperienced *KL* Otto Wermuth, and he had sailed from a layover in Kristiansand on March 4, about five weeks before the *U-234* had left that Norwegian port.

The two skippers shook hands and conferred over cognac in Fehler's cabin.

"What is your plan?" Fehler asked the much younger officer.

"I have jettisoned all my armaments, including ciphers and so forth, and am turning south toward Argentina to buy some time and possibly intern my ship. Do you have a better idea, Hans?" His eyes blazed with desperation, and his teeth were gritted in a beard-grizzled young face.

Fehler shook his head slowly. "I wish I could advise you, Otto. I continue to maintain radio silence, but listen avidly, in case there is further action out of Kiel, but I have no more incoming information than you probably do."

"But you continue on your mission?"

Fehler said nothing. He was becoming more and more unsure of that fact as the hours, no, even the minutes passed.

"My major responsibility now," Wermuth said laying his fist across the table and staring bitterly into space to one side, "is to ensure the safety of my crew. I cannot think of a smarter thing to do."

Fehler felt sorry for him and patted his shoulder. "You are doing the right thing, I am sure." He could not mention the critical cargo. In any case, from the wartime habit of knowing everyone had secrets, Wermuth did not ask any questions. "Good, then, Hans, I will get along. The dispatches, such as they are, have been exchanged."

The two men shook hands. "*Alles gute*," they told one another, "All good things to you."

The two subs parted company in the middle of the night, and *U-234* continued her lonely journey.

General Kessler and Fehler met in the skipper's cabin at Kessler's request. "*Ka-Leu*," he said, removing his monocle, "this situation reminds me of 1918." He looked stoic, but grim. He wore a casual but dignified blue-green *Luftwaffe* fatigue uniform with submariner's deck shoes.

Fehler nodded slowly. "Twenty-six years gone by, and we are back to that."

"Full circle, but far worse," Kessler said. "This time, Cossacks will ravage the nation. It is unthinkable what they will do to our women and children. We must keep cool heads now, Fehler, and do the right thing."

"And what do you propose that to be, General?"

Kessler folded his arms and laid forth his thoughts. "It is clear, naturally, that Doenitz cannot hold the show together. He is a far better man than any of the jackals Hitler surrounded himself with, but he is simply a place holder. He will ready the Reich for total, formal surrender. I understand from some of the short-wave traffic that he is concentrating on keeping Baltic fleet units operational as long as possible to ferry German military and civilians out of Russian zone of influence and into British and American theaters." He paused a second, and Fehler knew the silence was to reflect on the loss, on January 30, of the *Wilhelm Gustloff* with over 10,000 men, women, and children. The former luxury liner had been torpedoed by a Soviet submarine and gone down in icy waters in the North Sea with the worst loss of life in maritime history. As horrific as Fehler found that to be, it was emblematic of what Hitler had done to the German people, or rather what they had allowed him to do. The relentless propaganda of Goebbels had convinced the average German that God spoke through Hitler. Now that the Austrian vagrant was dead, it would take time for people to get used to not feeling that constant drumbeat of fear and war hysteria that made rational thinking impossible. "Fehler, I anticipate Doenitz will surrender Germany within a matter of days. I could have gone along with our friend Wermuth to his fate in Argentina, if he reaches it, considering Argentina finally declared war on Germany on March 27."

He paused to let the bitter irony of that settle in, the cowardice of those nations that were lining up to kick the corpse of Germany, now that she could not gore them anymore. Stalin had finally declared war on Japan.

He continued: "But there is a more important consideration by far." He poured them each a neat little thumb-full of schnapps. "Think about it, man. We can actually do something good for mankind, and become heroes of a sort, *ja*?"

"My men will need a lot of convincing to be led in any more heroics, General."

"I understand perfectly. Now consider. During the past few weeks, a whole line-up of nations have declared war on Germany, clearly and cynically so they can participate at the victory table after doing nothing or playing both sides against each other. If you think the Japs can hold out much longer, you have got to live in a fantasy world. For all we know, we might arrive in Japan in another two or three months and surrender your sub to the Americans. Therefore, Fehler, I strongly urge you to surrender to the Americans now."

Fehler felt his jaw drop. "Under no circumstances..."

Kessler's face was contemptuous. "Why, Fehler? *Pflicht*? Or *Flucht*? Or just plain *zum fluchen*?"

Fehler looked down at his own knotted fists on the table and let the other man's savage wordplay tear through his mind: "Duty? Or flight? Or just plain curses our bad luck?"

Kessler stabbed his forefinger repeatedly down on the tabletop for emphasis. "We have to think clearly now, Fehler. Stalin is Germany's mortal enemy, whether one is a Nazi or not. The Soviet Union sits a few hundred kilometers from the Japanese islands. Siberia is but a short sail from Japan. Now think of this. The greatest naval humiliation in history was the total destruction of the Czarist navy just 40 years ago at Tsushima. The Russians have a big score to settle with the Japs. You understand, Fehler? We have no friends in this world, especially not after what we have done. Our only recourse is to obtain mercy from the victors, and it won't be from Stalin. We must throw ourselves and your crew on the mercy of the Americans or the British, the sooner the better."

"No!" Fehler said, thinking of his Pacific islands.

"Yes!" Kessler said. "We carry the material that Stalin can capture to make *Wunderwaffen*, super weapons, to annihilate entire German cities. Do you comprehend what I am saying? The danger is not that the Japanese will irritate America by blowing up a few cities. The danger is, worse for us, that Stalin will capture U-234 and pulverize Berlin, Frankfurt, Hamburg, who knows how many German cities, in his revenge. There is a man who is an even greater monster than Hitler. Stalin murders anyone who even thinks a disloyal thought, and in many cases totally innocent people. Stalin is totally mad, insane, and we cannot allow this cargo to fall into his hands!"

Fehler was silent a long time. "I will think about it, General. I believe we have a few days to think. We continue to run under radio silence, here in the South Atlantic, as I decide what to do with my boat."

The debate that raged among the guests and officers was fierce. It went on for days, with Kai Nieschling and his fellow Nazis more determined than ever to do some unnamed heroics, while Kessler and Fehler, as well as First Officer Karl Ernst Pfaff, began to think of throwing the Nazis overboard and letting them swim home through shark-infested waters.

None were more stoic and silent and dignified than the two Japanese officers: Air Force Colonel Genzo Shoji, an aeronautical engineer, and Navy Captain Hideo Tomonaga, a submarine architect by profession. Whatever was going through their minds, Fehler knew, it wasn't pleasant. Given the Japanese reputation for drastic action under this kind of pressure, in fact, Fehler began to carry his Luger service revolver in its leather holster and belt, over his rumpled black service fatigues, in case he had to stop them from some dramatic effort to seize the boat and ram the nearest Allied warship in a suicide gesture. Just in case, Fehler armed Pfaff and several key trusted warrant officers and chiefs, to be ready for any eventuality. But it wasn't to come to that.

On May 7, the short-wave service reported that Grand Admiral Doenitz had unconditionally surrendered the German Reich from his temporary headquarters at Flensburg on the Danish coast. It was an ironic choice of places, Fehler thought grimly, thinking that "Flensburg" sounded a lot like the German "Flehensburg," which would mean a city of weeping if there were such a place. When Fehler made the announcement over the loudspeaker, in fact, one or two chiefs looked at each other like old men hard of hearing and asked "What did he say? Weeping?" By now, everyone was done with weeping, and the Nazis had fallen strangely silent as they began to consider the world of reality for the first time in their careers. Half of them had ever fired a shot in anger or been shot at, living instead in the airy rhetoric of their late hero. The sight of tough, bitter, strapping young sailors armed with pistols and grim expressions was enough to unnerve and cow them into silence, above all the frumpy and precise Kai Nieschling.

No more arguments at the mess table.

Fehler knocked on Kessler's cabin door.

"*Eintreten*," Kessler snapped. "Step inside."

Fehler stepped inside and closed the door. "I have considered your thoughts, General, and I wish to report that I concur. We must surrender to the Allies as soon as possible."

"Excellent!" Kessler said, standing up from where he'd been crouched in the cramped cabin, writing notes while reading Frederick the Great's memoirs.

"It gives me absolutely no joy," Fehler said.

"Of course not," Kessler said briskly, rubbing his hands. "Excellent choice. Best thing we can do under the circumstances. So—you tell me—what is the best way to reach the Allies?"

"First things first," Fehler said.

He had the sailors begin filling canvas mail sacks with priceless items—the Enigma machine; cipher books; the ship's log; any documents that might be incriminating or give away Reich secrets; the *Tunis* RADAR detector; the *Kurier* transmitter. The sacks then had ballast added in the form of metal machine parts, ammunition belts, typewriters, anything heavy, and were tossed one by one into the sea. Several chiefs walked the length of the decks on each side with boat hooks. They made sure no sack had snagged and might be hanging in the water ready to be plucked out by their eventual jailers.

For Fehler, the most melancholy part of the entire operation now came, as he went aft to the passenger cabins to inform Shoji and Tomonaga of his decision. The two Japanese, who had been whiling their time away quietly reading and talking, jumped up from their bunks in horror and began remonstrating with him. Between their broken German and their high pitch of excitement, they had a hard time making themselves understood. One thing was clear: they were desperate to have Fehler continue his journey to Japan, and at one point one of them was on his knees, in tears, beseeching Fehler to change his mind. When Fehler tried to reason with them, they became all the more irascible, so that he called on a chief and several sailors to take away the two Japanese officers' pistols and swords. He ordered them confined to quarters, under guard, for fear of mutiny or sabotage.

The dual nature of their distress was clear. First of all, they were fanatically dedicated to the cult of their emperor, whom they considered a living god. Secondly, by offering to surrender to the Americans, he had unwittingly pronounced a death sentence on these two men. He realized this with a pang of regret, though he was still steamed up about their earlier seeming unreasonableness. But he must put the well-being of the ship and its complement above the decisions these men were about to make for themselves.

The naval officer, Tomonaga, spoke for both of them. "It becomes necessary for us, then, to follow the path of honor prescribed by Bushido, the code of the samurai warrior. We cannot surrender to the enemy. It would be a betrayal of our emperor and nation." As Tomonaga spoke, both men bowed repeatedly from the waist. Their faces looked grim, their eyes black with anticipation of their fate.

"This is your choice, not mine," Fehler told them. "I have reasons for doing what I consider to be the right thing for my crew, my boat, and my own nation."

They bowed again, and Tomonaga said: "Please, Captain, we ask only that you respect our passing and do not interfere with our way."

Fehler felt anger welling up, but there was so much death and destruction these days, and he had so much to do, that he could not waste time trying to dissuade these men. Nor did he feel he had cause to do so. It was his boat, and he had a power of life and death over anyone on it, but this matter seemed beyond his right to interfere. Many a patriotic German officer had recently taken his life rather than face humiliation again as Germany had in 1918.

About an hour later, a sailor came to ask Fehler to come aft to see his Japanese passengers. With misgivings, Fehler followed the man. He found a small knot of curious men gathered outside the cabin door, along with the guard he had posted there earlier. Pushing his way inside, he found the two men lying side by side on their bunks with their arms linked as if they were jumping together into the unknown.

On the floor nearby lay an empty bottle, which Fehler picked up and examined—Luminal, a brand of Phenobarbital. The two men had overdosed themselves.

"Is there a pulse?" he asked the medical technician who stood nearby.

The man shrugged and checked their wrists. "Faint. They are still alive. There is a note for you from them." He handed Fehler a letter, which Fehler opened with a hopeless feeling. He read the letter with trembling hands.

It took the two Japanese officers more than a full day to die.

At the following daybreak, Fehler led an all-hands Christian funeral for them, although they had been Buddhists and Shintoists. The two bodies, tied into weighted canvas sea bags, lay on deck during the service, draped with the Rising Sun colors that the *U-boot* was supposed to fly on her bridge upon entry into Tokyo Bay. Under the flag, in their burial bags, both deceased men lay dressed in their best uniforms, complete with *samurai* swords. The two men had been good guests and had never made of nuisance of themselves. They'd shared all hardships without complaint, and left a pathetic little will bequeathing various little personal items to crewmen they had befriended. To Fehler they had left a small sum of money with which to contact their relatives in Japan to inform them that "We are dead, but did not disgrace ourselves in dying." Their bodies slid off the wet deck, down into the sea with two small splashes quickly drowned by the deep ocean waves.

Soon afterward, the radioman came running topside. "Sir! Sir! I have raised an American Navy vessel!"

"Let me see," Fehler said, tearing the sheet of flimsy from the man's hands. Sure enough—it was the *U.S.S. Sutton*, responding to their calls. Fehler was secretly glad. He'd been afraid maybe another *U-boot* had been dispatched to sink his boat before the Americans could seize his cargo and crew.

U-234 Towed to Portsmouth, U.S.A.

The enormous submarine awed American sailors and officers on board U.S.S. Sutton (DE-771). At 1,763 tons on the surface, 2,740 tons fully loaded and submerged, U-234 was more massive than the destroyer escort that had come to apprehend her.

U.S.S. Sutton was a modern Cannon Class Destroyer Escort displacing 1,620 tons fully loaded. She was 308 feet long, slightly longer than the submarine's 280 feet. She measured 36'8" (across) at the beam, and carried a complement of 15 officers and 201 enlisted crewmen. She was built for speed, with two diesel-driven screws capable of cranking out 21 knots zigzagging around to protect the clanking ships in convoys. She was lightly armed with three inch guns, depth charge tracks, and torpedo tubes. She was a relatively new ship, built at Tampa, Florida, and commissioned 22 December 1944.

Lieutenant T. W. Nazro, skipper of *U.S.S. Sutton*, was impressed by the behemoth. His ship and another DE, *U.S.S. Neal A. Scott* (DE-769), had been taken from patrol duty on 9 May to accept the voluntarily offered surrender of *U-1228*. *Sutton* left *Scott* to take charge of *U-1228*, a 1,545 ton, approximately 230-foot boat of the IXC/40 type.

The sub rode easily in the water with her hatch open and a sprinkling of human figures visible on deck. She was flying the German navy war colors and black and white surrender pennants. Nazro regarded her long and cautiously through binoculars, from a distance. Beside him, his officers did the same. All felt the same prickling under their collar. They'd been dealing with the fascist war machine for at least four years now, and wouldn't put anything past these fanatics. Was it possible that some of these Krauts were actually going to surrender peacefully rather blow themselves up and take as many enemy with them as possible? But surrenders were happening all over the Atlantic theater now that Hitler had committed suicide and Doenitz had officially surrendered. Would these Krauts be any different? Was their urgency real, or feigned? Nazro had the deck gun aimed for the sub's waterline under the conning tower. The mine layers were ready in case she dove suddenly.

Someone on board the sub spoke English, the stilted, schoolboy, pseudo-British kind, but it was well-inflected and easy to understand. "We have important materials on board," the voice said.

"Yeah, yeah, so do I, you pricks," muttered Nazro to himself.

The added flash came: "Important flag officer prisoner on board."

Nazro sent back: "Acknowledge flag officer. Stand by for boarding."

Standing by, came the signals.

Nazro ordered his First Officer: "Ready a launch, and keep those bastards on that sub under the gun."

Minutes later, a boat was in the water, manned by sailors in helmets and flak jackets, several with Tommy Guns. A squad of Marines in fatigue uniform, similarly armed, were in the boat, and her small outboard motor started whining as the boat bucked up and down in the huge mid-ocean swells. Trailed by a bluish exhaust haze, the boat moved toward the sub.

During a tense quarter hour, every eyeball on the *Sutton* was trained on the *U-boot*. From the three inch deck guns on down, everything that could shoot was aimed at them. Many a man paused to wipe sweat from the orbits of his eyeballs, before returning a blinking eye to the barrel of his gun and a trembling finger to the sweat-slicked trigger guard.

A lot of things could go wrong now, instantly, causing a conflagration that would end with one ship or both going down. Every man knew it, and the chiefs kept walking up and down muttering, behind the men's backs as the men leaned over the rail on the main deck: "Steady...steady...fingers off the triggers...nobody twitch, boys...if you gotta itch, scratch it with your trigger finger so you don't make a mistake and let loose..."

On board the sub, a number of men stood silently waiting. The more relaxed and beaten they looked, the more the Americans worried, suspecting a trap.

"Have them all raise their hands," Nazro ordered.

The signal crossed over, and the Germans complied. The Marines positioned themselves in the protective shadows of the sail with their side arms and Tommy guns aimed at the line of Germans who filled the main deck—about 40 of them, Nazro estimated, wiping sweat out of his eyes.

Nazro anxiously kept looking back and forth from the boat to the sub and back to his men in the boat. The *Sutton* stayed far enough out of reach that any detonation on the sub would not hurt the destroyer escort. Most importantly, the *U-boot*'s deck gun was pointed away, with a canvas cover over the barrel, a sign that the German skipper wanted to play fair.

As Nazro watched, the Germans dropped rope ladders and the Americans swarmed up onto the deck. So far so good. There was an exchange of salutes, and a brief conversation. A U.S. signalman on the sub flashed over: "Wants to retire colors."

Nazro had a man signal back: "Okay but secure deck hatch first."

There was another brief consultation between the German skipper and Nazro's officer. Two U.S. sailors dragged a heavy chain toward the hatch on the conning tower, along with a padlock, to secure the hatch open so the sub couldn't suddenly dive. It was something of a futile gesture, Nazro knew, because if the Krauts were bent on suicide, what better way to go?

The Germans stood at attention on deck while the red, white, and black colors came down. That was not a Nazi *insignium* and would be stored on board the sub along with the captain's papers if the bastard hadn't already destroyed those.

Sutton and her crew and captain were fairly green, but one grizzled old chief had done duty with U.S. subs until 1944, and he crossed to the *U-boot* with the *Kapitänleutnant* and his first mate to secure the boat for towing to Portsmouth, New Hampshire. Nazro's first mate and the German first mate descended into the sub, with the old chief, and were in there for about an hour.

The launch ferried over a handful of passengers under the watchful eye of a Marine guard. Several of these carried what looked like sea bags.

Nazro's yeoman signaled: *Did you check the Germans' baggage?*

Aye, came light signals from the launch, flashed by a yeoman instructed by the chief petty officer in charge.

Did you frisk them for side arms?

Aye, all unarmed and secured.

A quarter hour later, the Germans came on board under the watchful eyes of armed U. S. sailors all around. Most of the Germans were ordinary seamen, glad to have the war over with—bedraggled, smelly, oily submariners with beards and dirty faces. Nobody exchanged salutes. The officers appeared sullen. Their eyeballs cut left and right, like razors, with fear and rage and humiliation. It was almost spooky, Nazro thought, and a chill went up and down his spine. Were these guys really human? He noted their dark faces, fierce eyes, and stiff body carriage, and felt a touch of anger as he stepped forth to meet them unceremoniously at the DE's midsection. The Kraut skipper saluted, and Nazro returned the salute with a brief flick, a dismissing motion of his fingertips over his eye brow, nothing more. The Kraut seemed to take it in stride. Hitler had dismissed the U.S. as 'decadent' and 'negrified.' Now they were breaking their Hunnish sabers in defeat. *Good on us*, Nazro thought.

The most arresting figure among the Krauts was a tall flag officer in leather coat and boots with the peaked cap, monocle, the whole nine yards. Several American sailors tittered, and one or two muttered obscenities. Nazro didn't like the breach of good behavior, but he understood his men's emotions and shared them. "Keep a lid on it, you guys," he said from a corner of his mouth. "We're not grammar school girls. Show them we're bigger than they are."

The Kraut skipper seemed loose enough, introducing himself as Failure. Failure in turn introduced the Hun general, Kessler, who bowed slightly and clicked his heels. "At your service, Captain."

Nazro felt like telling Kessler, *don't click your heels on my ship, Nazi, or I'll shoot you like a dog*, but only nodded and managed to say in a thick, strangled voice: "If you people plan any tricks, you'll pay for it."

Failure understood this and said: "I have only the well-being of my crew in mind, Captain, thank you. We thank you for your hospitality."

Kessler remained ever the stiff Hun. "We are prisoners of war and officers. We expect to be treated with all the respect and hospitality due us under the Geneva Convention and standard military courtesy."

Nazro said: "General, you'll be treated fair and square. Under the same conventions, if you step even one inch out of line, I'll clap you in irons and stick you down in the hold on bread and water. Do yourself a favor. Don't click your heels on my ship, Schnauzer. It annoys us. *Capisc'*?"

Failure grinned a bit, and in contrast with Marshal Krepp he seemed almost like an okay guy. "I assure you, Captain, we will behave ourselves."

Kessler said darkly: "No unpleasantness will be necessary."

"Good," Nazro said. "Look around, General. We're the soft guys, remember? We're all armed and would not hesitate to shoot you if necessary. With that in mind, leave your barking and goose-stepping at the doorstep." He wanted to add, *we'll treat you better as prisoners than your people have treated ours*, and that might be true on board ship, but he'd heard stories of American mobs jeering at and stoning captured German submariners being offloaded at Portsmouth, New Hampshire—where they'd be headed now.

"I have information of the utmost importance," Kessler said. "It must be relayed to your superiors under the tightest security immediately."

Nazro ignored him and turned to the bridge. He yelled up: "What's the progress on board that iron sausage over there?"

A yeoman hollered down: "Chief says it's looking good, Sir. They're going through with a mallet and a crowbar, disabling the weapons systems. He says there are no torpedoes or mines on board—it's all cargo storage."

"Good. Tell them to take their time and make sure she doesn't dive again."

Kessler stepped forward in a convulsive, red-faced rage: "Captain, you must not—"

Immediately, a dozen safeties clicked and one could hear the scrape of men's rubber soles as they shifted their bodies in preparation to fill Kessler with lead. Kessler froze, dark as night, with those spooky white-gray eyes looking up left and right. He reminded Nazro of a rat that has gone after some cheese and realized at the last split second that it has one foot on the mechanism of a giant trap that is about to snap its back in half.

For a split second, every soul on board was frozen stiff.

"Easy," a chief muttered to nobody in particular in the silence that filled the air.

"We're the soft guys," Nazro said quietly. "You forget."

"Yeah, we wupped your asses but good," somebody in the crew said.

"Sorry," Failure whispered, then told Kessler softly: "*Immer sanfte, immer sanfte.*" Easy does it, easy does it.

Kessler stood back. "Sorry. There is strategic cargo of the greatest significance on board, which must not be lost or delayed. Your superiors at the highest levels will concur, Captain." He added in an imitation American drawl: "It's your ass if you screw up, Captain."

"He is right, Sir," said the Kraut captain. "Please listen to him."

"All right," Nazro said. "You two." He pointed to Kessler and Failure. "In my board room." He pointed to his nearby master at arms and told the chief: "I want two armed men on each of these two every second, understood?"

"Aye sir," said the khaki-clad chief with his white pistol belt, a skinny man in his mid 30s with graying hair. His name tag read *Shapiro* and there was no doubt how seriously he would take Nazro's order.

Nazro took out his .45 and cocked it, loudly in the silence, then held it at ease, pointing upward. "In case you don't understand. I'm not risking my men and my ship over some piece of paper you jackals signed someplace and then violated every chance you got. If I see the slightest sign of trouble, I'll kill you myself and take the consequences afterward. I make no jokes."

Kessler closed his eyes and nodded his head forward ever so slightly in an implied and infinitely pained heel-click of the chin.

"There is dangerous cargo on board," Kessler said. "They must not break open the cargo without knowing what they are doing."

Nazro considered this briefly. If there were some trick involved, it didn't make sense that Kessler would warn about it. "Very well, General." He holstered his automatic, and yelled an order up to the bridge. The order, to start securing the sub on a 200-foot tow line, and close her hatches, was semaphored immediately to the watch on deck of the sub.

Nazro gave orders for this first mate to sort out the Germans, based on the sub's cargo manifest and a list of passengers and crew the German skipper provided. From the spelling on the manifest, Nazro understood now the correct spelling of his counterpart's name—Fehler. He was already beginning to like the bright-eyed, regular skipper type a bit. They understood each other in a way that the stiff-necked general never would. The man cared about his sailors. The general was a staff type who'd never had a fighting crew under him. That made the gap between Kessler much bigger than between Nazro and Fehler.

They trooped down the ship's corridors to Nazro's stateroom, which had a fairly sizeable conference table and benches, with an actual window overlooking the sea. The thick blackout curtains were up, and might not be lowered again in the ship's lifetime except under drill conditions.

They sat around the table and a yeoman brought a coffee service. Kessler waited until the yeoman left. "Can you clear out the guards for a short while. They must not hear what I have to tell you."

Nazro looked at Fehler.

"I believe it is the right thing," Fehler said. "It is a matter of the highest security. I suggest you and the general speak privately for a few minutes. You will understand."

Nazro said: "Okay, here's what we'll do. Chief, you keep Fehler under guard. I'll take Kessler down to my private wardroom for a few minutes and see what he has to say."

Nazro and the general trooped around the corner, along another corridor, to Nazro's private quarters. A cook carrying a pot of beans, a mechanic wiping his hands on an oily rag, a pharmacist yeoman with a first aid box, all stepped aside to let them pass, but glared after them before going on with their duties.

Nazro closed the door as Kessler stood in a corner of the small room. Nazro sat on the bunk. "All right, General. What is your story?"

Kessler for the first time dropped his arrogance and spoke pleadingly. "Captain, you must relay a message by the most secret means possible to the highest echelons of your War Department. What you must tell them is that *U-234* carries a cargo of uranium oxide. That's all you need to tell them. Do you understand?"

"I think I can remember that," Nazro said. "Uranium oxide? I think I remember that—"

"It doesn't matter," Kessler interrupted. "With all due respect, Captain, don't trouble your mind over it. The less you know, the better. Just get that message off as fast as possible. Also, make sure the *U-boot* isn't lost, because your government will be anxious to have its cargo. And make sure nobody touches any of the cargo holds, understood? The consequences would be dreadful."

Nazro, who had an engineering background, understood that uranium was radioactive and figured in advanced particle research being conducted since the work of Marie and Pierre Curie in the early 1900s. Newspapers occasionally carried stories about the theories of Bohr and Einstein, though come to think of it, little had been broached in the popular press since the early days of the war.

"Hurry, please, I beg of you," Kessler pleaded. "Oh, and Captain—"

"Yes?"

"Captain, the ones you want to keep an eye on are Nieschling and a few of the junior officers. Fehler will give you a list. I can assure you, I hate the Nazis as much as you do, obviously for different reasons. Fehler and I pledge that we will keep the Nazis under control. Their fangs are gone, and their bark is nothing now. Don't worry about them."

Still mistrustful, Nazro put his hand on the doorknob. As a last private gesture, he said softly: "Okay, General. I'll take your word for it."

"Thank you," Kessler said. "Captain—"

"Yes?"

"If I am put on trial, please, if you would mention that I cooperated in every way..."

Nazro began to see where the German was coming from. It seemed rather pathetic. "I read you, General. I'll tell the truth if anyone ever asks me. Just behave yourself, and keep the rest of them in line. I'll be fair about it."

📖

A skeleton crew of U.S. chiefs and German mechanics stayed on board U-234, whose hatch was closed in case of rough weather as the ships trundled north-northwest toward New England.

Apparently, as Nazro learned, Kessler and Fehler had not been joking.

Nazro's transmission up his chain of command resulted in a frantic flurry of transmissions, and then radio silence.

Shortly, they were joined by two other Cannon Class destroyer escorts, *U.S.S. Carter* (DE-112) and *U.S.S. Muir* (DE-770). The three American warships steamed alongside *U-234* in a protective triangle as if doing dangerous Atlantic convoy duty.

Nazro learned nothing more of his cargo, but his own Navy's actions spoke louder than any words.

Before the convoy reached Portsmouth, Coast Guard cutter *U.S.S. Argo* steamed up at full speed, lay alongside, and removed Kessler and some of the officers and civilians who had been on board *U-234*.

At the same time, *Argo* left a platoon of eager, unmilitary looking scientific types who started crawling around on the sub. *U-234* was briefly sequestered offshore as a determination was made whether to remove her cargo there or bring her to shore first. All three destroyer escorts cooled their heels, and their crews remained on the highest alert as if an enemy attack were expected any moment.

Once in Portsmouth, *U-234* joined several other U-boats at dockside--moored by another surrendered German sub, *U-805*.

Nazro had heard through the grapevine that only three days earlier in Boston, the skipper of *U-805* had committed suicide in his cell by breaking his eyeglasses and slitting an artery, after he and his crew were paraded through the streets of Boston and pelted with insults and garbage by irate citizens.

No such treatment would be accorded this German crew. The boat herself was brought to dock and tied up under strictest security. Armed Marines were stationed all around with fixed bayonets, keeping curious and angrily pressing crowds at bay.

Even news reporters were forbidden to set foot anywhere near the boat, and Nazro and his crew were debriefed and ordered to keep their mouths shut tightly or face federal felony charges including treason.

Nazro wondered quietly: if not from the Nazis, then from which quarter?

The Japs?

But that seemed unlikely.

The Japs were busy defending their backyard in Okinawa and hardly had the resources to attack halfway around the world.

Then who?

Maybe Uncle Joe?

Wild Bill Donovan in Trouble

Major General William Donovan, head of the Office for Strategic Services, knew he was in trouble.

He'd seen it coming for a long time, and it was a freight train along whose front bumper was written *J. Edgar Hoover*. Hoover, the little bulldog who decades earlier had taken command of an obscure police agency of the Justice Department, the Bureau of Investigation or B.I., had made himself a leading Washington power broker. Upon the death of FDR, whom Hoover had loathed, Hoover's first action had been to call his office (now the Federal B.I. and soon, he hoped, the World B.I. or something equally grandiose—he had already staked his claim on the entire South American intelligence territory) and request the full dossier on Harry S. Truman. He had a dossier on everyone in Washington, D.C. For Hoover had learned over the years that the way he could exert power over people was to gather as much information on them and keep secret files. Everyone had some nasty little secret, and Hoover made it his business to know.

Donovan, trained as a lawyer but more recently evolved into a fairly flamboyant, innovative spy master and war hero, had managed to overcome naive America's slavish cultural devotion to the parent country, Great Britain, and had launched his own version of Britain's MI5, MI6, and Special Air Services all rolled into one: O.S.S., the Office for Strategic Services.

Hoover had been on the crime beat since World War I, and he'd cleaned up a corrupt bureaucracy to create a first-class law enforcement agency. Its law enforcement had been directed all sorts of crimes—alcohol trafficking during Prohibition (1919-1934), as well as drugs, gambling, racketeering, espionage, treason, and sabotage. Hoover forayed against both the German and the Red menaces. Hoover's single most visible case was the Lindbergh baby kidnapping in 1933, during which he managed to elbow aside the Treasury Department and other law enforcement agencies, and claim at least part of the credit for bringing Bruno Hauptmann to justice.

William J. Donovan, Hoover's second in command for a time, was the man Hoover most feared as threatening his position. Wild Bill Donovan was one of the most decorated soldiers in American history. A hero of World War I in Europe, he held all three of the nation's top decorations: the Distinguished Service Medal, the Distinguished Service Cross, and the Congressional Medal of Honor (CMH). He'd been awarded the CMH for heroism as a lieutenant colonel during the battle of *Landres-et-St. Georges* (France, 1918), for personally leading the Fighting 69th in an attack while seriously wounded. That regiment of New York Volunteers, famous for their service to the Union during the Civil War, was federalized in World

War I as the the 165th Regiment of the 42nd Division, or 'Fighting Irish,' who would lend their name to the Notre Dame University football team. Donovan was one of the founders of the American Legion. His credentials were impeccable. Upon his return to civilian life, he made an unsuccessful run as Republican lieutenant governor of New York State. Factors cited in his loss included that he was Irish-American and Catholic. He served as a District Attorney in western New York, and confided to his friends that he had ambitions far outstripping his origins. He dreamed of one day becoming the nation's first Catholic president. It was not to be, and now he was fighting to hang on to the espionage network he'd created.

Hoover's lifelong hatred of Donovan was born during Donovan's time as Coordinator of Information, when he had to mesh the intelligence activities of the FBI, the military departments, and other agencies. Hoover made sure Donovan, even after he became chief of OSS in 1942, was kept out of South America. McArthur kept the OSS out of the Philippines, which MacArthur saw as his personal fief. Thus began a war of machinations by Hoover that now, in mid-1945, at the peak of his accomplishments, had brought Wild Bill Donovan to an abrupt precipice that was about to end an illustrious career.

J. Edgar Hoover had what one aide called "a terrible patience," and he could wait for decades, patiently biding his time until he found the moment to destroy an old enemy. Hoover never forgot or forgave, even imagined slights. A very insecure individual, he compiled huge dossiers on the private lives of every politician and public figure. There was nobody in Washington, whether friend or foe of Hoover, on whom there did not rest a complete file—be it FDR, Donovan, Eisenhower, Eleanor Roosevelt (slandered by Hoover for alleged lesbian dalliances and other infidelities), or the most flagrant Communist.

Donovan, meanwhile, thought he had freed himself of Hoover's clutches in striking out to create the first real U.S. international intelligence agency in 1942. The exploits of O.S.S. around the world throughout World War II were legendary, though the agency itself would be kept secret for many years.

The earth suddenly shifted: Donovan's patron, FDR, died of a cerebral hemorrhage on April 12. Soon, Donovan realized that his dreams were coming to an end. Hoover had quietly and methodically built up a power base that included Supreme Court Justices as well as officials of the State Department, including the naïve Edward Stettinius. More importantly, Hoover had let Truman know—and Donovan as well, through back channels, for intimidation—that he had a dossier on Donovan. The most serious accusation Hoover could, and did, bring to newly sworn-in President Harry S. Truman—who knew next to nothing of Donovan, but believed Hoover—was that Donovan's organization was hopelessly infiltrated by Communists.

Donovan, hearing this charge, had to reflect that a good intelligence chief did indeed seek whatever bed partners he could in executing his mission. The primary mission remained defeating fascism by any means possible. The nature of successful espionage, as his British and French seniors had taught him, was to fight dirt with dirt. Hoover was a master of these arcane arts, yet managed to trump Donovan by adopting the accepted sanctimonious piety. With Nazism on the ropes, all that was left was a monumental, religious crusade against the infidel Communist. Too late, Donovan realized how far ahead the 'terribly patient' Hoover had been thinking all these years. Donovan saw it was too late to salvage the brilliant organization he had cobbled together. That would now emerge as the Central Intelligence Agency under someone else's tutelage. But would it be under Hoover?

Now, as Donovan awaited a business visit by Ivor Crane, a colonel he'd recruited in London from U.S. Army's Military Intelligence Corps, he reflected that the handwriting was on the wall, and there was little he could do to save himself. He still had a mission to fulfill, and he'd continue fighting to the last, like a good soldier. When Crane knocked at Donovan's apartment in Manhattan, Donovan rose in stocking feet to open the door.

In the evening of a drizzly spring day, in May 1945—one of those days when it was still cool, but there was hint of the coming summer humidity in the air—Donovan held a coffee cup in his free hand as he pulled the door open. There stood Crane in a business suit with his tie loose and a newspaper casually hanging from under the elbow from which extended his wooden hand, while he held a briefcase in the other hand. The two men exchanged greetings in the foyer as Donovan closed the door.

"Come on in, Ivor," Donovan said. "Coffee?"

"I just had dinner," Crane said shaking his head. "I didn't want to arouse any suspicion by coming earlier."

"Oh?" Donovan's interest was piqued. He went around closing drapes and straightening furniture. Unlike the lavish Paris digs he'd just given up at the Ritz, this Government-service apartment was austere. It was simple, but secure, located in a row of brownstones in Uptown Manhattan. It had a secure entrance below, and another secure entrance halfway up, before a visitor could even knock on the deadlocked door. Not that Donovan spent that much time here. His agents had set the place up as a safe house, but now with the severe budget cuts Truman had visited on his agency, he was just letting the lease run out and was using it as a crash pad during his visits to New York City.

Crane, favoring his prosthetic arm, threw his coat over a chair and poured himself a short, neat whiskey from a bottle Donovan kept for visitors. With this, Crane walked over to a window in the living room and looked out over the glimmering Manhattan skyline. "You know that Hoover is smearing you."

"I understand that."

"Those of us who know it are outraged."

Donovan chuckled quietly. "I've had 16,000 people under my command and we helped save the world. I lost fewer than 200 agents, far better than my Infantry days in France during the Great War. Now this vile little bulldog is trying to impugn my reputation. And he is doing a damned good job of it." Donovan sat his long, rangy frame down, set the coffee aside, and mussed his graying hair. "Time for me to get out, Ivor. I got through the first war alive, and I tossed all kinds of manure in this one, but I don't have the stomach for the kind of crap that gigantic bureaucracy in Washington shovels around."

Crane sat down hard in the couch opposite as night fell outside. "General, it's not over. You can fight. You can win."

Donovan shook his head.

"What's the matter with you, Sir? Give them hell."

"Too honest," Donovan said ironically. "I want to spend some time with my family. I just don't have the stomach to exchange hairballs with Hoover for the rest of my life."

"Listen," Crane said, looking around. He suddenly said, "I assume Hoover doesn't have any bugs on us here."

Donovan chuckled again. "Wouldn't that be—no, I've had the technical people go through the walls. It's clean."

"I have some interesting news," Crane said. "I picked up a top secret wire that the Navy picked up a Nazi sub in the Atlantic. They brought her in to Portsmouth, New Hampshire. This sub had on board a huge amount of weapons-grade uranium headed for Japan, along with jet airplanes so the Japs could energy-bomb our cities. They've flown the Krauts to a secret facility down near Washington to interrogate them, including a *Luftwaffe* general."

"So?" Donovan said with a shrug. "Sounds like ONI is handling it. Hoover will get his fat little pug face into it somehow—nothing we can do about it."

"No, but listen," Crane said. "As I see it, right now you stand at the crossroads. We have a new super intelligence agency, the Central Bureau of Intelligence. The two most qualified people to run it are you or Hoover. As I see it, it's fifty-fifty, but you've gotta go fight for it, General. You can't sit back and let this twisted little pervert take you to the cleaners. It's downright un-American the way this creep operates. Don't take it lying down."

Donovan shook his head and put his feet up. "You're an optimist, Ivor. I think the game is over already. I agree, Hoover is a sleazy fellow. You'd think those in power would dump him. It's been tried, to no avail."

Crane grew agitated. "That's because you have naïve people like Eleanor Roosevelt and Ed Stettinius trying to run the show."

"Stettinius!" Donovan said with a snort. He liked Eleanor, but he had little use for the man who had said "Gentlemen don't read each other's mail," in regard to a spy coup OSS had managed to pull on the Soviets. Stettinius, as Secretary of State, had forced Donovan to give back to the USSR a top secret code book that had been found on a Finnish battlefield, with which OSS could have followed Stalin's constant treachery. Naïve people like Stettinius kept sabotaging the espionage efforts of the U.S.

"Get this," Crane said. "They've taken the Krauts down to Washington to turn them upside down and empty their pockets. Meanwhile, my people have been able to track some interesting movement on the part of some of the Useful Dupes around New England. It seems that this shipment of uranium oxide is going to be sent west somewhere, top secret, way beyond my range of visibility. What's interesting, though, is that we might be able to pull off a little trick or two of our own by tracking it and seeing who tries to steal it. We already have a suspected CP on the move."

"Who?"

"Goldman, a physicist from M.I.T., who has been working at Berkeley since last year on some top secret project. The Manhattan Project, which sounds like a fancy cocktail."

Donovan's professional interest briefly overcame the cynicism and depression that he'd been fighting off for the past few weeks as he realized that Hoover was about to get his head. His one real hope now was that, if he himself couldn't get the prize position as the head of the new Central Intelligence Agency, then Hoover shouldn't either. Rumors reached Donovan that it was already a done deal. Truman was going to create a vast new espionage bureaucracy, but he was going to name someone completely new and unknown to head it. The really bad news was that Donovan already knew OSS was about to be disbanded. OSS had existed despite the turf wars of the military branches and the State Department. It looked as though they would dismember his organization, and return to the old ways of petty divisiveness. Truman believed in a separation of powers to keep everyone honest and prevent anyone like Hoover from ever acquiring the kind of power Hoover had, and so Truman was going to take from Hoover the jurisdiction for all activities outside the United States—intelligence, counter-intelligence, and otherwise—and limit Hoover's range of operations to the domestic front. That would mean Hoover would lose the entire South American espionage empire he'd set up. Donovan had heard a rumor that Hoover, in his infinite pettiness, was poised to destroy his South American FBI intelligence operation rather than let it fall into an opponent's hands. "He would have done so well in Byzantium," Crane once groused to Donovan over Irish double-malt whiskeys before Donovan's trophy-laden home fireplace.

The best news was a rumor that, once the world war were over, Truman planned to launch a consolidated global, exterior spy operation in the mold of Britain's external Secret Intelligence Service (SIS), or MI6. The worst possible news was the rumor as to whom Truman was planning to install as the first head of this new agency: a civilian with zero military background, and with almost no intelligence background, whose current job in life was as chief executive officer of the Piggly Wiggly supermarket chain.

Now, as Crane began to propose a desperate new counter-intelligence gambit, Donovan sat forward with his hands folded between bony knees, and listened intently.

"To begin with," Crane said, "I will visit the commander of U-234. If I get lucky, I might have a clue as to what happened to his uranium."

U-Boot Captain at Fort Hunter

By the time Johann-Heinrich (John Henry) Fehler was headed toward Washington, D.C.—under guard, but not chained, on a U.S. Navy DC-4 along with General Kessler and the rest of the technical officers and civilians from *U-234*—Fehler's appreciation of the world had changed.

For one thing, he was amazed at the wealth possessed by everyday citizens in the United States. He was amazed at the strange division of classes based on race. Blacks appeared more prosperous, certainly, than most Germans after the war. At the same time, coming from a racially homogenous nation, Fehler could not get used to this idea that an entire class of human beings could float around unseen like ghostly, dark-skinned shadows. Their very existence went unrecognized in motion pictures, novels, newspaper articles (unless it was about jazz musicians using heroin, and at that the actors were whites with black face makeup). They did not officially exist, these blacks, but they were cooks, train porters, airline skycaps, maids, anything menial that the whites did not want to do. One of Fehler's first experiences with race in the United States had been at a restaurant. Taken on a bus with several other German and Italian POWs from the naval base to a U.S. Navy-run airport near Portsmouth, there had been a stop for lunch. The Shore Patrol guards, loyal U.S. military men, all Negroes, were not allowed into the restaurant, but were forced to eat C-rations sitting outside in a park, wearing their ponchos, in fog and drizzle. There was plenty of room in the warmth inside the restaurant! These class divisions made the U.S. seem truly alien to Fehler. He'd been to places like South Africa, where the blacks lived in squalor under white overlords, but these blacks in the U.S. were supposedly full citizens. They had voting rights, but weren't allowed to vote—at least in the former slave-owning South, which apparently never forgot its grievances, no matter how out of touch with reality. Fehler now had time to ponder such things, given that he was no longer a warrior chieftain, constantly responsible for serious missions and for the lives of his crew and passengers. Especially, what impressed him and weighed on him as he traveled toward Washington, D.C. was his growing realization of the sheer vastness of this nation. How could the delusional and stupid Hitler and his crew of narcotic-ridden misfits have imagined that little Germany, with its 65 million inhabitants in a land area half the size of France, could ever hope to conquer so much of the world? Against a U.S. that had, at the height of the war, rolled two bombers an hour, two warships a day, off of its many assembly lines, without straining itself? He got the impression that even the Americans, be they little people in little towns, or important officials, uniformly seemed not to understand what a giant they were upon the world stage. In many ways, they seemed delightfully naïve. Europeans, who had first encountered significant numbers of Americans after the Great War, called them child-like. And then there was the fact that they thought of their nation as 'America,' forgetting Canada, Mexico, and South and Central America. The beer was watery, the bread like cardboard (*Papp*), the candy a mix of chemicals and sugar, but the beef was great, the whiskey superb, and the countryside gloriously beautiful. Many of the women were delightfully obese, despite rationing— unlike emaciated *Frauen* clambering in rags amid the ruins in the Fatherland, lucky to find food in garbage cans.

Fehler, a good-natured, bright man with an optimistic view toward the future, could only grin to himself and enjoy the food (of which there seemed to be limitless supplies), the fun music (to which even the top Nazis had secretly tapped their jackbooted feet), the attractive women, the whole crazy culture with its contradictions and its ups and downs—and a clearly patriotic population that believed just as fanatically in their national mission, and successfully so. As he sat in a plush seat on the DC-4, enjoying civilian life, he sipped on a container of chocolate milk and looked out at the brightly lit cities, patchworks of yellow and amber light, slowly revolving below. More than ever, he realized the futility of the sacrifices he and the other Germans had made for a decade in the service of one man's insanity and one party's evil, or both. But, dammit, here he was, comfortable, no longer at risk for his life! He was delightfully and wonderfully and deliciously free of all responsibility for life and death. He no longer had to sink Allied ships and try to save their passengers or let them die. He no longer had to write letters home to bereaved mothers whose sons he had held in his arms while they died, crying, from terrible burns. A million things—the whole weight lifted off his shoulders! Yes! He could indeed smile.

Fort Hunter, so Fehler learned, was a secret installation outside Washington D.C. The fort, whose origins dated back to the time of George Washington, had been one of the defensive sea artillery forts surrounding the capital. The British in the War of 1812 had burned Washington. This had demonstrated the need for such defenses. It had been made a battery (Sheridan Point) around Civil War times, and only taken out of warlike service by 1917. Now it served as an all-purpose Government facility, and one of its wings was a special interrogation camp for German *U-boot* officers.

Fehler was housed with several of his former colleagues, among them Werner Henke.

Kessler was taken to a different wing, and Fehler saw very little of him anymore. *Good riddance*, Fehler thought. Kessler had big fish to talk to, and Fehler could only relate his tiny part of the story the Americans were after. Like Kessler, the civilian and military technical passengers of *U-234* were taken away to other processing points.

Judiciously, as much as he bantered with his comrades, Fehler kept his mouth shut about the secret mission of *U-234*. They all had lots of bittersweet and poignant memories to talk about—comrades lost in battle, wives and children lost in bombing raids while the men were at sea, parents who had died during the war, a lost world that would never come back again. Some of these comrades were still unreconstituted Nazis who saw no error in their ways. A free thinker could meet a mysterious and violent end in the prison camps, which were often secretly run by former Gestapo and SS operatives in their relentless zeal to keep Hitler's spirit alive. Others had long ago gotten wise to Hitler's folly but soldiered on because it was the German way of doing things. All felt the crushing blanket of defeat on their backs. All suffered the shame and taunting, even the light-hearted humor of the invisible blacks in uniform who seemed to be the glue holding this society together, doing laundry, cooking, escorting prisoners. Fehler developed new friendships with a few Jews and a few blacks. These fellows were all just fine in their own right. Some of them, like Goldblatt, a camp doctor, who really cared about his patients, and always listened extra long to your chest with his stethoscope, as if listening to a ballgame of his beloved Yankees; or the easy-going Smitty, a tall Negro cook who always sneaked you an extra pork chop, with a big smile, no strings attached, if you looked hungry or homesick—what golden hearts!—these were *Kumpeln*, *Kerle*, regular guys!

Not everyone among the German prisoners felt this way. Fehler coughed up his share of secrets and was transferred back to Portsmouth, where he was put on light duty, administrative tasks, helping out the Americans as they prepared their vast hordes of German prisoners for expeditious return to a shattered Fatherland. The more difficult *U-boot* prisoners were sent to a special camp at Papagalo, Arizona where they could be maintained under heavy security.

Then there was *KL* Werner Henke, commander of *U-515*, who could not tolerate what was happening to him and his fellow prisoners. There was a paranoid rumor mill that always reported the blackest news. Now they said the Germans would all be gassed eventually. One evening in June, Wenke suddenly broke free from the exercise yard and sprinted through the dusk toward the barbed wire at the edge of the Fort Hunter preserve. As other POWs watched in shock, a volley of rifle fire rang out from the guard towers. Wenke just managed to reach the barbed wire in view of civilian houses not far away, when his body was riddled with rifle bullets and he hung bleeding to death in the wire for at least a quarter hour before Marine Corps troops pulled his tangled corpse out of the steel thorns.

That, in turn, caused all sorts of shadowy commotions—like the man who came to visit Fehler a few days later, a tall, graying intelligence officer who introduced himself as Colonel Ivor Crane of the United States Army. Fehler was about to return to Portsmouth, and was looking forward to the change. He thought nothing of this visitor, having had plenty of such interviews. They sat opposite each other in a small visitation room, sharing cigarettes. Crane had smuggled in a six-pack of watery, lousy American beer, for which Fehler was nonetheless grateful. Crane must be a brave man, for he'd lost a hand, and he carried himself like a warrior. Crane seemed a sinister warrior, and that caught Fehler's observant eye. "Infantry?" he guessed.

"El Alamein," Crane replied. Crane seemed a rather odd duck, probably not the regular Army M.I. though he introduced himself as such. Crane kept looking strangely aside, as if he expected to be overheard (by what? A hidden microphone? A counter-spy?) They were in a small room with night-black windows running with rain. The banging steam radiator should blank out spy pickups. "This radioactive material," Crane said. "How many boxes?"

Fehler told him, while feeling a bubbling up of mirth. "What? Don't tell me your government has lost a box or two?" Fehler had delivered it to these stupid Yanks, and there wasn't much more he could have done to save them from an Axis atom bomb, much less a Communist one. As soon as he laughed, he regretted it. Immediately, he had a picture of the Soviets atom-bombing Berlin. "Colonel, are you people complete fools or what?"

"Captain, I have my reasons for coming here today. You are to speak to nobody of my visit today, do you understand?"

Fehler could only shake his head helplessly as it became apparent that the Americans seemed to have lost their minds, and their bomb. Then another possibility occurred to him, which was truly horrifying. Stultifying in its brazenness. What if Crane were a Soviet agent, and the Russians were trying to intercept the material somehow, take it to Moscow? The result would be a Soviet atom bomb. Too horrifying to contemplate. Fehler broke into a sweat. He knew Crane had his back covered. If he, Fehler, made some wild accusation to his masters in this prisoner of war station, it might go badly for everyone involved. There was nothing he could do but keep his mouth shut.

He rose. "I think we have talked enough for today," he told Crane.

"Hold on a minute," Crane said angrily.

"*Gehen Sie zum Teufel.*" Fehler said, "Go to hell." He turned and stalked out of the room. He left the beer on the table.

Ivor Crane, *Main-en-Bois*

On a drizzly spring night, Ivor Crane tossed his newspaper into a trashcan and strode purposefully along through the market square in Alexandria, Virginia. He did not see himself as a bad man or a traitor. He might be a Soviet double agent, but he was determined to help his boss out before OSS went down the drain. Thousands of men and women working for Donovan felt this way, while thousands in the employ of Hoover were anxiously waiting to jump ship and go over to whatever new super-spy agency President Truman was about to sign into being. Pug Hoover was right—there were a lot of progressive thinkers in the spy business, coming as they did from elite colleges, where they were presumably exposed to actual thinking as opposed to the usual rehash of capitalist brainwashing.

His visit to Fehler at the submarine officers' interrogation lab in D.C. proved largely fruitless. He had a hunch that Fehler was onto him. Had he dared sneak a weapon in with him, he might have assassinated the German just to be sure. Now he had to gamble that Fehler might decide to remain silent. Why should a captive German care what transpired between the Americans and the Soviets? Rather than risk blowing his cover, Crane decided to try other venues. One way or another, that uranium oxide would wind up in Soviet hands. First, though, he had to find it. It was as obvious as the nose on his face that the U.S. government had spirited it away from Portsmouth to be added to its own stockpiles. So the trick was to find those stockpiles, which would be wherever the Yanks were developing their own wonder weapon.

📖

"We could be put in jail for talking about it," Foucault said as he used a trembling hand to dip a cookie into a little chocolate sauce.

"It's imperative that I understand what they will do with the material," Crane said sitting o the edge of his seat. He still had his hat in his hands, spinning it impatiently. He suddenly realized he must seem rude, and laid the hat down on the oriental rug between his feet. "Help me, Dr. Foucault. Help the U.S. government."

Foucault ran a crippled hand over his liver-spotted temples. "Well, let's see. They are doing this research in centers all across the country, keeping it decentralized, I suppose. From Oak Ridge, Tennessee to Hanford, Washington to Yale University in New Haven to Berkeley near San

Francisco. I imagine they have central facilities somewhere. I suppose that uranium could have gone just about anywhere." He thought for a moment. "Tell you what. Check out the background on a company right here in Manhattan called ChemCor. I seem to remember they were hot and eager to get radioactive fuels, and it seems to me the FBI came to me a year or two ago asking about them. They had a Belgian cargo ship tied up at a Manhattan dock for a long time, interned with some Congolese yellow cake. Maybe that will get you going."

"Thanks!" Crane said, jumping up grabbing his hat. He hugged Mrs. Foucault on the way out. "Best cookies I've had in a long time."

Mary beamed after him, closing the door.

Crane sprinted down the stairs, out the front door, and into the street. His coattails flapped as he sprinted for the nearest subway station. It was a beautiful plan. He could help himself, help the world-wide workers' movement, help Donovan, hurt Hoover, and sow more dissent among the American amateurs who had no real idea about how to do world-class espionage. Too mired in their childish ra-ra idealism and their ridiculous crusade to colonize the world for U.S. corporations to plunder. As an apostate Russian Orthodox, and an atheist in the service of communism, he had no use for religion—which Lenin had called 'the opiate of the people.'

Along the way, he stopped at a phone booth and called Donovan at the apartment. He had to be very careful what he said, for the line might be tapped by Hoover's minions, and most likely he was being followed.

"Yeah," Donovan said in a curt, dry voice.

Crane said cryptically: "ChemCor. Land of the $24 beads for land deal with the Manna-hata. Check them out. I'll follow up with you. *ChemCor.*" He hung up after spelling the name as Foucault had done for him.

Jaguar in Portsmouth

The damp chill at night created a gray fog that drifted over the spooky masts and sails of docked U-boots at the naval station dock in Portsmouth, New Hampshire.

Sitting beside *U-508* was *U-234*, recently arrived in the company of Coast Guard cutters and Navy destroyer escorts. Sailors with loaded shotguns stood guard at dockside, squarely in the middle of the boarding ramp.

Nearby in the water was a fifty-foot sailing vessel with her engine housing covered by canvas and her large sail furled. Her lights were off, and several men in watch caps and dark clothing waited eagerly. When a U.S. Navy patrol boat puttered by, manned by young sailors who were tired of war and only wanted to go home, the men waited tensely with their American-made revolvers. The Americans never quite caught on that there was a boarding party less than a mile offshore waiting to go in, quickly do its work, and head out to sea where a Soviet submarine waited to pick up them and their precious cargo.

Somewhere, a dog barked. Traffic flowed past a mile away on the public roads. Out there was a town, a city, filled with civilians celebrating the recent fall of Berlin and the approaching climax of the war with Japan.

There were plenty of people who felt it was going to be about the same kind of punch and go as Patton's drive in Germany. Many expected MacArthur to do in the Pacific what Eisenhower, Patton, and others had done in Europe. Still, there were always those frightened and conspiracy minded individuals for whom the glass was never half full, but always half empty and loaded with poison. The sailors traded laughter, rumors, colorful jokes, little anecdotes about home and girlfriends, pictures of babies, worries about when it would all be over. Shifts came and went. Most of the Germans were either in POW camps by now, but a few had been kept in Portsmouth for interrogation, and some of the higher ranking ones, including Nazi civilian stuffed shirts, had been flown away someplace for interrogation by high U.S. brass. Some rumors had it they'd been flown directly to Washington, and some of those were the kinds of rumors that seeped through the walls of secrecy and security by way of mouth—the guards on special Navy flights, the colored cooks, any of the thousands of little mice who weren't noticed when the big boys were nibbling captured cheese.

There were also plenty of brass sniffing around, and there were at least two dozen or more intelligence agencies involved—both known quantities like Military Intelligence, Office of Naval Intelligence, and newer outfits nobody had ever heard of before. Many were small intelligence sections lost in the copious layers of middle management in regular civilian agencies.

When, therefore, a quiet, dark-eyed U.S. Army major began sniffing around, hardly anyone took much notice. The major was a man in his late 30s, with an ageless sort of face. He could have been ten years older or younger. Only one guard at a gate casually checked his I.D., and thought nothing of it. The major's face and I.D. went out of the guard's mind before the major had even stepped away from the guard shack and passed through the outer security perimeter to examine the stacks of boxes on the dock around the captured German submarines. The security guard was a young kid who couldn't wait to get out, who often came to work half sloshed on cheap whiskey, and who preferred to listen to radio music rather than diligently scan the harbor with his binoculars as he'd been trained to do.

The army major had his collar up, his brim down, and his hands in his pockets. He had an ID badge clipped to the lapel of his raincoat, should any other guards question him. None did.

The guard at the gate was busy, bent over his radio to bring in the station more clearly to hear Al Trace And His Silly Symphonists play *Mairzy Doats*. He'd play it loudly until the sergeant of the guard came by to tell him to turn it down or turn it off, but that wouldn't be for another hour at least.

Meanwhile, the man who had signed in as Major Robert Malone strode carefully around the dock, eyeballing the German subs before showing his badge to the boy with the shotgun, who then let the major inside to clamber into the submarine as she sat disabled at the dock.

Which the major did, quietly, with a tool in his pocket to unlock the mine shafts and determine if General Leslie Groves had already removed the cargo to use in his top secret weapons program at Oak Ridge.

The splatter of leaking rainwater on metal inside the dead boat was the first thing the major heard as he clambered down the ladder. He knew exactly where to go in the dim reddish maintenance lighting inside *U-234*. It was cold and damp in the gloom down here. Shadows ran around him like ghosts. Water dripped from broken fixtures, and shattered glass lay under extinct dial faces. Using a flashlight, he followed its wavering and stabbing beam deep into the bowels of the sub. He opened two of the shaft doors and stared at empty metal floors, and scratch marks where heavy gold-lined boxes of yellow-cake uranium had been dragged out. Was there a shred of hope the stuff was still here? He had to be sure. *No.* He pointed the flashlight here and there. The stabbing beam found nothing. *Gone.*

No time to lose. He turned and hurried from the *U-boot*. Viktor Mutsev, the man known by a variety of handles including Jaguar, climbed hand over hand up the steel ladder leading from the ghostly interior of the submarine. They were too late to steal the material now. He must wave off the boarders and the submarine, then immediately turn to his chain of command in the *rezidentura* to learn where the shipment of uranium oxide might be headed next. His guess: the American atom bomb project, and he had recently learned that was being carried out in two centers: Hanford and Oak Ridge.

His best information was that the material would be going to Oak Ridge, for technical reasons involving the type of bomb material. He understood the stakes perfectly, and was highly motivated. For Stalin, it would mean possessing an atomic bomb. For communism, it would mean a step closer to world victory. For himself, it would mean a promotion and perhaps a nice *dacha* outside Moscow in that hazy paradise of the future when the dictatorship of the proletariat was in full force. The thought of these things made him salivate, and he pressed on all the faster, his hands blurring on the cold, damp rails as he emerged into the night air like a drowning man gasping for oxygen.

Ivor Crane: Double Betrayer

Within two days, working with OSS, Crane had established that the shipment of uranium had been offloaded at Portsmouth, put on a civilian charter plane flown by Army Air Corps pilots with top clearances, and taken somewhere out west. He relayed this information to his handlers.

Crane followed up at a feverish pace, for there was no telling how many bombs the Americans already had, or when they might start using them. Crane learned that a Russian émigré named Bernard Rossakoff, who had worked as a chemist for ChemCor before it went bankrupt after a Federal investigation in 1943, had revealed it was a front for the NKGB technical branches.

Crane hopped a Navy charter DC-4 out of Norfolk, Virginia and was on his way to San Francisco.

Part Five: Sailor, Pilot, & Spy

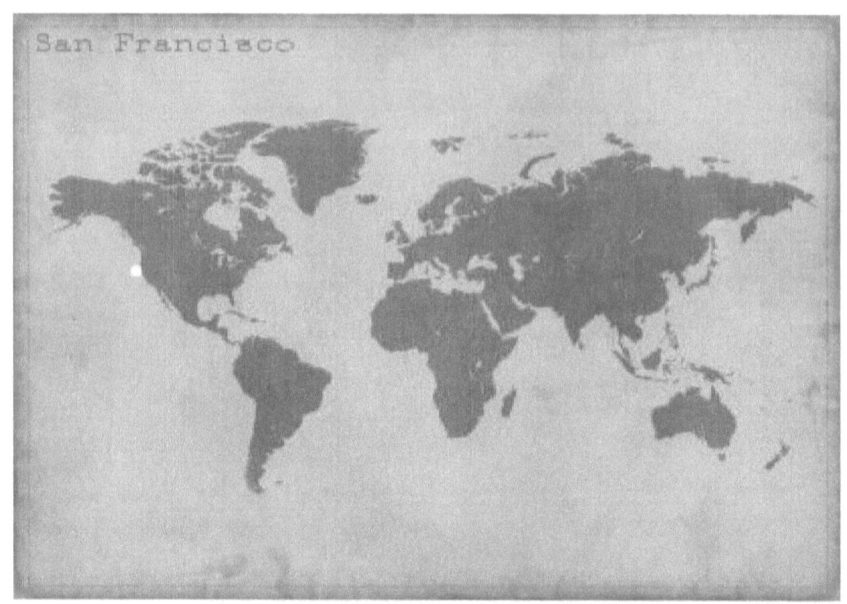

San Francisco—Tim: Mystery of Corie & Meg

Tim Nordhall inhabited a sensuous twilight-world in which time seemed to stand still. His relationship Corie and Meg had a logic all its own. One afternoon, as he sat in the living room reading Pearl S. Buck's 1941 novel China Sky, he looked up to check the time on a little military travel alarm clock he'd picked up at the PX, and laughingly saw it draped with a woman's silk stockings drying after the wash—no idea which woman's.

Tim was willing to let time slip a few cogs out of gear for a while. He was weary of conflict, of fear, of treachery. His past was a violent and murky movie, filled with the blast of torpedoes and the red haze of pain, followed by endless hours of drifting amid salt water and seaweed off the African coast before being deposited naked and unarmed on the beach. Then there had been the dread of being picked off by marauding lions that lived on the edge of the desert. He should have died there, he sometimes thought, but some hand of fate, some unseen giant hand, maybe God, had plucked him out of that purgatory and deposited him back in civilized London where he'd survived German bombings and dated English women and drunk Irish beer. That was the good side.

The future was what? For millions of Americans under arms, pondering a bloody and costly invasion of the Japanese homeland, the dreaded move further into the Pacific and the terminal battle for the Japanese homeland seemed to evaporate in hopeful and wishful thinking that Japan was rapidly slipping the same way Germany had. If there was to be a new push in the Pacific, it looked as if it would pass Tim by. Why not? Had he not seen enough of war? The future was some unknown black void down the road when he'd be out of this military twilight and back in the civilian world where one had to work harder and smarter...but what did anyone really know of that, given that the normal world if there was one had ended in 1929 followed by years of deprivation, fear, and despair for more than half the population. What would it be like to live in boom times after a great victory like the one that seemed to be shaping up? Tim had no idea—like many Americans, he wasn't old enough to remember much about the world before Depression and World War. He'd been sixteen when the stock market crashed in October, 1929. From there, he counted eleven years of Depression and five years of war—half his life, all of his adult life. He had no idea what peacetime and prosperity were like. He imagined it was a bit like this dreamlike existence.

He lived from hour to hour, day to day, wandering to and from work, writing up reports on Japanese, German, Italian, Russian screws and grommets and assemblies and gazintas and all manner of esoteric parts list items. ('Gazinta:' this gazinta that, which gazinta a larger assembly, and so forth).

The fair fruit of young women in uniform dangled before his eyes, but he was no Adam and they were no Eves, and work was no Eden. Rather, he was satisfied with the care he got from Corie—when she was there, and Meg was good company as well.

Corie would disappear about every four days or so, returning as mysteriously as she'd gone, two or three or four days later. Generally, she had a sour look, and she would kiss Tim briefly and then hold him at bay while she went through a cleansing ritual. She would immediately, almost frantically run a hot bath with lots of bubbles. She would soak in there for a half hour and emerge with wrinkly fingers and toes. She couldn't say where she'd gone, and he knew better than to ask. She would towel herself dry and take him to bed. She'd hold his head in her hands and kiss him inch by inch starting with the top of his head and ending with each toe, not missing anything in-between. He would start that same path on her, inch for inch, with the same devotion—only the truth was they never made either journey in one pass because usually by the time they got down to the nipples, or working the other way, up to the groin, both were moaning with pleasure and desire and they would collapse into each other's embrace. "Hold me," she'd whisper, desperation mixed with passion.

Tim hardly ever spent a night at the V/BOQ.

At other times, Meg seemed to be the one gone most of the time, while Corie was at home, and Tim felt almost like a married man. It was an interesting sensation, since he'd not had the opportunity to settle down— well, one or two girls in London might have liked it if he had, with them, out of a bunch he'd dated, but the passion wasn't quite there in him, and Uncle Sam had unceremoniously transferred him in any case. Corie had a few days off, and spent them cooking, sewing, walking, reading, listening to radio. She spent every available moment with Tim when he was off, and they made love several times a day, always with an urgency that she might be called away, or worse, might never come back.

He liked the warmth of her breath on the back of his neck. He was tired and this was all a dream. He never turned around, but enjoyed what she had come to offer or take. That was all there was too it, and it had a unique beauty all its own, like a mathematical equation or a hermetic chord that reverberated in its perfection. There was nothing more and nothing less. He was a man with two women. It might have just been a brief story of a sailor on shore leave, who meets two remarkable women and has an unusual fling before being reassigned to his death in some wartime Pacific nightmare. Instead, he was living this dream that sometimes seemed too good to be true. When Meg and Corie were around, he'd go out with both women to a movie or a restaurant or dancing.

Tim and his women went dancing together under reddish lights while big band brass wrapped its long notes sinuously around them and the rhythms made the blood run a bit faster. He took turns dancing with his two women, and sometimes they danced with each other, always laughing and easy. Once in a while some rangy Texas GI in Army uniform with loose tie and hard knuckles would cut in after a long awkward wind-up, and either Corie or Meg would be gracious and give him three dances before skipping out with a high sign to Tim to join them outside. That way there was much less likelihood that some enlisted brawler's knuckles might connect with Tim's jaw, and Tim preferred it that way. One black trumpeter gave Tim a knowing look one night, grinning as he wiped his mouth with a handkerchief and told Tim: "You are a lover, boy, not a fighter. That's all right. That's all right." Tim and the women would hop a few bars and take a taxi home. Like people everywhere, they were tired and had to go to work early in the morning.

Every evening, the ritual was the same. He would come to the courtyard and standing waiting in the wooden bower among the hydrangea and frangipani, among the jasmine and the bougainvillea, until either Meg or Corie came to fetch him. The fetching was done silently—a shadow behind the glass door, a flash of white nightgown, a pretend-bored look, a furtive glance—and whoop! Up the stairs they went together, he and his guide woman. Week after week, each day this ritual.

The two women set him up in their little living room; just a night table with room for a few books, his writing things, a few clothes, toothbrush. Corie laid out a pile of blankets for him and a pillow, on the premise that he would sleep on the couch like a good chaste fellow, but he never did. Even when Corie was away, he slept alone in her bed.

He protested, saying he really did not want to impose—and he thought, *what if Meg wants to entertain a man?* But she never seemed to entertain anyone, and Corie put a finger on his lip: "Don't ask. Don't speak. Just say yes and make two women happy." Later over vanilla milkshakes in a late night joint she explained: "Meg can be very lonely, and it makes her feel stronger to know you are there."

"She has that little bit of an accent," he said probingly one night.

Corie put a finger over his lips. "*Shhh.* If she wants you to know something, she'll tell you."

Corie and Tim made love when Meg wasn't there, and stealthily sometimes late at night, hoping not to wake Meg who was asleep in her room nearby. He and Corie made love early afternoons, sneaking home from work and back to work again; or in the late afternoons, before Meg returned from her own mysterious job with the new United Nations Organizational Planning Agency (UNOPA) whose stationery lay around the kitchen with Hang-the-Man games doodled in ink scribbles amid coffee stains.

If Meg heard anything or was disturbed, she never said anything. She seemed to loosen up and come out of her shell. She stopped being imperious, and actually become affectionate. It was all part of the odd ask no questions, *c'est la guerre* atmosphere, Tim was going to go along with it. Meg seemed to enjoy his presence around the apartment, though she was gone a lot and gave them plenty of leeway. She never complained about his presence and in fact once or twice, when the three of them were drinking late in the evening, came to sit beside him and once actually kissed him behind the ear, stroking his hair, before abruptly rising and walking away, not to leave her room that night. Those little moments were rare. Tim remembered one or two, like a sunny afternoon when the wind chimes lightly tinkled outside in the orange trees, and a plane droned distantly over a picture-pretty blue bay. Corie was home, reading a book in the plush chair by the living room window. Tim was there, doing mundane things like washing his socks in the bathroom sink and laying them side by side on the window sill hundreds of feet above Octavia and Lafayette Square. Meg was joking with Corie, laughing about something, and walked by, stopping to look over Tim's shoulder. For a second she laid her chin on his shoulder. For a second she touched his rear end, just long and lingering enough not to be an accident. Then she had a book and a cigarette and plopped on the couch opposite Corie with her feet up to wriggle wool-stockinged toes.

Then one morning Corie said over breakfast at a nearby hamburger joint: "I'm going to be gone for a few days, Tim." She sucked on her yogurt spoon, then waved it in the air as she said spoke. Her hair stuck out in several directions at once.

"I'm going to miss you."

"Me too," she said rubbing her ankles against his under the table. She leaned forward: "Stay at the apartment and take care of Meg, okay?"

He shrugged. "Sure." No big deal.

"No, I mean, she feels alone, Tim."

"I keep thinking I'm in the way."

"You're not in the way. We'd tell you if you were."

"Is it the war?"

"Is what the war?" She spooned blueberry yogurt, and had a white mustache. Her eyes were wide and frank.

He touched a little scar on her cheek, where there was a speck of blueberry. "I mean, do two women really live with one man?"

"People do what they need to."

He felt awkward at having voiced an inner question. "Never mind. I just want to make sure—"(She stared at him with innocent eyes)"—want to make sure that it's all okay."

She set her spoon down, pushed her cup away, and licked her fingertips one by one. "It's what we make of it, Tim. Yes, it's the war. It's a lot of things. I could crash a plane and never come back."

"Is that one of your secrets—why you are who you are?" He leaned forward and extended his palms. She placed her hands in his. "Yes, I think so. When you fly a lot, in the military, sometimes planes that have been repaired or planes with radical new designs, things go wrong. A lot. And then people die." He tried to trap her hands in his, but she pulled them away. "It's part of how I live, Tim. I can't live any other way."

They both put their hands under the table, each between their own knees, and looked away pained.

"Come on, walk me to the trolley," she said.

When they were walking on Sutter, she slipped her hand through his arm. "You and I are just like any other couple, Tim, except that I sometimes go away and do secret stuff." She stomped her foot lightly. "I wasn't supposed to say that."

"Secret kept," he said, glad to have had a peek at her secret life.

"You don't know the half of it, poor guy."

"Just tell me it's the Government."

"Is what the Government?" She appeared genuinely puzzled.

"Why you go away when you do and come back when you do. All of it. Whatever the secret is."

She slipped her arm more tightly around his and tugged, several times. "It's the Government, Tim. Yes. And you must never ask again."

"I won't." It was really all he wanted to know, whether it was true or not. What did he care if she was flying some chunk of steel with a weird acronym in circles over some desert air strip?

As he waved goodbye to her, and she waved with a secret little grin from the packed window of the trolley, he reflected that he'd always supposed he'd marry an attractive young woman in an apron who'd have children by him and stay in the kitchen, waving as he went off to work in his car. This was all a dream. Supposedly people were going to live like this when all the fascist dragons were slain. He shrugged and started on a long healthful walk down the hill to work. It was good this way, to enjoy what offered itself each day, in this impermanent and fantastic twilight world. If nothing else, one day he would have interesting memories. Deep inside, he knew—and didn't want to think about—how it would hurt when he lost her. Maybe she was right. Maybe he didn't want to know why.

📖

Sometimes he thought it was because they felt so utterly comfortable together, and yet at other times he wondered if something was bothering her under that opaque, attractive surface. Meg was a lousy cook, but she tried hard. Usually she'd make some variation on slightly scorched macaroni and cheese, sometimes with bits of pastrami mixed in from her sandwich at noontime. She'd always make enough for two, and they would sit quietly at the table. He'd read the paper and she'd read some fat 19th Century novel. When she read, she wore light blue plastic framed glasses that kept sliding down and she'd absently point her index finger at herself, right between the eyes, and push them back up. It made her look momentarily cross-eyed. The bridge of her nose was wrong for the glasses.

She looked up suddenly one day and said "What, Tim?"

"Your nose." He'd been staring across the top of his newspaper and noticed that she had a wide bridge, and the tip of her nose had an interesting almost middle-eastern downturn. "I didn't say anything, but you must have felt me thinking about you."

She feigned annoyance but looked pleased at the attention. She returned to her book. "I sometimes look over at you," she said.

He suggested: "Different glasses, maybe, you wouldn't have to push them up all the time."

She had a melodious voice from somewhere deep in her throat. "Well, either I spent a second pushing them up or I go through a big circus getting an exam, getting fitted, going back several times...who has time?"

He nodded at her logic, and she returned to her reading. He was tired that evening and sat up listening to the radio in the dark of the living room. Meg went into her room and closed the door. After a while, the bar of light at the bottom of the door turned off. She must have gone to sleep.

Tim read a while, until he dozed off sitting in the plush chair by the window. He awoke to some noise from outside, found that the air had grown chill and damp. He rose, pushed down the window, and staggered off to Corie's bedroom. He shut the door, felt his way through the darkness, and descended into the familiar world of her smell, her sheets, her perfume, the faint something that she brought with her machine oil, cockpit leather, something. He felt a pang as he thought of her, and wished she were here with him. Was he falling in love with her? He hoped not. But he longed for her. So he fell asleep, with one arm sticking out into the air.

Sometime during the night he had a dream. He dreamt that Meg came in quietly, glowing in the moonlight. Her gown was like a lantern, very faintly translucent, the planes of her body bluish shadows underneath. Her footstep was inaudible, made with solid feet with painted burgundy toenails cut straight across and chipped in a few places. Her fingers smelled of that matching burgundy nail polish that he knew so well. She came in with her black hair hanging straight on both sides. She slid in behind him, warming his back with her belly while her feet were cold against his legs and he curled up tighter. He felt her arms interlock around him, felt the pressure of her palms against the flat of his stomach, and heard a sigh of contentment. He smelled something vanilla on her breath, something stale also, something flat like old smoke, and smelled fresh shampoo in her fluffy still vaguely damp hair. She pulled up the sheets over them so it got warm, and he drifted off in her warmth as though he were drunk. This was what Corie must have meant. Meg held him to her like a stuffed animal and he slept soundly. And when he woke in the morning she was gone. But he knew it was not a dream because she had firmly tucked him in.

He felt well rested and sat on the edge of the bed rubbing his beard stubble, and wondered if the bed's warmth smelled more of Meg or of Corie. Shrugging, he shuffled off to the bathroom to brush his teeth and shave and shower. Along the way he saw that her door was a few inches ajar and her bed was tightly made and she was gone to work for the day.

Once or twice he saw Corie around town when she was in one of her absences, and some instinct told him not to contact her. Perhaps she would not want him to. Then one day Tim became paralyzed with grief and fear when he saw her with a man who held her hand. They sat in a restaurant having coffee and pie. Tim happened to be walking near the Ferry Depot during this lunch hour, and just happened to see her reddish-brunette head through grayish gauzy lace curtains. She had that same sunny smile he knew so well, and he stepped close happily to greet her. Then Tim's smile crashed away and his stomach lurched, for he saw her and a man inside—they had their heads together in some humorous affectionate conversation. They exchanged passionate kisses. The man, who was of medium height, slender build, foreign-looking by the cut of his suit and the length of his blond hair, put his hand over hers and whispered something intimate, to which she pealed with laughter—silently, from Tim's perspective where he stood across the street almost urinating in his pants. She kissed him behind the ear in a manner that left nothing to the imagination. Tearing himself away, Tim strode the whole distance back to work without stopping to eat at the lasagna shop where he'd planned to have lunch. He pictured himself berating her angrily for deceiving him, but she had not deceived him. She had warned him not to snoop. There was nothing to say.

Crank paper into typewriter. Agonize for a long time. Rip paper out, ball it up, and throw paper across the room. Nothing to say.

When he saw her again two days later, he let it slide like a bad dream. He remembered how talking had ruined things with Anna. This couldn't be happening again. It wasn't possible. Now he understood why she bathed and cleansed herself when she returned home. Corie seemed no different once she made that transition. She devoured him with greetings and kisses, and he melted back into her world feeling sick and beaten, but a prisoner of desire much as he'd been a physical slave of Nasr Tandileh in Mauritania. Rather than confront her, rather than ruin everything, he kept his wound hidden from her. He took his hurt inside someplace where he stored it with the other hurts of his life, like on a shelf in an antiquarian shop, but he became snippy and suspicious and followed her secretly sometimes, even when he wished he wouldn't. He resolved to live minute by minute if necessary until the war was over and he had to leave from here when life got back to normal. He sought each other all the more passionately in bed, and she seemed both puzzled and pleased by his new attention. As he rocked in her breakers he felt it was all okay. For some reason, it was all just fine. She might not come back alive one day and he must swim in her bay, he must sun himself in her cove, he must play in her sand while he could. She stayed for a week this time, while Meg left them alone to the apartment. Had Meg found a man of her own, finally?

Tim also found out quite accidentally that Meg's name was Naomi Meged. One of her names. Apparently she had several. Now that was strange. Both these women must be crazy. *I must be crazy*, he thought as he found Meg's passport on the floor under her powder-blue blazer, which hung on a kitchen chair one day while she scrubbed the soiled collar of her blouse in the bathroom. Tim absently picked it up a dark blue Canadian Commonwealth passport with her name on it and the insignia and regalia of the British Crown. It lay face down and he glimpsed its inside before laying it on the table. It was her picture in there, looking dim and pained like all passport snapshots, but the name underneath said Hasmig Saghome Varkidjian. He stared at it as she came out of the bathroom. No wonder she had an accent, however faint. *What the hell am I doing here in this crazy situation?*

"Staring at my secret life?" she said, startling him. She took the passport from him, grabbed his belt, and shook him in gentle admonition, without anger.

"Sorry," he said. "Armenian?"

"How did you know?"

"I knew a watchmaker named Vasserian once. He told me most Armenian names end in that way. I'm sorry, it's none of my business."

"Just don't talk to anyone about this, okay?" she said and walked away, leaving him wondering ever more.

Corie came from her bedroom just then and sat at the kitchen table with a pencil and the crossword puzzle. "What's a bitter vetch?" she asked.

"Some kind of turnip," Tim said. "From Armenia."

Meg came back from her own bedroom, carrying a small greenish document. "Tim, darling, if anyone ever asks, you do not know about the other passport. Look here, sweetie." She waved the greenish passport, which had a gold-embossed half moon on the front along with a star and a sword. "*Turkiye*, you understand? My name is Eyne Fatima Usluk, do you understand?"

He backed away slightly. "So which is it? Which are you?"

She made a sphinx face. "Both."

"I don't understand, but it's okay, right? One of those things we're not supposed to know."

Meg flipped the passport in her pocket. "Honey, don't worry about it, please. I was born here, and I love this country. I'm as American as you are. It's just that I—grew up elsewhere." With that, she grew mum.

Corie hardly looked up. "It's okay, Tim. Just accept that we're a little different, honey, okay?"

"As long as we don't wind up in jail."

"We won't wind up in jail," Meg said with a reassuring grin, which did make him feel a bit better. "Guaranteed by Uncle Sam."

"Promise!" Corie added, assuredly folding her hands together on the table. Yet, she looked pained. Tim remembered the walk along the Thames with Anna. Talking about love had changed everything. They should have shut up and continued their blissful, dreamy existence. Or had that been a delusion in itself, inevitable to come crashing apart sooner or later?

Oak Ridge, Tennessee-Jaguar

The man sometimes known as Jaguar drew near his target of opportunity, an NCO assigned to work at the nearby top secret plant.

Sergeant Nilo Pemble was enjoying his usual breakfast at Mom's Diner on Main Street, not far from the top secret installation where he worked as an armed guard and highly cleared driver. Nilo Pemble was a man of habit, which was one reason he appealed dearly to the security apparatus devised by Lieutenant General Leslie R. Groves to shelter the top secret work going on at Oak Ridge. Pemble liked his eggs sunny side up on toast, the toast medium and buttered. He liked a short stack of buttermilk pancakes on the side, along with orange juice, black coffee, and a ladleful of chipped beef over the eggs. He had a big job coming up, for which he'd been ordered to put together a squad of men, and a backup squad to boot, for one of those occasional extra-secret special trips across country. Everything was going his way. Wasn't life sweet? He fairly glowed as he hummed to himself, pouring sugar into his coffee.

Suddenly a shadow fell over the table, and he looked up. There stood a tall, dark-haired Army major in dark green Class A tops and pinkish trousers, looking like one of them Ivy League officers. All he needed was a riding crop and an attitude. Since the Civil War, the army had been run by a corps of Northeastern officers in the Anglophile mold, and Southern NCOs evoking Celtic and Confederate heritages. For a second, Nilo Pemble felt like snarling, until he remembered his place.

"Hello, Sergeant. The place seems to be full. You and I are the only single military men here, and I was wondering if you'd let me join you." Without awaiting a reply, the man slid into the plastic booth opposite Nilo. He had with him a tray on which sat a cup of black coffee and a bowl of dry cereal.

"Yessir," Nilo said belatedly. "Be my guest."

"Thanks," the major said. His name tag read Malone.

"You work on post, Sir?"

"I go where I am needed, Sergeant."

Viktor Mutsev (Robert Malone, or Jaguar, or whatever identity suited the moment) nodded. "Yes, I work on post." Through local informants, he'd received the information pointing him to Pemble. Nilo Pemble was the NCO usually charged with leading crews of enlisted men when fissile materials had to be transported long distances. This would be his only attempt to physically get near Pemble. There was little time to waste. None, in fact. He needed to know where Pemble was about to travel. He would gladly have taken Pemble to a dark place at night, tortured the information out of him, and left him dead, but he just needed Pemble to somehow tell him where he was going so the shipment could be intercepted. He suspected it would be San Francisco. Mutsev said in nearly flawless English: "Yes, Sergeant. I'm with the Public Affairs Office." He chuckled. "Keep the public misinformed, right?"

Pemble laughed. "Yeah, that sounds about right. For their own good, the dumb shits."

"My feeling exactly. You on travel?"

"Why do you say that?"

"Wearing your Class As and all."

"Oh yeah. Yeah, I'm headed out west. Say, where you from? Sounds like you got a little trace of an accent."

Mutsev laughed. "I was about to say the same about your Alabama drawl. I'm from upstate New York near Lake George." A total lie, but that sidelong glint of suspicion left the other man's eyes and the sergeant nodded, relaxing.

The two men ate in silence. Mutsev knew Pemble had stopped at the Travel Office on his way home last night, without making any other stops, and had the plane tickets for his group of enlisted men someplace with him. Mutsev had already jimmied Pemble's 1938 Chevrolet open and searched through it for the tickets, and then restored the car as if nothing had happened. The tickets weren't in the car. That meant he had them with him, the dumb bastard, unless he'd forgotten them at home.

"Gotta go take a piss," Nilo Pemble said delicately, making a hitching motion at his pants with both hands while getting up.

"I'll guard your eggs for you," Mutsev said with a wink.

"Thanks; you do that, Sir."

As Pemble strode off, Mutsev looked around with a quick flick of the eyes. The restaurant was filled with cigarette smoke drifting in blue and gray layers. Waitresses hustled about taking orders, and men and women sat in profile in the high-contrast light, silhouetted as they leaned close to one another in conversation.

Mutsev reached over and lifted one lapel of Pemble's dark green Eisenhower-style jacket. Sure enough, there in his inner pocket were the tickets, eight of them, neatly bundled. Mutsev rose, fiddling in his pocket as if looking for change, then quickly pulled the lapel aside once more. In a glance, he had memorized the flight details.

His source had assured him the Americans were no more sophisticated than that. The tickets would not be a blind or a ruse. Sergeant Nilo Pemble was about to travel to San Francisco on the date and time indicated on his ticket. He'd go to the army airfield indicated, aboard a special charter plane, and from there it would be a matter of simply diverting his cargo in a direction more convenient to the workers of the world rather than the capitalist interests of a small number of wealthy Americans.

Satisfied, Mutsev sat back down to finish eating. Nilo Pemble came out of the john, hitching his pants up again. He stopped at the counter to chat with the waitresses, none of whom liked him. He smoked an entire cigarette there, and finished a cup of coffee, before returning to his seat.

Mutsev calmly finished eating, left a tip, and rose to leave. He brushed past Pemble on his way out. Pemble still stood by the counter, trying to impress the waitresses who had their arms loaded with heavy plates, perspired, and quite obviously wished he'd go away. Pemble took no notice of Mutsev, and Mutsev quietly left, but not before picking a toothpick from the dispenser beside the cash register, and nodding coolly to the lady cashier, who gave him an insincere squint meant to be a smile, but otherwise took no particular notice of him.

Mutsev, emerging in the parking lot outside, was elated. He had just done a month's worth of intelligence work.

His first trip was to a gas station, where he changed into his civilian clothes. He drove a few towns over to sent a telegram to the legal *rezident* in San Francisco, advising the time, date, and location of the arrival of the set of classic Charles Dickens novels a client had asked for—at a certain U.S. Army airfield outside San Francisco.

Then he drove to the next town, where he ditched the stolen car and hotwired another one, with which he drove to Kansas City for a flight to Laramie and thence to San Francisco.

SF May-June 1945 Tim: Reconciliation

Tim began arguing with the two women, following his discovery of Corie's infidelity, and moved back into the V/BOQ. He'd seen Corie twice more, now that he had an idea where (obsessively) to lurk and watch.

What really set him off was the discovery, one day, that the blond man was either living in the room he'd been forced to vacate, or friends with whoever lived there. How convenient, so easy to slip in and out for a little sex. Jealous and bitter, Tim had much trouble sleeping nights in his lonely room at the Presidio, thinking about Corie, and also about Meg. Sometimes he asked himself if he'd lost his sanity. He'd lie awake looking up at the slot of moonlight that fell in through the skylight, and ponder how something as normal as love could be so strange. And so hurtful. Corie seemed to be out of town or else didn't care. She didn't call.

Tim went about his daily work routine like a bird with a broken wing. He'd go out after dark for a few beers around the corner at a dock workers' bar with sawdust on the floor and rough men in cheap suits and bleary faces hunkered together discussing racing forms. Tim didn't hear from the women for a few days, and steeped in pain and anger. Then Meg left a message at the desk, then several messages which he read and discarded. Each was a simple note, written in her round, feminine hand, with just a hint of her perfume in the paper to tell him for sure it was genuine, as if it were some document smuggled to him in an espionage plan. Each simply said something like: *Dearest Tim. Miss you very much and hope you'll come around again. We should talk about things and then maybe they will be clear as mud. Trust me—you are deeply cared about. Love/Meg.*

Finally, he called one day, but nobody was in. He left a brief telephone message with the concierge at the Hotel Auger, and then went about his business. No word from either of them. He ate lunch alone at a hamburger place near the shipyards, dinner at a Greek restaurant on his way home. He was beginning to convince himself that he'd been childish, maybe even selfish. They had not known each other long. They didn't know each other at all yet, really. How could he expect her to devote her heart to him alone? He made a trip to the Hotel Auger to leave a note in person.

The next day, when he arrived at the V/BOQ, Meg was sitting on the bus bench in front. She looked younger and thinner than he'd remembered, though her face was rounder than Corie's. The dark red lipstick and the light blue shadow around the eyes seemed girlish. She was fashionably dressed in a dark suit with matching gloves and purse, high heels with ankle straps, and a wide hat with a red flower in its folds. She rose and stood with the purse over her thighs, regarding him with that hurt, hungry glitter in her eyes, and a matching amount of quiet, distant defiance.

He walked up to her, thrusting his hat back on his head, and put out both hands. She let the purse swing away on her shoulder, and put her gloved hands in his. Her hands were warm. "Hi, Tim," she said with a bit of music in her voice, as if she'd been afraid he'd send her away.

He sensed her vulnerability and pulled her close. "I passed by and left a note. I wasn't sure you got my message," he said quietly, aware that the eyes of young sailors and jealous older men were on them.

She cocked her mouth to one side and flicked a glance at him before looking down at their joined hands. "Wasn't much of a message, Tim. *Hello, thought I'd call and say hello, oh well you're not home so there. Goodbye.*"

He laughed at her paraphrase. He put his hands around her shoulders and pulled her to him. She came readily, laying her cheek against his collarbone and touching his neck with her fingers as if they had been lovers. It was good to hold her like this.

"I missed you," she said.

I missed you too, he thought, *and how.*

He rubbed his hand gently along her back, feeling the thicker, denser mass of her around her shoulder blades, unlike bony Corie. "I've been confused, I guess."

"I know," she said in a low voice, "and angry, I'm sure. I don't blame you." They held each other for a while. She added: "We are all three confused."

He felt like a drowning man, gasping for air as he clutched her to him, knowing at that moment that it was the happiest thing he'd done since walking out the door on them. She seemed to sense his innermost thoughts, running her lips along the throbbing artery in his neck in a long kiss that was intimate and direct. He knew exactly what he desired at that moment. Not necessarily what he wanted or what he thought best or what even made sense. Just what he desired fervently, like someone hungry for good bread. He cupped her head in his hands and brought her face to his. Her eyes were closed and her face was upturned, as if it were raining and she were enjoying the strange delicious smell of fresh droplets on her cheeks and forehead. When their lips connected, her mouth was all over his, and her hands roved across his back, pressing him to her. She gasped audibly, as if enjoying that same good bread for the first time, as if she'd been starved for it. So they stood together for a time, silently speaking in that language that renewed itself in a new fervent attack with each new inhalation, and then spent itself in a series of ragged exhalations.

They took the tram back toward Union Square, and then the cable car up Nob Hill. Arm in arm, they walked the last few tortuous blocks through shady, hot little side streets where golden afternoon light lingered long into the evening. Several times they stopped to nuzzle, enjoying the heat of each other's breath and the sidelong messages of one another's eyes.

"Corie—" he started to say.

She put a finger on his lips to silence him. "I know what you saw. I know what you are thinking. I know you are hurt. She loves you something crazy, Tim."

He held her finger to his lips with his thumb and index finger, as if kissing something sacred. "If I could only believe that in my heart. I want to, so much."

She murmured: "I wish things were more like they seem and less like they are. You've been burned before, someplace, poor guy."

"Yeah." *Anna.* "It's no fun feeling hurt and confused."

"No, it isn't," she said. "You must believe me that we both love you."

He walked slowly, feeling her body press against his. He felt her elbow in his waist, her shoulder against his upper arm, her warmth, the sincerity in her eyes.

"You can be a lucky man, Tim, if you understand we have both fallen in love with you." He absorbed her information without understanding, as if she were speaking a foreign language. She continued: "I know it's not supposed to be this way, but then neither are people supposed to kill each other by the millions." Her tone grew halting as she got closer to their truths. "I've talked about it with her, and we both agree we just like being with you and we don't want anything to change."

"I saw her with him. She was all over him."

"It's the job, Tim."

"What do you mean?"

"She's been trying to tell you, without being able to."

"She's seeing this guy because—?"

"We can't talk about it. There is much, much at stake. It is an extremely secret operation. We can't walk away. We have to finish the job."

"We?" He couldn't imagine Corie in bed with another man. He remembered Jaguar. He remembered Claire Denby. He tried to picture himself, afterward, at a baby christening in some big church, with all sorts of sanctimonious hoods with swords. It didn't work for him. *Operation?*

"Maybe one day soon we can explain it all to you. It's nothing, really, depending on how one looks at things." She pulled her arm to squeeze his arm. He pulled in response. She said: "The only judges who have the right to say anything are you, I, and Corie. We are the three people who love each other. Oh don't look so shattered, Tim. You do love her, don't you?"

They walked into the shaded courtyard.

"I saw her with that other guy."

"I know you did, baby." She stopped in the gloom of the big eucalyptus tree and put her hands on his shoulders, looking up into his face as if he were a dumb giant. "Sweetie, don't you get it? It's something we can't discuss. But our real feelings are bigger than all that. Honey! Darling!" Her gaze flicked left and right involuntarily. She pressed her hands against his collar bones, looking up at him with sincere, pleading eyes.

He held her, because there was nothing else he could do. He could close his eyes, smell her soap, and pretend everything was okay. But could he pretend? In a way, it was a relief to know that there was some kind of underlying rhyme or reason to Corie's mysterious behavior. He understood that she was sleeping with the man, and he found it almost impossible to understand or forgive. He'd never in his life, for a moment even, contemplated loving a woman and sharing her with some strange man who owned a different piece of her life, a piece from which he was forever barred. Meg seemed to sense his agony, for she made a pitying face. "Poor baby."

He said thickly: "She told me not to fall in love with her."

"Nobody can tell another person such a thing," Meg said.

"She warned me it could only go so far."

"But your feelings fell off the dock, poor man." She added: "And ours did too. So now we are all stuck." She grasped his hands. "It could be worse."

He grasped Meg's hands with both of his, almost to push her away and storm forever out of the gloomy courtyard with its suffocating jasmine and lilac smells. Perhaps it would be the only reasonable, logical thing to do. The safest thing. The least painful. She did not have the strength to pull free, but her face and her eyes betrayed terrible anxiety as she looked up at him, biting her lip, willing him to stay with her looks.

He stayed.

She took his hand and unlocked the door. She led him up the stairs, towing him the way Corie had not long ago.

"Will she be back?" he asked. Maybe it was all over and he'd be with Meg alone. Maybe that would work.

"Yes she will," Meg whispered. "She loves you, Tim, even if she can't say so. She is such a straightforward girl. When she tells you she loves you, she wants it to be after this is over. She doesn't want to lose you. Neither do I."

"You know?"

"I know her very well. She's cried about you, and about herself."

They entered the hallway, then slipped into the women's apartment. Meg locked the door. They stood facing each other. For the first time with her today he felt awkward rather than passionate. "Something will happen, won't it?" He wasn't sure what he meant—something to break the impasse, to make the world normal. She shrugged, closing her eyes briefly, not knowing the future any better than he did. "Something always does, Tim. Meantime, we live."

He knew exactly what she meant. As he unbuttoned his tie, he stared into her face and saw the same truth etched there. He remembered the feral lions roaming on the beach, the last of their kind, unmindful of their extinction just around the corner. They were magnificent beasts who should be masters of the world rather than a pitiful remnant. Meg helped unbutton his shirt. She squatted down to undo his belt and pull his uniform trousers open. His dark, gold-braided jacket landed on the floor with a thud. He guided her face in his hands while she took him out with eager, firm fingers and took him in her mouth as if that was what she had been wanting to do all along. He felt her warmth and wetness around himself, felt the gentle

ridges of her teeth around the ridge of his pleasure. He reached down and
felt her rich hair pouring through his fingers. He saw her blunt, bare knees
peering from under the modest hem of her dull uniform skirt. He raised his
face up, closed his eyes, and listened as she painted wet sounds on the gray
shadows beginning to grow long on the chairs, the window sills, the kitchen
counters, as the window glass grew cold with evening. Nuzzling her lips
against the tender skin under his nipples, she signaled for him to come to
her now. She took him into the comfort of her affection, and gently rocked
him to a fuzzy climax. "I've wanted you so," she whispered, rubbing the
back of his head while she pressed her face against his and feverishly kissed
his cheek, his ear, his neck. "

"You're both—?"

"Yes. We have to. They are going to destroy the world. The U.N.—it's
already full of crooks and traitors. Our government is just beginning to get a
handle. Honestly, darling, try to forget all about it. We were trying to shield
you. And always remember—we both love you. You poor guy, stuck with
two complicated women."

He buried his face in her warm, fragrant shoulder. He wasn't sure he'd
be able to do it. He wanted to. He was afraid he might go crazy and jump
out of his office building and swim, no, fly, to China or something to escape
his own feelings. With Meg's arms firmly wrapped around him, he wasn't
going anywhere, and he didn't fight her. He held her tightly. She let out a
long, shuddering sigh, and held his head to her, and whispered: "Baby." He
could feel her breath in his ear, like a spring breeze in the flowers around
the Hotel Auger.

June-July 1945 Oak Ridge: General Groves

The Director of the atomic bomb project, Lieutenant General Leslie Groves, was in Washington, D.C. at various times in May 1945 because, just as technical issues of critical mass were being resolved in building the bombs, so metaphorical critical mass issues were beginning to take shape in the political, philosophical, social, and economic arenas.

Newly inaugurated President Truman had been shocked to learn of FDR's development of at least two types of atomic bombs (uranium-235 and plutonium-239) and that the development was as far along as it actually was. The transitional leader between FDR's death and Truman's ascendancy was Secretary of War Henry Stimson, who helped usher the development along at the topmost political level. There were even higher considerations being broached by the developers, including their chief, Dr. Oppenheimer.

A lot of agonizing went on. For one thing, the fiercely destructive firestorming of Japanese cities was costing hundreds of thousands of civilian lives. Stimson felt much moral anguish. Profound questions continued to be raised—was firestorming, like Dresden, truly cost effective (in the cost of human lives vs. political result) in the destruction of the Third Reich, or had it simply been a cruel adjunct? Would destroying hundreds of thousands more Japanese lives produce an intrinsically more meaningful result?

Groves was having breakfast at his Washington apartment with David Hawkins, a young philosophy graduate from Columbia and Berkeley, whom Oppenheimer had insisted on installing as his assistant. The gesture struck Groves as pointed. Oppenheimer—hamstrung by the constraints of wartime development, and knowing he was under serious surveillance as a possible Soviet spy, in large part because of his own past involvement with the Soviets, and his wife's and his brother's active membership in the Communist Party USA—had suggested that on humanitarian grounds the President share his information with Stalin. Truman had laughed out loud.

Like his OSS counterpart Wild Bill Donovan, Groves was a pragmatic, results-oriented man. Both Groves and Donovan had distinguished themselves as professionals and business executives before the war. Groves had accomplished a miracle of civil engineering and wartime mass organization by building the world's largest manmade building on schedule and under budget—the Pentagon. Donovan, disliked by the military establishment as an amateur and a civilian at heart, had built for FDR an espionage structure that was the equal of any in the world—except that it was reputedly riddled with Communist informants—so said J. Edgar Hoover, a man with an agenda.

The same accusation was often made against Groves' organization, even though Groves had surrounded himself with a cadre of his own intelligence operatives. Part of it was anti-Semitism. Groves felt, on a pragmatic level, that the Soviets had been desperately fighting for their survival for years— first against famine and economic collapse following the disastrous end of World War I and the Czarist regime they had overthrown, and then against Hitler. Russia had lost a fifth of her population (easily a third of the losses due to Stalin's purges, pogroms, and mass murders. He well knew that many of his Jewish scientists and their families had emigrated from Russia, and were still true to the socialist ideals that the Soviets had co-opted. Many were torn in their loyalties. Some remained patriotic Russians. For others, idealism overcame national allegiance. All Groves could do was ride the tiger, appreciate their genius, shield them from Hoover, and hope they would become regular U.S. citizens. It didn't help that many of them had experienced raw, physical hatred on the streets here in the U.S. from people who called themselves Christians.

Groves had created a sprawling and highly secret infrastructure employing at least 100,000 persons across the nation at various facilities. Few persons other than Truman, Stimson, Oppenheimer, and now Hawkins (who was also under surveillance as a possible Soviet agent) had a complete overview of how widespread the industrial network was for producing the bomb.

There was not one bomb, but there could be at least three: uranium, plutonium, and uranium-deuterium. The last of these, brainchild of a team led by Edward Teller, had been abandoned as impracticable. The world's supply of H3 (Deuterium, or heavy water) was negligible, and there were too many practical reasons against the project. This was the version that Hitler's scientists had been developing, until the Allies in a risky and brilliant series of operations had destroyed the Norsk facility in Scandinavia and sunk a barge containing much of Nazi Germany's supply of heavy water.

Uranium-235 was being made into a bomb at Oak Ridge, Tennessee, while plutonium-239 was being weaponized at Hanford. It was a shotgun approach, in other words, using the best minds and research results in the world (including Einstein's) in the hope that at least one approach would stick.

Groves had a special message for Hawkins to take to Oppenheimer this morning as they worked on black coffee and poached eggs. "I have a big surprise for Oppie," Groves said, using the unsentimental nickname Oppenheimer had earned over the years. "We have our hands on a fresh supply of very high-grade uranium oxide."

"Oh? What source?" Hawkins might not be a trained physicist, but his scientific background was adequate for dealing with technical issues.

"German."

"I thought we had all that covered. Donovan sent teams out across Europe and they earmarked every major dump the Krauts had set up."

Groves fully understood the implications of Donovan's findings. In one case, they'd found, in a French laboratory, hundreds of drums of abandoned uranium ore, some of it in barrels that had rusted apart in an open-air dump. "This is different. It appears to be very high grade material from abandoned Silesian silver mines."

"Percentage?" Hawkins licked his spoon.

"Over fifteen per cent."

Hawkins whistled. "Wow. That's outstanding. How much?"

"At least 560 kilograms. Enough to refine down to build at least one critical bomb mass. Maybe several."

Hawkins thought about this. "It's a bit late in the game."

"I understand. We're less than three months away from usability, assuming the C-in-C approves."

"Stimson will talk him into it."

"I think you're right. I'm not worried about it. The consideration of losing a million fighting men to put the Japanese down will be more than any president or political party in this country will want to bear."

"So what are you suggesting, General?"

"I'm suggesting we can hop on this stuff, get it refined, and have it fissionable in time for transport." He was thinking of the small island of Tinian in the Marianas, where the Seabees had been busily constructing a forward base—kind of a Manhattan Island in its own right, or a giant aircraft carrier—for launching the hopefully final super raids on a mortally crippled Japan.

Hawkins knew he was being used as a messenger, and would let the technical objections if any rest with Oppie.

Groves pressed on: "I'm suggesting we use the German material as the trigger. That will increase the output of our uranium bomb by at least 20 per cent if not more."

"Do we have time for the added complications?" Hawkins grumbled.

"Logistics aside," Groves said, "we don't know if it's going to work at all, do we? We're shooting blind here, so why not give ourselves the best shot in the arm we can."

"I'll have to run it by Oppenheimer."

"You tell him I said to do it. None of his endless arguments. I've already sent the stuff to Oak Ridge for enrichment." Groves slapped his napkin down, hefted his appreciable bulk erect, and walked huffily from the room. "It will be on its way to San Francisco very soon for shipment to Tinian."

Hawkins sat in his chair and stared after the general's retreating figure with equal frustration. He had great misgivings about the use of these weapons. On the wildest side—and who was he to know?—a few scientists had expressed fears that if a sufficient concentration of fissionable uranium-235 were in one place, the chain reaction might conceivably spread and set the earth's entire atmosphere on fire, incinerating every shred of life forever. The majority of scientists involved had poo-pooed this possibility, but it pointed out to an ethicist like Hawkins how dangerous the one-sided determination of a bunch of generals and politicians could be.

So far, not even top military leaders like Eisenhower or MacArthur knew how far along the U.S. was to having the atomic bomb.

Now Stimson was helping Truman organize the political and economic discussion regarding the bomb's use.

At the same time, Truman was about to address the world's leaders in a new organization that would hopefully be more effective than the lamentable League of Nations. On June 26 Truman would address the fledgling United Nations in San Francisco, whose first and Acting Secretary-General was a highly placed State Department official named Alger Hiss.

Before his death, FDR had made concessions to the rapacious Stalin that many leaders considered tantamount to treason. Like Donovan and Groves, FDR had been guided by the overarching needs to get the job done with a minimum of philosophical shavings being thrown off.

In that spirit, in July, the U.S. participated in the Potsdam Conference. Truman had no idea Stalin knew the U.S. had the atomic bomb. The groundwork was well under way for a long, insidious war of stealth and bluff that would go on for decades, with smaller hot wars being fought in proxy nations around the world. Stalin was determined not only to have the geopolitical advantage of territory and United Nations control. He would have the latest and most powerful atomic weapons in his grip.

The uranium bomb and the plutonium bomb each had their advantages. The uranium bomb was exceedingly difficult to refine into a fissionable state because it required the rare isotope of atomic mass 235, which had to be refined to 97% purity by the most advanced and complex methods known—or being developed on the fly by the world's best scientific minds. Once the critical mass was in one place, the rest was relatively easy. In fact, theoretically, it was possible that enough pure Uranium-235 could assemble naturally, and create a non-manmade fission explosion—though none had yet been found or documented anywhere.

The plutonium bomb was theoretically easier to build, and it might be more powerful to a slight degree, but it was more complex to maintain and explode.

Groves' answer had been to build both types.

The plutonium bomb would be tested June 15 in a live run called Trinity.

The uranium bomb was considered such a sure thing that a test was considered unnecessary and would only deplete the only supply of material on hand. Supplies of the pure fissionable material were too slight, including precious material luckily obtained from the captured *U-234*. The German material would be a valuable backup, a second trigger, in case something went wrong with the one already on hand for the first device to be dropped on Japan.

June-July 1945 Tim & His Women

The language of gestures and silences sometimes speaks louder than that of words. Tim tried to grit his teeth and pretend he wasn't insane with jealousy. Oddly, it made love all the more intense. If there was a pivot, it was when he came to their apartment for the first time in a while. He sat on the couch, tense and closed in on himself. Corie knelt before him in her bathrobe. She put her hands in his lap. He wouldn't touch her. She looked up at him, mouth trembling, eyes shedding tears like large raindrops that had hung in a sweltering summer cloud. She whispered: "I want you to know. I love you. Only you. Totally." Then she threw herself in his lap, face to one side, crying heartbrokenly. He touched her poor, heaving back, petted her, stroked her. She kept sobbing and crying with all of her heart. Eventually, she just cried sporadically and threw herself on his mercy. He held her to him, until he thought she must have fallen asleep. Meg came in and sat beside him, putting an arm around his back and sitting closely. Her free hand rested on Corie's head, stroking her hair gently, as if to take some of her pain. "Not much longer," Meg whispered, to both of them.

Tim began living with Corie and Meg again. For a glorious few days, life was perfect. Corie was home from her ordeal (the mystery man from State was off to Washington, plundering more secrets for Uncle Joe). Meg seemed upbeat, Tim's work was otherwise quiet and uneventful, and for all of them the continued victories in the Pacific suggested that the world would soon be able to stop holding its breath. Life would return to normal. For a moment, time and space seemed to hang in suspension.

They went to movies together, arm in arm. They went shopping. The women would leave Tim to guard their paper bags while they strolled among the bright new counters of the trendiest department stores.

Corie now said odd things at odd moments. One day, sitting in the lobby of a swanky hotel, dressed in their finest, they were waiting for Meg to return with some movie tickets. Corie very properly folded white-gloved hands together and whispered in his ear: "I am totally yours. You are my love and my redemption." He took her hands in his and didn't know what to say. He wanted to say *I love you* but the words didn't come and her eyes looked bulldozed.

Most of the time, they ignored the world, though they were part of its gritty wartime reality, even here in the city of love and sunshine, of oranges and breezes, of palm trees and jazzy music and young people.

One night, they came back together, having had a few cocktails at the Drake. Laughing, they let themselves in, shooshing each other, and locked the door. Within minutes they were all dressed for the night and threw themselves on Corie's bed. Tim was last, bringing a tray of drinks and pretzels. They laughed and huddled together while the radio played softly.

Outside, the city was a living and breathing entity that seemed to cry out gently in its dreams. The moon hung like a huge melon half-buried in clouds, showing its cratered underbelly to ships passing under the Golden Gate.

Meg lay back, yawning, and turned off the light on that side of the bed. Soon, Corie and Tim did the same, turning off the light on the window side.

They lay quietly, letting a cool night wind wash over them. Distant ships' horns talked to each other on the sea. Soon, Meg's slow breathing filled the air as she slept. Tim reached quietly and ran his hand along Corie's bare belly, up to her small breasts, down again, and she sighed contentedly, snuggling against him, raising one thigh slightly to invite his hand to further adventures. He crawled close and nuzzled his lips against her cheeks. He smelled faint tinges of lipstick, tobacco, and citrus on her breath. Her breath was heavy and irregular as she turned to him in the silvery moonlight. Her eyes were open wide with hunger, then closed as passion crept up on her like a drowning tide. He stretched, feeling her alongside himself, knee to knee, buttock to groin, warmth to warmth, moist to moist, trembling to trembling. She craned her neck as her mouth sought his. She twisted slightly, leaving her openings close so he could take her as he wanted. Her arm reached back so she could stroke his hair. Their lips sought each other's and drank hungrily, tongues intertwining. His fingers roved over the topography of her slim little body. Her breath came in raspy, steady, urgent sawing sounds. Quietly, so as not to disturb Meg, Tim used his hand to part Corie a bit and enter her wetness from behind. She moaned softly, stabbed by pleasure. Together they writhed in slow motion, very subtly, and the loudest sounds were the sighing of their skin on linen and the breath that rasped from their tortured mouths.

Tim gradually became aware of another touch, one that at first, in the confusion of his passion, he thought was Corie's. Locked in pleasure with Corie, spooning, perfectly joined, afraid to move for fear of disturbing Meg, he nonetheless felt the different touch of Meg's heavier, bigger hand, practicing new calligraphies of sensation on his back. Meg pressed against him from behind, so that they three were now spooning. Meg's breathing was hungry and out of control. Tim stopped in his writhing for a few seconds, letting this new tide wash over him. Corie arched her back, still enjoying him in her, and reached back over him. Her fingertips brushed Meg's fuller, heavier thigh, pulling her closer. Meg needed no urging, but pressed against Tim from behind. Now Tim found himself enclosed between walls of desire and heat. Corie moaned softly and Tim felt electric waves running through her before she fell back, exhausted. All the while Meg, aware of Corie's gratification, wrapped her arms tightly around Tim's belly and pulled him backward toward herself, so that his rear rested in the softness of her belly. Her fur tickled him.

Now came a shift of ballet. Corie turned toward him, leaving him limp and aching slightly from the friction of her gratification. Gently, as if in a dream out of the Arabian Nights, Tim turned in place so that he faced Meg, with Corie spooning from behind. Meg held her hands up to touch his face. She looked beseechingly up into his eyes, afraid that he would reject, hoping he would accept. Corie wrapped her arms around him from behind, pressing her groin and thighs against his rear so that he nestled in the softness of her belly. Meg groaned, realizing that he wanted her now. Corie held him as if she were giving a gift to Meg. Tim ratified the dance of the three by seeking Meg's mouth with his own. He felt hands on his key without knowing or caring whose eager but gentle fingers cupped him. Meg pushed him back into Corie while her tongue invaded his mouth with urgent demands. Tentative and exploratory, Corie's hand reached around Tim's ribs and her hand fastened on Meg's breast, taking her nipples between childlike fingers that sought only to hold, as if it were a daffodil or a daisy. "Go on," Corie whispered to Tim. "Go on," she urged Meg. "You know how much you want him." Tim took charge, rolling on top of willing Meg, wanting Meg, thrashing and crying Meg who opened wide (Corie gently stroking her soft knee). Meg pulled Tim onto her, into her. She rocked wildly with long-suppressed desire. She slammed her wide hips up at him as much as he thrust down with his narrow, muscular midsection. She grew very wet for him. They slapped together softly in the delicious shadows thrown by a Venetian blind. Corie crept close several times to share the kisses of Meg and Tim. Their cries mingled in a soft delirium as they crested in fulfillment. Meg lay for a time, legs wrapped around him to keep him hers, and pressed his face between her palms as she looked into his eyes. Tears ran down her cheeks. She seemed to want to say something, but her lips were wet and spluttery and blubbery and her eyes overflowed. Her body spoke for her. Her body racked and spasmed with sobs that were silent at first, then loud and wailing, but soon silent as she held him like a life preserver. She wasn't letting go. Feeling Corie's arm sympathetically draped over his back as if comforting her through him, Tim pulled up a corner of the bed sheet and lovingly dabbed Meg's eyes. He wrapped himself around her like a bandage and kissed her to her innermost, trembling, wounded soul. That moment, for the first time, he realized the depth of her suffering. He whispered: "I'll make it good." She looked up at him with utterly true, vulnerable eyes. She was like a child who had been unjustly struck, a puppy that had been kicked. It was Corie who breathed in Tim's ear: "Oh, thank you for taking her. Please love her, Tim." Tim couldn't speak. He brushed a light kiss over Corie's mouth, and then put his face beside Meg's. Her skin was wet and sticky with tears, and still she sobbed, from deep within, but she had her hands on his shoulders. Her fingers kneaded his shoulders as if he were a large, comforting stuffed animal. At last, looking quenched and comforted, she pressed her face into the security of his neck and stayed like that until all three fell asleep. But they were wired with electricity from their new connections. All through the night, various architectures sprang up where there had been only the austere combinatorials of a man or woman lying alone, a man and woman rustling together in the sheets. New complexities were possible that had not been there before. There was no text book. The movies did not offer guidance. Chocolate boxes were only for a boy and a girl. A thousand and one nights were not enough. The intoxicating richness became its own addiction, sweeter than any other.

In the morning, Corey complained of a happy exhaustion as she left early in her flight suit. Meg and Tim slept late and sat together by the open kitchen window, enjoying sunshine and lilac scents while having coffee and toast. Meg had showered, and now sat wrapped in a bathrobe and turban. They said very little, but huddled close. At one point, she leaned close and said softly: "You are the sweetest, kindest man I've met in a long time." She squeezed his hand. "Thank you." With that, she walked out of the room and started cleaning house. As she made Corie's bed, loudly fluffing the sheets and playing loud jazz on the radio, Tim could swear he heard her humming happily to herself.

📖

One day at the office, Stan Kehoe remarked casually: "I saw you with your two wives the other day." Stan was bent over his engineering drawing board, fixing the shading on a Japanese hex nut done badly by a U.S. Navy civilian who probably didn't care. "You guys are quite an item."

"Oh?" Tim froze, and then looked up. Stan might be the canary in the coal mine. Cold ice water light poured in through the early morning window. The wrong word, the wrong ear, and he could be court-martialed. The women's mission could be exposed. *Shut up,* he inwardly told Stan, gritting imaginary teeth. *Shut up!*

Stan laughed. "Or are they your sisters?" He looked closer. "Say, are you living with those two chicks?"

"We've become good friends," Tim said carefully. His groin still tingled with the exercise of the night before. "I grew up with a house full of sisters."

"If you're dating the pilot," Stan said shaking his head as he returned to his drawing board, "maybe you could set me up with the Jew."

"The what?"

"The juicy dark one."

"She's Armenian."

"That would explain it," Stan babbled innocently while he kept working.

"She's seeing someone."

Stan shook his head sadly. "Too many guys coming home. I'm having trouble latching up with any more good ones. Used to be a free-for-all not long ago. You'd better work fast, bud, or you'll be a swinging bachelor for the rest of your life."

"I won't lose any sleep over it. Say, what do you think about the Brooklyn Dodgers this season?" He changed the subject, and Stan went for it. Baseball was his passion, and he lit up as he abandoned the more awkward and painful topic of amatory conquest.

Nobody else ever made a remark in the weeks that followed. Tim was careful not to touch either of his women in public, or even to exchange a kiss. They, in turn, seemed like a pair of giggly girls as he watched them at the beach or in a store over a milkshake together, and he supposed someone looking at them for the first time might think they were small-town friends bringing their freshness to the big city. It dawned on him, one afternoon when the women were away shopping together and he sat on the couch enjoying a hot cup of tea and reading a book, that he would miss them terribly when this ended. Did it have to end? Would they ever talk about things? What did one do in his situation? There was nobody to ask, nobody to talk to. The women did not let on whether they spoke about it between themselves. Nights came and went with the same uneventfulness as breakfasts and dinners, workdays, trips to the store, rides along the beach with neon winking on and off on a sphinx-like lovely Meg or Corie f looking out over boulevards gliding by, alive with America's power and spending and her people's wealth.

As he sat on the couch a week later, he reflected: had anyone in history ever been in this situation before? Did one marry both women somehow? In Nasr Tandileh's world, you could marry up to four women. Millions of households around the world worked like that. Maybe they could move to Mauritania—God forbid and forget that stray thought! He remembered the lioness, the slavers, the sleazy schoolmaster.

"I love you, Tim," Meg said to him one night when they were alone. She lay facing him, head propped on her hand, elbow in the pillow. The fingers of her free hand traced through the hairs on his chest. It was a casual gesture, as if they were married. Corie said it too, one afternoon when they were alone together in the kitchen. He was eating cereal, in underpants and T-shirt, reading the nonsense on the back of a cereal box, when Corie crossed her arms around him from behind, in an X over his chest. She buried her mouth in his ear and whispered: "I love you, Tim."

He said it to them, too, passionately, at odd moments. One time, they lay together in bed on a sunny Sunday afternoon listening to a baseball game on the radio. The game was right there in Kezar Stadium a mile or two away. Tim lay face down in the middle of the bed. The women lay on their backs, one on either side of him, and he had an arm over each. "I love you both," he said, never taking his contented face out of the pillow, and they each reached up silently to stroke his arms in affirmation.

One afternoon, while Meg was away somewhere (not to ask, not to wonder), Tim met Corie in the tap room at the Drake. In the darkness that smelled of beer and smoke, they sat together at a small table sipping beers and listening to a ball game on the radio behind the bar. "Feels like a date," Corie said with a giggle.

"I want to marry both of you," Tim said lightly.

"We'd be willing," she said with dark humor.

"How would we do that? With an imam maybe, in Egypt or someplace." He stared dreamily into mysterious hieroglyphics made by water circles in the grime on the tabletop. They both knew, at that moment, it was impossible. How would one do such a thing? And then live in some tiny town someplace? People knew all your business. He laughed. "You know, the three of us are country mice. We just don't know how to behave in the city."

She laughed and wrapped her arm around his, laying her cheek on his shoulder. He pressed his cheek against the top of her head, smelling soap bouquet mingled with sea air and leather seat cushions in her fragrant tousle. He could have cried.

The air smelled of cotton candy, fried fish, gun smoke from a little shooting gallery, and kerosene from a Maya Indian woman fire-eater who awed the largely blond or brunet tourist crowd not only by her antics but by her exotic appearance. Meg always had a veiled something, Tim found, even when he felt close to her. She had a mystery. It was a wounded thing that lay cat-like in the slits of her eyes. She too was exotic. Where Corie's pleasure was like the sun, Meg was like the moon—alluring, bright, yet full of shadows. By moonlight, a prick of a rose might draw blood but that cut would remain indistinguishable, just another dark tear oozing black liquid like shadows running from shadows.

"Do you feel trapped with us?" Meg asked when they were alone together.

"No. I feel...perfect."

"Like it was meant to be?" She tightened her arm around his, pulling him closer into the curve of her waist. Her hand lay on his chest, her fingers playing in the sensitive skin under his larynx.

"I'm afraid if we talk about it, it will go away."

"It will," she said. "We must never talk about it." She shook him gently. "You can go out with us one at a time. We won't mind. And we're not interested in each other in that way, if that's ever occurred to you."

"I wondered a few times. You're just pals, right?" He stole his hand over her behind under her loose shirt. "I like having you both sometimes."

"Like a lion with his bitches," she said in a low, satisfied voice. "We get carried away when we are with you."

"I don't think lions have bitches. Lionesses, maybe. Or even lionettes."

"Lady lions. Never forget we are ladies first and lions second," she said, "or I will have to roar at you. *Raaa!*"

He tamed her with a little kiss, which she meekly and un-lionesslike returned. A little later, he thought she did look lioness-like as wind ruffled her long dark hair.

"How do we do this?" he asked.

"Do what?"

"Go on."

"I don't know."

"Do we?"

"I don't know."

"I want us to."

She was silent, considering the squiggles on the sea, the steam around the sun, the innocent screams of little girls with their cotton candy. Her eyes looked gray with uncertainty and some unknowable pain. "It would kill me now, for us not to. Or if you ran off with Corie and left me alone again."

📖

Corie's hair bounced and she squealed as she ducked a peanut that sailed over her shoulder and ricocheted off the red plastic seat.

They looked around, noticed eyes on them, and settled down, hand in hand over the table, faces close together.

"I needed a roommate after I got here from England," she said. "The Navy housing office fixed us up, and there we are. That's almost a year ago now."

"That's it?" he asked.

"Should there be more?" The waiter brought wontons and steaming egg drop soup in small heavy white china cups. They ate silently, playing with each other's feet under the table. "To answer your question, no, we never slept together before you parked your butt between us." She nibbled on a wonton, getting soup on her nose. "Neither of us ever thought about being with another woman, and I don't think either one of us would ever be interested. You are just special, I guess." She trailed off, eating. After some thought she added: "I don't think she ever had any luck in love either. She was kind of bruised up from—"

"From?"

Corie looked down, wiping her nose with a napkin. "She will tell you if she wants to. She was married to a man in Turkey. Oh yes, Meg has traveled. She had some kind of big man over there, arranged by her family, and he beat her until she ran away. I shouldn't tell you all this, but I love you both. She was going to have a baby, and he beat her. She lost the baby, and ran away."

"Her family is in Armenia?"

"In Turkey. Armenia has been carved up between the Soviets and the Turks and whoever else over in that part of the world. My geography stinks." She laughed briefly. "Meg lived in Napa most of her life like any nice American girl. Wine country. Northern California. The Armenians have money. They make good wine, her family. Then they sold her off to this Ismet creep."

"Where is this creep now?"

"Somewhere back in Anatolia, probably figuring out new rackets now that he can't smuggle guns to the Nazis and the Italians anymore. From what she told me, he's that kind of guy."

Tim nodded to himself slowly. He had wondered about that look Meg sometimes got. Mistrustful. That was the word. Pained. There was more to this story, he was sure. "I'll be happy just to be a stupid band-aid," he said. "I would never hurt either of you."

"We know!" She laughed in his face, as if throwing flowers. If they were five years old, she would have run away just then, leaving him standing. Instead, they each fell silent and ate their soup.

At one time or another, either Tim or Meg or Corie stalked silently from the apartment with pink cheeks and outraged eyes over some minor thing, slamming the door and leaving a wounded silence. The funny thing about it, Tim found, was that it was a lot like two people having an argument. No matter who was mad at whom, the three of them would then silently part, leaving each other alone, and only drift back together when the anger or the hurt had dissipated hours later. At worst, they slept in the same bed together without speaking or touching. That only happened two or three times in a matter of several months. One time, Meg slept in her bedroom and Corie stormed off to the living room couch. But they always made up.

How brief the days were. How fast time fled. Never more than a few hours went by that they were not back together, in the slow opiate of that cream-thick love among night-glowing walls.

Meg told him one Sunday morning when they had slept together alone, Corie being off on one of her trips: "Promise me, Tim, if you ever look back, you'll never be angry at anything that happened here."

He looked up from his comic pages. "I'll do my best."

"You can't know everything. It's not important." She toyed with her toast. Her fingertips glistened with butter, and crumbs stuck to them. "We are very sincere, Corie and I."

"I am too." He put his comic page down. "What?"

"Nothing. There is nothing I can say. Just trust that I love you, Tim. I have never loved a man like I love you. It's weird that I have to share you with my doofy roommate, but there it is."

He sighed deeply, and sat forward leaning his elbows on the table. He rubbed his eyes with his hands. "At risk of repeating myself, I love you both. I'm content. I'm happy. Are you worried?"

"Yes." She looked more vulnerable than veiled.

"I want it go on forever." He reached across to take her hands. He always had this feeling there was a deeper secret—something terrible— many terrible things maybe—just under the surface, just out of reach. She started to cry. Big droplets ran down her round cheeks. Droplets pooled on her upper lip and fell among the crumbs in her egg on her plate. He massaged her thick little fingers with his own. "Trust. Now we are in love, and we could hurt each other, so we have to trust. That's all part of love."

She nodded.

"Am I enough for both of you? I worry too."

She shrugged and looked into the abyss of her uncertainties and made a not-knowing shake of the head. It was a scary moment, because it made him wonder if he would love either one of them alone as much as he loved both, and supposed not. It seemed a recipe for losing one or both. Then he grew angry and guilty with himself, as he often did. How dare he do this, when it was against all the regulations and dictates of the world he lived in? He remembered that dreadful Tandileh, who had kept him chained to a wall. Was this the kind of world he and these women were creating for themselves? No, dammit. There must not be justification, explanation, philosophy, guilt, a lot of stupid talk. This was how it had been willed to be, and it was good. He could love either woman for herself, alone, as a man loves his wife or his girlfriend, and it was just different, that was all. Is a large cup any more full than a small cup? This was a very large cup fate had placed before him, and he wanted to drink from it every day as fully as possible, without a lot of dumb questions, in case it ran dry the next day. Or in case it broke, as cups sometimes do.

Broken Cup

The cup broke one afternoon when he left work early because the building's power failed and the boss sent everyone home.

He heard laughter as he walked into the courtyard, and recognized Meg's voice. He quickened his stop, thinking to catch the two women—not stopping to wonder why they were home at this hour—and then he froze with ice wrenching his gut. They were with their tall, blond man in a fine suit, who held one of them on each arm as he strode through the courtyard with them. They looked up at him and laughed, much as they did with Tim, and in a flash the three of them were gone through the small passage amid the ivy. Not before Creepo had his hands on both their asses, squeezing.

Like a wounded lion, Tim charged after them. Heart pounding in his throat, world collapsing around him, he followed the sound of their laughter, the sound of the man's seductive voice, and trailed them out onto the next street. There, he emerged just in time to see them climbing the steps of a large building together. They were still arm in arm and looked too happy for Tim's cozy dream world to be true.

📖

He did not go back to the apartment. The V/BOQ awaited him with its cold and noise nocturnal charms. Its mop-wielding, choristic black men sang in sublime voices that echoed like those of monks in some cathedral. The V/BOQ awaited with its communal toilets and silent shaving men and small snarling arguments over a soap dish or a too-loud radio. It was a monastery of shared cigarettes, a dirty joke filled with empty desire, or contempt for the unreachable. He did not return to the apartment that night, but came to gather his shaving gear and leave a note saying he was working a lot of overtime and would be in touch. Any other woman, he would have said goodbye with a short bitter speech. This thing, he wanted to leave open a door to his pain, not close it all off forever yet, the amputation was too severe, the shock would kill the corpus.

He had time now, and began to skip an hour or two at work. Nobody cared much since it was all under control and he was now a section chief. His boss didn't ask questions as long as he showed up for the daily and weekly briefings and Admiral Lemney was happy. So Tim was free to roam, and roam he did. He reverted to his London skullduggery. He became almost feral in spirit. He could not rest.

He researched the history of the Hotel Auger. No surprises. Government contract, bought out by the United Nations commission in early 1945 to house diplomats. Other housing for diplomats: every spare hotel room, every spare apartment in San Francisco. The Charter foundation was holding its meetings here beginning in April, with the declarations to be made in late June. The city was filled with men in turbans, men and women of all colors speaking all languages, even men who looked like the recent goose-stepping enemy. Tim recognized Berbers and Moors and Almohads and other rulers of West Africa—time travelers from the distant past, who continued to hunt rare predators on the beach and trade in human slaves and keep multiple wives, living as they had in the Dark Ages, while making hollow pledges in this city of the future. While siphoning off vast sums in foreign add money that ended up in their private, secret Swiss bank accounts.

Meg and Corie left messages at the V/BOQ desk for Tim, and he did not return them. Instead, he made contacts, phone calls, visits. He kept bumping up against secrecy and security connected with the gathering union of the world's nations, particularly since the President himself was due to participate in the launch a few weeks off. Slowly, carefully, he probed, and found there was indeed a Hasmig Saghome Varkidjian who worked as a receptionist with the Armenian consulate. She was never there when he phoned, saying he was with a delivery service. He offered a vague description of her, and was told yes, that must be Miss Varkidjian. Young, attractive, dark-haired, shapely, solid.

Likewise, there was an Eyne Fatima Usluk attached to the Turkish delegation as a receptionist. Young, attractive, dark-haired, shapely in a solid way.

He trusted nobody by now, and checked everything he could. He found out that there was indeed a Captain Corinthia Johnson, WAFS, assigned to the Presidio Naval Station, but attached for duty to some outfit in Oakland, and he got lost in a maze of acronyms, numbers, and gobbledygook, as he expected he would. He could not track down pay, billeting, or other allowances information through the local Bureau of Personnel or the pay office.

He hated himself for doing so, but he began to shadow them. More than once, he thought he wasn't the only one. Once it was a dark glance from some guy in a slowly passing car, looking him over as if eyes were knives that could carve flesh. Once it was an attractive, tall black woman with both hands in the pockets of her long brown coat and her chin tucked down so that he couldn't make out her features under a tightly-wrapped yellow kerchief. Once it was a policeman keeping pace on the opposite side of the street. Another time, a rainy afternoon, he recognized Corie and the blond man on a street downtown, speaking with a tall, thin, urbane looking man in a suit whose face looked familiar. It took Tim a few moments to place the face, from newspaper accounts—the Acting Secretary General, the first leader, of the United Nations, a high State Department official named Alger

Hiss. Was this affair of such great consequence? Tears and rain blinded Tim as he stood watching.

At one point, he followed Meg from a United Nations office building to a long black car with Bulgarian insignia on its diplomatic license plates. He took a taxi and followed—right back to Nob Hill, around the corner from the Hotel Auger. He watched Meg emerge from the car in the company of that same blond haired man. The car, driven by a chunky dark-haired man with heavy beard shadow, sped away. The blond man put his arm around Meg, a hand on her buttocks, as they walked to that building on the other street.

Tim got himself a cup of coffee in a large paper cup. He bought a half pint of cheap whiskey and poured it in the cup. He sat on a bench in a small park halfway up the street for hours, waiting. Fog rolled in, a light fog that coated everything with tear drops and made him shiver in his damp clothing. He waited, stepping from foot to foot, while wisps of fog drifted silently around the street lamps and etched gargoyle horrors in darkened windows.

He saw Corie emerge from the ivy tunnel. He saw her brunette hair and quick gait. She wore white high-heeled shoes, a flowery dress whose hem crossed her mid calf, a hat with a feather, white gloves, a matching little purse. She strode to that doorway, rang a bell, and was buzzed in. She didn't seem to be suffering at all.

Tim waited. And waited. By one a.m., after five hours standing around, it became clear that both women were spending the night.

He stood in the street alone and wretched. What had he done to get himself into this hell? Was it even possible that he was hallucinating and none of this was happening? He'd been betrayed somehow, but unless he could figure out why, nothing else made sense. Maybe he'd been used; but that too didn't seem possible. All that misery with him, and then these happy hooker looks. What the hell! He stormed off.

📖

For a while, he watched the steady rhythm of the bartenders in their red vests as they flew busily through the motions of handling bottles, glasses, napkins, stirrers, the cash register. Waitresses came and went in skimpy dresses and high heels. Gradually, Tim noticed an attractive blonde a few stools away. Men stopped to make comments, and she shook her head. She was in her mid-thirties, still pretty, but lined. Her eyes had a sad heaviness. She still managed a cute smile, but her mouth was beginning to set in a hard line. She was nicely dressed, in a white fluffed out skirt, with a white fuzzy sweater draped over her shoulders. Every so often, she'd look over at Tim and smile innocently. He nodded back, even waved his drink in a toast. After a while, she picked up her purse and walked over. "Mind if I park here for a while?"

"Sure," Tim said, offering the second bar stool out. There was no sign about ladies not being at the bar. He had a hunch about her. She signaled subtly to the waiter, who brought over her drink, her doily, her change, a stirrer. He took a dollar from her pile and put it in his pocket.

"How are you?" she said. "My name's Mona."

"I'm Tim. Out for a quiet little drink?"

She had a smoker's deep voice. "Sort of. I got stood up."

"Oh, I'm sorry to hear that. Someone important in your life?"

She laughed dismissively. "How about you, Tim? You look like you got sent out into the rain."

"More like I walked out."

"Will she take you back?" Mona grinned sympathetically, lighting up. A man came up from behind, big guy in a white suit, and lit her cigarette. "Thanks," she said over her shoulder, "not this afternoon." The man glowered at Tim and left.

"I guess we'll talk when we're good and ready."

"That's the spirit," Mona said. "You look like the marrying kind of man. You look the right age, too. About thirty?"

"And you, Mona?" he asked innocently, only half interested.

"I have never been able to settle down," she said. "I make good money doing what I do. People tell me I'm a fool to waste my good years and my good looks."

"Just haven't met the right man yet, I guess."

She laughed again. "Honey, I meet lots of men. None of the ones I meet are the kind I'd want to marry. But the surprise is—some of them are priests, bankers, upstanding citizens."

It dawned on Tim that she was a hooker. "Mona, do you work here?"

"You're not interested in me, honey." She gave him a hard look. "You know why I came over here to sit by you? Because I'm tired and I want to be left alone. I just want to have a drink and sit quietly for a while and talk with a nice guy. That okay with you?"

"Sure, be my guest."

"I'm what you'd call a pricey girl. I was supposed to meet a city official here for a date, but I guess his wife had other ideas. I can do you for an hour. Twenty five dollars, but let me finish my drink."

"Honestly, Mona, no. I'm not interested. But thanks."

"That's fine. Kind of a relief, actually."

He put twenty dollars on the counter. "Can I ask you a question?"

She looked at the money and at him. "That's the other part of this job. Counseling men about women." She slugged down her drink and waved to the bartender for another. Tim raised a five dollar bill to indicate he'd pay. The bartender nodded, delivered her a drink, and took Tim's money. "Keep the change."

"Thanks, Mister."

"Generous," Mona said. "I like that in a man. So what's your grief, Tim? Can't understand your woman? Are you married?"

"I'm in a weird way, Mona. I've got two girls."

She laughed. "That doesn't sound like a problem. You're a nice looking man. You know what? I can see it written in your eyes. You're ethical. That's eating you up. So you have to pick one?"

"No, not quite." He didn't want to go into detail. "Mona, here's the question. How does a woman do it? I mean—what you do. See, the problem is that…" She looked at him uncomprehendingly. "Okay, here's the thing. Suppose a woman were working for the government. As a spy, let's say." Mona laughed, then saw he was serious. "So she ends up having to sleep with some Communist creep to get information. How does the man she really loves, who loves her, get around that without going crazy?"

"Oh, you poor guy. This is for real, isn't it?" Mona sucked on her cigarette and thought. "Does your woman really love you? Which one, by the way?"

"Both."

"Oh come on, you're kidding."

"I wish I were."

She raised her eyebrows with a chilly laugh. "You're weirder than I am."

"I'm sorry I asked."

She smoked furiously. "I'm sorry. Let's start over. What is it you want to know?"

He stared at her.

She looked at him with dawning realization. "You are in love with both of them, and they're screwing some Commie that's in town with this U.N. circus."

"You are a smart woman, Mona. How do I handle it? Do I run away? Do I wait?"

"Honey, if they love you, you wait. You'd be a fool not to. Look, women wait all the time. I've been waiting all my life."

"How do you square it with yourself?"

"Put the money away, Tim. This is free advice. I have my morals too. I want to feel like I did a good deed today. Are they nice girls?"

"I think so."

She scrutinized him. "You're smart, handsome; nice personality. You'd have better judgment than to get involved with some gold diggers. Here's what I'm going to tell you. Those girls are hookers for Uncle Sam. So's that waitress over there, only she's just selling her smile for a tip. We're all selling a piece of ourselves every day. When you bought me this drink, you were selling yourself to me because you want something. You want information. Your girls want information. You know what? You just do it, and walk away. Pretend you went to the store for a pack of cigarettes. It's nothing."

"I see. Just put it in a box and stick it on a shelf and don't think about it."

"If I were a street hooker, I'd tell you something a little different, because they see the world from their angle, and it's different, but in the end it's all the same. A street hooker would tell you men are all about fighting. Mostly they fight about their pride, especially over a woman. Women are a commodity. They can influence things behind the scenes, but they have to pretend the man has all the power. So being a woman is a lot different from being a man. We don't have antlers to go crashing into each other. A woman has to always be afraid—of going out at night, of being alone, of getting assaulted. It's not like that for a man. You may be afraid of getting jumped, but you'll get a black eye or get knifed. The other guy isn't going to rape you. That's what a street hooker would explain to you."

"So what does it all mean?"

"Tim." She put a hand on his wrist. "Tim stop worrying about yourself. Worry about those girls. What they are doing must be killing them. I'm used to this. I can send myself a thousand miles away while the john has his little five second orgasm. I know how to get it over with as fast as possible, from as far away as I can. Worry about your girls." With that, she patted his cheek, sliding her fingers along his jaw with a woeful smile, and walked away into the mists of her life.

Navy Nurse—Tim's Heart

Tim deliberated about Mona's advice. He was still smarting, not ready to call either Meg or Corie. As he left work the next day, he heard a woman call out his name. "Tim!"

Standing across the street among throngs of pedestrians was Anna Stokowska in a smart, dark U.S. Navy uniform that made everyone passing by stare at her long, crisp figure. He did a double-take. His heart wrenched as he crossed the street. "Hey, what a surprise."

She glowed. "Tim, I couldn't believe you would be so easy to find."

They embraced, and he felt the familiar long curve of her back. The taut spirals of her low back were exactly as he'd left them. She smelled good. He inhaled the scent of a light milled soap and a touch of floral perfume full of mystery and enticement. He buried his nose in her neck, deeply inhaling her linen blouse collar. "Oh my God, it's good to smell you again."

"Smell me? What about see me? Whoa!" she said jauntily, under her Navy Nurse Corps cap. "You've been doing without! I can tell, from that hungry growl. Kind of hard to believe, a nice looking guy like you."

He shrugged, looking upward. "War is crazy. I thought you were in Greece, getting married or something. How did you get into the U.S. Navy?"

"I'm getting U.S. citizenship," she said holding her purse before her as they walked slowly. "I have to confess, I met a fellow after you left, an American Navy type who reminded me a bit of you, and that started the wheels rolling. But, you know how it is with sailors."

"I can imagine."

"Oh, you sailors are all alike." She pushed his shoulder lightly.

"Let me guess. He broke your heart."

"That was already broken, Tim. You know about Erek. Erek is now in Soviet hands. You and Erek have been the two loves of my life."

"Oh my God."

"Yes. The Russians overran Poland and took all the military people for internment in the Soviet Union. I heard from him earlier this year. He got a letter to me through the Red Cross. He says he has been very sick, and wishes me to live my life without him because he doesn't feel he will make it back."

"That's very sad."

"Yes. But I'm always game. I knit, sew, darn, and damn, whatever it takes, and put it all together again. You know what? I have no photos of Erek, and I can only picture him as a young, healthy man, almost a boy. If he comes back to me, I will spend the rest of my life with him. Even if he is in a wheelchair."

"And the Greek?"

"That was a lie. I wrote that to free you stop of me. There was no Greek, ever. There was only you."

Tim's head swam at this. "And the American?"

"A misadventure. His name is Harry, and he is a very senior Captain."

"Still in England?"

"Yes. He didn't want to leave his wife, it turned out. I didn't know there was a wife, but darn it, I should have known. He's a sailor. So, anyway, I already had the papers in. I don't know what I was thinking. I was so lonely. Sometimes I felt—I still feel—as if Erek is dead already. Isn't that terrible? A girl has to go on with life. I would have been miserable with Harry, and he with me, so it's best that he turned out to be a sailor. The Navy was happy to get me. Harry was glad to help me get out of the country and out of his life." She pointed to the gold bars on her collar, and the twin gold braid and star on her epaulets. "They made me a Navy Lieutenant right off, because I have a strong background in treating burns, and there are so, so, so many terrible burns at Letterman."

"That's where you are going to be stationed?" They spoke of Letterman Army Hospital at the Presidio.

"Yes. So—wanna take a girl out for a milkshake or something?"

"Yeah."

She winked. "Yeah?" she imitated him in a deep, accented voice. "Is that all you can say?" She did the deep voice again: "Yeah, baby."

He offered his arm and she took it. "Can I invite you for that shake, and maybe a burger?"

"I'd be delighted."

"I promise never to hurt you again."

"Oh, I knew you weren't in love with me, and that's okay. I had no right to tie you down with my silly dreams and all. Silly, that's all it was. I think I'm a lot more worldly now." She took him to her car, a humpy gray Ford, and handed him the keys. "You're the man. You drive."

Along the way out of town, he said: "I'm really sorry, Anna. I sometimes think about you. I wonder how it could have been."

"Well, I'll be around. We can date, and see how it goes."

He put his arm around her waist. Was it possible to resurrect their relationship? Could they fall in love this time and go all the way? "I would like to find out, Anna."

"Don't fret, Tim. I'm easy. Buy me a nice hamburger or something."

He did. After stopping for lunch, they drove down the coast. They rented a hotel room near Half Moon Bay and walked to the beach. He felt an odd tugging as they walked on the same beach where he'd walked with Corie weeks ago—or was it ages ago? Funny how time slipped by in different quanta for different purposes. Long wavelengths for bad times, short wavelengths for good times, and all gone before you had time to register a sine wave.

"You didn't hurt me as bad as you think," she said as they sat on a low wall by the beach, with wind ruffling their hair. "You weren't ready, and I could tell that. I couldn't get any more serious with you than I did, being married and all. And I did feel I was part of the Free Polish war effort. So it ended the way I expected. I was very broken up over you, but it wasn't your fault."

They talked about her hopes and dreams in the United States, while he stayed quiet about his. "I hope you'll call me," she said as they walked together holding hands and picking seashells on the beach. Gulls cried and whirled, and the surf scrolled in.

"Of course, Anna. I can't stay away from Navy nurses."

"There is one thing," she said.

Of course, he thought, there is always one thing.

"My friend. The guy I almost married? He's being assigned here too. I don't know what I'm going to do if he calls me."

"You're still in love with him? And he's still married?"

"I'm not in love with him. It's just—uncomfortable. I'd prefer to never speak with him again. He's a big surgeon, an admiral, and I may have to work with him. I'm not looking forward to it. It will mean being discreet."

In a way, Tim felt relieved. He wasn't about to fall in love with Anna, at least not recklessly or easily. He felt comfortable with her, and the idea of her sleeping with or waiting for another man did not bother him so much, now that he'd been through this thing with the Auger twins, as he was beginning to refer to his former harem.

They left the rest of her thought unspoken, and ran together, chasing each other in wet brown-sugar sand, laughing.

They spent Friday night and Saturday night in a motel park, then went for a long drive further south toward Santa Cruz. There, they ate lunch at a seafood shack on Almar Avenue, with outdoor tables, and went for a long walk along West Cliff Drive and out onto the ocean view point before heading back into San Francisco. She did not press him. She was easy, as she'd promised. They made love at the Santa Cruz hotel, like old times. She lay beside him, still, touching his arm with those eyes brimming with desire as a voltage accumulates on a copper terminal, and she grasped him when she was ready, as before. He remembered exactly how to make his fingers circle her bush, and she came explosively at least three times before throwing herself on her belly for her famous snoring exit. He did not have the energy to go for the dessert, but lay beside her, touching her rear and falling asleep also.

In the morning, as they dressed and got ready to leave, she winked. "You did some things I don't remember you doing before. You must have found a good teacher somewhere, to satisfy a woman so much. I hope I can put in a reservation for next time, soon."

He drove back to San Francisco, and promised to call her very soon. She was any man's dream, and yet Tim again felt that slight hollowness. Something about her just didn't seem to be there with him, or was it him not being entirely there with her?

Before she drove off, leaving him at the V/BOQ, she stroked his cheek. "I'm yours if you want me, Tim."

📖

"Tim." It was Meg, breathless.

He hung up.

At noon, Meg waited for him across the street. She wore a plain white dress and carried a brown purse. Her dark frizzy hair was brushed pack into a rouge fan, Asian style, and her mouth had a bitter touch of red lipstick, like blood, like violence. She looked more Asian than ever. Her features were lovely, and distorted with emotion. He wanted to walk the other way, but some magnet pulled him toward her. She towed him along. He walked beside her on the crowded sidewalk in the noon heat. "We have to talk," she said.

"Meg, I can't deal with it." If anything, he had been pondering Anna's offer to make things as they had been in London, and that would mean the Thing and Erek and he wasn't sure he wanted that either.

"Tim."

"I saw the three of you together," he said bitterly.

"I thought so. I promised to love you. I wasn't lying." She strode along. "You said you loved me," she said, sighing in pain and resignation.

"I said that. So did you."

"Please. Let's go where we can talk."

"Oh what the hell! I'm overdue to meet a nice, simple, uncomplicated girl and just have a date or two." He kicked a crumpled paper bag aside. He couldn't hurt her, or Corie, nor did he want to hurt Anna again. "I just can't handle it. I hurts me more than it hurts you." Without touching her, he followed alongside as she led him up the street, around a corner, down an alley, and into a dark back apartment overlooking an Asian style garden.

Two Chinese women carrying large ceramic pots nodded to her, and she spoke briefly with them in some western Chinese dialect, almost Turkish. In the back of the Chinese restaurant, he saw sweating men, cheap labor, hefting huge noodle pots while sweating in a back kitchen. The place smelled of Asian food and cooking oils. At the moment, the place felt as alien as the emotional street on which his dislocated heart was limping.

Meg led him into a small gloomy room containing a bamboo table, two chairs, and a little table with a potted rubber plant on it. The décor was Mandarin. A window overlooked a tiny courtyard that could have been in Shanghai or Mongolia, for all that Tim knew.

They took seats opposite each other. Meg laid her purse aside and lit a Pall Mall. She offered, and he accepted. They smoked silently together, Tim feeling light-headed from the unaccustomed tobacco.

A young Chinese woman with a beautiful face came, with a veiled look and averted eyes, bearing a stack of bamboo wicker plates, covered. One by one she removed the lids, revealing dishes with rice, marinated ginger, a dozen exotic treats. A man brought steaming green tea. A child laid white linen napkins and chopsticks before Tim and Meg. They withdrew, leaving Tim alone with Meg.

"I know what you have seen," Meg said. Tim picked at a shrimp lacquered with sweet and sour sauce.

"I've tried, but I can't stand it."

"I know you are hurt, Tim. I am too, though you may never believe me."

"I do, Meg. I understand." He remembered Mona's advice. "I worry more about you and Corie than I do about myself. It still hurts, and I'm just trying to get right with myself."

"Losing you would be very painful for me. I have suffered some bad things in life, but losing you would be a bad one. We were so happy."

" I think Corie had it right. Now is not the time to fall in love. "

"She's right, darling. Except that people don't choose when to fall in love. I think once the U.N. is rolling, this will be over. Other people will take over."

They sat silently picking at their food. They sipped tea. Out in the garden, a frog chirruped. It was like letting your eyes get used to the dark. This was a matter of letting your ears get used to the silence. You heard the whisper of wind in grass, the splash of water in a tiny fountain, the flutter of a bird's wing in a tree—all very chilly in this shade, despite the hot day. He thought again about the sacrifice Claire Denby had made—Madame Lady Haw-Haw or whatever her real name was, now probably having tea and crumpets with the Queen of England and pretending she hadn't spread for randy old Grimsby and wandered down the street puking all over herself while he walked behind her, trying to grab her ass and pee through his half-open fly at the same time. He grimaced at the memory of her sodden skirt and his pale pickle-tip waggling before stained trousers.

"Tim, my name is really Naomi Meged, and I am a Jew." Nothing would have surprised him, even if she'd said she was from Venus. "I am all the things I've said. I was born in California, I am also Armenian, I have a Turkish name, and I am in love with you."

"How is all that possible?"

She picked a shred of tobacco from the tip of her tongue. Her eyes glittered with tears and humiliation. "I want to be honest with you. I have never loved a man as I love you. I have been in espionage for some years. It's a dangerous, dirty business. That man is a Soviet agent, and I let him stick his thing in me. It's not that I want him or care about his ugly implement. It makes me sick to lie there and let him do it. I could be killed for telling you this. He is a very high ranking agent. The Soviets are screwing the United States night and day while we go about eating hamburgers and having a good time thinking we have won the war and we are so great. I'm a spy, Tim. I am spying for the United States, sleeping with our enemy, now trying desperately to help save China from falling to the Communists. And helping to get a Jewish state set up."

"How soon will you be free?"

"When the job is done. When I have served the United States, the best way I know how, with my body, even as it sickens me. I have been in battle." She blinked at some memory. "I have killed men, and I could do it again."

Tim was still reeling from her admission where Herr Commie had been putting his implement. He thought again of Claire Denby. She and her husband must have weighed the same issues, heatedly, over tea at their palace or whatever. It had seemed to theoretical, so abstract, driving around in the rain with a drunken Stan Kehoe. Now it made brutal sense.

"Tim, the United Nations conference will be over in a few weeks and this guy will go back where he belongs. He doesn't even know my real name. He doesn't really care, because he thinks I am a simple secretary making some extra cash on the side as a call girl."

Along with our ditzy little red-head, Tim thought. "He pays you?"

"Like a whore." She laughed bitterly. "I prefer it that way. I wouldn't want him to think he is laying Naomi Meged. Or any fine Turkish or Armenian girl."

"And Corie?" Tim asked.

"I recruited her." Tim felt another blow. "He pays us each time. Fifty dollars extra for up the ass. There, now you have it. I'm sorry to be so frank. We tried to shield you from the truth. Now you know everything, and there is nothing more to hide. You can take us or leave us, my love." He sat with his head hanging, fists together on the table. He looked up, but couldn't look at her.. "This man likes duets, Tim. It's the least of my concerns. There was another one in Ankara who liked to maim girls, and I personally shot him to death when he killed one of my friends. No human being deserves what he did to my friend. I came up the stairs to check on her, in this place where he was renting a room while on garrison duty. Something told me to take my gun along. It was an old French 8 mm. Lebel revolver. I found her on the floor in a pool of blood. She died that afternoon in a restaurant below, where kind people put her on a table with a jacket for a pillow. A doctor came, but it was too late." She closed her eyes a moment, then returned to the tale of the captain. "He'd used a knife on her down below. Blood all over the place. He was still screwing her, stark naked, on her dying body, the monster, when I came in the room from behind and put the gun by his head. He thought I was joking and he actually laughed, tried to brush the gun aside while holding his dick with the other hand. That's when I fired for the first time. It wrecked his shoulder and he staggered back in shock, holding the shoulder with his good hand, and shielding his privates with the other, dangling hand. Suddenly he was a scared boy who had been bad. Very bad. I was going to blow his dick and balls off as he stood there facing me, leaning against the wall. He could see I was deadly serious. He wasn't laughing anymore. I didn't care what I did next. I just wanted to hurt him. I thought of the girl, and of my ex-husband who used to beat me until I lost my baby. I remember slipping on the girl's blood. I saw a kitchen knife in her blood. He backed up to the window yammering like a hysterical little bitch. I can still see his black hair hanging down into his forehead. Sweaty. He had a nice cleft chin with lots of blue beard on his jaws on and in his chin. His eyes were dark brown or olive green with a flat bluish haze in them. When you kill someone face to face, you forever remember them as if you saw them through a microscope. There is a camera in your head." She shuddered, wishing to yank the film out, and unable to do so. "He had one brown tooth and a few missing side teeth that he must have got smashed in battle from some Armenian rifle butt. He was an infantry captain, and his partial denture lay on his medals. I shot him right through the hand, taking his balls and his dick off. My gun wouldn't fire again. I took his gun out of his holster on the chair. It was a Turkish Nagant six shooter. I took my time, aimed, while he stared at me. He died scared. I had a clean shot through the head and put him right out the window head-first. He landed in the alley below. There was blood and brains on the wall of the opposite house. I threw his dentures after him as well as the gun, and then I ran like the wind to a Kurdish safe house where they knew me and took me in." She lit another cigarette, and sipped tea in quick nervous gestures. "We all have things we must not think about or we will go insane. If you can do that, I will finish with the spy business and be your woman."

"Oh, Jesus, Jesus, Jesus. And Corie?"

"She loves you." Meg shrugged lightly. "Before she met me, her worst nightmare was getting stood up at the malt shop in Ozone, Kansas. I dragged her into this. Tim, before I met you, I was just—empty. You woke something up in me. Something wonderful. Do you know: I have been on my knees, crying and telling her how sorry I am for getting her into this dirty business. She cried too. She forgave me. We wanted to go on with you. Then you left. Now I've found you. So, it's simple. You know everything now. We solve this problem the only logical way. Either you leave us, or you take us both. We give ourselves to you. She was afraid to come because you might be angry and say no. In any case, she had to fly somewhere far away. I am the messenger today. You can have everything, Tim, if you want."

Tim put his hand heavily over hers. She looked at him uncertainly. He put his other hand over all the hands and kneaded her hands as if they were dough and he were a baker. She gasped in relief, as if saved from drowning. Her jaws worked, her eyes blinked. She couldn't speak. Neither could he.

"We'll keep you warm at night and give you pleasure. We'll be wonderful companions for you." She saw his pensive, distraught look and darkened with concern. "She and I were just friends until we met you. She was just a tool at first, but I grew to like her, to care for her as a friend. She is a sweet person, you know that." He nodded. She continued: "You came along and it all fell into place. Now we'll finish with this Alger Hiss and his Soviet friends, to say nothing of this randy Ferenc we've been depleting of information, and then it's over." She bit her lip. "Now the air can be clear." She puffed hungrily on her cigarette, filling the air around her with smoke.

He coughed and waved his hand with a grimace. "Very clear."

She quickly stubbed it out. "Sorry. I'll try my best." She pressed her fingertip against his lips. "Don't ever speak of these things. I try not to have any feelings about it one way or the other. There have been other things like that. He is not the only one I killed with the partisans. I don't let it inside me, Tim."

"You mean—you put it on a shelf and don't think about it." *Mona.*

"Something like that, yes." She stared beseechingly at him through smoke-teary eyes. "This is war, my love. We are soldiers." Her face looked swollen and her lips trembled. "Can you forgive?" His tongue felt thick and wouldn't let him say anything, but he nodded. She put her hands over his and looked devoutly into his eyes. He started rubbing her hands because they looked heavy and sweet. She squeezed back. "It's a deal, sailor."

"Deal," he said. They settled into an exhausted silence, occasionally sipping tea. She said: "Corie flies her planes and hardly has a second thought about what she does." She imprisoned his hands in hers. "I will help the U.S., and the U.S. will help my people. There really is a shining star at the end of the road, called Israel. I will probably never see it, but hope was enough for Moses so it must be enough for me." She swallowed hard, stroked his hand. "But enough now. That's all you need to know. Too dangerous for you otherwise."

"So you are a California girl."

"I am, baby. Born in Napa. That much is true. My father is Armenian, which makes me Armenian. My mother is Jewish, which makes me Jewish. See?"

"Clear as a mountain spring."

"You just need to know that we both love you." Her hands felt warm around his, and he closed his eyes, remembering suddenly how good it had felt to be loved by them. "You need to know nothing more."

"What a fool I am," he whispered out loud. He hoped his heart was steering him right. And he was about to hurt Anna Stokowska again—and that was always such a heavy, complicated thing.

Meg pressed his hands between hers. "Believe this when I tell you. I would do anything in this world for you. I would give my life for you. You hear it from Naomi Meged, a soldier who has killed men: I would die for you, sailor."

📖

Corie was away on some secret flight (or whatever). The apartment was semi-dark, except for a candle flickering orange in a corner. Fresh air blew in, stirring the curtain and the candle.

Meg wore a silk Middle Eastern dress, and served him a tray of sweets and hot tea. He sat on the couch. She knelt on the floor and took off his shoes and socks. She brought a bowl of hot water with salts, and massaged his feet in it and kissed his toes and the bottoms of his feet until he almost peed his pants. She wiped his feet dry with a clean washcloth. She put the washcloth, the bowl, and the tray aside. She said to him in a low voice: "My love. My friend. Master of my heart." He rose toward her, to embrace her. She pushed him firmly, and he fell back on the cushions. She unbuttoned his pants, took him out, and put him in her mouth. Then, with her moist warmth wrapped around him, her teeth pressing pleasurably on him all around, she reached up and pulled his shirt tail from his pants, fumbled with the buttons, opened the shirt, and teased his nipples with her fingers. He groaned, resting his hands on her head, enjoying her frizzy hair against his palms. His fingertips roved, reading like Braille the bony contours of her cheeks, her temples, her jaws as she worked noisily on him. When he was about to come, she held him away from her and licked underneath. She looked pale, Oriental, the Asian that she was, from that massive continent whose eastern edge she wanted to save for the Kuomintang, and its western rim for the People of the Book. When he thought he could not take any more, she hiked up her dress and straddled him on the couch. Knees on either side of his head, she pressed her bush against his face and let him find with his tongue the cleft in her peach. With her index fingers she parted the leaves to reveal the stem of her apple, while with her other fingers she held apart the slices so he could taste the mother bed of its seeds. His tongue found the architecture of her deep offering, under the stem the tiny lubricated openings of what flows out and the tight doorway offering entry to that which wants to go in. She used one hand, palm splayed against the wall beside her upraised and transfigured face, to support herself, an elbow to pin up her disheveled dress, and the other hand to help him find what he urgently sought. Finally, he grappled her down. She guided his conquest, settling on her back with arms helpful. He entered her gate, whose threshold she had washed with welcomes.

"There is a lot going on," she told him. "The whole world is being made over. I only know a very tiny part of it. I do know that there are deals being made about how the world will be put back in order after the war, and I happen to wish that there will be a state for the Jews where we lived thousands of years ago. That's just a tiny part of it. The Soviets and the British and everyone else have spies throughout town, but nobody as many as Stalin. He wants everything, and someone has to stand in the way, even if Truman and his people are too naïve to fight now before it's too late later." She rubbed his eyebrows, his cheeks, kissing each spot that her fingers brushed. "This man, whose name you do not need to know, is a very high person with the Bulgarian delegation, and they are in Stalin's pocket. This man thinks we are just fancy bimbos, and he thinks he is in a safe, private place. The truth is that there are microphones and taps every inch in every room, and he keeps making phone calls that our people are listening in on." She nursed him gently, kissing the thoughts on his forehead. "If this were the Arabian Nights, you would not think twice about running away with two lovely courtesans, would you? If this were Topkapi, you would love to steal away two of the Sultan's finest houris, wouldn't you?" She pinched his nipples gently, twisting them in mock cruelty.

He touched her cheek, pulling her face to him for a kiss. "I can't bear the thought."

"I had a broken heart. I cannot tell you..."

He put his hand over her mouth. "Shh."

They looked at each other, she a poor *houri* (female angel, harem treasure, nothing at all to do with a similar Western term of contempt) whose tears welled up over the prison of his hand and then fell down the bars of his fingers. "Help me forget, Tim. You have already done so much to heal me."

He felt as though he must be crazy, but he said: "I promise:I will stay with you if that is what you want."

She went to the bathroom to wash her face and came back to snuggle beside him—an American girl suddenly. "Thanks, dear."

"Where is my other complication?"

"Corie."

"Yeah. My other wife."

She snuggled. "Corie is flying a crate to Montana."

"A crate."

"That's what she said. She talks like a man sometimes."

"Like a pilot," Tim said. They laughed. In a corner stood an orange crate on end, acting as a little bookcase with a doily and a vase on top. "I'll bet she could fly an orange crate," he said.

"She's such a pilot," Meg said. "Corie comes from a straight laced little town in the middle of Kansas someplace, like Toto and the Tin Man. We met as roommates. I developed her as material, and got her involved in this trade. She thought it sounded like a grand adventure, though it's caused her so many tears. It's not something you can just walk away from. In the end, we became true friends, and now we have you between us. Neither of us was ever interested in women. Without you in bed, we are just like any two regular girls. With you, it feels good. Not when we are alone; just when you are between us. You know, girls will sleep together, just to be warm and have company. Not to touch or get excited." She paused a while. "So that is the flight plan."

"That sounds like Corie," he said.

"She's a pilot."

"She'll fly any crate if it's the right one."

Two souls exhausted, they drifted off to sleep the morning away, side by side, tangled together and warm.

Confused, he struggled for balance as the bed jumped up and down and something pink flashed before his eyes. "Tim! Our Tim! You came back to us!"

Corie.

He took her in his arms and pulled her to him. She wrapped herself around him and flooded him with kisses. He was surprised how strong and wiry she was, in contrast with Meg's firm softness. Corie stayed on top, naked to begin with, and wrapped herself around him, enveloping him in her flower. He felt like a bee, trapped in the nectar inside an orchid or some exotic jungle blossom. But it was only her pink Protestant Kansas waterfall, foaming around his rocks, and together they slammed up and down making their own storm and taking comfort from it.

Meg stood in the kitchen in a filmy black sun dress with large sunflowers on it. A cigarette dangling from a corner of her mouth made her eyes water, as she made crepes and a rich, cheesy chicken filling with white wine. As Corie and Tim whispered in the living room, the house filled with the smells of sautéed onions and garlic as well as batter and smoke. And coffee. As evening fell, the windows stood open to the damp breeze, the radio poured out toothpaste swirls of rich band tunes, and it was all the way it should never have stopped being.

Except that the two women still had their mission. *Houris.* He might start drinking heavily if this didn't stop soon. He didn't know what to do about Anna, either. How could he hurt her again?

Meg slept soundly in her own room with the door closed.

Tim and Corie danced together in the living room to show tunes, and then sat on the pillow and drank martinis. "I don't think of it as sleeping with a woman," Corie said, a little sloshy. "Ick." She made a face. "I like men. I like Tim. Come here, Tim."

Tim cradled his martini, sitting beside her. "Uh..."

"Meg told you about our adventure with that slimy Ferenc."

"Yes."

"I can't wait to be done with it." She paled in her outburst and slammed her hand down. "I call him Ferret when he can't hear. Sometimes I call him that from another room. Hey, Ferret. Come here and lick the floor in front of me." She sipped. "I'm trying to dream up something nasty to say to him when I last see him, which can't be too soon."

"Do me a favor," Tim said. "Let's not talk about it again. I just want to pretend like it's before I really knew. Can you do that? Put things on a shelf and just pretend they don't exist?"

"What do you mean?"

"Like this. When you are here with me, that's all there is. When you are flying crates, that's all there is. When you are having a nightmare, that's all there is, in that place, and when you wake up you forget about it like it didn't happen."

She eyeballed him a little sloshy. "I can do that?"

"You have my permission." *Mona says so.*

"Then you'll stay with us?" She seemed relieved. "We are perfect together, we three. I hope it always stays like this. You won't leave us again, will you?"

He shook his head.

"It's one of those war things," she said earnestly.

Truth in Espionage

Tim was at work two days after his reunion with the women, when he looked up from his desk and saw a familiar looking woman across the courtyard in the next wing of his office building. Anna Stokowska wore a U.S. Marine Corps Women's Reserve captain's uniform that looked crisp and tailored on her fine figure. Her blonde hair was neatly bunned under a dark green cap.

How odd. He'd just that morning tried to call Anna and say he was sorry but he had to hurt her once more. The number he got was a wrong number, and he felt relieved. Not only did he not have to confront her with the truth yet, but he could buy some time in case the deal with Corie and Meg went nuts again. *Give it a week at least*, he suggested to himself.

Shocked, he dropped the pencil he was holding and half-rose. He stared out the window, across the courtyard, and into the opposite window in the next wing over. Anna Stokowska stood talking to a young female yeoman as if asking directions. The yeoman, a plump brunette wearing white blouse and dark skirt, respectfully explained something and pointed away down a corridor in the direction of the central plan archives, the rooms upon rooms crowded with files and shoebox-like receptacles filled with engineering drawings. Some of the archives were those of Tim's section, which were top secret and sensitive. The woman strode off in the direction the yeoman had indicated.

Tim hurried out the door after her.

In a flash, it all came to him. She'd been using him in London. She was trying to use him here. He remembered the night Jaguar had raided the map room. Was it an accident that Anna had postponed their usual Wednesday lunch to Friday evening dinner to keep him occupied while her fellow spy ransacked the Technical Section and walked away with that tube? Like bolts of lightning, other instances of sly deceit struck him. *How dumb could I have been?* She had to be connected to Jaguar, then. And that meant Jaguar was in San Francisco. Hard to believe. Had she really cared about him? Had he not hurt her then? Something told him it was more complicated than that. Things always were.

What is Anna Stokowska doing in a Marine Corps uniform? Even from 200 feet, through two windows, Tim made out the flash of twin silver bars on each shoulder, on the field green with red trim of a Class A uniform. How could that be, when she'd just reintroduced herself to him a few weeks earlier as a Navy nurse working in the burn unit at Letterman Army Hospital?

Something was seriously wrong here. He hurried down the echoing corridors, where passing men whistled tunelessly and the echoes of their whistling rose up through wrought-iron railings and wooden stairwells where clusters of Navy personnel hustled about at their jobs. Tim made his way through the central lobby of the third floor and spotted Anna's shapely behind moving along a busy causeway over the street below, a connecting tunnel leading to the files warehouse on the other side.

What to do? He bent surreptitiously over a wall fountain, still eyeing her. He let the water run, but did not drink. When she was far enough away not to notice, he trailed her. She showed a wallet badge at the information desk, and two young female clerks unsuspectingly directed her to where the research documents of Admiral Lemney's section were stored. Tim wished he were a fly so he could hover just over her shoulder and see where she was going, what she was after.

The opportunity presented itself in the form of Stan Kehoe, who was just marching in the opposite direction, carrying a sheaf of documents under one arm and a cup of coffee in his other hand. As always, he managed to look boyish and busy and sincere and utterly silly. "Stan!" Tim took him by the shoulders.

"Whoa! My coffee!"

"Stan, this is really important." In about two minutes, he explained the gist of it to Stan, who handed over the sheaf of papers to a clerk. "Isn't she your Polish girlfriend from London?"

"Yes!" Tim finished explaining. "She is up to no good."

Stan agreed to go back and keep an eye on Anna.

Tim returned to his office, closed the door, and sat back to think. What had she said? Navy nurse...he got on the phone and dialed the hospital. "Hello, is there a nurse by the name of Lieutenant Anna Stokowska?" he asked.

"Spell that please," said the yeoman at the security reception desk. Tim did, and the answer came back in a moment: "Yessir, Lieutenant Stokowska is assigned to the Ob-Gyn Ward, but she is off-shift right now."

"She's not in Burn?"

"No, Sir."

"I'll take her ward number so I can call direct."

"That's against rules, Sir. Nurses are not allowed to receive calls on the floor. You'll have to go through the Head Nurse's office."

"Okay, fine, I'll call back later."

"I'll be happy to connect—"

"Thanks, but I have a baby coming out, no time now." He hung up.

Jeez. What next?

As he sat holding his head, Stan burst in. "Hey, got my papers?"

"Over there." Tim pointed to the sheaf of drawings he'd placed on a chair near the door. "What was she after?"

Stan shook his head. "She wasn't. She walked right through the place heading for the next connector. I thought she was going to the ladies' room and kind of hung back, and then I saw her behind on the ramp, sashaying along—man that woman has a figure, takes your breath away—so I ran after her."

"I hope she didn't see you." Tim spoke with a falling voice. That was Anna—a face and a figure like that, wasted on dirty business.

"No way. She was on a mission, that broad. On her way to a section in the next building that I wasn't allowed to get into but she showed some I.D. and waltzed right in."

"What section?"

"Test records from the Radiation Lab at Berkeley. Whatever that means."

"Thanks."

Stan left, and Tim ruminated. How to check up on her without giving himself away? He strode down the hallway, knocked on Captain Martin Teague's door.

"Yeah."

He let himself in. "Martin, can we talk?"

"What trouble are you in now?" Teague sat behind an ocean of ledgers, puffing on his pipe like an oceangoing tug. He looked harried.

"Sorry, Martin. It's important." He explained about Anna. "I think we should put a tail on her, find out what we can."

"Yup," Martin said with pipe-bound lips, reaching for his phone.

Tim put his hand over Martin's. "Just remember—we don't know who is listening to whom, so don't say more than you need to."

Teague waved his pipe and looked put-off. "What are you, the FBI?" But he looked up the number and called an ONI connection. "Hello, Sam? Marty Teague here. Got a kind of an odd little thing I think you'll want to check out for us. Can't talk on the phone." Moments later, when he hung up, he said: "The run-around. What else do we expect? And he's a friend of mine! Imagine if I were a stranger. Where would he refer me then?" He wrote down a name and an address and pushed the slip of paper across to Tim. "He gave me this address for one of his agents—Billy Seward. He's a major in Army CIC."

"I know him," Tim said.

Teague froze. "You do?"

"Yeah. London. He broke up a spy ring." He remembered how dumb he'd felt, along with Stan Kehoe, being apprehended by Seward near the bodies of Admiral Todd and his wife. Disgraced, Todd had ended her pain and then avoided facing his own prison or execution. Saved his country a bullet.

"You've been a busy guy." Teague handed the number over. "Seward's people manage the Berkeley side of this racket. He'll talk to you. Good luck."

"Thanks." Tim pocketed the information and went back to his office, just long enough to grab his hat, leave a note with his secretary—that he was going on a medical appointment and wasn't leaving a number where he could be reached. Teague would field for him. With that, he set out to find the address on Grace Street.

"We meet again, Nordhall." As they shook hands in the doorway, Seward said: "Yeah, I'm the sports coordinator for just about any office, Army or Navy, within a mile of here. Come in and grab a seat. Coffee?"

"Yeah, thanks. Black, one sugar. This time, no dead man in the car."

"Oh yeah, that." Looking crisp in his neatly ironed shirt and freshly pressed tie, Seward stood at the corner sink and set up cups while waiting for the kettle to boil. "That all worked out okay." He pointed to the old building around them. "We're in an old office building here, slated for demolition. We're using it until Uncle Sam builds us another Pentagon on the West Coast."

"Nice," Tim said. The structure was an unexpected hidden spot of bureaucratic drabness, in the midst of an attractive neighborhood near Grace Cathedral and Huntington Park. One could smell tropical plants in the gardens in the park and hear macaws yelling their beaks off. Occasionally, one heard the thump of a tennis ball on packed clay not far away on the courts near the Pacific Union Club.

"So what's going on, Nordhall?"

"You introduced me to Anna Stokowska," Tim said.

"Oh yeah, that." Seward said, picking up a phone. He spoke briefly with someone and hung up. "This could be interesting. So Anna's back in town."

The kettle whistled and Seward brought their coffees to the desk. Tim accepted his cup. "I thought I was in love with her. I thought she was in love with me. Now I gather it was all another Claire Denby racket." Seward stared at him, eyes full of flickering cryptology. Tim continued: "At least tell me you're on our side."

"I'm on our side," Billy said. He stirred his tea. "She was crazy about you. It took a lot of reasoning to get her out of London, even under orders from the Free Polish Army."

Tim closed his eyes. "That's worse."

"What's worse."

"I was afraid I had hurt her. I wish she'd been faking."

"She was real. Did she tell you about Erek?"

"Her cousin? Was that all true?"

"Yeah. You see how weird these inbred aristocrats can be. He was her second cousin, and they were crazy about each other from the time they were children."

Tim said: "Then it's true. I don't know what to believe anymore. They had a few days in Königsberg or Danzig or someplace before the Gestapo took him away. She escaped and went to London to work for MI6."

"She was working all sides of the fence," Billy said. "She felt she had to, I guess. I was trying to play her against Jaguar. You were my one rook. She was supposed to be the other, except you two fell in love. She asked to be transferred, finally."

Tim was more stunned with each revelation. "She wrote to me twice. Once from Rome, and once from Athens."

Seward had a gravid undertone in his voice. "She was under orders to ixnay any further contact with you. She really loved you."

"Then it was true. And I lost faith in her."

Seward looked at the ground, as if his heart lay dying there. "I was in love with her too, but I couldn't get to first base with her. She stayed true to you the whole time."

"Oh my God."

"Yeah, my God." He rose, rinsed out his cup, and put it in the drainer. "For what it's worth, Nordhall, you were in over your head. We all were. Not just the matter of Anna. Claire Denby we played like a champ. Win some, lose some. But Jaguar and the Soviets had us wrapped around the axle. We didn't know if we were coming or going."

"What now?"

"We found out that the Soviets have Erek. They're still playing her."

They were interrupted as the building door opened. Two men in civilian clothes entered. One had gray hair and wore glasses. The younger one seemed the more authoritative and carried a thick brown file folder tied with string. Both wore flannel suits. The older one shook out a cigarette, offering all around, but nobody else lit up. Seward introduced them. "Major Pash," he introduced the younger man, "and Colonel Reventloe, Military Intelligence."

They all went into a meeting room and Seward closed the door. The four men sat at a large table under fluorescent lights.

Pash said: "Lieutenant Commander Nordhall, have you had any dealings whatsoever with Rad Lab?"

"No. What is it?"

"Have you ever been to Berkeley?"

"Nope."

Pash loosed the string on his accordion folder and opened it up. Tim saw documents, photos, memos. "I have access to a mile and a half of folders like this, but I picked this one on the fly because it pertains to your duty section. Interestingly, there's a folder on you."

"Doesn't surprise me," Tim said. Did they know he'd worked for OSS?

Pash frowned. "You came here highly recommended, top reviews, blah blah, from your boss, Captain Jack Stone, who is now happily retired and living in San Diego. Silver Star, all kinds of hash on your chest, action off West Africa, blah blah. What did you do in Katanga, Nordhall?"

Tim sipped his coffee and tried his best to be helpful. "I escaped from slave traders and made my way to the nearest friendly station to get back to my unit."

"Slave traders?"

"I kid you not."

"Hundreds of miles to Leopoldville. How did you do that?"

"Couple of Luftwaffe deserters with a stolen Ju-52."

"I see here—" Pash licked a finger and flipped through more pages. "Oh yes, *Top Secret. H.M.S. Sturner.* Hm, yes. And so on...sure, well it's the Dark Continent, so what do I know. Great. You're in Katanga, and you sell your soul to this fellow Crane, who is with O.S.S. Is that right?"

"Sounds sort of correct, except I think I still have my soul with me." So they knew at least part of his London story. They must have very high clearances.

"Right. Did Crane give you a talk about anything—say, minerals, rocks, that sort of thing?"

"Yes. He flew me to Katanga Province and he did talk to me about the importance of..." Tim had to think for a few moments, it had been so long. "Uranium, I think it was. He hinted strongly about an energy bomb."

"Tell us all that you remember."

"That's about all. He talked about physics, and about explosives. In fact we sat in a plane and he drew diagrams of how neutrons bounce around..." Tim had to stop and think again. "Critical mass. That was it. Well, it's the stuff you read about in Scientific American, for the few people that do. I happen to be a journeyman engineer, so that sort of thing interests me."

Pash nodded. "Very good. So there is a heavily censored segment here that I have no way of reading, that pertains to your services in London." He closed the file. "Nordhall, let me put it this way. I have a need to know and a clearance longer than from here to the moon. I need to know every breath you took, everyone you screwed, everything you ate, and the color of every shit you took, from the time you left Africa until the time you followed that Stokowska broad down the hall this morning."

Tim took a deep breath and exhaled. "Well, that's going to be a long conversation."

"We have time," Reventloe said. "Seward, how about some coffee?" Billy Seward rose and left the room. "An important conversation," Pash said. "You need to understand we can go all the way up to the White House. This is that important, okay?"

"Understood, Sir."

"I'm also not a major but a Brigadier General in the War Department, G-2. Intel. Reventloe is a Major General. We don't want to call attention to ourselves, so let's just pretend we're field grade officers. Please understand, again, how important this is. We already know about Stokowska. I know you were screwing her in London. No problem. She was screwing you too, and you didn't know it."

"General," Tim said testily, "let's make a deal. Don't talk to me like I'm an asshole, and I won't talk to you like you are an asshole. It will make things all that much smoother."

Pash was a hard man, but he seemed amused. "Okay. Point taken. I'm sorry." He turned to Reventloe. "I'll take that smoke, Carl. Looks like it's going to be a long afternoon."

Together, they relived Tim's military career from the time he set out on H.M.S. Sturmer to the present. The only detail Tim avoided was his relationship with Meg and Corie. Nobody would believe him anyway, so he told as close to the truth he could: he'd met and befriended Corie, then fallen for her roommate while remaining friends with Corie; and now he was just a friend to both women. Even at that, Pash and Reventloe exchanged prurient looks but did not pursue that leg of their questioning any further. Tim was too relieved to be offended by their suspicions.

Reventloe said: "I understand you are a ladies' man." He quickly raised a hand as Tim, tired and stressed, felt like clambering over the table to wring his neck, court-martial or not. "Easy, Nordhall. Calm down. Just so you know, I cannot ask you about the two women you are living with because they are under a shroud of secrecy from the State Department. Different jurisdiction, different fish to fry—and some very big ones, from the size of the Do Not Disturb sign hanging outside their case file."

"Okay," Pash said, "I think we have a good framework to run with, but things are still blurry and sketchy. This spy stuff is frankly a bit baffling to us. Not something we're used to. Not very American. We see ourselves as security people guarding a national secret to which you are partially privy, thanks to our friend in Katanga. I checked and found out that he was killed in a plane crash barely a week ago off the coast in Virginia. He worked for General Donovan, whom you don't know."

"Oh yes, I had lunch in London with Crane and Donovan."

"You do get around, Nordhall. Then you understand—the Jaguar operation, your sideshow away from Jack Stone's shop at Tining Mallow— that was one of Donovan's ops. We now realize that it was compromised from the start."

"No kidding."

"It's beginning to look like Crane was a double agent, working for the Soviets. We thought we were feeding him harmless information in return for his bad info, hoping to nail down his contacts. Instead, he and Stokowska and the rest of the ring were stealing real secrets. You were handing real information to the Soviets at St. Dunstan-in-the-East."

"Sorry."

"No need to feel like a dope. We all have pie on our faces. These people are slicker'n snot. Stalin has more spies in the U.S. than he has people in Russia."

Seward just happened to come in and sit down. Tim said: "About Anna Stokowska. Billy, you introduced me to her. Did you know from the start—?"

Seward explained for the other officers' benefit: "That she was working for them? Yes. She's a patriotic Polish girl. She wanted to be on our side, but the Nazis were holding her fiancé, a very important Free Polish Air Force officer and political prisoner while she was stationed in London. They threatened to kill him if she didn't cooperate. She had access to you and Jaguar, and I thought I could turn her. Didn't work. Not in love nor in war."

"If I'd had any idea—." Tim thought about how close he'd come to being in love with her.

Seward shook his head. "You would never have really had her. She will always love her cousin." He threw up his hands and sat back, defeated by life. "I like evolution, you know? We're all just chimps in suits. Everyone stiffed her, and all she had left was her love for you, and you stiffed her. Life has treated her badly. She is one of the most beautiful women I've ever seen."

"I didn't exactly stiff her," Tim said. "It was complicated."

"Yes," Seward said. "It was." From his tone, there was little blame in the air. Maybe jealousy and irony. "She was supposed to use you, not fall in love with you. I wonder. If she'd been in love with me, would I have thrown everything away for her?" He looked at the generals. "In my business, you have to think of all the angles. A lot of us become quietly heavy drinkers. I play a lot of sports and take cold showers." The room rustled with uneasy but relieved laughter. "Working with her was like being in the room with a great work of art. You know—Primavera steps down from Botticelli's canvas. Same thing with Claire Denby. So if Anna's back in town, then can Jaguar be far behind? I'd say Ivor Crane, but you tell me he's dead."

Pash asked: "Does the name Elizabeth Bentley mean anything to you?"

"British luxury car."

Pash and Reventloe exchanged glances and smiled.

Pash said: "American traitor."

"A spy code-named *Umnitsa*." Reventloe produced a pipe, which he tapped on his leg to empty it of old tobacco. "Do you read much economics?" Tim shook his head. "Professor White? Harry Dexter White? Name ring a bell?" Tim shook his head. Reventloe reflectively shook his head in the momentum of questioning and began filling his pipe.

"Silvermaster?" Pash asked. Tim shook his head, and the momentum of questioning went back to Reventloe. As the hours progressed, Tim noticed a pattern. The generals worked together, but Pash seemed more interested in matters involving the newly forming United Nations, while Reventloe kept circling carefully (without giving much away) around scientific matters. Atomic physics was mentioned a few times.

"Have you ever been to Canada?" Reventloe asked. "Montreal?"

"No."

"But you're from New England," Pash injected.

"Yes."

"New Haven. Home of Yale University."

"Yes. Two years of Teacher's College."

"Ever do any work at or near Yale?"

"No, I'm just a humble clockmaker." Tim laughed. They laughed too. "What are all these questions about?"

"Clockmaker. Great. That's funny," Reventloe said.

"Sorry, we can't connect the dots for you," Pash said with a remote, veiled unpleasantness in his voice, which Tim couldn't decipher. Meanwhile, no doubt, the phony woman Marine Corps Reserve officer was probably walking off with the nation's secrets. "From New Haven, did you go to Manhattan from time to time?"

"Hardly ever."

Reventloe puffed on his pipe. "Ever hear of Amtorg?"

Tim shook his head.

"Chemator Inc.?"

"Joe Weinberg? Gregory Kheifitz?"

"No, no, no." Tim was beginning to get funny tingles about his conversations with Crane in Katanga, and he said so. The conversation spun through a number of names that Tim wasn't familiar with. Reventloe was interested in Tim's nodding acquaintance with nuclear physics and tried to pin him down on something, but couldn't. Tim knew he was clean, and didn't worry.

Pash brought the conversation back to Ivor Crane. " It will be a few years yet before this country realizes how thoroughly those bastards have infiltrated every nook and cranny of our government, our military, industry, you name it."

Reventloe added: "Sounds paranoid, but you have to remember the Communists have been losing the industrial battle from the very start. Even though, for a brief moment in the early Depression, American workers were so desperate that thousands migrated to the U.S.S.R. for work. Ever since then, the Reds have had to beg, borrow, and steal to keep up with us. Then Hitler comes along and together with Stalin murders a quarter of the Russian nation. They are going to be like cornered animals for the rest of the century, trying to prove the fantasy that their dictatorship is better than a liberal free market system."

Tim had had enough coffee to last him a week. "I bailed out of the spy business back in London last year. I hope you can read that in my records. All I wanted to do today was tell you to keep an eye on my ex-girlfriend."

"We will, Nordhall," Pash said darkly. "Thanks." He rose and extended a hand. "We'll be in touch if we need to talk more."

"Go easy on Anna," Tim said. "She is a good nurse and she helped a lot of people. She's had much grief in her life."

The two security officers regarded him with patience and pity as they trooped into the outer office and kitchen, where Billy Seward was practicing making baskets with wadded scratch paper. Seward said: "The FBI is tracking Anna Stokowska's every move."

"Go easy on her."

Pash dusted himself off. "Nordhall, people like her cost lives. Sometimes lots of lives."

"I know." Tim felt sad. "We need to forgive. This is America."

"Philosopher, eh?" Pash modulated his sarcasm a bit. "I'll see what we can do, short of putting her in front of a firing squad."

Reventloe gave a sniff and hitched up his pants. "I was an infantry commander from Anzio all the way up the road to Bastogne. I have no sympathy for traitors. We'll make sure she hangs."

"Maybe a trial first," Pash added with grim love. Tim saw the game plan. He felt anger directed at himself. They hated her for betraying her country, but they hated him more—for having been loved by a beautiful woman. Their jealousy was a poison just about as dirty as a desperate and confused woman's treason.

📖

"What do you mean?"

Meg pulled him in and slammed the door. She stood in the small kitchen wringing her hands. "I have to tell you this. I know you won't like it, but the Bulgarian...he...doesn't know I understand Russian. He was on the phone all excited, talking with his people. He's here to help spy on us and the U.N., but he was just pulled off on a more important case. Something about a Bullet. Do you know anything about that?"

Tim took her wrists. "What about this bullet?"

She shook her head. "He knows Corie. He knows where she flies to sometimes. They now know we aren't whores. He mentioned her name. I don't know how long, but they're turning the tables on us."

Tim shook her wrists. "Yes, and—?"

Meg held her hands over her mouth and looked pale. "He grabbed his coat and ran out the door. Something about a bomb. What did he mean? Do you know? Are they going to blow up the U.N. or something?"

Tim held her away from him to quiet her while he tried to think. "A bomb...a trigger...no, it's not the U.N. " The energy bomb.

"Yes?" She tried to follow him.

He put his hand on the door, and held the other hand up to stop her. "This is going to get really dangerous now. Stay here and don't go out, okay?" With that, he hurried out into the hall and down the back stairs. Emerging in the courtyard, he sprinted out into the street and found the nearest pay phone. He dialed Seward's office, since Pash had set Seward up as his contact. "Seward, it's Tim Nordhall. I have to talk to you right away. This could be really important."

"Really. We're having trouble finding Anna Stokowska. Any idea where she might be?"

"Not an iota. Can you pick me up? I need to talk with you."

📖

Tim wore a dark civilian suit, gray felt hat, and long grayish-tan overcoat. He stepped off the curb, pulled the car door open, and got in. Immediately Seward had the car in gear and moving with traffic. "What is it now, Nordhall?"

"This is really important, okay? I have a friend who overheard a conversation."

"The Varkidjian broad?"

"Yes. How did you know?"

"We had her under surveillance until the State Department pulled us off it. People way up in the clouds. Are you part of their network?"

"Oh no." Tim waved both arms. "Listen, I'm practically a civilian. I get out soon, and I think I'm gonna go home and build clocks in New Haven."

"Okay, skip the drivel. What is it?"

"I have reason to believe there is a gadget on its way here. Something important connected with the work Reventloe is doing. The Soviets are going to steal it."

"How do you know all this?"

"Putting two and two together from what was said. Meg overheard this Bulgarian say he was being pulled off his U.N. work, which we have to assume is very important. He ran out the door in a flash...so what would you assume?"

Seward nodded, pursing his lips in thought while absently flowing with traffic outside the hermetically sealed and quiet windows. "He's got a new assignment. I'll tell Pash." He reached under the dashboard, pulled out a dully finished green metal box, and put it on the seat. The box had an articulated cable running under the dash. Seward opened the box, took out a black phone, dialed, and listened—a wireless field phone, on batteries yet. Would wonders ever cease? "Pash, it's Seward. I have Nordhall here in my car. He's babbling something about an *ombbay,* got that? Something about a *riggertay.* That make any sense to you?" He paused. "Got that? Good!"

Seward glanced at Tim several times while continuing absently to negotiate corners, until they were driving along Market going in a big circle back toward Nob Hill. Seward hung up and put the box on the floor out of the way. "Pash couldn't say much. It's over my head."

Tim raised both hands and implored: "My friend Corie is a pilot, and Meg thinks she may be involved somehow. I'm worried for her."

Seward didn't soften. "You and the women."

"Billy, be a pal. Help us out."

"The U.S. Army is on the case, okay? Go back and take your girlfriend out for a milkshake or better yet, a bottle of scotch, and sit tight."

"What are you going to do?"

Seward pulled a .45 out from under the seat and palmed it over. "In case you need it."

Tim checked the clip—it was full. "Thanks." He put the gun in his pocket.

"I have a softball game. Army-Marines. Wouldn't miss it for the world."

Tim slapped himself on the head with both hands. "Seward!"

"Okay, Nordhall. I will tell you this, and if you tell anyone, I will personally yank your tongue out with pliers and set it on fire under your dick. You got me?"

Tim nodded.

"Pash just told me that Stokowska called in last night. She wanted to make a clean breast of things."

"Did she turn herself in?"

"Yeah, the FBI's got her. I don't know if they're house sitting her, or if they've got her locked up. She's afraid the Soviets will punish her fiancé, but she loves her new country—that would be the U.S.A.—and she loves its people—that would be you, I imagine—and she told us everything she knows. That's why I don't have time for you Varkidjian story."

Fighting himself inwardly, Tim said: "Let's be smart this time. Remember London. Jaguar is still out there, and he's smarter than the rest of us put together."

"We're watching out for dirty tricks," Billy said. "Go have a beer or something. You're all worked up. I'm on call in case we have any action." He pulled up near where he'd picked Tim up. "I appreciate your enthusiasm and patriotism, okay? Now get out of my car so I can go do some important stuff."

"Thanks, Seward."

"Bye."

"Oh, Nordhall?" Tim was halfway in the street, and turned.

"I was crazy about her back in London, not that I got to square one. I still care for her too. I'll do everything I can to see that they don't hang her. With any luck, she'll get life at hard labor." Billy Seward drove off.

📖

"Yes?" Meg answered in a scared voice.

"It's Tim. Where do you think Corie is?"

"I don't know. There are a dozen airfields around San Francisco and Oakland for starters. I have absolutely no idea."

He thought—desperately—and couldn't come up with anything. "All right. I'll call you if I get any ideas. Keep an eye out for her."

With that, Tim stood helplessly on the street corner. He thought of Anna Stokowska. He had her phone number in his pocket. He wanted to see her just one more time. He went back to the pay phone and called the operator. "Can you tell me what part of town this prefix would be?" The operator told him, simply, "San Francisco, Sir."

"It's a big city, but thanks." He smashed the receiver on the hook and paced up and down. What to do? Desperately, he called the hospital again, and asked for the Head Nurse's office. An older woman answered.

"This is Doctor Shilfmx," Tim said running his fingers over his mouth.

"Doctor who, Sir?"

He rubbed a fingertip over his teeth. "Shilfmx, Thostedorx Falx."

"I'm sorry—? Can you say again?"

"I need to get in touch with Army Nurse Captain Stokowska."

"Oh," the woman said with a growing tenor of conspiracy and vicarious delight, "Doctor Hershbein, I didn't recognize your voice."

"I'm eating a sandwich."

"Of course. Anna did leave a number in case you called."

"Let me have it, thanks."

The woman dictated S-U-tter 1231.

"What part of town is that prefix?"

"Civic Auditorium, Sir."

"Thanks." Tim put in another coin and dialed the number. The phone rang and rang, but nobody answered. He dialed the Operator and asked for an address to go with the number. The Operator sounded grumpy. "I don't have a listing that way, Sir. Oh, okay, I'll skim through my directory real quick...here it is..." She gave him a street address in the downtown area and Tim took the first cable car down that he saw. He ended up in a quietly elegant neighborhood, on a tree-lined street with new, glossy cars parked on the slope, and flower pots in window boxes. He found the house—a quiet, gloomy town house—and walked up the stairs. He knocked on the front door. It was a dark green, glossy door with shiny brass lion's head knocker, looking well maintained. Nobody answered. After knocking without luck several times, over about five minutes, Tim stepped back down to the curb. He looked around, spotting a phone under a shade tree, and walked over to call Meg. He crossed the stately street with its fine fronts and well-kept sidewalks.

"Meg?"

"Yes?"

"Just checking on you. Any word from Corie?"

"No. I'm worried sick. Where are you?"

"Downtown. Looking for someone who may have information." As he spoke, he spotted Anna Stokowska down the street. What was she doing loose on the street? She walked closer on the opposite side of the street, without noticing him, and looking very preoccupied. Her beautiful face was pale. Her eyes were cavernous. She'd lost weight. She wore a long overcoat, and carried a heavy shopping bag. She had a kerchief over her head that made her look like an old woman, but Tim recognized her. "Call you back," he told Meg and hung up.

He was about to cross the street and call out to her, when he noticed a man walking the other way toward her. Something made Tim and stop and pull back into the shade of the willow on the sidewalk.

It took him a minute but he recognized the stiff hand first, then the face.

Ivor Crane, the suave older O.S.S. officer he'd last seen in London. He had not died in a plane crash off Virginia. He must have faked it, and led the War Department hounds off his scent. Then the ring was still in operation, now in San Francisco.

Anna hurried up the stairs to the green door fumbling with her key. Crane strode along, as if herding her, with his hands in the pockets of his black suit. Crane walked right up the steps behind Anna with his good hand on her back. For a moment, Tim wanted to run to her rescue. Then he realized that she was willingly with Crane. Her expression was unreadable. Was she glad to see him? She embraced him with both arms and pressed her cheek against his chest. He seemed to be comforting her. She unlocked the door, and they stepped inside. Anna might think Crane was on her side, but for Tim the pieces suddenly clicked into place. Pash and Reventloe had been right. Crane might be old school and big money, but Crane was on the wrong side. Even as the door closed, Tim was on the phone. He dropped his remaining coin in, before he realized that Seward was probably gone already. He dialed the number, but nobody answered. Gone home for the day. Fine way to run an intelligence operation. He'd furnish Seward the address of this place, and the FBI could get a toe-hold on tracking this nest of spies.

Meanwhile, what to do right now?

A large, black car glided to a halt outside the town house. A jowly heavy sat at the wheel. He blared the horn briefly. The curtains parted, and Crane leaned out. Crane signaled for the man to wait, and the car backed effortfully into a parking spot under nearby tree shedding leaves.

Tim waited, not knowing what to do. As he waited, he saw shadowy shapes moving in the apartment. He saw Anna, taking off her coat. He saw Crane berating her. Anna went left and right, trying to escape him, but he hit her. She went down. Tim gritted his teeth and balled his fists. He reached into his back pocket for the .45 Billy Seward had given him. Now Crane had Anna by the hair and was pulling her along. She cried out and extended her bare arms to brace herself on the floor. She disappeared for a moment, and Tim thought Crane had killed her. He stepped forth with the impulse to run across the street, over the fence, right into the apartment.

Before he could draw the automatic, or dash down the stairs, a man's harsh voice said: "Stop right there, bud." A hand like a shovel gripped his arm and easily pulled him back. A dark steel .38 loomed at his temple. "Get back in the doorway," said Howard Lemon, the FBI agent who had evicted him from his apartment at the Hotel Auger. Lemon arm-barred Tim and shoved him back against a recessed door. "You blow this case for me, and I'll shoot you. Right here, right now. Like a fucking dog."

"Mr.—"

"Special Agent Lemon, FBI. Say, aren't you the joker from the Hotel Auger?"

"Yeah, that's me. That woman across the street—"

"She's giving the guy a blow job. What's wrong with that?"

Tim stared across the street. Over the low window sill, there was Anna Stokowska on her knees with her face buried in Ivor Crane's crotch. Tim saw her blonde hair and clasped hands, and she looked as if she were in church praying. Then Crane hauled off and slapped her audibly. Her head went to one side, and then she submissively resumed her task. Crane gripped her hair—which looked painful—and shook her head as he pressed her mouth onto him. Tim felt a rage to kill him. As he tried to reverse bar Lemon, Lemon cocked the trigger and pressed the cold steel to Tim's forehead. "You make a sound, you blow the case, I blow your brains out right here, right now."

"Help her, please."

"No dice. She sold her soul to those people."

"She turned herself in. She's working on our side now."

Another loud slap could be heard, followed by a heart-rending wail from Anna. "You guys tried to turn her, but they're on to it. They'll kill her."

"Oh yeah? Well, you're out of the game, permanently." He gave Tim a little shove for distance. "Your options are closed. Can you behave yourself?"

Tim had no choice. "Yes."

Lemon uncocked the trigger. "Listen, fella. I'm going to give you a chance to get away clean. You don't want to be involved in this mess." He pointed up the sloping sidewalk. "Start walking and don't look back. Go someplace far away and have a few beers. Kill an hour or two. Then get on with your life."

Tim hesitated, and Lemon shoved him down the stairs, gave him a painful whack on the right shoulder blade with the side of the revolver. "Get the fuck outta here. Go on."

Tim grabbed him by the lapel and pulled him down toward him. The two men stared at each other at an impasse. Tim released his grip and walked away. Lemon stood smoothing his rumpled coat.

Tim looked back once as he walked. Crane and the woman were gone from the window. Probably raping her in the bedroom, he thought as the sidewalk curved out of sight of Lemon, into the cover of leafy trees. What to do? He must do something to help Anna.

He had no more coins for phone calls. It was too risky to leave to get help. He walked up the street, his heart pounding, and had a desperate idea. He was about to do something that could get him arrested, but he had no choice. Looking furtively around, he tried door handles on cars, until he came to one that was unlocked. Looking around, he pulled the door open, got in, and bent down to pull the ignition wires out of their harness. It was something he'd seen done before, when a fellow engineer had forgotten his key and was too drunk to think straight. Easy as pie. He touched the two wires together that would normally go into the ignition. The car started with a powerful roar of eight cylinders, and Tim wheeled away down the empty street. No car owner came running after him, so he might just get away with this. He waited up the street, half a block away. He hoped Lemon wouldn't spot him.

He did not have long to sit there. The green door opened, and out came Crane, bounding down the steps while Anna stood anxiously waiting with folded arms as if she were cold. She still wore that coat, and was tying the babushka back around her bruised head. The next moment, Howard Lemon burst out the door and took her by the wrist. She had one small suitcase. She offered no resistance as Howard Lemon hustled her to the car with the jowly driver whom Crane had earlier ordered to wait. So Jowls wasn't waiting for Crane. He was waiting for Anna. And what did that make Howard Lemon? Howard Lemonoffski?

Tim intended to run Jowls off the road and save Anna. As Tim sped down the street, Crane pulled out in a dark blue 1940 Oldsmobile, coming between Anna's car and Tim's. Anna's car turned a corner and was lost to him. And with it, a piece of his heart. By the time Crane got going, there was no sign around the corner of the car with Anna in it. Tim's only hope was to follow Crane at a discreet distance, and hope he would lead Tim to Anna. *God help her*, Tim thought. There were so many possibilities. What was going on? He remembered the cruelty of Pash and Reventloe, and had an idea. Maybe they'd sold her to the Russians in exchange for something—information? Or maybe they just wanted her to punish her for turning on them? And he'd told Howard Lemon that, like a fool. *I betrayed you again*, he thought bitterly. *I promised not to hurt you again, and I have.*

What had Meg told him so earnestly? *I am a soldier. I have killed men. Hear what Naomi Meged, soldier, tells you. I would die for you.*

He said out loud: "I would die for you, Naomi, or for Corie, or for Anna." With so much courage in these women, he had to do something now. *Something.* He couldn't reach Seward, and he couldn't call those bastard generals, but he had Crane in his sights.

It was getting late in the day. A few cars already had their lights on. Crane drove steadily and fast, heading out of town as Tim followed.

Change of script. Man walks into empty room and sits at typewriter. Cranks in sheet of paper and starts typing. Fingers hunt and peck. Letters hammer down on platen, as inked ribbon jumps and rolls under determined and steady keystrokes. Man clatters urgently away.

City gave way to countryside. Luckily, the gas tank was three quarters full. Telephone poles flashed by with monotonous regularity. Crane drove on, and Tim was beginning to wonder if he were being led on a wild goose chase. Abruptly, Crane signaled to pull over, and Tim had just time to snap out of his reverie and do the same. Without signaling, Tim pulled right into a country driveway between wire fencing. It was a rutted dirt road with grass growing down the middle. Off to the side were pastures and farm equipment. Tim did a quick, bouncing U-turn with his lights off and glided quietly to a halt at the edge of the road.

Three dark cars sailed by and parked in tandem behind Crane's car. Crane walked back to consult with the drivers of the other cars. Then Crane got back into the Olds and resumed his trek. All four cars headed east, with Crane leading and Tim following at a distance.

As the late sun lay on the horizon in the west, it became apparent what the destination was. With the window open, Tim heard loud buzzing sounds and looked out to see several military cargo planes taking off or landing. A sign confirmed that they were approaching an airfield: *Livermore Naval Air Station*. At a nearby intersection, the street signs read East Avenue and Greenville Road. While Tim stared at the street signs, he almost missed the sudden turns made by the cars. All four cars drove past the airport a short distance and turned around. Tim had to avoid being noticed, so he turned left into the airfield itself. He followed a wide service road around the field. At the southern end were the control tower and other structures, and north of them a broad square with planes parked at the ends. As he watched, a silvery cargo plane droned in from the east. It was a C-47 Skytrain, military version of the Douglas DC-3. As Tim watched, the Skytrain flew down to a landing with its flashing lights rotating on top and underneath. Could this be what Crane and his cohorts were waiting for? Tim had nothing to lose. He felt desperate to do something, anything, to find Anna and make sure she was safe.

As the plane taxied down the runway, several dark green military cars left the control tower area and sped down the runway—three sedans, running low to the ground because they were filled with the dark shapes of men in uniform. The fourth car was an armored car with a white star and other military markings—probably an Army paymaster vehicle. Helplessly, wishing he knew what was going on, Tim watched as a side payload door opened in the plane. Technicians with upturned earmuffs hung in the open door, waiting as the plane turned at a slight angle and stopped. The sedans slowed down and stopped nearby. The armored car drove right up under the cargo door. Men climbed out from all the cars, carrying machine guns.

A Military Police jeep pulled up. "What's the matter, pal, are you lost?"

Tim's scalp prickled. Here he was, on a military airstrip, in a stolen car..."Yeah, sorry. I just came to watch the planes a little bit. Is that okay?"

"Naw." The MP, a little man in a gray windbreaker, with white helmet and leather, looked like an Irish pug. "Get back on the public road, Mac, or we'll have to haul you in."

"Yessir!" Tim said, putting the car in gear and rolling along with an apologetic wave. The MP jeep trailed him all the way around the airfield until he reached the main county road. He left the jeep sitting on the service road and turned right onto the county road to shake him.

He glimpsed activity at the recently landed plane. Men in overalls lowered a heavy-looking wooden box from the plane. It took several men to lower it, straining, whatever it was. It took several more men on the ground to carry it to the armored car and put it in the rear.

Tim only had to wait about five minutes before the armored car and its three companions came around the bend and turned onto the road headed toward San Francisco. Having seen the heavy object, he guessed it was the purpose of the entire operation. What little thing like that could possibly warrant so much attention? Could it merely be a harmless payroll transfer, with him sitting here as a complete fool?

If so, he was about to implicate himself in a robbery.

Crane's cars emerged from a side road. Tim had no way of warning the men in the government cars.

Crane's men drove alongside the Army cars. Four and four. Tim's spine prickled. Was it possible Crane's people could have known the exact number of escort cars?

The last three of Crane's cars turned on flashing red lights and sirens. Obediently, the Army convoy pulled over. Crane's vehicles blocked them.

Crane's lead car pulled up alongside the armored car.

A heavy moving van lumbered along, out of nowhere. It rammed the Army sedans one by one, forcing them into a ditch. One of the Army sedans actually rolled over. As dust drifted across the landscape, the drivers ran from the Crane cars toward the armored car. Crane had the armored car blocked off, and now he and his accomplices pulled the driver and his assistant out by the collars of their leather jackets. Army security men swarmed from the ditch, where Tim surmised a few others lay injured. The security men had machine guns, but Crane's men were quicker. After a brief, noise gun battle during which machine guns blazed, and the security men dropped back pulling their injured and dead with them.

Meanwhile, the two leather-jacketed drivers on the road each received a vicious blow of a pistol butt to the head, and lay motionless.

Within ten seconds, the armored car and one sedan screamed away down the county highway toward San Francisco. Several security men stood in the road, shooting, but they were stranded, beyond radio and telephone contact.

Tim stopped with a screech of tires and told the security men: "I saw the whole thing. Get in." The car rocked as they piled in. Tim sped off, with doors still closing. One of the security men was bleeding from the shoulder, and held it to staunch the blood, while still gripping his pistol with the injured hand. "Thanks!" one of the men said. "Who are you?"

"A U.S. Navy officer with a stake in all this. We'll flag down some cops along way," Tim said. "What's in the crate that they're after? Pay Muster money?"

"Some kind of energy bomb. Supposed to be really powerful and dangerous. Roadblocks are already set up," the men told him. "We weren't expecting an ambush, but we have the route blocked out."

Tim shook his head. "They get their info from inside sources, from spies and traitors. They aren't taking your routes. Look!" As he spoke, the armored car and the sedan left the road in a cloud of dust and plunged onto a country road that led up into hilly brown countryside. Tim made a split decision and screeched to a halt. "One of you guys get out. Flag down an MP or a highway patrolman who has a radio dispatch car. The rest of us will chase them."

Moments later, his car bounced along in the wake of the armored car.

"You have enough gas?" one of the men said worriedly.

"Half a tank."

"Press on!" someone said. The men had the windows open, had guns out, ready to shoot if they could get close enough to riddle the tires.

Abruptly, a half mile ahead, Crane changed tactics. They headed up a wide, gradual hill going west. A last bluish gleam of daylight lingered over the hilltop. The slope on which the cars raced was falling into shadow.

The armored car was the slowest of the vehicles.

Crane turned his sedan sideways and stopped to block Tim's car. Several men got out of Crane's sedan. The armored car kept on going.

The sedan was just a nuisance. Tim made a wide circle around it. Shots rang out, muzzles flashed in the dusk. The agents in Tim's car returned fire. Nobody seemed to hit anyone. Tim emptied his .45 at them. Empty shells arced smoking through the air.

Poof! One of headlights went out. Shattered glass *ting*ed against the windows.

Up ahead, the armored car reached the crest of the ridge and stopped. Tim saw men in silhouette against an orange-black sky and swirling clouds. They climbed out, opened the back doors, and wrestled out their heavy wooden crate.

On the distant horizon, a dark shape droned closer. It was a two engine plane, coming in low and slow with his flasher lights off. The pilot flew with firmness and skill. Suddenly, two large, glaring headlights blazing away.

The roadblock sedan's driver, realizing Tim had succeeded in running around him, started his engine and headed in an oblique path to ram Tim's car.

The plane, a B-26 Marauder medium bomber, came in low and fast. The pilot was hot—going to make a one shot landing. The men with the box stood ready. Their leader—Crane, Tim was sure—stood waving a revolver and looking directly at Tim's car.

The intercepting car roared up the hill, gaining. The agents in Tim's car were all on that side, shooting away.

Ting! Ting! Ting!

Bullets sang as they shattered windows and whizzed through the car. One made a hideous whistling sound as it raced by Tim's field of vision. The man beside him flew to one side, head hitting the window even as the window splattered with brainy gore.

Tim grabbed the gun from the dead man's hand and fired at Crane on his left while driving. He was right-handed, and had to fire resting the gun over his left elbow as he kept the gas pedal floored and his left hand on the wheel. The sedan bounced with screeches of tortured metal.

Blam! Blam! Blam!

Tim emptied the gun and dropped it on the floor so he could grab the wheel with both hands.

The car kept gaining.

Ahead on the ridge, the Marauder landed, bounced several times, and rolled to a stop near the armored car. It was too dark to see details. Silhouetted against the swirling orange sky, Tim saw figures moving, a shape being lifted on a steel bar by means of heavy straps.

A security man behind him screamed and abruptly fell silent. The intercept car seemed to be out of bullets. It was a powerful vehicle, and it gained steadily. Now it drew closer and Tim could see the gritted teeth and wild eyes of its driver as he gripped the wheel with both hands.

He rammed Tim transversely against the left front fender. Instead of crumpling, Tim's heavy car rolled smoothly over on its right, several times. Tim hung on to the ceiling straps and hoped for the best. He had the wind knocked out of him, and felt his body flying around as the car rolled over and over. Tim's eyes filled with grit, and his mouth became dry with dust from the field. Glass crackled like hot popcorn cooking, and bits of it sailed through the air. Tim covered his eyes. The car started to teeter as it rolled wildly, and gradually came to a rest on its side. Tim grabbed the gun out of a still figure's unmoving hand and climbed up through the driver's side window to offer combat.

"Stop him!"

"Drop the gun!"

"Don't shoot him. We need him!" *Whose male voice was that?*

"You're finished!"

"Stop right there!"

Tim was surrounded, and he slowly raised his hands. On the ridge, several men struggled with the box. The Marauder waited, idling its engines, feathering its propellers. Its headlights were off now, and the plane sat ready to kick up loudly roaring engines as it waited to take off. The pilot seemed patient and in control. Several men, holding guns on Tim in the fresh evening breeze amid grit flying in the prop wash, dragged him down from the car. Tim lay on the ground, face down, with his hands behind his back. A man's boot sat squarely in the center of his back with a heel on his left shoulder blade.

"Don't kill him. Malone wants him," Ivor Crane said.

Malone. Tim looked up, and saw Jaguar jogging down the hill waving a gun. The corners of his dark suit jacket flapped, and his hat flew off. "I want him!"

While Jaguar—or whatever his real name was—came closer, Ivor Crane regarded Tim with a certain haunted look in his eyes that said the game was over for Crane. "How did you know?" he asked Tim quietly.

Tim said: "It took me a year or so, as we were having bangers and mash back at that pub in London, to realize that you gave your game away long ago. When we first met, you said that the real Malone got a knife in the back in Mauritania."

"Yes?" Crane looked genuinely puzzled, and tense as if wondering what else Tim knew about him. No doubt there was a lot to know about Ivor Crane.

"You couldn't have known that. Willi didn't make it out alive, and he was the only one besides me who knew how Malone and that Belgian woman died. You knew, because you stabbed them. You made it back to Leopoldville before I did."

"Yes, and so?" Crane stared at Tim. "If it makes you feel any better, you nearly killed me with that Kraut's Luger. You missed by a hair."

"Too bad." Tim stared in turn, remembering the shadow who had stepped out of the bush and fired the shots that killed Willi and nearly finished Tim off too. "You killed them. Why?"

Crane grinned. "Malone was getting out of hand. Donovan didn't know Malone had gambling debts and was getting desperate. Malone was a smart intelligence officer and he was onto me." He shrugged with the fatalistic finality of one who had betrayed his family, his army, and his nation and had no rear exit left. "He had to die. The woman was just there."

"So you killed Malone and the woman. You stuck that knife in his back and I came along at an inconvenient moment. You could keep the drugs you were delivering, and keep their money, and so get paid twice." Tim spat at Crane's feet. "You had me impersonate Malone, and now this guy Jaguar is impersonating me—or Malone. Which is it? Quite a valuable guy, Malone, even though he's been dead for years."

"You poor, brainwashed, capitalist fool," Crane said. He stepped aside as Jaguar reached them.

Tim didn't know Jaguar's real name, and he could readily assume it was Russian, but he'd forever think of the man as Jaguar. He told Crane: "I hope you'll be happy living in Uncle Joe's worker paradise."

"Put him in the plane," Jaguar yelled hoarsely to the men, waving his gun at Tim.

Crane put his gun away and pulled his raincoat shut. He nodded to Jaguar and started to walk toward the plane. Without preamble, Jaguar loosed several bullets into Crane's back, and the man dropped onto the grass, where he lay in a weirdly twisted position, like a crumpled question mark of shock and betrayal. *He had to die*, Tim thought. How ironic. *Live by the sword, die by the sword.*

"And you," Jaguar said grinning. "Are you afraid to die?"

Listen to Naomi Meged, soldier who has killed men. I would die for you, sailor. "No," he told Jaguar directly eyeball to eyeball. Even Jaguar blanched a bit at Tim's steely coldness, but he recovered. "You have courage," Jaguar said, "but do you have courage for your girlfriend? Want to see her die?"

Anna? Tim thought.

"Lucky man," one of the men growled at Tim in a foreign-accented voice. "You get to live. Into the plane!"

"How convenient that you would show up just now," Jaguar told Tim. "You will add insurance that our little pilot does what she is told. Get in!" He motioned with his gun.

Corie! If he'd suspected she was the pilot, in the back of his mind, he was relieved that apparently she wasn't with them of her own will. He clambered up a steel ladder entering the bomb bay.

"What about the poor slobs in the car back there?" someone said. Several of the speakers had European accents.

"All dead or injured. They can't hurt us now."

"Leave them. Their pals will find them soon enough." Jaguar laughed and added: "They'll think Crane died gallantly in the line of duty, and they'll give him a hero's burial." Several men joined him in laughter.

As Tim boarded the plane, he entered into the central loading bay. Already sitting on the floor of the plane, strapped to a ring in the floor, was the wooden crate. It was a heavy pine box covered with phony shipping tags. It had heavy rope handles on four sides, and several tags signaling danger—no warnings of radioactivity, but Tim was sure if the box were dropped, and if the lead container inside broke, its handlers would die horribly.

The interior of the plane smelled of aviation gasoline and burnt welding flux and dirty canvas. Its sides were hung with olive-drab quilting and equipment. Tim was bundled into the plane and someone tied his hands behind his back with a thick, dirty rope.

Jaguar's four men climbed on board, carrying a badly injured fifth man. The dead ones being left behind would have no identifying papers. Jaguar's men threw large bundles on board and climbed in.

The bomb bay door slammed shut, and the plane jerked forward. It was designed for fast take offs, Tim knew from his casual reading in magazines and newspapers. A tricky plane to fly, which required highly skilled piloting, it could carry cargo or a bomb load of 3000 pounds, over a range of 2000 miles, at up to 300 mph, at a service ceiling around 20,000 feet. It would carry five crewmembers and offered as armament four 0.30-inch machine guns poking through at least one Plexiglas blister on top of the fuselage behind the wings. It was powered by two gutsy Pratt & Whitney R-2800 engines and when it took off, it shot along and zoomed up into the air fast enough to slam the unwary back in their seats.

The heavy crate strained at its anchoring bolts. The men in back held on to whatever they could. The deck pitched at a 45 degree angle as the plane climbed, piloted by a female *virtuosa* who would land in the dark on a bumpy hilltop with barely any lights, and take off into the unknown without fear.

Tim rolled backward and landed against a quilt-draped bulkhead.

"Tim!" a familiar woman's cry reached the cargo bay. Tim looked forward and there, through a Plexiglas interior window above a hulking storage unit, sat Corie in the pilot seat. She had a large shiner staining one side of her face, and her cheek bone looked as though someone had none too gently put a boot to it.

"Are you okay?" she cried.

"Yes! Just drive and watch where you are going!"

"We are heading for Montana!" she yelled. "I had to do it or they said they'd hurt Meg. I'm sorry, Tim!"

"Shut up!" Jaguar yelled.

"They're Soviets," she yelled to Tim. "Don't trust these lousy Commies." She yelled at Crane: "What are you going to do, shoot me?"

She rolled the plane left, right, left, yawing angrily in powerful snapping motions that sent men and equipment tumbling about. "Try me, you stupid dong. You hurt him, I'll kill all of us. Do you understand me, you Communist hyena?" She added: "They are making me fly to Great Falls, Montana, Tim."

Jaguar had a dark expression. He appeared to swallow hard, and he abruptly put his gun away. "We don't need any nonsense," he said. As the plane leveled out, he walked over to Tim and sat down. "Okay, Nordhall. How did you happen to get from there to here? I thought you were a dumb bastard, the way we led you around in London."

"I guess I learned a few tricks in the meantime."

Jaguar rubbed his palms up and down his face with a huge sigh of frustration. "What a nuisance."

"You hurt him," Corie said, "and I'll fly this tub into the first mountain I spot. Trust me. I don't make jokes, especially with larvae like you."

Tim noticed again, as he had in London, that Jaguar spoke excellent American idiom, but now Tim recognized the slight accent—*Russki*. He told Jaguar: "I finally did figure out you were not exactly on our side. What's your plan, Karl Marx?"

"I'll ask the questions. Don't press your luck."

Tim kept trying to assess the other man, looking for an opening, some weakness to exploit. Jaguar projected an air of seeming relaxed, but with some solid inner armor, some monumental self-assurance. *Another fanatic,* Tim thought. *Our age is full of them. Nuts on the right, nuts on the left.* "Looks like we're all trusting our luck here in this flying hand grenade. What's in the crate?"

Jaguar grinned, picking up on the metaphor. "The biggest hand grenade you ever saw. Pure German uranium oxide. Crane was working with my side the whole time."

"And you shot him."

"He was one of legions like him that work for us. You people don't stand a chance. The Socialist world will think back on you as we look back on cavemen."

"Pause for breath," Tim said. "You're turning blue."

"Bah!" Jaguar said. He waved to his men and said loudly. "Relax, everyone. This will go smoothly. Let's not waste our energy." He walked into the cockpit and sat in the empty co-pilot seat. He said loudly to Corie, so everyone could hear. "Let's make a nice deal, eh? You get us down in one piece, and I'll give you and this capitalist bitch a chance to run for your lives in the forest later. You'd like that, wouldn't you? Everyone wins. Do we have a deal?"

She glared straight ahead and said nothing.

He took out his pistol, cocked it, and aimed it long-armed at Tim's head.

She thrust her jaw out stubbornly.

He rose and walked toward Tim, keeping the gun aimed at Tim. "You want your little friend to live...?"

"Okay!" she yelled at Jaguar, while looking toward Tim the way the lioness in Mauritania had looked toward her cubs in the tower.

Jaguar grinned at Tim. "I was right. You're the perfect bargaining chip with this little spitfire."

Corie said: "It's a deal. Leave him alone!"

Tim said nothing, thinking that by now someone must have stopped to help the security man he'd left on the highway. Soon the government might figure out that a plane had landed to make off with the armored car's cargo. The tracks near the abandoned armored car alone would tell that story. From there, top-secret new radars could track the lone plane as it cruised through the sky.

Jaguar kept Tim and Corie apart. At times, Jaguar would go sit in the co-pilot seat and check the navigation maps and instruments. Tim, meanwhile, sat tied up by the rear bulkhead—insurance that Corie would do as she was told.

The Soviet agents opened some of the bundles they'd thrown in, and out came heavy clothing. They started dressing as if they were going to some Arctic *rendez-vous*...or maybe Alaska, Tim thought, and then Siberia?

As the hours passed, and the night wore on, Tim wondered if there would be a refueling stop, but he remembered the specs on the plane—because he'd worked on some retrofits and logistical spares concerns for all the major U.S. and Allied warplanes. If she were fully fueled—and he had no reason to think she wasn't—if these guys had planned right, then she could cruise 2000 miles on a fuel load. That would get them to Great Falls, no problem.

Great Falls...that would be the home of Malmstrom Air Force base. Tim's office in San Francisco had sent cases full of documents to the Russians via courier plane by this route. Given the horrific losses of ships on the North Atlantic convoy routes in 1941-3, FDR had set up a northern air route under Lend-Lease, sending everything but the kitchen sink to the Reds. The Soviets would load supplies at Malmstrom. U.S. pilots would fly the planes to Alaska, where Soviet pilots would board and fly the planes the rest of the way into Siberia and points beyond, anything from Anadyr to Leningrad. Tim had heard complaints that the Soviets had sticky fingers and tended to stuff anything that wasn't nailed down, including high-level secrets, into diplomatic courier pouches that were then immune from U.S. or Canadian search and seizure. Suddenly, the reason for the gunny sack with Soviet markings became apparent. This had to be one of the most audacious coups in history—stealing part of an atomic bomb right out from under the noses of the Americans—even as they were convoying it through San Francisco to the docks for shipping into the Pacific Ocean, to finally end up devastating some Japanese city—and then using U.S. aircraft under Lend Lease to fly the stolen parts to Soviet territory with impunity. It could become the most critical detour in history if Stalin's agents and fifth columnists got away with it.

"Where are we now?" Tim asked.

Jaguar waved gun at Tim. "Shut up. You don't want to know."

Tim kept his silence, but he was planning frantically. How to derail this plan, while saving at least Corie and, with luck, himself?

He had no way of talking with her. Any signals they sent each other would mean the other men on board would also see them. What to do?

He sat back, racking his mind, trying to remember details of the aircraft from his review of parts lists, catalogs, diagrams, photographs, manuals, anything that would provide a clue.

He tried to picture various scenarios, but they all ended up with him and Corie dead and the bomb materials lost.

Jaguar walked around handing out bomber-style breathing apparatus, but ignored Tim. Jaguar and two aides wore masks tied to the main aircraft oxygen supply. They dragged a large, bulky package toward the bomb crate—a parachute. It was a drogue chute, the kind used for dropping bulky things like crates of ammo or food or water close along the ground. They untied the satchel from its anchor ring. Then the men carefully and methodically prepared their satchel for air drop. They weren't going to land in the middle of Malmstrom Army Air Field and taxi around with stolen atomic bomb material. They were going to drop the satchel in the wild within a few hours' flight time. They'd recover it by automobile and drive to a secret location, where it would be properly repackaged in a sealed container under diplomatic immunity. Then, and only then, would Russians fly it to the airstrip at Malmstrom, as if it were coming directly by air from back east.

Jaguar and his men were anxious to get on with things, and they did not want to be caught short on time. They had their crate sitting on the deck, pretty as a present with a bow in it, ready to air drop. Yes, and the plane was a bomber, Tim thought, which meant it had a bomb bay. He watched Corie, and wondered what she was thinking. Corie studied the proceedings from the corners of her eyes, looking for an opening. Her blazing determination was scary.

The Rockies fell behind. The plane flew over Idaho and into Montana. Jaguar had his men open the double bomb bay door. The cabin whirled with cold, fresh air. Tim began to feel light-headed. Below, Tim knew, was a four mile high column of wide-open atmosphere and, sprawling below that, a wilderness of icy forests, mountains, and plains. If one were to lose a bomb in there, say by throwing it out prematurely, one might never see it again.

Jaguar's men pushed the heavy crate so that it rested by the open bomb bay.

The Soviet agents rigged explosives on a timer on the bank of oxygen tanks supplying the plane with breathing air. Tim puzzled about this, until he realized they weren't planning to land at all. That, in turn, meant Jaguar had lied, which was no surprise, given that he'd murdered Crane in cold blood. So what did it mean? They planned to parachute out with the uranium and let the plane explode in mid-flight to cover up any further evidence. That meant they must have quite an operation down on the ground. No doubt they were shipping everything to the USSR via Malmstrom except the Statue of Liberty, and that might be next. They seemed more frightening than the Nazis.

The fifth man had died, and Jaguar's men carried the body to the cockpit. They propped the dead man up in the co-pilot's chair and strapped the body in. He had been changed into Army flying togs and looked quite authentic. Jaguar's intention, it seemed, was to fake a plane crash. As a charred mess of fragments, who would ever know the real truth of what had happened here at 20,000 feet? Tim felt an ever greater sense of urgency, not only to abort their mission, but to save Corie's life, and his own.

Jaguar, who had been studying the navigation map again, seemed to feel Tim's thoughts at the back of his head. "Don't worry," he told Tim, "I have a plan to fix you right up." He told Corie: "If you choose to kill us all at this point, my people will recover the crate anyway, so that's no longer a threat."

"Let him go," Corie said to Jaguar, about Tim, as she shook with anger and fear. Her black eye was darker than ever. Her teeth were gritted with determination.

Jaguar and two men maneuvered the quarter-ton crate closer to the bomb bay. Their hair whipped in the wind, and they looked alien with their breathing tubes dangling from black snouts. Tim watched the other two men as they readied the bomb sight. This was going to be a precision drop, probably into some mountain valley where other men might be waiting with a pickup truck.

Tim lay helplessly against the bulkhead where they had tied him. Icy cold wind shot in through tiny cracks in the metal around him; the plane had evidently seen a good deal of use. The metal itself was chilly as a refrigerator.

Jaguar stepped around the Norden bombsight and peered into it. The highly secret apparatus was capable of logically computing factors such as velocity, altitude, and more, in conjunction with the operator's precise visual aiming at the target. "Ten minutes over target," newly appointed bombardier Jaguar announced. A slight wind current bucked the plane. Jaguar glanced up. "Don't try anything cute," he growled at Corie, who still flew loosely with both hands on the controls so that her whole body rocked in sympathy with each bounce. She was perfect, Tim thought—a symphony pianist at her clavier.

The Soviet agents started putting on parachutes. Now Tim understood the heavy leather clothing and goggles. They weren't going to Alaska or Siberia just now. They were about to parachute into the night above Montana...right near some Soviet lair outside Malmstrom airbase.

"Goodbye, Corie," Tim said. "I love you." He signaled for her to get her chest breathing pack ready.

"I love you too, Hon." She fluttered her eyelids like signals. "Sorry, I can't do anything to help us now."

"Steady on course," Jaguar growled. "Remember our deal."

She retorted: "I'll remember it if you do. Give him air, you asshole."

"All right," Jaguar said. He tossed a breathing pack with a small tank at Tim. Then he bent down to untie one of Tim's hands so Tim could work the mask over his face if the need came. The mask covered the mouth and nose. It had an articulated hose that could be plugged into either a chest oxygen pack or to a system of pipes supplying oxygen to various locations within the aircraft. Tim would not be able to reach the nearest outlet. "No tricks," Jaguar said as he freed Tim's hand while keeping a gun pointed at him.

Jaguar stepped back to the ongoing operation by the open hatch. "Steady," he said, looking down into a bombsight. The other men leaned against the crate containing the bomb material in its heavy container, wrapped in the parachute.

Tim and Corie exchanged desperate looks. Both were calculating, split second by split second. Their situation stood at the edge of hopeless. Jaguar and his men were all wearing parachutes now. It was clear—they'd drop the bomb, jump ship, and maybe throw a grenade as the last man dove out the hatch. Tim and Corie were doomed—minutes from death.

"Steady," Jaguar said. "Two minutes until the drop."

For a second, the other four men were frozen in a posture to push. They bent forward, ready to strain against the pallet holding the bomb. Breathing tubes hung from their faces.

"One minute," Jaguar said, holding his black snout against his face as he looked down into the bombsight.

Suddenly, Jaguar and his minions backed away coughing and yelling. They tore their masks off and doubled over, choking. Jaguar turned red as a beet, and his eyes were wide in horror as spittle dribbled from his tomato-red mouth.

Corie laughed as she waved a piece of tubing, while winking at Tim. He saw what she had done: of the various conduits running along the bulkheads, she had disconnected an elbow joint in the main oxygen line. She had similarly disconnected some other line—probably the fire extinguishing system, with its unbreatheable and no doubt toxic contents—and then she'd hooked the two together using the breathing hose from her own node of the plane's central breathing system. She'd switched to a free chest pack from under her seat.

Still tied up, Tim strained desperately to reach the nearest of the agents in the hope of snagging a gun. *No luck.*

Corie used her booted foot to shoot a weapon across the steel-grated floor at him: a flare pistol.

Jaguar and his men were still choking and helpless, but they wouldn't be for long. Jaguar had boundless determination. Every split second counted now. Jaguar had no time to shoot Corie or Tim just then. Already, Jaguar hung over the bombsight like a drowning man over a life preserver, wiping his eyes with his sleeves while staring down into the aiming viewer. He dribbled mucus, saliva, tears, even flecks of vomit onto the glass surface. "Come back around!" he yelled at Corie.

Corie said "Your ass!" and stepped from the cockpit. Her parachute straps dangled nearly to the floor as she ran to Tim's side. With a wicked-looking utility knife, she cut him loose from the bulkhead.

Jaguar screamed: "Damn you!" as he spotted a pistol on the ground. As he reached for the weapon, Corie wrapped a heavy-duty cargo strap around herself and Tim. Together, Tim and Corie sidled toward the bomb bay.

Jaguar's companions were recovering from their own vomiting fits and came running around the side of the crate. Tim shot them with the flare gun, and they backed away screaming in a bundle of flaming greenish-yellow phosphorus and waving arms as their flesh dissolved. Their goggles looked otherworldly as they screamed and batted at their flaming clothes.

Jaguar aimed his pistol and fired. The shot went wild.

The plane bucked, and Jaguar staggered back against the bulkhead, holding his arm up to shield his eyes.

Corie threw the knife, hard—and it stuck in Jaguar's shoulder.

She and Tim worked their way past the burning crate and jumped into the night.

Above them, the plane sailed away, with the men inside screaming. The plane glowed like a lantern about to explode.

A single parachute fluttered away. "Damn! That's got to be him!" Probably the unstoppable Jaguar, Tim thought. Malone dies again, only to be reborn again some other time.

Tim clung to her, and she to him, as they were jerked about violently in the freezing wind. He nearly blacked out. Without oxygen at this altitude, he'd be dead soon. Corie shared her breathing pack with him, swapping the black rubber mouthpiece back and forth.

Their last view of the plane was as it sailed away glowing, and trailing smoke, a roiling funeral pyre. When it was a good five miles away over empty mountains, its fuel lines caught, and streamers of bluish flame licked around the plane. Then a shower of sparks. A powerful explosion that sent the wings flying off and buckled the fuselage in half. The wing tanks exploded, and a deluge of fire and radioactive dust tumbled down through the atmosphere.

Tim and Corie sailed silently down into the bosom of an enormous impenetrable pine forest, and he bet that forest rangers would find them before Jaguar's accomplices did.

Change of script. Man sits typing. Yanks copy off roller, lays it next to typewriter, inserts new sheet. Keeps typing. Keys hammer down under fingertips, inked ribbon jumps and rolls under determined and steady keystrokes as words pour onto new sheet of paper.

July 15, 1945 Jaguar comes for Meg

Meg waited until dark before she started to cry—Naomi Meged, man killer.

As the sun sank down into the Pacific Ocean, she stood looking out over the city and considered what she must do. Her choices were limited now. She loved Corie and Tim—but she would never see them again.

Ferenc, the blond Communist ick, Alger Hiss' sidekick, had spoken of using Corie as pilot for some new venture. What could it be that was so important that the *Rezident* had pulled Ferenc off the UN case and put him on this new thing? She had decided to blow her own cover. She had gone to the FBI and told them about the uranium. What else could she have done? Now, however, the Soviets were probably on to her. It was only a matter of time before they came, to take her away to the USSR for a final date with Stalin's torturers. They had a long bill of accounts with her, and she would pay dearly. She knew all this, but at the moment she could only think of how lovely life would have been with Tim and Corie. She smoked cigarette after cigarette as she thought about these things. She carried a hankie wadded up in one hand. It was soaked with tears she had cried. Her stomach was full of twisted knots.

Meg stood at the high window and contemplated the yawning, dizzying distance down into the courtyard below. Only days ago she had stood there with Tim, passionately kissing. Now that all seemed so far away. She looked down and contemplated taking the quick and easy way, rather than letting NKGB do their creative work inside Treblinka.

San Francisco seemed to feminine, so pretty, so safe, such a mix of Occident and Orient. Every breath of life here brought exquisite pleasure to one who knew she was condemned to die soon.

Soon enough...

For now, she stripped her clothes off and prepared a long, hot bath. She sat in the bath tub smoking and drinking, but it gave her no pleasure, no relief. Her entire life was a lie, a horrid mess, even when she was trying to serve her new country and do right. It would all turn out badly in the end.

She felt the water growing cool around her, even as the walls and the windows dripped with perspiration.

She toweled herself dry and went into the living room. She poured herself a full martini glass of vodka, and threw in a slice of lemon. She didn't bother to add ice in the American manner.

It was just a matter of waiting now. Soon, all too soon, it would be over.

She turned on the radio and sat in the living room listening to Glenn Miller. In her soul, she took a ride on the A Train. How she loved America! She loved every breath of its air, every beat of its music, every grin of its raw and trusting but powerful heart. She loved the U.S.A. as she loved life itself, even with her shining dream of a future Jewish state. Tears ran down her cheeks. Eyes closed, she sobbed. Their ghosts were there, laughing around her: Tim and Corie, her loves. Would they understand how much she loved them? Would they understand she had spared them by not trying to contact them now?

Then, too, there was the new baby growing in her womb. She turned the radio off and stubbed her cigarette out. What use was anything? She wiped her eyes with her sleeves, sniffling. She did the only thing she could then, and started packing a small suitcase. No baby things. Not yet necessary. She'd left her last set of those in Ankara. What few things she had hidden way, saved up from the long-ago summer when she'd almost become a mother, but for the kicking and beating by the Turkish monster, when he'd thrown her down a flight of stairs in Ankara. Sobbing in slow, continuous hiccups, she placed her clothing into the valise—a piece at a time, carefully folding each item.

Then came the knock at the door.

She whirled. *So soon!*

The knock came again, more urgently.

"Yes?" she wailed.

"Miss Varkidjian. Open this door now." It was Mutsev. He 'd come for her as she had known he would. He was following orders, as she had been. He must be NKGB. Then it was all over. They could not be stopped. "You use more names than I do." He pounded on the door. "Open up right now!"

She walked over and turned the latch. She let the door shudder open, and he pushed it open gently but relentlessly, the way peasants drowned unwanted kittens. "Are you ready?" he asked.

"I'm ready." She put into the bag a small doll of Corie's, and a book Tim had been reading. Things to remember them by. Then she closed the suitcase. She put on her long, drab overcoat and green hat with the feather in it. She looked at herself in the mirror, and noticed that Malone and two other men were waiting silently. Like rocks, these NKGB men. They knew they would own the world soon enough. She picked up her valise and turned out the light.

The men waited in the hallway.

She took a last look around and then pulled the door shut behind her.

Mutsev took her elbow and pushed her along. The walk down the stairs with these big, rock-like men, through the courtyard, took minutes but seemed like hours. Her heart felt as though it must burst out of her chest with sadness as she looked for the last time on this lovely free city, from the car, as they took her past the *Rezidentura* at the Soviet Consulate—no need to stop there; all the arrangements were made, she was sure—and then down to the harbor. There, a ship awaited, *Kalinin*. In a few weeks, the ocean would lie behind her, with this whole glittering world, and the vastness of Russia would swallow her into its bosom, never to let her go again.

Carrying her valise, she walked from the car to the gangway, followed by the NKGB men and Mutsev/Malone/Jaguar/whoever he was. Fog roiled up as she walked across the rickety wooden bridge, and a sailor leaned above, looking down at her with his arms folded on the damp steel railing. Here and there, under greenish tin shades like Chinese hats, glowed small islands of light, 75 watts against the vast night and the sea.

When she walked into the dim corridor that smelled of sweat and cabbage, she knew she was almost home again. Not in the home she had chosen, but the hell from which she had escaped, from the Middle East to the lower Caucasus.

On the empty dock outside, fog swirled in. A single light stayed lit a while, and then it too winked out.

Change of script. Man sits typing. Yanks copy off roller, lays it next to typewriter, inserts new sheet. Sheets beside typewriter multiply. Man keeps typing. Keys hammer down under fingertips, inked ribbon jumps and rolls under determined and steady keystrokes as more words pour out.

July 15, 1945 Tim: *U.S.S. Indianapolis*

Tim burst into the apartment. Everything was terribly wrong. There was an emptiness, a coldness, that had not been here before. Silence weighed the air like a smothering blanket of frigid Arctic air. Tim stood still and listened. His shadow fell across the fine wooden floor, head bowed, as he listened to a distant piano music whose plaintive notes fell, one by one, like raindrops, into the moonlight that played on glowing oak floorboards.

"Meg?" He knew she was gone, but he rushed to her room anyway. He noted the drawers hanging partially open, half empty. He noted that her suitcases were gone, her perfume table half empty. The place still smelled faintly of her—Chanel No. 19, Shalimar, Matchabelli—but it was a faint essence, as if she'd gone weeks or even months ago.

He looked in the bathroom, the living room, everywhere, and her dear effects were gone. She must have left in a hurry, perhaps under duress, for she'd taken only essentials. His book was gone, as was Corie's favorite doll.

Another shadow fell across the doorway. Mutsev/Malone/Jaguar, the man of a thousand identities? No—Ivor Crane. "Looking for someone, Nordhall?"

"Yes."

"She's gone, Tim." Crane lit a cigarette without effort despite the prosthesis, ever so carefully, snapping the lid on the flat silver case shut, slipping it in his pocket, then clicking the Zippo open, licking off the blue flame before clicking the lighter shut and letting it sink of its own accord beneath the waves of his pale raincoat pocket. He exhaled a long grayish flume that curled in midair and expanded under the wan overhead light.

"I know," Tim said feeling beaten. Without her, it seemed of little use to go on. He stood with his head lowered and his fists balled at his sides.

"The FBI will be coming for you now."

"I don't care."

"Oh, but there is still Corie. You should come with me. I have a safe place for you."

"Let me get a few things." He picked out his kit bag, the small one that resembled a bowling ball bag. He threw his shaving gear, some underwear, a few essentials in it. He took her smallest perfume bottle for the memory— the Shalimar that had been nearly empty for so long it seemed bone dry, but it still smelled of her. And there was a little keepsake of Corie, a tiny silver spoon she'd had as a baby; he took that too.

"Hurry," Crane said.

Tim paused in the doorway, taking a last look. He knew this was a place he could never return to. Even if he spent his last years building clocks in a drafty warehouse down in New Haven Harbor near the Quinnipiac Pier, that would be less painful than ever facing this again.

He switched off the light and pulled the door shut. The walk down the stairs took forever, it seemed, and like life itself was over before he'd begun to fully be aware of its happening.

They walked down together, through the courtyard that smelled of jasmin, and to his car parked at the curb with an official U.S. Army tag in the window so no cop would think to ticket him. Crane put him at the wheel, reminding him with a little mime that he had a gun in his pocket, so no tricks. Tim drove down the cobblestone streets in silence. Tim felt the tires slipping a little on the damp trolley rails. Crane lit another cigarette. He chewed gum at the same time, and slouched lazily in his seat, American style, the Yank casual style that the world loved so much now, which said goodbye to all the horrors of war that had cost so many millions of innocent lives.

Soon they arrived in the harbor, at a checkpoint outside a tall wire fence guarded by MPs with rifles and dogs. It was foggy, and a slight drizzle moved in. He could hear the stealthy, cat-like rattle of tiny drops on the glass and the roof as he got out.

Crane threw his cigarette butt aside and came around the car. He stood looking at Tim, who held his lapels together and stood looking back. Crane extended his good hand. "Goodbye, Tim. Good luck."

Tim reached out and shook the other man's surprisingly strong, dry grip. "Thanks. Who knows. We might even bump into each other again some day."

Crane smiled thinly. "I doubt it, Tim. But it's been swell." He looked up at the ship's huge black steel rear. Shadows and light played under the snappy brim of his hat. "The *U.S.S. Indianapolis*, Tim. She's going to carry the fissionable material to an island not far from Japan, where technicians will put together those two bombs. A uranium bomb and a plutonium bomb."

They heard a faint, distant droning sound in the sky. Both men listened. Crane said: "Some of the material is going by plane." Tim and Ivor Crane looked up as a dark shadow passed noisily through a bright area where the moon poked through between huge dark clouds. "That will be Corie now in her B-29, flying the bullet that you two saved from the Russians in Montana. She'll be waiting for you when you arrive in Tinian." He patted his hand against the black hull, which made a bottle-like twanging sound. "This is the only place we can hide you, Tim. You'll be safe here. This is the only place where the people who took Meg away won't be able to reach you."

Tim nodded and stooped to pick up his bag. "So long, then."

Crane waved, and Tim walked away into the fog.

He could smell the seaweed, the stink of low tide, could hear water and trash and kelp slapping against the cruiser's thick stern keel section as he crossed the gangway. A sailor standing guard with a loaded M-1 saluted, and Tim nodded as he waved his I.D. card and stepped onto the deck.

Change of script. Man yanks another sheet off roller, lays it next to typewriter, inserts new sheet. Sheets beside typewriter multiply. Gray shadows dance around the room as man keeps typing. Keys hammer down under fingertips, inked ribbon jumps and rolls under determined and steady keystrokes as words pour out. It is a melancholy night music.

Captain McVay came down to see him several times. McVay was pleased with himself for the record speed and the good morale on the ship. The war was winding down, and both Tim and McVay understood the terrifying cargo the ship carried. Good thing it was in the right hands.

Wind tousled McVay's graying hair as they stood side by side on the bridge. "You are welcome to stay on Tinian."

"No thanks," Tim said. "I think the war will be over soon and I want to go home. I'm going back with you on the ship."

"Do you have someone waiting for you at home?"

"Maybe. I'll have to go home and see. One woman, anyway. There were two."

"Every sailor worth his sea-salt has at least two." McVay grinned knowingly, knowing nothing. "Does that special one love you?"

No point explaining the incomprehensible. "As far as I know."

"You love her?"

"Yes."

"Then that should work out just fine." Faintly puzzled, McVay slapped him lightly on the back. "Sounds like you'd prefer two of them, sailor."

"No," Tim said softly, "that can only happen once in a lifetime."

She was I-58, a Japanese submarine that would live in infamy.

U.S.S. Indianapolis, now serving as a troop ship carrying over 1,400 men, many of them wounded, crossed in front of her bow tubes two days out of Tinian. *I-58* released her final salvo of the war. The troop ship got off one short signal under the wheel of the Milky Way: *May Day, May Day, May Day...* The first torpedo blew off her bow, severing her radio mast and preventing any more transmissions.

Naval headquarters at Pearl Harbor and other locations received her distress call, but thought it was a Japanese hoax, and refused to send planes or ships to investigate. Three hundred men went down with the ship immediately. Another 900 bobbed in the sea for over five days. They were hungry, thirsty, and harassed by sharks. The wounded went down first, then the healthier men. Sharks would circle in and pull a man down by his legs from amid his mates.

At one time, the men thought they heard the droning of a circling aircraft, but it never landed. Some swore they heard its engine sputtering far away as it flew off. Others said it was merely in illusion. One of many illusions. Some sailors went mad with thirst and drink sea water, which made them die choking in an agonizing death under the blistering sun by day or the cold silver moon by night. Others tried to bite open the necks of living shipmates clinging to flotsam with them, to drink their blood.

After nearly a week, Navy carrier planes spotted the drifting flotsam and survivors. A rescue mission got underway, but only 316 men were pulled from the water alive. Tim Nordhall was not among them.

July 15, 1945 Corie: Liberator

Corie and her co-pilot, an older WAFS, took turns at the controls. In the back were a half dozen Army nurses in their off-green uniforms, playing cards and laughing and smoking. The weather was uneventful through the whole trip. The giant B-29 droned high up in the sky over miles and miles of Pacific Ocean that looked like rippled dark green-blue glass.

Locked in a special compartment way in the back was the bullet that would be shot into the world's first atomic bomb used in war.

Corie knew she should feel relaxed, but she felt an odd sense of foreboding through the entire flight.

Only Corie had clearance to know about the secret cargo. She went aft three or four times to sit with the bomb, which had been retrieved from Montana and specially reassembled at Berkeley Radiation Lab and shipped to Tinian as part of the drop on Japan. She'd flown to Oakland on a B-24 Liberator piloted by a couple of joking civilian Lend-Lease pilots, with the bomb. Or, as some Army Air Corps colonel with a doctorate in physics loftily and vaguely explained to everyone on board, it was a spare trigger for such a bomb. Tim had sat next to Corie through the whole flight. She wanted to hold hands but it wasn't permitted. At Oakland, Corie had kissed Tim goodbye—a lingering, melancholy kiss, full of longing for them to be back together, and troubled by the ringing and ringing and ringing of the telephone at the Hotel Auger. Why wasn't Meg answering? Was she sick? Was it another horrid session with the blond ick? God, how she longed for it all to be over.

Then, as she sat alone, piloting the plane over the vast Pacific Ocean, she'd looked up at the stars and had that strange premonition that she'd never see Tim again. That tore through her heart like a knife. And Meg? What of her?

Next morning, she awakened groggily on a cot in back. The other WAFS had been flying the box for several hours and wanted to be sure Corie could co-pilot in case something went wrong.

The descent and touchdown were flawless.

Several scientists and colonels in jeeps met the plane. A deuce and a half truck lumbered up, its canvas cover half off, its wooden ribs exposed and shaking.

Several privates under the direction of a corporal and a major lifted the device off the plane and into the truck waiting below. Then they closed the canvas and off they all went, leaving Corie to her thoughts.

It was lonely without Tim and Meg. She tried having a drink at the base club, but only caused a fight between two groups of sailors. She sneaked out the back door as the MPs and the Shore Patrol showed up waving their white billy clubs. She heard one more chair fly through the air and shatter glass as she stuck her thumb out on the busy main drag and hitched a ride to the V/BOQ.

The dead man, Crane, came by and spoke with her. "You should get back to San Francisco. That's where Tim is headed on the Indianapolis after they pick up more wounded at Leyte."

"Is that where he went?"

He nodded, looking at her in grave manner with his forehead lowered and his eyes boring into her soul, before he walked away with his hands in the pockets of his pale raincoat.

Next morning, a low pressure cell pulled in fronts of rain squalls.

Orders arrived for her to fly a B-29 back to Frisco, but she demurred, saying she wasn't up to it. If she had trouble on her mind, its name was Tim. She inquired about him. The travel office informed her: "Yes, *U.S.S. Indianapolis* sailed out of here three days ago headed for Guam. Should be long on her way to Leyte by now with your man safely on board."

Corie scratched her head, thinking something was wrong here. "Has there been any message or anything?"

"No," the young Navy yeoman said, hustling back and forth in his white crackerjack uniform. "They are all under strict radio silence." He made a face and looked left and right. By instinct, she stuck her head close to listen, just as he stuck his head close to whisper: "There was a distress call, but it was just a single short message, and GHQ is sure it was a Japanese hoax to draw innocent rescue ships in and then torpedo them."

Corie stood on tiptoes. "Didn't they send up at least one plane to check and make sure they're okay?"

The clerk sadly shook his head. "Can't spare a single aircraft."

Corie hitched a ride back to her room from a fat sailor in a jeep. She dug her orders out of the trashcan and walked and ran down the runway to the travel section. She stood in line, twiddling her hair nervously, and when it was her turn, she shoved the orders across. "These came when I was still in the air. I missed this flight. Can you set me up with a new one?"

The clerk, a female lieutenant with freckles, checked her notebooks and a clipboard. "Hmm...Ma'am, there is not another B-29 ready to go. I do have a B-24 Liberator that's got to go to Leyte."

"Perfect! I'll take it."

"Oops. I don't have a co-pilot lined up. You'll have to wait a day or two for a flight plan."

"Can't."

"But Ma'am, regulations..."

"Gotta go, honey. Just clock me in and I'll sign any paperwork I need to. I'll bring my own co-pilot and navigator, don't worry."

She left the young officer looking perplexed as she rushed to the airstrip. There, she checked in copies of her orders, signed in, and then got suited up for her flight.

A B-24 sat on the flight pad—checked out, fueled up, ready to roll. Mechanics just finished oiling one of its four powerful engines. She was an aesthetically lovely craft, with big strong wings on a silver fuselage, and a twinned tail like two coins standing on edge. Handled well, had a lot of range.

Corie hotwired a jeep under an overhang. *Girl's gotta do what a girl's gotta do.* She drove the stolen jeep, no lights, top down, through stinging drizzle out onto the tarmac, far from the tower. Water ran down her head, dripped from her nose and chin, blinded her eyes. She wiped it absently away as she raced under the wing. She climbed from the jeep without bothering to shut it off.

Corie climbed on board. Quickly she put on overalls and a heavy parachute. She started up the engines and checked out the systems one by one. A mechanic came on board and said: "Ma'am, where is your flight crew?"

"They'll be here any minute. I'm just warming her up."

"Let me know if I can help," he said, looking cocky, showing off.

"I'll be fine," she said offering that sunny little wink that made guys like him wilt or want to conquer worlds for her. "You can finish checking out the wing fuel pods and the RADAR scoop. But first, would you take that jeep I came in, and drive to the tower to pick up my flight crew. They'll have the papers. Then you can drive the jeep to the motor pool and you're free to go."

"Will do, Ma'am. Thank you!" he said, clambering happily down the ladder. That would keep him busy long enough, Corie thought as she busied herself in the cockpit. To rescue Tim, she must have a good, operative airplane. Satisfied, she slammed the cockpit door shut and put on her earphones. She strapped herself in and put her feet on the floor pedals. She'd flown at least two dozen missions in this type, and she knew the plane well. It took her five minutes of walking her fingertips around to get rid of the feel of B-29 and whatever else she'd flown lately and get the Liberator feeling back in her soul. Humming to herself, she released the brakes. The plane began to taxi. She radioed the tower and told them she and her flight crew were ready for takeoff.

"Negative, Liberator. We do not have a flight plan on deck for you."

"You have it right there in front of you."

"Liberator, negative."

"Take another look. It's right there where I put it not 30 minutes ago."

There was a brief silence. She cranked up the engines.

"Liberator, stand down."

During that time, she revved the four engines and they laid down a deafening carpet of noise on the otherwise quiet and empty night strip.

"Liberator, return to base. That is a direct order."

Corie took off her headgear and dropped it by her side.

Liberator, Liberator, Liberator…

Gripping the wheel with both hands, working the foot pedals, she took that big stallion between her legs and started down the runway. *Get out of my way.*

Soon, she was doing over a hundred knots. The engines roared and everything shook and rattled. Corie rocked and rolled with the flow, her hands easy on the controls, her cap firmly above one eye. The plane's nose tilted up, , ready to start gulping clouds.

She caught a brief glimpse, far back and below, of twirling red lights pouring out of a hangar and following her down the runway but she reached up and adjusted her ailerons. It was a little bit tricky working foot pedals, side sticks, and overhead levers, but she'd brought in planes on one engine, planes on one wheel, planes with half a wing missing, and this was nothing. She grimaced determinedly as that big bird drew laminar airflow over its skin like a woman wanting to be caressed. Steadily, she thundered up, higher and higher, into the night sky and then leveled off at 30,000 feet in the direction of Leyte. That would be a long haul, but she was well rested, and she'd take her lumps when she landed. They might ground her, but they needed all the pilots like her that they could find. Besides, after the war they'd want to send her back to a sewing machine in Kansas, and that would be impossible for her. Not after helping to win World War II. She had nothing to lose. All she wanted was to find Tim.

She flew into a high, solid gray front. It looked like a wall of gray smoke, reaching out to embrace her, to welcome her into its dour embrace.

Lightning flashed.

She turned her radio receiver on, and skimmed the airwaves for any news of *U.S.S. Indianapolis*. Nothing. Not a peep. She caught Tokyo Rose, AFN Pearl Harbor, a short-wave sender from Seattle—no *Indianapolis*.

She thought she heard a man's faint voice amid all the scattered whistles and clicks and squelches and tweets of a disturbed radio air. Very faint:

May Day, May Day, May Day…

Probably just hearing things. She'd have to drop down and look visually.

Rain started peppering the window glass. The Liberator had a high, generous cockpit with plenty of overhead visibility. She could put it on autopilot and go down to peer through the machinegun blisters in the nose, tail, top, and under the fuselage. She thought about that, tongue protruding from a corner of her mouth, and decided not yet.

Wind buffeted the plane. Water rocketed around her. Corie strapped herself in and flew lower. The lower she went, the thicker and rougher the air got. Rain smashed against the windows. The fuselage made loud banging and pinging noises as its skin changed shape, cooling down on its metal skeleton.

Once or twice, the whistling on the radios seemed to be interrupted by static, and amid the static she could hear voices talking. Sometimes it was Japanese, sometimes English, sometimes Dutch, sometimes Venusian or something. Yiddish? Armenian? Hard to say.

Her dials jumped in unison each time she hit a little bump in the air and the plane rattled as if it had flown through someone's window. She heard a crash like broken glass, but it was just the equipment, the radio tubes, the glasses in the aft galley. Once she heard a crack, and glass falling, and figured a mirror must have broken in the mid-fuselage head. Not worth getting up to check.

By her reckoning, she was now in the area where *Indianapolis* should be if the ship were still steaming full flank to avoid Jap subs. Dread gripped her gut again. That, and the baby she was carrying. It was Tim's, no doubt about it. She must find him and make him understand he must come back.

The storm kept smashing against the fuselage, and the wings whipped up and down as if she were a bird trying to flap, but this bird was built to endure, and she kept on gloriously flying through the night.

By dawn, the storm's fury had lessened. The lightning had stopped. Gray dawn light poured down into the cockpit, where Corie sat singing to herself. "Rock-a-bye baby, in your crib..."

She looked out at the citron sun ball trying to poke through bad cigar clouds and sang: "Tim, darling, talk to me baby, talk to me honey, give me a sign..."

There, in the water, she spotted a box. The box, with one corner sticking up, rocked strongly up and down in the waves. She circled around several times, but could not make out any symbols. Dammit, too bad this wasn't a clipper or she'd set it down and clamber down to look. The awful truth began to dawn on her as she saw more bits of wreckage. A big ship had gone down here. A black slick, yellow with sunshine, spread its evil and frightful fingers on the sea below. It was full of lumpy things. She soared down for a look, skimming as low as she dared. Not a soul waved to her. Nothing, nobody alive in all that fuel and diesel oil. She roared in a wide circle, spewing up foam.

She bit her lip, and a tear rolled down. "Tim, your baby and I are here. Where are you?" She picked up her headset and twiddled the dials, but the radio was out. Silence or not, it didn't matter any more. She circled for hours, navigating by the sun and her chronometer. Rain squalls came and went, peppering her windows like tears. One thing was sure now. *Indianapolis* wasn't going to make Leyte, not today, not this week, not in this lifetime. And that was all she had, this lifetime.

She got the short-wave working, and tried tapping out a Morse code message, but no reply came. She kept tapping out S.O.S., S.O.S., S.O.S., and the coordinates, until one by one the engines fell silent, and in one last lunge the plane made some clunking noises as the wings cooled, and down she went, in a cartwheel, sending up emerald sheets of spray full of lace stitchings like a sewing machine, and that was that. How cold it was here, like this. *Tim, it's your baby and me...looking for you, honey...*

Water poured in—huge jade waterfalls of it. Japanese wind chimes tinkled—dark, and sinking fast.

Moscow, 1991 Moscow: Countess & Colonel

Marianne sat in the Aeroflot passenger liner, watching rain dribble down the window as her giant aircraft nosed in at a terminal in Sheremetyevo International Airport. The Soviet Union was breaking up, faster and more completely than the world could have imagined. The land of mystery, with its purposely false maps and huge espionage budget and paranoia, had opened its windows, and fresh air was blowing in. The air, however, was not that of the West, but of Russia—the real Russia, not the Communist house of cards, not the land of Stalin's hammer and Lenin's sickle.

Marianne was surprised—shocked—that she unexpectedly felt a crushing sense of her personal history and destiny in the heavy, damp air around her. As soon as the doors opened, there was an inrush of fresh air, smelling of exhaust fumes, rain, and wet soil. Mother Russia was the womb from which Marianne had been born. She had sprung from the bloody, muddy, fish-rotten, mosquito-gnawed, tragic, vegetal fecundity of Siberia. The minute she stepped through the door and inhaled fresh air, she had a strangely exhilarating, intoxicating sense of being reborn—of relief, almost, of being closer to the truth. She was home—body and soul.

She was part of this unparalleled super-nation sprawling across eleven time zones and embracing much of Europe and Asia. These exotic people were her countrymen and country women. She shared deep parts of herself with them, which she had not realized until this moment. She thought of her dear mother, and held a small airline blanket as she cried quietly to herself.

Like a sister, a beautiful blonde stewardess with Mongol eyes, who could have been Auntie Dora's daughter, came and knelt beside her, put her arm around Marianne's shoulder, and held her while she cried. The stewardess asked no questions. Maybe in Russia it was expected that you cried amid glory and catastrophe. Marianne leaned against the young woman, who rocked her gently with one shoulder. Marianne keened into the damp folds of the blanket, as wind sings through ageless forests. She inhaled the woman's scents of sweet flower soap and starchy uniform linen, and thought she was home. She lost track of time, but soon she rose, reinvigorated, and her briefly spawned sister drifted off, carrying a piece of Marianne with her as she aided other passengers, while Marianne carried a piece of the unknown Siberian girl with her.

📖

The plane looked remarkably like a Lockheed Tristar with the third engine at the top rear of the fuselage, Marianne thought as she carried her two small valises off. The Soviets had copied superficialities from the West, without changing Russia itself. She was about to meet an obscure agent whose code name in London during the war had been Jaguar.

There was a muted, enduring sense of continuity as the attractive Slavic stewardesses in their dark uniforms, and the handsome young cockpit crew, stood shaking hands and wishing passengers well. I'm home, her mind sang to itself, in a daze

Whatever was coming with the breakup of the Soviet Union, it just didn't seem possible that civilization could be swallowed up just because some corrupt old men in the Kremlin were lost in their vodka dreams. Marianne nodded and exchanged well-wishes with the flight crew in her broken and heavily French-accented Russian. It felt as if it came welling up from the heart of her Siberian childhood. She'd been born in this vast nation. Eleven time zones, was it, crossing half of Europe and all of northern Asia? The ground itself seemed to reach up to reclaim her soul like a long-lost spirit that belonged in the frozen forests and the steppes and taiga of a land in which superlatives paled. There had been Romanov dukes who gave their duchesses mountain ranges for birthday presents. Ignorance and totalitarianism had kept this breathtaking behemoth shackled and crippled. She hadn't realized how excited she would be. Then reality set in.

The trip through customs was long and boring and she liberally handed out five dollar bills under-hand to keep things moving. For a little money, men with families to feed, men with jobs that did not always pay on time, men with pinched narrow faces and big hungry dark eyes, could work wonders in cutting through bureaucratic red tape.

The wind outside was mild. People hustled to make a living, as they did everywhere else in the world. Why not here? It was her first time in the capital of her native country, and she felt a strange sense, almost suffocatingly, of going back into a dark past that she did not want to revisit. Her mother had been exiled in the most horrible and cruel manner, and had been desperate to leave.

But there were pieces of the puzzle here, and Marianne was armed with the information she needed to extract just one more bit of the truth out of the jaws of old age and deception. She checked her own small travel valise in a lock box, to be retrieved on the way back to the West and her continuing search for her father. Her mother she had found anew, though she'd long known where her grave lay.

📖

She knocked on a dark wooden door and waited. She verified several times: the curling, yellowed slip of paper in the name slot read, in Cyrillic, *Mutsev V.*

Finally the door opened and a pretty female eye smeared with mascara peered over a dangling metal chain. "*Da?*" The girl had a listless tone. The eye looked puffy.

Marianne introduced herself as best she could in her broken Russian.

"You have dollars?" the girl said, switching to heavily accented English

"We can talk about it."

"No guns. No knives."

It took Marianne a moment to realize that the tough-sounding girl was scared of the neighborhood in which she was being raised.

"I am unarmed, a woman, alone. I came a long way to see him."

The chain rattled, and the girl opened the door. She was young, maybe 19. She had rings in her soft smooth skin—ears, nose, lip. Her short dark hair stuck out in rebellious points, streaked in deliberately jarring vermilion and kelly green. Her eyes were a lovely dark blue, but shot with red from last night's drinking binge. Marianne could still smell the mix of stale smoke and cheap vodka or beer. She wore a russet tunic and tight jeans. She was barefoot, with dirty feet and big, ungainly toes that a lady should cover up. Maybe she would learn to become a lady one day, Marianne thought to herself as she shook hands with the girl.

"Jane," the girl said. "I am really Marina Viktorovna Mutsev, but who gives a fuck about stupid name like that."

"It's a nice Russian name," Marianne said.

"Jane is from American rock song about freaky girl and vampire lover boy."

"Ah, Countess Didier," a frail voice interrupted from beyond the girl, cutting into what had almost become a conversation. A man shuffled out from a back room, holding a newspaper against his stained herringbone pants. The atmosphere about him was homey and clubbish—entirely opposite the Bohemian chaos radiating from his post-Soviet granddaughter.

Viktor Mutsev's voice was still crisp with humor and cleverness. He wore a rumpled gray shirt and pushed his suspenders up as in a nervous, unconscious habit. Past 80, he still had dark blue eyes like the girl. His thin white hair showed a pink scalp riddled with gray and brown skin cancers and eczemas. "We were expecting you, Madame." He took charge at the door, and let her in.

"Colonel Mutsev," Marianne said, extending her hand.

He stood stiffly and bowed from the chest, as if they were old nobility greeting each other in a hall of mirrors from a lost ghost era. "Countess Didier. What a pleasure. Did you bring us anything from the victorious West to brighten up our poor lives?"

Marianne set one valise on the table, but kept the other in hand. The girl flew to open the valise, snapping its latches with eager, grimy thumbs. She exclaimed in flurried whispers. Inside were several rows of gleaming metallic paper containers of fresh French coffee, American cigarettes, English tea, German and Belgian candies, German razors with blades, Italian shaving soap. The labels were still on there from duty free shops at JFK, Heathrow, Bourget, and Düsseldorf.

"Any Jack Daniels?" the girl asked.

"Sorry, no. Couldn't get it through customs."

"Fuck!"

"Easy, *Marinka*," the old man said. "We have to be thankful for all that the great lady brings us."

The girl snapped up a carton of cigarettes and flounced off into a back room.

Mutsev made light motions with his hands, as if dancing in a ballet. His eyes were filled with bright hilarity at the irony of it all. "The lady is great aristocrat, come to visit us in our dictatorship of the workers." A less refined Russian would forget to add the seemingly useless articles—*a, an, the*—of English, but Mutsev had passed as a native Briton or American. His articles were almost impeccable.

"I am Russian by birth," she countered. "I am on the soil of my mother's grave."

"So you are, *Timofeyevna*, so you are." He looked over the valise, nodded with punctilious satisfaction, and flicked the lid shut. "You have another valise that you'll leave with us if I make you happy."

"That's the deal, Colonel."

"Fair enough, dear lady. Would you like some tea?"

"Please."

"Sit over here by the window," he said, delicately taking her jacket and helping her to a s small table with two seats. "We are so international these days. Remember that your dear mother was Polish, and that somewhere in Poland she first saw the light of day in all the sacred innocence of a child."

"Yes," Marianne said. The window by the table overlooked that same playground below where puppies and small children played in their brief dream time of eternal genesis, like frail embers floating in the formless void where space and time begin.

"They grow up with more than we ever had," Colonel Viktor Mutsev said as he broke open a Twinings packet and took out two little teabags. "But what of their souls?"

"They have it hard," she said, shivering despite the mild weather. She thought of those proud May Days, those parades, the rockets, the goose stepping soldiers, the red flags with yellow hammers and sickles, the patriotic marching songs of the first nation into space...and now this dreary poverty. "I have not come to embarrass you, Colonel."

"I know that," he said matter-of-factly, as if it was all just nothing—a momentary inconvenience, a scrape of the knee, a lump in one's pudding. "The world changed in 1945," he said softly. "This is nothing in comparison."

For a moment, it was as if they had known each other for many years. It was that same home coming for her again, as she'd found on the kind shoulder of the stewardess. I would like to be buried there one day, Marianne thought, thinking of her mother's grave, of Siberia, of the woman's smile and Yupik eyes.

Mutsev—a predator who had become a survivor with a soul—put heavy, black-framed glasses on so that he could peer at the proper setting on the gas stove. "At least we have gas, but not electricity," he muttered with elegant patience. "Tomorrow, we have no gas, but a million lights like the stars of the cosmos. Our story never seems to change, no matter who is in power."

Water began to grumble in the pan. He sat across from her, folding his hands on the table. Taking it from nowhere, it seemed, he pushed a little piece of paper across. On it, in painstaking blue ballpoint, he had written a name, phone number, and address in Western script. "Here is what you need."

She pulled it across to her with a trembling hand. "This is what I came for." It was a question, a declaration of wonder. Her toes *kribbelten*, a German expression, in the sense when toes tingle in memory of long-ago frostbite.

"I thought I would surprise you," he said kindly. "You will get more than you asked for today. That man, whose name is written there, he will take you to your destination. Your journey will be over. Who knows, maybe a new one begins."

"This is…it?" she whispered, holding the piece of paper in both hands.

He nodded meaningfully. "*Da.* That's it. But I hope you stay for tea and stories." He rose to prepare a proper tea service. No samovar, but a nice stainless steel kettle from Germany would serve handsomely.

"I bet you have many stories." She watched him, feeling overwhelmed and chilled. Mutsev must have been a tall, handsome man once. She could picture him as Tim Nordhall must have seen him in World War II London, looking like a black-suited, bowler-hatted, brolly-wielding bank employee. But how many of his stories were true, and how many were falsehoods like the murderous life he had lived in the service of one of history's deadliest madmen—Uncle Joe Stalin?

"I hope you stay a little while," he said. "I have very little company here in my old age."

"Please tell me everything you know. I would love to listen."

"You can be proud of your parents." He nodded with a spark of happiness. "You look just like your mother, you know. She was one of the most beautiful women I have ever seen. Such a tragic beauty. Her love goes with you, *Umnitsa.* Everywhere you go, she is your guardian angel."

"I think so," she said softly. "You called me *Timofeyevna.*"

"Yes." He read her trembling hopefulness and said with equal softness in the semi-dark room: "Yes, that is correct. *Timofeyevna* is the patronymic name, your middle name, customary for a girl whose father happened to be named Timofei or Timothy.

At that moment, Marina hurried out without a word of goodbye. She wore a dark pea-coat with bulging pockets, presumably to carry gifts of cigarettes to her friends—or more likely to buy drugs. Marianne didn't ask, and the old man ignored her. The door slammed. Her feet could be heard, clattering down the stairwell.

Mutsev smiled at the memory of World War Two. "That was something. I was working in the Congo with the American Colonel Ivor Crane, one of our double agents, when a Luftwaffe deserter brought us this American Navy engineer they rescued in Mauritania. That was your father, Tim Nordhall."

"Who was this deserter?"

"Willi Märzig, a fine German lad from Kiel, who stole a Junkers-52 from the Afrika Korps, and defected to Mauritania. I met him in the Belgian Congo, where I had an operation going. Long gone now, like all of them." He prepared to bring tea and cookies. "My operation covered the Belgian radium mines, and let to interesting developments when Stalin, Hitler, and Tojo all decided they must have the atomic bomb. Of course, Uncle Franklin got there first, as the Japanese well remember. My life became much more interesting, given me an outlet for my talents. Your father was brilliant, say what anyone will, because he influenced the way the world changed in 1945. Your mother even more so. I must tell you a long, long story with many twists and turns. Some of the twists and turns occurred naturally, and others are man-made."

She felt puzzled. "What does that mean?"

Mutsev brought a tray loaded with tea and goodies to the table. "War and espionage, dear Countess, are full of strange twists. It is like someone writing a script and changing it all the time. Well, I should begin with a ship that got torpedoed by a Nazi U-boat off the coast of West Africa." Bit by bit, as the day grew long and wan, and no Marinka came back, the two sat alone. He had many things to tell her, about Katanga and London and Portsmouth and San Francisco, and she held his hands—the hands of this killer, this old lion who was the last of his kind, this jaguar who had prowled the ruins of London during the Blitz and bedeviled her father.

As they talked, Marianne held his hands as if he could pour out data transmissions into her of all that he knew, and he knew so much. The transmission went on for a long time, while rain dribbled outside, the world licked itself clean of its wounds, and silence fell around the gray projects except for the occasional slammed door (or gunshot?) or drunken howl of laughter.

He grew tired as he wrapped up his tale. "We almost got Hitler's atomic bomb stuff. We had it in our hands, ready to transport to Siberia via Lend Lease air lift, when your father and his women spoiled it all. Your mother was the one above all—I turned her in London, but she turned tables on us all. She lost terribly in the end."

Marianne was still a beat behind. "His women?"

"His two wives, and your mother—she was the third woman. These two women, they never met your mother. He probably never told them about her. I think he loved your mother all his life, but she disappeared into Siberia. Her Polish cousin, her husband, died not long after the war. Anna—your mother—was Erek's child bride, his wife, after all, and the love of his life. Do you realize that Erek himself was a Polish noble, and an officer in their proud but tragic resistance to the *Kraut-fresser*?" She had been brought up to refer to Sauerkraut, marinated cabbage, by the French border term of *choucroute*. Fressen, in German, was a reference to animals; the term for people eating is essen. "Erek died soon after the war. Stalin had him murdered in a POW camp when the poor young man could not tell, under torture, where his beautiful young wife might be found. Stalin wrapped everything in a cloak of secrecy. We were so paranoid that all of our maps had false information so they could never be used against us in an invasion. Try driving somewhere using a Stalin era map." He laughed out loud. "Our spirit was lost in the maps of Stalin's distorted landscape."

He stopped to sip tea and break a cookie. "Tim's two women were spies working against one of our other sections. We did a lot of sabotage to the UN in those early days. We would have done more, if it weren't for the two women." He confided: "In the end, I saw one more chance to throw Anna at Tim in San Francisco, but she betrayed us and saved him. Stalin got to her. The Americans sold her to the Soviets in a spy swap that went bad. No consequence. Stalin was delighted. He would have killed her, but he sent her to Siberia as bait in case your father went looking for her. Problem was, his agents had no idea where to look for Tim and his women to plant the bait. It was a waste of time and lives, a loss of happiness and human rights, for nothing, but none of that mattered to Stalin." He grew dreamy and repeated himself a bit. "We had teams of men looking for your father and his two women. We were ordered to kill them. Stalin kept a personal dossier on his desk, updated every day by NKGB officers, so much did he personally hate your father for preventing him from stealing Hitler's lost atomic bomb materials from the captured U-234. We never did find your father. Stalin died, and our people quickly lost interest. I loved Anna, too, and assisted various people in the FBI, including a gnome called Howard Lemon. Together, we have all known for many years where Tim and his women live—and we have sworn to protect them."

"I know," Marianne said. "I visited his family—my aunts and uncles— in New Haven, Connecticut, and they said they were still sworn to secrecy."

"Secrecy is a blessing sometimes, as much as it is often a blight and a virus. Look what secrecy did to Russia under the Soviets. We invented disinformation. The Americans had their CIA by then, and they spread a lot of manure around, also disinformation. I am happy for them."

His long ramble petered out. They finished their tea and cookies. Marianne carefully folded the precious paper away into the innermost pocket of her purse. A while later, they stood at the door. She'd given him both bags as she planned, not wanting to carry them.

"You look very much like your mother," he said again.

"Did you know my mother well?"

"Not intimately, but I met her in London. She was working for the Nazis, she was working for us, and in the end she was working for the Americans and the British and the Soviets. In all my life, I not known another agent like her. Crane, he was a double, working against his own Americans and for the Soviets. I was a triple, working for my country, and leading on both the Allies and the Axis. Your mother was a quadruple agent. Not because she wanted to be clever, but because she was desperate. She loved her cousin, and she loved your father. She tried to play all the sides, and lost in the end. I will tell you this, Timofeyevna Anyanovna. Your mother was a good, loyal woman. Her virtuousness is what undid her. She could have had any man in the world, but she was true until death to the two men she loved—Erek, and your father. No matter what anyone tells you—remember that about her. She was the most beautiful, and the most loyal, and the most courageous soul I have ever known. I tried to own her, Countess, to be clear. I ran her, so why should I not have her sexually like any other woman whose life I ran? In the end, it is clear, she was running me. But she was a wild mare. She could control the many riders on her back, but she got in over her head. Any man would give his everything for a woman like that. She was as unyielding, as strong, and eternal, as a tall mountain covered in fresh snow."'"

"Thank you, Colonel Mutsev."

"I tell you this also. She was the true love of your father's life. As much as she lived for him, torn toward her beautiful love in the Polish sphere—had Hitler not destroyed all that and so many lives besides—just exactly so much he was torn about her. His sphere contained these two other magnificent women who devoted their lives to him. Your father too had his measure of greatness too, as I knew him. He had that same innocence she did. He was smart, but he could not think like an evil man. That is necessary in the spy business." He laughed out loud. "They were like children. Good people find good people. You will learn all this for yourself." He clapped his hands together, as if dusting them off. "More tea, more talking, but not with me. Don't lose the piece of paper I gave you."

"I won't." She touched her coat, where the address was deeply stashed in an inner pocket. "Thanks for everything, Viktor. I leave you with the valises, and please do not hesitate to contact me if you need anything else." She added softly: "For Marinka."

"Thank you, Countess." He bowed from the waist, fully doubling over for a second or two, as if he were inviting her to a very formal dance step.

In another time, she thought, he might have made a strapping Czarist officer, and done much better for himself unless caught up in 1917 events. "Good luck then," she said.

"And you, *Umnitsa*. Take with you all the love of your motherland. A harsh mother, but a good one."

"What will you do, Colonel?"

"I will soldier on to the end. Now my duty is only to one unruly girl who may yet become the *umnitsa* that I love." He struggled to contain his emotions. "It has been a good life. I retired on a good pension for that time. I married and had two children. One of my sons, Igor, was wounded in Afghanistan and is now manager with Gazprom. My other son, Boris, is divorced and drinking himself to death. I am raising his daughter for him, not doing a very good job. What can we do?" He raised his hands quizzically.

Change of script. Man yanks another sheet off platen, lays it next to typewriter, inserts new sheet. Sheets beside typewriter are stacking up. Gray shadows dance around the room as man keeps typing. Keys hammer down under fingertips, inked ribbon jumps and rolls under determined and steady keystrokes as words pour out. Is that a spark of light in the window? Is morning here, or is it another of these many ghosts bearing a candle? Someone in the audience coughs softly. The play is nearly over. They have been spellbound.

Aug 6, 1945 Tibbets: Hiroshima

On the morning of August 6, 1945, a lone B-29 piloted by Major Paul Tibbets flew over Hiroshima, a moderate sized Japanese city unremarkable in every way.

The plane was named *Enola Gay*, and on board was a uranium bomb about the size of a car, nicknamed *Little Boy*. Nurturing it were several elite scientists who called themselves *weaponeers*—a dark jargon for the genesis of a new age.

The Japanese, who did not have fuel or aircraft to spare, did not even bother to shoot a few A-A rounds into the air. The few who noticed the plane assumed she was taking photographs high up where no fighters could reach her.

From nowhere, a spectacular ball of light blossomed. Slowly, a vast mushroom cloud roiled up into the stratosphere. The plane was already gone. The city was a wasteland of flattened, scorched rubble. Often, the only sign left that a certain man or woman or child had existed was that their shadow had been holographically etched into whatever marble or stone happened to be behind them. Leaves, birds, and butterflies made similar shadows. It was a dark art form for a new age. Four days later, a plutonium bomb named *Fat Man* exploded in Nagasaki, with thousands more dead. The emperor went on radio and declared he was not a living god. Japanese forces everywhere were ordered to surrender. World War II was over—a new *Iliad* of whose rage the goddess will sing for thousands of years, when much else is buried and forgotten.

The audience claps as the play nears its end. Man stops typing and rises. Taps sheets of script together, forming a neat pile. End of script. Man turns and bows to a clapping and delighted audience. Man throws sheets in the air, and they sail around him in unruly and comedic confusion.

Marin County, 1991—Billy Seward

Marianne, Countess Didier rented a car and drove north into Marin County, using the information Uncle Viktor Mutsev—Jaguar—had written down for her. She was well-rested for a change, and she had eaten a light breakfast in a fast food restaurant. She'd carried out a cup of cola with ice on it, which sat sweat-beaded in the drinks container beside her. It was midmorning on a flawless day—sunny, blue-skied, warming to a balmy temperature. In the misty blue of San Francisco Bay, under the Golden Gate Bridge, pleasure boats rode hard in the wind with their masts leaning forward and their bright sails stiffly full of wind.

Wearing a conservative, nicely cut Navy-blue women's business suit and white blouse with a little bow tie, Marianne nervously drove a half hour or so north into Marin County, through the increasingly lush green countryside that distinguishes north coastal California, and into the low verdant vinyards and orchards of Napa and Sonoma. She drove into the wooded back areas of Santa Rosa, and found a small country lane buried under great redwood trees. She cruised slowly along the country road, sipping the last of her soda, until she found the driveway of the house she was looking for. She pulled in behind a parked boat on a trailer, and a large off-roader SUV with grills over its lights and overhead fog lights.

The door opened as she walked up the driveway. She felt a pang in her stomach, sensing each step took her closer to that other, missing book end in her life. The man standing in the doorway was old, like Mutsev—at least 80, and he braced himself in the doorway. He wore an eye patch. He must have been a strong man in his youth, and he still had a fierce glint in his good blue eye, and a determined jut to his white-stubbled jaw. He wore work shoes, rumpled denims overalls, and a white T-shirt. "You the lady that called?"

"Yes I am. Can I visit with you for a few minutes?"

"I don't see why not." He stepped back to let her pull the screen door open and join him in a living room that smelled faintly musty. If he had a housekeeper, she was not be good about washing clothes and cleaning up. Dirty dishes were stacked on a coffee table, and a television set flickered with the news. He pressed a button somewhere, and the TV went black. "Have a seat."

"Thanks." She found a palatable spot on a doggy-smelling couch under the front window, thinking the light and the brightness would separate her somewhat from the gloom in which the old man was spending his last years.

"What was it you were after?" He helped himself about awkwardly, leaning on things, and favoring a stiff left hip. "Doggone it, Randy! Randy!" he bellowed to someone in back. "Roger!"

He returned to the living room and sat down hard. "My dog and my grandson. Can't rely on either one of them. Dog's probably out chasing a rabbit. The boy's probably playing hooky from school—maybe out in back smoking a joint. I can never be sure which."

Marianne introduced herself as briefly as she could. "Do you remember a man named Tim Nordhall?"

Billy Seward thought for a moment. A defensive switch seemed to click on somewhere deep inside of him. "Sure I do," he said. "How could I forget? Navy boy, as I recall. Some secret defense work, is that right?"

"Did he have two wives?"

"Now what kind of question is that?"

"I think he was my father."

Seward looked startled, and examined her with his one eye. "Yes. I can see that. You're the spitting image of Anna Stokowska."

"My mother."

He said carefully, putting his hands over his cheeks, and with great emotion in his eye. "I searched for her a long time. Didn't find out until a few years ago that she died long ago in Siberia. I didn't know until a few days ago that she had a little girl named Anna Timofeyevna Samsonov."

"Jaguar must have called you."

"He did. We have worked together for many years to protect your father and his women. He does it in memory of your mother. Well, so do I. You were that little girl, eh?"

"That's me. My mother married a drunken fisherman in desperation for his small paycheck. My stepfather drowned at sea. My mother died not long after of TB. Vadim Samsonov's sister raised me—my Auntie Dora. His family were part Russian, part Yupik. She was old, and made sure I was adopted by a well-off French couple, who raised me in Europe. I became Marianne Didier, and here I am."

Billy Seward's gaze was far away. "Anna Stokowska," he said reverently. "What a gorgeous woman. And you look just like her. I mean, twenty years ago maybe you looked like she did as a young woman. Forgive me if I sound rude."

"Truth is truth."

"You are seeking the truth. I see. You are still a beautiful woman. Saw you in the magazines and talking head shows."

"That's long behind me. I am embarrassed."

"Don't be. Looks like you had a wild time." His thoughts wandered on. "Three women in his life—the first an exotic Middle Eastern spy, the second woman one of those dashing women pilots, and the third woman your mother—how could he choose? Stalin took the love of his life from him, so he took both of the others. And they went along with him. They were both powerful heifers each in her own domain. One was a man killer, the other a derring-do pilot. Either would have made an ordinary man happy."

Marianne tried to bring him back to the moment. "All three of them did survive the war, didn't they? The man, the two women?"

"What makes you think so?"

She hoped she was right. It was a long journey, full of anguish for her, and all for nothing, if she were wrong. What if Mutsev had misled her just to get the coffee and liquor? "Supposedly they all perished in 1945."

"That's right," he said. "Naomi Meged was abducted by the Soviets. Nordhall died on the *Indianapolis* when a torpedo from the Japanese submarine I-58 hit her. And the little brunette WAFS was lost at sea searching for him."

"But none of it is true, is it?"

"Is it? How would I know?"

"It's been half a century, Mr. Seward. The Soviet Union is finished, Stalin is long dead, the war's been over a good half century, and the secrets are starting to look silly. Why don't you help me out?"

"What makes you think it was a lie?"

"Jaguar."

Seward sat upright. "Huh?"

"You heard me, Mr. Seward."

"Oh yes—him."

"I have all the old news clipping from the time. They all contradict each other. The news clippings and the police reports and the War Department memos tell a story that can't be. Supposedly the same man was in three different places at the same time. I've been to Moscow and talked with the man himself, Viktor Mutsev, Jaguar, Malone, who knows what other names and disguises. He told me for sure those were all planted cover stories. He gave me your name and promised you would help me."

"Okay," he said. "Look, you have to understand that we all protected Tim and his women for years and years. Old habits die hard."

"Please help me, Mr. Seward. I've been searching my whole life long for him." She was ready to cry. How horrible if she was to get this close, and no closer. The piece of paper from Mutsev had its limit here, in this room, now. She might as well throw it away now.

He stared at her. "What do you want me to do?"

"Maybe," she said, "Catherine Franzese might want to know what happened to her brother."

He grinned. "Catherine called me to tell me you visited her."

"No."

"Yes. A number of us have been covering for Nordhall for a long time. Maybe it's time to let go now. For his daughter, at least."

"What do you mean?"

"He was on Stalin's most wanted list. He kept the Russians from stealing the radioactive material from *U-234*. We couldn't stop the Reds from developing the A-bomb. We had plenty of traitors in our midst that took care of that. But Tim slowed them down for a few years. He and his women."

"And my mother."

"Your mother above all."

"What were their names again?"

"Naomi Meged and Corinthia Johnston."

"That leaves"

"Yeah. Anna Stokowska, the Free Polish Army nurse."

"My mother."

"She was the other great love of his life."

"You sound like you knew him personally."

"You could say that."

"Then you knew all along what happened to him."

"We knew Stalin would have had him killed. We knew" (his eyes seemed to grow cloudy) "that your mother was in danger, but there was nothing we could do to help her. I mean, my section. There were some other people—the U.S. was riddled with rival counter-intelligence services. That was mostly Hoover's doing, but the generals and the State Department shirts had a hand in it. Weakened us badly. Some secret branch, masquerading as FBI, turned her over to the NKGB. Their agents took her away, as directed by Stalin, but in the end, Siberia took her, and millions of souls like her. Here you are, a very lucky little Siberian orphan."

Marianne struggled with tears. Seward handed her a box of tissues, and took one himself. He pretended he just had to blow his nose. His eye was wet and red. She dragged out one tissue after another to mop the big round tears that fell liberally down her cheeks. "Why did nobody help me all this time?"

"We had no idea he fathered a child with Anna. She disappeared and nobody could find her. Stalin kept a lid on everything. Your mother was from a devout Polish Catholic family. Her middle name was Maria. She must have named you after herself. The French turned it from Anna Maria to Marianne. Easier for you to blend in. You've had a good life."

His guess startled her. "My Didier parents spoiled me. They carried an old title dating to the Sun King monarchy—Trois Roses, Three Roses. They gave me a wonderful life, and I loved them like my own parents. I always thought...My stepmother's sister was an old spinster named Marianne. They thought it would make her happy, since she never had children. Later, they explained to me, and it all made sense from the little fragments of memory I carried deep in my soul."

The old lady had lived to the age of 90 in a little house near Rue Cortot, a Montmartre back street in the *XVIIIe Arondissement* of Paris, near the tiny home of composer Erik Satie. Marianne had often gone walking with her to the church of St. Jean, around the artists' stalls; and under the white dome of the *Sacre Coeur*, wrapped in incense smoke and choir music. Another life entirely.

"Who knows? Like the stories we spread about Tim. The truth is whatever works best." He coaxed her back from that memory, gently:

"Your mother tipped us off, and saved that uranium from going to Russia. We were all crazy about her. Tim was the lucky stiff she loved. I called San Francisco P.D. to the Hotel Auger *tout-suite*, but it was too late to save Anna. Tim and the girls put the kibosh on that plane headed for Montana."

Marianne wiped the last tears away and sighed deeply, a shuddering sigh as she waved a balled up piece of wet tissue. "So what really happened then if all those stories about shipwreck and plane crashes weren't true?"

"That's right." Seward kept tapping his fingers, until he forgot about them and dropped his hands in his lap. "He and the little pilot, they recovered part of the atom bomb that went to Hiroshima. The other girl, she helped expose Alger Hiss and saved the country from getting screwed worse than we eventually were. Government swore me to secrecy, of course, but I was a law officer, hunting Nazis and Communists for years, and that was just second nature to most of us good decent cops. Did my part in New Guinea before that, you know, came home with a piece of shrapnel in my hip, but I stayed in the Army. Wound up on desk duty in London with CIC, then in San Francisco as they got the UN set up in 1949. Most of us felt that way. Wanted to do everything we could to help the country. Your father and his women are national heroes. I'm one of the few who really know anything about them. I made sure we saved them, no matter what. I still feel terrible I couldn't save your mother."

"Then they didn't split up? She flying the plane to Tinian, he taking the ship? Meg being kidnapped by Soviet agents?"

"No, no, the spy boys planted all that baloney in the files knowing the Soviets would get in there to look. It was all a put-on. We had Uncle Joe baffled, and the Reds swallowed it for a long time. After Stalin was gone, their man Jaguar actually helped us. I suppose because he was nuts about your mother like we all were."

He excused himself and went to another room far away in the back of the house. She heard him make a phone call. His voice was guarded, but familiar as if speaking with a very old friend. Soon, he returned to be with her. He brought her a glass of water, which she accepted..

She asked: "And my mother?"

Billy Seward sat down, holding his glass of water. Ambient light shone in their twin waters as captured sunlight and inevitable truth. "She was the greatest hero of all. She tipped me off on the plot to steal the uranium, which could have made six atomic bombs. It cost her life and happiness, though she took you with her to that miserable beach town in Siberia. The Japs would have destroyed a half dozen U. S. cities. Stalin was even more eager to get his hands on Hitler's atomic bombs. Your poor, beautiful mother saved the world." He took a deep breath. "Now let me tell you what happened in real life, as opposed to those cock and bull stories."

He grew animated, and his eyes lit up, as he leaned forward to tell the story, and Marianne leaned closer eagerly to listen. "It was the war, you know," he began. "The crazy, crazy goddamn war..."

Aug. 1945: Wild Night Ride

As Billy Seward told this part of the story, it wasn't Mutsev at all who came to kidnap Meg. Rather, two carloads of NKGB agents cruised down the street and pulled up at the side entrance of the Hotel Auger. Looking right and left, eight men in long overcoats got out. They had their hats pulled down and their hands in their pockets. Leaving a driver in each car with the motor running, they paraded through the courtyard and approached the back door. One pressed the buzzer, while the others gathered around him and looked upward.

In the window several stories above, in a darkened apartment, Meg looked out with a feeling of devastation. She saw the men below and knew who they were. She knew they were armed and that they were operating right under the noses of the American police. Not since her disastrous marriage and the loss of her baby had the world looked so utterly bleak. Her country had promised so much, yet failed to protect her. America was failing her again now. What was there to live for? With Corie and Tim gone, what was the use?

Hearing a knock at the inside hall door, she turned and waited. She was ready to die.

"Miss Meged!" someone said sharply. "Miss Meged! Open up!" Startled, she realized from the accent that it was an American voice, a familiar gruff one. She rushed to the door and fumbled with the latch.

Below she heard a crash as the Russians forced the metal door with their shoulders. Men's rough steps clattered coming up the fire escape outside. In two minutes, they would be here, and she'd be on her way, pinned helpless between them—to a ship back to Siberia, as had happened to others like her in the past. The NKGB never forgot, never forgave, and never gave up.

She opened the hallway door, and confronted the American police.

"Miss Meged!" It was that military detective Billy Seward, cutting a heroic figure with his pirate eye patch, poised in the doorway with a .38 in the air. "Hurry. We can make it if you come now." He grabbed her hand and pulled. Behind him stood several husky San Francisco policemen in blue, sporting heavy night sticks and Tommy guns. They looked grim and determined.

Meg heard the Soviet agents' voices now, the rumbling of their shoes, the click of more than one gun safety being released for action as they came to the landing outside that would admit them into Corie's bedroom in the apartment.

"Let's go!" Seward said, towing her across the hallway.

By then, some Communist's shoulder rammed repeatedly against the door at the top of the fire escape. As the door splintered, Meg glimpsed dark hats and shapes beyond it. Across the hallway, a door opened under the hands of the old Chinese-American man. Beside him, an ancient face looked out, that of Josephine Auger, in her wheelchair. "In here, kids. Quick!"

A distant siren keened. "The law's on the way," said a police sergeant in an Irish brogue. "We'll need all the help we can get, lads. Get ready for a fight."

"No, no," Seward said. "They won't get here in time. We're outgunned." He shoved Meg into Miss Auger's apartment so that Meg stumbled and landed on one knee at Mrs. Auger's feet. Behind her, Seward closed the door as quickly and quietly as he could and locked it, double-bolted it. "Get away from the line of fire in case they start shooting," he whispered, waving at Mrs. Auger and Meg.

Mrs. Auger just had time to take Meg's hands in hers. Meg rose as the Chinese-American man pulled the old woman out of the way. They heard angry voices in the hallway outside. The sirens were slowly getting closer, and multiplying as more flying squad units equipped with radios joined the race toward the hotel. The Soviets would have to back off now.

"They have nerve, these Communists," the Chinese-American man whispered. "I called Seward. You can trust Billy Seward." He grinned. "Seward loves good *lo mein*, and he's been a customer at my cousin Yeo's restaurant on Grant Avenue for years. These Commies, they just don't get it, man. They don't grasp how America works. They can't defeat us with their lies and murder. Honest people make good food for good people. These truths are self-evident."

Miss Auger agreed: "These foreigners just don't get it."

While the elderly man held forth, Mrs. Auger took Meg's hands and pulled Meg to a safe spot in the bathroom. They three peered out from the dim recess where moonlight gleamed on the white tile floor with mosaic tiles in black.

One heard crashing noises. The sergeant said: "They'll be in here any second."

"We have to make a run for it," Seward said. "Ladies, there ain't time. We gotta go. Say *adios* and off we go."

Mrs. Auger looked tearful as she gripped Meg's hands in her gnarled ones. "I'm sorry, my dear. I had no idea that you were working for us all."

Meg leaned down and planted a kiss on her forehead. "We all do what we must, Mrs. Auger, and you've done your duty now. Thank you for saving me."

Mrs. Auger was trembling so hard she couldn't speak. She could only reach out with both trembling, palsied hands, but Meg was beyond her grasp now. Meg blew a kiss goodbye as she and Seward let themselves out on the black iron fire escape. The old Chinese-American man waved.

Voices resounded outside as more San Francisco Police officers in their blue uniforms poured up the stairs with their guns drawn, a captain with gold braid in the lead, to surround the Russians. The Soviets refused to surrender or even hold up their hands, claiming embassy status. SFPD had been groomed and lectured about diplomatic immunity. The captain knew enough to let them go rather than contribute to an international incident so close to this critical time of the founding of the United Nations.

Instead, about two dozen San Francisco cops formed a ring around the dozen Soviets, and pressed in so hard the commies could hardly breathe, much less make speeches.

When one of them tried to bluster and protest, a night stick came out of nowhere and bounced lightly on his head, just enough to stun the sullied Soviet into sullen silence. A cop said: "Put a rag in yer yap, you effin' shitbird."

After a five minute stand-off, the captain called out: "Okay, boys, I think we have questioned our wonderful effin' guests long enough. I am assured that they are men of good quality and Christian will. If they're not, I'll throw their moth-eaten sacks of tripe off this balcony myself."

The Russians mumbled and straightened their coats. They surrendered their shooting irons with some angry murmuring, but they knew they had been held up long enough for the enemies of socialist happiness to escape. They were now more afraid to report to the spiders masterminding their foul dens, and thinking of the punishments and tortures Uncle Joe would mete out. *Sprechen sie Gulag?*

The captain's parting words to the alien agents were, in Gaelic: "We just finished pounding the piss out of the Nazis, and we're going to kick the Japs in the ass, and then your Uncle Joe better watch his own keyster because we have the means and the motive to stuff a few boots up in there. Get out of here, you unshaven atheists and sectarians."

Even the most nervy, hardened Russian stared in confusion. What kind of place was this? Gaelic cops, *lo mein*, a pirate cop right out of the comics. It was like a madhouse nation, and they fled down the stairs without their prize—Naomi Meged. But another prize had been promised to them, and now they headed to the docks to take her.

📖

Seward half ran, half backed down the stairs, pointing upward with his revolver. "My duty," he told her. "I am going to get you out of town safely, or die trying." Several detectives met them at the bottom of the stairs—strong, silent men with determined faces. They packed black, military-style automatics and waited with their long overcoats blowing in the damp air.

"Come on, boys, we've got someplace to go in a hurry."

The uniformed police and the Soviets faced off on the other side of the building—SFPD herding the Reds out through the courtyard and back to their waiting cars, which now needed a tow truck because a few passing firemen, listening in their hook and ladder truck on the same radio frequency, had let the air out of the tires just to be helpful.

While this went on—anything to slow down the Mongol herd from Moscow—Seward and his detectives hustled Meg out through a small hedge entrance on the other side of the property, to a big black unmarked police car that sat running with steam puffing from its exhaust. The car happened to be the police chief's own souped-up armored cruiser, a veritable battle ship of the streets.

The titanic car barely rocked as Seward, Meg, and four detectives piled in. The rear doors softly slammed shut as the big powerful car roared away with a slight chirp of ripped rubber and a deeply throttled engine that sounded like a plane's.

When they got a few blocks away and were heading down the main streets to get out of town, the driver put on the siren. The wailing echoed up and down, bouncing off house and store windows. Traffic screeched to a halt on all sides as they tore through intersections without slowing—with red lights blinking left-right, left-right, left-right inside the front bumper grill and in the back window. On top was an array of lights and sirens meant for a huge fire engine, and the effect radiated for blocks around. Every dog in San Francisco began howling as if the world were about to end.

It was the flight of the damned. All that was needed was that the car be on fire, with devils shoveling coal at it. People froze in place and stared when they saw the SFPD panzer coming. Dogs and cats fled for their lives.

Red lights flickered hysterically off shop windows left and right, and a triple-throated, ear-splitting keening tore through the night.

Was it a replay of 1906? Had Tojo invaded?

Seward and another man knelt on the back seat, watching in the rear window for pursuers. The rested their drawn guns on the back rest.

The cruiser picked up several escorts along the way—motorcycle cops, squad cars, even a couple of park rangers on horses.

Their route took them out of the main part of town, and into the eastern suburbs, a bit south toward Oakland and always heading toward the mountains and deserts of the vast homeland.

Their local escorts melted away. Nobody was following.

"We're clear," Seward said after a while. He told the other men: "Keep an eagle eye out."

"What is happening to me?" Meg cried. She rubbed her hands over her face. No tears came. She felt overwhelmed.

"Turn off the noise," Seward ordered the driver.

Lights flicked out; sirens died down in a long, low, raw rasp.

Seward turned to Meg. "Just a few more minutes, sister."

The car roared through empty intersections on the way out of town. They passed

A few more blocks later, they pulled into a gas station. As Meg watched, mystified, they pulled around the small brightly lit pump island, past the gas station, and around the corner into a gravel parking lot shielded by tall hedges and lit by a single overhead light, on a telephone pole, under a metal hood.

Another large car—a big brown Chevrolet—sat waiting with its lights off but its engine running. Beside the car stood several persons in long dark coats, with down-turned hat brims shadowing their faces. Several carried Tommy guns.

Two didn't. For a moment, Meg thought they were prisoners.

Seward's car pulled up alongside.

Meg recognized two unarmed people standing there. She threw the door open and jumped out. "Tim! Corie!" Tim and Corie opened their arms. She flew into their embrace. They laughed and cried and embarrassed all the big, gruff detectives.

"Jaysus," muttered one, "ye'd think it was an Irish wake."

Seward still held his revolver and paced uneasily up and down. "Come on, you three. I want you out of town as fast as possible. We'll tail you for a while to be sure you're safe. Then you're on your own." He waved his gun eastward. "It's a big wide open country out there. I gave you the government phone number of you know where. They'll keep you safe as you find a new place to settle down." If he meant to say more, it seemed he couldn't because his voice became gravelly and he had to clear his throat. He handed the .38 to Tim, along with several olive-green, canvas cases, U.S. military issue, each with a full ammo clip. "I keep handing you guns and you keep losing them."

"Thanks, bud. I'll hang onto this one." Tim climbed into the big brown Chevrolet. Corie rode shotgun, and Meg sat in the back. "Thanks, Seward," Tim called out as the car started rolling.

"My pleasure. We'll be right behind you for a while. Good luck to you!"

Meg threw herself happily against the front seat and hung her arms over it, putting a hand on each of her companions' shoulders. She wanted to tell them how happy she was but all that came out were tears.

Behind them, the detective car followed like a destroyer escort. Its lights and sirens were off, but the dark shapes inside were armed and ready for anything. Several men brandished Tommy guns out the windows. A brawny brown arm hung from a window, brandishing a night stick.

Nobody followed them. After about an hour the police car winked its headlights several times and then pulled over to turn around. Last Tim and Corie and Meg saw, its dwindling headlights were pulling out into the road to do a U-turn.

Ahead were safety and a new life together in the vast and comforting emptiness of the continent. And that was as it should be. They had each served and served well. Now their country would serve them in turn, and it would be a good life for Tim and Corie and Meg.

San Francisco 1991: Umnitsa

Marianne Didier followed as Billy Seward walked her to the door. He said: "Good seeing you, Countess."

They stood in the doorway together. Marianne was waiting for him to furnish her father's telephone number and address. She was eager to complete her long journey of so many miles and so many years. "At least I had those three years with my mother," she said. "We were very poor, and conditions were very bad. She got sick and died when I was tiny. But I remember she loved me. We lived near the water front, and sometimes on a foggy night, we'd take a walk together, hand in hand, and listen to all the fog horns out at sea. Did you ever marry, Mr. Seward?"

"Oh yes. I had a good woman. Mexican-American gal I knew in high school, named Carina Sanchez. We had a good life together. Lord, I miss her. She died on me after thirty years. Woman cancer. I have three boys and five grandchildren. They live in the area and visit often enough." He said in a big, husky man voice. "I loved your mother too."

"What?"

"I knew her in London. She was the most beautiful woman over there, and there were a lot of beautiful women. I would have loved to take her on a date, but..." He paused, rifling through his many secrets, deciding which to tell her. "I never got to first base with her. She loved your father and, if circumstances had been different, would certainly have married him. She had eyes only for him."

"Except my mother was married to her cousin. And my father loved those two women."

"They came later. They are very nice too. Not as beautiful as your mother, but your dad's a true blue kinda guy. It's the soul he cherishes. He was a fox in the hen house with the women. He had his pick."

"He is a good man?"

"The best of men, lady."

"You'll give me his phone number and address? Is it a long plane flight?"

"Oh, not at all." He fumbled in his pockets. "Come on, I'll give you a ride to their house. It's just about two miles up that dirt road in the back country."

She held her hands over her mouth. "What?" For some reason, she was thinking about Berna, the beautiful and gentle young blonde granddaughter of old *Ka-Leu* Fehler, whom she had met in the *patisserie* in Berlin. How that child had clung to her grandfather! How they had held hands! How she took care of the old man. Child nothing, the girl was practically a doctor already...

Billy Seward jiggled his car keys. "Tim and his women got tired of living in Bucksnort, and moved back to the coast. They like to stay out of sight, you know, old habit. So I bought a piece of property up there snuggled between an Indian reservation and a state park. Nobody bothers them up there, and they can get into the city for shopping."

"I'm so nervous," said as they got into his big old car, which had cracked leather seats and smelled of dusty air conditioning ducts.

"Don't be. He'll want to know everything about you. You'll have plenty of time to talk. All the time in the world. I guess you probably don't know you have four brothers and three sisters." His words rained on her, only half understood. It was all so overwhelming. "They're a little younger than you. All turned out fine. All married, with good jobs and educations, in their late thirties, early forties. I think Tim has about fifteen grandchildren by now."

"Make that eighteen," she said, thinking of her own three children.

"You have kids too?"

"Of course. I'm divorced. Didn't you follow the tabloids? Or we'd have had more. They're all grown up living in Europe and Israel with their families. Actually, so my father has great-grandchildren."

Billy Seward whistled. "Wow. He'll want to hear all about them. The more the merrier."

It's like a dream, Marianne thought as the car bounced over dusty, uneven roads.

The air here was fresh, the sky blue, the fields full of butterflies.

They turned at a driveway and pulled in close to a wooden porch. The house was old, and rambling, but looked in good shape. "I put it in Tim's name," Billy Seward said. "Every two years or so, the girls pick a color, and he and I paint the place. Gives us something to do. We polish off a case of beer and talk about old times, the Dodgers, the Raiders, all that sports stuff. Or we used to."

Billy Seward gave the car horn a tap to let those in the house know they had arrived.

As Seward and Marianne sat waiting in the car, an elderly woman opened the door of the house.

Another elderly woman peered out behind her in the doorway.

Then a man appeared between them. He was frail and stooped. He was white-haired, and hobbled slowly with a cane.

"He's got arthritis." Seward regarded Marianne. "You should know that he has cancer, and will be gone in a few months. You got here just in time." His eyes were a bit moist.

Marianne held her fingertips to her lips as tears blinded her.

"Let's go meet them." Seward called out through the open car window: "Tim, here she is. Your daughter."

He and Marianne stepped from the car onto crunching gravel in the simple driveway. The wooden porch was overgrown with trumpet vines, ivy, and Bougainvillea in a riot of rot and color.

The two women looked happy and stayed close as they helped elderly Tim Nordhall across the porch and down the steps.

Corie and Meg waved to Marianne. "Hello! Hello! Welcome!"

Seward said from the corner of his mouth: "Take your hands down. You're covering your face. Let him see you."

She felt like a car going 60 in the rain—so did the tears fly from her eyes as she removed her hands to look at them more closely.

Tim Nordhall stood in the driveway leaning·on his cane. His two women stayed by his side. He looked confused and cloudy. He blinked at Marianne. He rubbed his eyes, as if he couldn't believe whom he was seeing.

He gaped as if seeing a ghost.

He reached out to her with a gnarled, trembling hand. "Anna?"

All her life, Marianne had ached for this moment.

She rushed toward her father with open arms, and he awaited her with his arms spread in love and acceptance. This was all she had ever wanted. She hoped she could be as good a daughter to him as Berna was a good granddaughter to the old U-boot captain.

Umnitsa.

A good girl.

Epilog

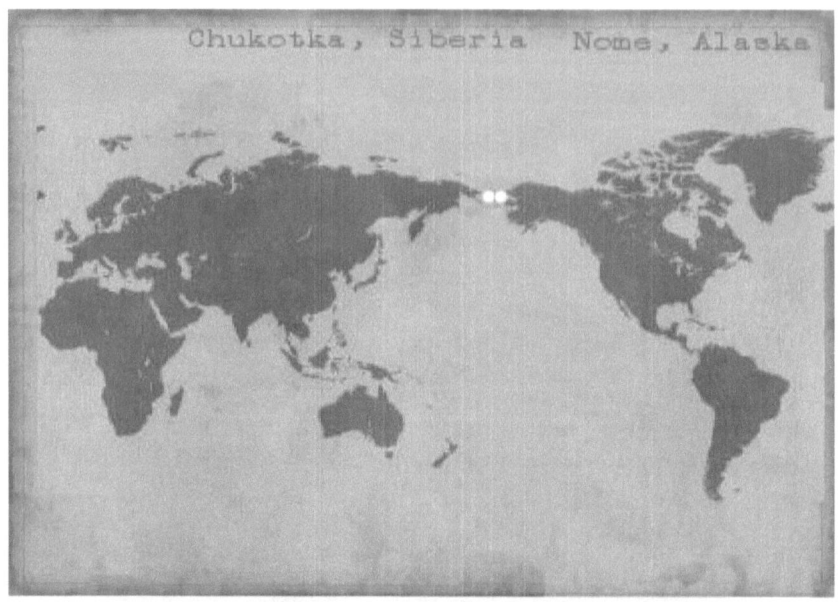

Hunter's Point 1945: World's End

A distant fog horn sent its deep blare long over the ocean. Other ships answered in high notes, low notes, short blasts, primordial snorts.

On a floating San Francisco dock, a half dozen NKGB men and matrons waited before a Soviet cargo ship that cold, damp night in the fall of 1945. It was two minutes to midnight by an industrial clock hanging on a union house wall. Weak lights glowed greenish under hat-shaped enamel shades on telephone poles. These small islands of light hovered, hemmed in and overwhelmed, beneath the rust-streaked hulls of freighters.

A large black American sedan with official plates pulled up two hundred feet away in a shady spot where they would not be easy to ambush. That was okay with the Soviet agents. They stood in the open, under bright lights, to show their amiable intentions. Most of them had just been disarmed by the San Francisco Police, and had little fight left in them. They were far more scared of their commissars than they were of these chaotic and inscrutable Americans.

FBI Special Agent Howard Lemon alone led their silent prisoner, holding her elbow. Two other agents stayed far back, by the car, smoking cigarettes and easily cradling Tommy guns. They had given her a needle with morphine in the car, and she was beyond fighting them. She looked pale and stricken. She had only a small suitcase, the baby in her womb, and the clothes on her back.

Howard Lemon stopped where he was supposed to. She staggered numbly toward two waiting matrons. Lemon slipped a hand into his pocket, fingering the gun there. The Soviet group never acknowledged the Americans. They led Anna Stokowska away over the swaying wooden dock.

Looming above was a black metal hull bearing a red star and the Cyrillic legend *Kalinin*. The ship's decks were deserted and dark, but her engines were running at throttle, ready to run from the dock without tug boats.

The Russians walked alongside the ship, until they came to a rectangular opening into the ship's hold. The matrons searched Anna, and a man looked through her valise. He pulled out a photo album full of old brown pictures. Flipping through the pages, he shrugged crudely. Pictures of Polish capitalist swine in their big cars, uniforms, and palaces. Finding nothing of value, he tore pages from the album and flung the album out over the water where the scattered pictures sank out of sight. If Anna noticed, she was unable to gesture or cry out. They bundled her and marched her across the dock into the ship.

The ship smelled of pallet wood, heavy hempen rope, diesel oil, packing grease, rotting fish, and cooked cabbage. As they stepped inside, a wall of fog drifted over the docks. City streets in the hills, blocks away, offered stray cheers to celebrate news of another victory in the Pacific, or a win at a ballgame, and horns tooted as if saying goodbye. The hands on the clock on the union house wall passed across midnight, from the old day to the new. Minutes later, as the fog thinned, one could see that the steel cargo gate on the ship had been closed. Condensation dripped down the riveted and brutal hull. Not a soul could be seen outside.

Another wall of fog rolled in, hiding the ship. Her diesel engines revved up to full racket, and oily smoke drifted through the fog. The dock trembled.

"Hey, Howard," one of the men with Tommy guns said. "Come on."

Lemon stood strangely transfixed. He turned slowly and walked back to the car. His shoes crunched on wet, glistening gravel. He took his hand from the gun in his pocket and pulled a pack of cigarettes from another pocket. Flicking a cigarette out, he shook it to his lips and put the pack away. With a tiny orange flame from his Zippo, he lit it and inhaled deeply.

As cigarette smoke drifted away behind his head, one of the men said: "What the hell was that all about? Why didn't you back away?"

"Well," said. "For just a second there, I had this crazy idea. I was going to shoot her. Not for what she did to us. I felt sorry for her and wanted to put her out of the misery I know those bastards are going to put her through. But you can't just shoot people." He shrugged. "This is America."

The men opened the doors to get into the car. All the doors slammed shut but one, and the motor started up. The men were eager to get in out of the cold and damp. Lemon took another puff or two and flicked his cigarette butt away. Leaning on his still-open door, he turned and looked once more at the ship.

The dock was empty, as by a magician's trick. The ship had vanished.

He climbed in and slammed the last door. The car drove off.

Now the whole place looked like somewhere at the end of the world, or before the world had been—empty, populated only by ghosts and memories.

Thick fog rolled in again, twirling damp wraiths full of ghosts.

The fog brought in its moist embrace a low booming of ships' whistles.

Ships whispered to each other over the curvature of the earth, far out at sea, where it seemed time was just a cloud without minute hands or second sweeps.

But then again, the earth is round, and everything that drifts beyond its horizon must eventually drift back from behind in a circle, to start everything over again.

📖

The galaxy wheels immutably over the moonlit night sea.

The moon looks down with a shocked but familiar face.

If one looks out to sea, there is someone—a little girl, just four years old, standing on the opposite shore. Because the world is round.

It's really all very simple, God, and I will help you make it so if you let me, if that's how it's meant to be, oh please...

On a lonely beach far, far away, full of pain and wonder—staring back. Holding her mother's hand, and hoping for a great big beautiful dream, that her daddy would come to save them both, and that her parents would live happily ever after, together with their good and clever little girl. Because it must be so. How could it not be so? How could it turn out any different? It must be so. It must.

Else, why do all the farmers till their fields, and all the fishermen go out to sea, and all the clouds roll endlessly in the sky? Why do people with briefcases in the cities of the world ride trolleys to work each morning? Why do all the fish swim in the oceans, and all the birds fly in the sky, and all the lions and tigers roar in the jungles?

It just must be so. How can it not be so? It must, it must. Oh please let it be so, and then everything will be so very much all right in the whole world, stars and clouds and all the boys and girls whose moms and dads tuck them in every night with a prayer, a kiss, and a story.

Homecoming

The Boeing 747 airliner with Air France markings thundered majestically toward a landing at Orly in Paris. Marianne sat by a window, her face grimacing in sunlight. Below, she could watch the gray mist of an ordinary, slightly foggy, drizzly day in Paris float up toward her.

Sunlight flickered out as the plane dropped through a low, thick cloud deck. A shadow descended across the interior of the crowded plane as it left ethereal space and reentered the world of the living. It was the everyday world of pleasure and pain, of deflections and hopes, the will to live and dream and march onward as long as the cosmos willed it.

Minutes later, feeling light of body and soul, Marianne stood in line with strangers shuffling down the stuffy aisle to meet loved ones, to resume their daily lives, to be with loved ones.

Hundreds of feet pounded in the sky bridge, herding toward the arrival lounge. There, amid bright signs and neon lights, amid orderly confusion and the temporary purposes of waiting, walking, milling, or looking uncertain, stood her family—those who loved her, those she loved. Finally, she was complete, and bringing them news of the universe. In her small suitcase were the notes that she'd lugged for months, for years. The bloody deaths of Lenka and her brother and cousin near Anadyr, and the discovery and loss of her half-brother almost in one day, were still raw—but she could feel them fading. The familiar world she had grown up in--of old Three Roses title and Didier wealth but most importantly, her children, her family, her grandchildren—waited for her.

A dozen persons waited for Marianne: her three sons, their wives, their children including the new baby, at least two little cousins, and elderly grand-mère with, yes, a Gitanes smouldering in one gnarly paw. They smiled as they circled around her with embracing arms, and she lost herself in the love of their closeness. Together, they wandered hand in hand, arm in arm, toward the exit, toward the van that would take them home to the big house in the suburb of Passy. Marianne ignored the muted mumbling of announcements about all the comings and goings of airliners from and to the great cities of the world. She would not need to journey any more for a long time. She was home. She did not look back.

❧ fin ☙

Worlds of John T. Cullen

John T. Cullen's main core Web presence is at:
www.johntcullen.com
from where the majority of his fiction and nonfiction can be traced outward to numerous websites, retail sites, and other venues.

John T. Cullen is a novelist, journalist, essayist, and science and history writer living in San Diego, California. He is the author of more than 30 books, as well as dozens of articles (nonfiction) and short stories (fiction). He has written at least one scholarly paper for peer review, about the ancient Sator Rebus—an enigma for which he has provided the first plausible translation and explanation.

He has lived in various countries across North America and Europe, and is conversant in a number of languages including English, German, and Luxembourgeois. He translated Goethe's Faust (Part I) from German into English in an edition to appear from Clocktower Books in 2012-2013.

A San Diego author, he has been the first to plausibly explain one of the region's (and nation's) most intriguing puzzle—the ghost story at the Hotel del Coronado, associated with Kate Morgan; but more importantly from his standpoint, the true crime of 1892 that led to the so-called Beautiful Stranger's dark and violent death amid allegations of foul play and sexual dalliances with men in the highest places. The owner of the Hotel del Coronado at the time was John Spreckels, one of the nation's wealthiest men. Spreckels was in the White House with President Benjamin Harrison, negotiating the future of the sovereign Monarchy of Hawai'i, when in the author's opinion Kate Morgan and her accomplices attempted to pull of a blackmail attempt gone horribly wrong. The result was a cover-up, and a murky, colorful legend that has intrigued the world for over 120 years. The author has written *Dead Move: Kate Morgan and the Haunting Mystery of Coronado, 3rd Edition* as a scholarly analysis with over 120 footnotes. He followed this up with *Lethal Journey*, a noir mystery thriller based on his notes and the most gripping elements of the long-standing myth. See www.coronadomystery.com for more information.

John T. Cullen holds a B.A. in English (University of Connecticut, Storrs), a B.B.A. in Computer Information Systems (National University, San Diego), and an M.S. in Business Administration (Boston University). He has a workmanlike appreciation of Latin, and a nodding acquaintance with ancient Greek, for research purposes.

He has been an Internet publishing pioneer since (Clocktower Books, 1996+). He was for years author of the acclaimed Sharpwriter.com (in 1999 named by Writer's Digest as one of the top 101 resource websites for authors). He was also, for nearly a decade, publisher and editor of Far Sector SFFH—during its heyday, the world's oldest professional web magazine of science fiction, dark fantasy, and horror.

He is being recognized as the first person to plausibly decipher and explain the mysterious ancient Sator Square, an enigma that has puzzled historians and archeologists for centuries. As an Active Member of International Thriller Writers, at a recent annual convention in New York City, he was probably the only author present who had ever actually deciphered a mysterious, ancient inscription of great importance, found all over ancient Roman empire—and lived to tell about it.

For more information, visit Clocktower Books at:

www.clocktowerbooks.com